WE ARE WORTHY

ALISHA WILLIAMS

Book cover design: Books And Moods
Editor: Geeky Good Edits

Created with Vellum

AUTHOR'S NOTE

Welcome to Calling Wood, where Alphas come to form their packs and find their Omegas.

We Are Worthy is a very sweet and very steamy contemporary omegaverse. This is a standalone that ends with a HEA. However, characters from We Are Worthy will appear in other's books set in the same world. You will have to read one to understand the other. But, if you want to read the other books, start with We Are Worthy.

If you want sweet, nerdy virgin alphas, a beta who's more alpha than anything, and an omega whose goal is to show her alphas just how much they deserve to be loved and desired, then this is the book for you. Add in some MM steamy goodness, lots of knotting, and some sizzling hot heats.

WE ARE WORTHY

CHAPTER 1

OCTAVIA

"Tia, honey, is everything ready to go?" My mother, Marie's musical voice says, never failing to put a smile on my face.

"Yup." I turn around to face her as she stops in the doorway of my bedroom and give her a beaming smile. "Everything's ready to go."

Her eyes start to water, the emotion of me leaving getting to her again, but she keeps her proud smile in place. "I'm going to miss you, my sweet girl," she says. Her voice is a soft whisper as she steps into my room and over to me, cupping my face. "I'm so proud of you." She places a tender kiss on my forehead, and I have to force back tears of my own as the reality hits me. I'm going to be leaving, moving away for the next few years, or at the very least, until I find my Alphas.

"Thank you." I wrap my arms around her, giving her a

tight hug as I take a deep inhale of her scent. Warm vanilla, it always helps me relax when my nerves act up.

"For what?" She lets out a chuckle as she holds me tight.

"For being the best mom a girl could ask for," I say, giving her a soft smile as I pull back to look up into her green eyes, which mirror mine.

"My job was pretty easy, having an amazing daughter like you." She tucks a piece of my bright red hair behind my ear. "It's not going to be the same without you."

"You still have Spencer." I grin.

"Did someone say my name?" My younger brother says, popping his head into my room.

"Yeah, just telling mom that the world isn't over because she still has you." I laugh.

He enters my room and makes his way over to me, throwing his arm around my shoulder. "Well, yeah, she's going to be fine; the best child is still here," he jokes, then ruffles my hair.

I might be older by two years, but he's a good foot taller than me. We look nothing alike. He takes after our father, Russell, tall with shaggy brown hair. And I take after my mother, both of us short with long, red hair and freckles for days. We have three dads; Russell is a Beta, while Jim and Robert are Alphas. My mother is an Omega like my brother and me.

Omegas are rare as it is, but having a family with three is one in a billion. Three Omegas under one roof has had its challenges, even though we each have our own space in this huge house. Thank god, too, because I do not want to be anywhere near my parents when my mom goes into her heat.

"Only for two more years, then you'll be joining your sister at Calling Wood," my mother points out, causing more tears to fall. "Then I'll be all alone."

"You won't be alone, you'll have our dads. Plus, it's only an hour away. We will be by to visit all the time," I reassure her, pulling her into a hug.

"Not if you're too busy with your new pack," she sniffs.

"Mom, this is me we're talking about. No Alphas of mine will keep me away from my family," I say, pulling back to meet her watery eyes.

"Good. I know some Alphas can get very possessive." She wipes at her tears.

"I might need and crave the basic things, but I'm not your average Omega. I'm my own person, and I don't *need* Alphas. I want them. There's a difference."

As much as I love my mother, I don't want to be like her in the sense of wanting to cater to my Alphas' every whim, be a housewife, and pop out babies. I want to have my own career and not *have* to rely on anyone unless I choose to.

But I *am* an Omega, after all, and I do have needs. Calling Wood is a school where Alphas, Betas, and Omegas attend. It's designed to be a safe place where attendees can meet their pack, find their mates, and live happily ever after. And that's exactly what I plan on doing. I want to meet my Alphas, but I won't just take any pack. I won't settle for the first pack who promises me the world. The dream would be finding my scent match. Call me crazy because that's almost as rare as Omegas themselves, but I believe in fate, and hopefully, it's on my side. I mean, our family is already full of miracles; my mother found her scent matches, so why not me too?

It's not a deal breaker, but if I can't have my scent match, I'll be putting time and thought into who I choose as my pack.

"How's everything going in here?" My dad, Jim, says as he steps into the room. He takes one look at my mother's red rimmed eyes and is across the room in seconds, pulling her into his arms protectively. "What's the matter?" he growls, and I take a step back. That's another thing about a house full of Omegas being around Alphas, we all react. He looks over at me, noticing my reaction, and his face softens. "I'm sorry, it's just..."

"You saw your Omega upset and wanted to make her feel better. I get it." I smile, shaking off the odd feeling and wrapping my arms around them both.

"I'm okay, love. Just sad to see our baby girl go," my mom reassures him, patting his chest.

"We all are. Your fathers were upset they couldn't make it to see you off, but there was an important meeting at work," Dad says.

"That's okay. We will see them soon. Your job is essential to our community, and I get it." I smile up at him. They really do. My dads own a company that helps rescue Omegas from the underground rings. Let's just say sometimes Omegas are not as lucky as me, getting to attend Calling Wood. It's not something I like to think about, but

I'm glad there's people in the world like my dads to save and assist them.

Everyone takes a bag and helps carry my stuff downstairs. Most of my stuff should already be at the school and set up in my new apartment, so I only have a few things to take with me.

With the help of the driver, we load everything up into the car Calling Wood hired to drive me. I turn to see everyone standing on the curb in a line, their faces holding a variety of emotions.

"I'm going to be okay." I laugh as I hug my dad.

"I know you are. You're strong and smart. You don't take shit from anyone, even Alphas. You're going to be fine. But that doesn't mean I'm not going to miss my little girl," he says, his scent of sandalwood taking over my nostrils. I need to get some air without offending him because while my mother might enjoy that scent like it's a drug, it burns my nose. So I move to my mother next. She starts to cry again, this time heavier sobs that rack her entire body. We say goodbye, and my dad wraps her in his arms, guiding her back into the house while soothing her with all the right words.

"Well, looks like it's just you and me," my brother says with a sad smile.

"I'm gonna miss you." I mirror his smile.

"I'm gonna miss you too. But you're twenty-one now, you need to go. Or this house will be pure hell to live in." He chuckles.

"You've got another two years before you're going to be in the same boat." I laugh.

"Don't remind me," he groans. "Good luck, sis. I hope everything goes well for you."

"I'll be fine. I have Ivy there. Even if she's busy with her pack and their Omega, I know she would be there for me if I needed her."

His face drops at the name of my best friend, and I curse myself for bringing her up. I knew he always had a thing for her, but when Ivy came out as an Alpha, she left for Calling Wood right away, leaving my brother heartbroken. Spencer just came out as an Omega earlier this year, and I can tell it hurts him that she has a pack with her own Omega now. One that's not him.

We give each other a long hug before we let go. I get into the car, buckle up, and turn to look out the back window behind me as the car drives away. Spencer moves to stand in the street, waving goodbye. I wave back until I can't see him anymore, then I turn around and look out the window.

I'm going to miss them all, but I'm excited for this new chapter in my life. I've watched how my fathers are with my mother. I want that. I want to be treated like I'm the most precious thing in the world. To have my mates look at me like they're starving and I'm the only thing that can feed their hunger. Someone to tend to my sensitive moments, to hold me when I need it.

And, my heat. God. I've thought about what it would be like the first time, getting lost in the frenzy, all the scents, my slick, the knots. Biting my lip, I try not to perfume at just the thought of taking knot after knot, sex for days until my body is spent and my bones are jelly.

I'm a horny, little virgin Omega. I'm woman enough to admit it. And that's one of the main reasons why I'm going to Calling Wood. At eighteen, we find out if we're a Beta, Alpha, or Omega. At twenty-one, Omegas go into their first heat, usually a few months after their birthday. There's just something in our biology that says, *'hey, you're old enough to reproduce, it's time to have babies and settle down'*.

I'm not really looking forward to the whole being a mom thing yet. Maybe someday, but right now, I'm too young. I'm not ready for that kind of commitment, but I'm down to practice all night long. Yes, please, sign me right up. I do want to find my pack and start my new life.

Closing my eyes, I lean against the cool window and drift off to sleep to the vibrations of the car.

When I wake, it's to tapping on the window.

"Miss Lockheart. We're here," the voice of my Beta driver, Emmett, sounds muffled through the closed car door.

Blinking my eyes open, I take in my surroundings and remember I'm in the car. Stretching, I make a dramatic noise like everyone does because the stretch just feels so good after keeping your muscles locked in one position for so long.

Unbuckling my seat belt, I open the car door and step out. A gust of warm California ocean air hits my face, and I smile, grateful that I still get to be near the beach.

Emmett gets my bags and places them on the curb in front of the tall stone gate. I can't see the building behind it, but there's a sign that states 'Calling Wood'. And under it says, 'Our mission is to give every Alpha, Beta, and Omega their happy ending'.

Smiling at their slogan, I can't help but hope that's exactly what they will do for me.

The big steel gates to the right of me start to open, and I perk up. A man dressed in a security guard's uniform, along with an older woman in a pencil skirt, white blouse, and a fancy bun, steps through.

"Miss Octavia Lockheart," the woman greets. "I'm Dean Benson. Welcome to Calling Wood."

CHAPTER 2

OCTAVIA

Mrs. Benson holds out her hand for a shake, and right away, I know she's a Beta. I take her hand in mine, giving it a firm shake with a bright smile. "Hello Mrs. Benson, it's so wonderful to meet you. But please, call me Tia."

"Tia." She gives me a beaming smile of her own. "It's our pleasure to have you joining us here at our school. We hope you'll find everything you're longing for within the next four years at our institution. Please, come with us, and we can go to my office where I'll explain the rules about how things work around here. Then Knox can bring you to your apartment in the Omega compound."

My brows crease at the mention of the name. She must understand my confusion and steps aside. "This is Knox Hunter. He will be your private security. All unmated

Omegas must have protection when outside the Omega compound for safety reasons."

I get my first good look at the man before me and fuck me. I really hope these scent blocking panties are doing their job because if not, everyone here will know just how wet I am as I take in the fine ass man in front of me. He's tall, over six feet. His black and white uniform hugs the bulging muscles that threaten to rip through.

"Miss Lockheart," his deep voice says, doing nothing at all to help snap me out of my little trance, but I do manage to find his face. *Fuck, it's even better.* He has a cocky, playful smile like he knows exactly what he's doing to me. His toothy grin shows off two cute little dimples at the corners of his mouth that I just want to trace with my tongue. My hands twitch with the need to run my fingers through his dark locks. And... is that ink I see peeking out of the top of his shirt? Fuck me. Like please?

"Tia," he repeats, and the use of my name has me finally snapping back to reality.

"Oh, umm, sorry. Foggy brain from the nap in the car," I lie, hoping they believe me.

He just grins wider and shakes his head.

"It's lovely to meet you, Tia," he says, holding out his hand. I look at it for a stupidly long time before extending a shaky hand and placing it into his. As soon as we make contact, my eyes widen as they fly back to his, and I let out a little whimper. His boyish smile is gone, replaced by a heated look, and if I don't let go of his hand right now, I may just climb this man instead of waiting until I find my Alphas to lose my virginity like I've been waiting for. I think I just might be in trouble here.

We both let go like we've been shocked and take a step away from each other.

"Looks like we're off to a good start," Dean Benson says. I look over to find her watching our little interaction with a satisfied grin.

Knox clears his throat before turning around and heading back through the open gate.

I have no idea what just happened, but I want to feel it again and more often. The rush of arousal my body received and the intense connection made by only one touch. But no matter how much I want to climb that mountain of a man, I just got here. I need to relax and let nature take its course. *This has to mean something though, right?*

The Dean informs me that the main way of transportation around Calling Wood is golf carts. As the main part of Calling Wood comes into view, I suck in a small gasp, and my eyes widen, taking in the view around me. I read up, as much as I could, about this place on their website, and from what I saw, the place is its own mini town. I easily spot the main school building. It looks like it was plucked out of a fairy tale. It is a legit castle. The photos on the website don't do it justice.

"Knox can take you on a tour tomorrow after you get some rest. Classes start on Monday," Dean Benson says as the golf cart stops outside the front of the school. Another man that seems to be waiting for us steps forwards. "John, please get Miss Lockheart's remaining luggage to her apartment while we have our meeting."

"Yes ma'am." John nods his head at the Dean, then at me before taking Knox's place in the cart and driving off.

"This way," Knox's husky voice says as his hand lightly touches the small of my back to guide me forward. I bite my lip, holding back a moan, loving the warmth of his large hand through my thin t-shirt.

I keep my eyes facing forward, not even bothering to check out the school as we walk down the halls. I'm too hyper focused on Knox's fingers and his thumb rubbing lightly against my back. *Why hasn't he moved his hand yet? Does he want to make sure I don't get lost as we make our way through the twisting halls, or does he like touching me as much as I do?*

"Here we are," Dean Benson states, turning to me with a bright smile. We've stopped at a wooden door with a little sign next to it that says 'Dean Of Calling Wood University, Mrs. Nancy Benson'.

Looking around, I curse myself for not paying attention. I hope Knox includes her office on our tour tomorrow because I have no idea where in the building we are.

I follow her inside while Knox stays outside and closes

the door behind me. With him out of sight, I can breathe a little more easily. Normally, Beta scents don't affect me, but he has a sweet smell to him, with a hint of mango. And fuck if I don't want to have a taste of him.

"Please, sit," Dean Benson insists, pointing to the chair in front of her desk.

Taking a seat, I cross my legs, trying not to nervously play with my fingers like I usually do.

"So, let's get to it." She smiles at me before looking down at the papers on her desk and shifting through them. She grabs a big, brown envelope and hands it to me. "This here has all the information about your classes, schedule, maps, hours to the shops around town, and anything else you might need, as well as your apartment keys. Of course, you can always come see me, or call Knox if you have any questions."

"At Calling Wood, we try to provide a safe environment for our Omegas. But to ensure that, there are rules all students must follow. For any unmated Omegas, there are more precautions set in place. Omegas, Alphas, and Betas all live in different gated compounds to ensure safety. Alphas are not permitted, under any circumstance, to enter the Omega compound, mated or not. If you would like to meet your Alphas or a pack you are courting, they must wait for you at the gate. The only Betas allowed within the Omega compound are assigned guards. However, Omegas are allowed within the Beta compound."

"What about Omegas going into the Alpha compound?" I ask, shifting in my seat.

"It's the same as the Omega compound. But we have houses for mated packs if they are so lucky to meet their mates and choose to attend the school further. Most leave and start their lives once they form a pack, but you are more than welcome to stay and continue your studies."

I let out a sigh of relief. "I'm glad to hear that. As much as I'm looking forward to meeting my pack, I would really like to get my full education here."

"The school, shop, and other places within Calling Wood are open to all, but Omegas must be with their Beta guards outside the compound until they're mated. After that, it is the Alphas' job to keep their Omega safe and protected. We do not tolerate unruly Alphas, but unfortunately, when it comes to Alphas and Omegas, sometimes things happen. That's why we have so many policies and protocols in place to prevent such things."

"What about Betas?" I shift in my seat again, the reality of my new life slowly starting to hit me.

"What about them?" she asks, her brows pinching in confusion at my question.

I clear my throat. "What if you mate with one too?" I ask, then chew on the inside of my cheek.

Her face smooths out into a knowing grin. "If you happen to mate with a Beta, that's perfectly fine."

"What if that Beta is your guard?" My cheeks must be as red as my hair right now because here I am asking about my guard... the one I only met less than a half an hour ago like I'm already planning our mating ceremony or something. "Does he become another Omega's guard even if he's mated?" Oh, I don't like that idea, not at all. Dean Benson must smell the jealousy that I have no right to feel rolling off me because all forms of amusement fall from her face.

She gives me a reassuring look. "If a Beta guard turns out to be mated to an Omega, he or she will be reassigned to another position. That is if the Omega and their pack are still attending Calling Wood. And once you are done with your studies, they will, of course, go with you."

I relax at her words, knowing that if something happens between Knox and I, he won't get fired, and we would be free to be together.

"What about my heats?" I ask, finding my face red hot again.

"We have a few options. Your apartment is sound and scent proof. We will provide you with everything you might need to help you through your heat if you choose to do it alone. If you are unmated and would like an unmated Alpha or their pack to help you through it, we have isolated houses you can use with a nest that is always thoroughly cleaned and washed in desensitizer. Otherwise, if you are mated by then, you would just spend it at home."

"Okay. That's good to know." I nod and look down at the packet she gave me. I really hope I meet my Alphas before then. I don't want to go through my first heat alone, being in pain and never having the relief my body craves.

"We have a program to help unmated Omegas find a pack that works for them if you're interested. We would set up a meet and greet with unmated packs. It's helped quicken the process in the past. We've had quite a few happy Omegas come out of the program."

I think about her offer. *Do I want to try to meet them on my own?* It could take forever, and I might not meet them before my heat. "Why not. What could it hurt?"

Dean Benson goes over a few other things with me before I thank her for everything, and with everything she gave me in my arms, I leave her office, finding Knox waiting for me just outside.

"All good then?" I could listen to him talk all day. I just got here, and I already know my life is going to be very eventful. I never thought about being mated to a Beta before. Although looking at Knox now, seeing how he's looking at me like I hoped my Alphas would, I'm really loving that idea.

"Yeah." I give him a shy smile. I look down both sides of the hall. "Umm." I blush. "Do you mind leading the way?" I laugh nervously. "I don't really remember the way we took to get here."

He lets out this deep chuckle that has me feeling weak in the knees. Holy hell, if I'm this bad with a Beta, I have no freaking hope with my Alphas. I'm going to be a horny little puddle of slickness. I kinda can't wait.

CHAPTER 3

OCTAVIA

I trail behind Knox, trying to take in my surroundings as he leads me back out to the main entrance of the school, but my eyes keep drifting back to his ass. He has a nice ass. Honestly, I'm a little jealous at how toned it is. His black slacks hug it in just the right way. It's almost impossible not to stare.

"And here we are." Knox's voice snaps me out of the silent stare down with his back side, and my eyes shoot up to his. My face flushes at the sight of his sexy side smirk. I've been caught perving. *Great, Tia. You just met the man under an hour ago, and already you're thinking about taking a bite out of that perfect peach.*

"Sorry," I awkwardly offer, shifting from foot to foot. "When we go on that tour tomorrow, I umm..." I chew on the inside of my cheek. "I think I'm going to need you to show me how to get to the dean's office again."

His smirk only grows, and my belly flutters at the sight of those dimples again. "Sure thing, Omega."

He turns and pushes open the door, holding it open for me to pass him. His hand lightly grazes my back as he guides me down the stairs and to the golf cart. I didn't need any help going down the stairs, so something tells me he's just looking for reasons to touch me. Not that I mind. Although just being around him has my mind going haywire with feelings that I'm not quite used to, but not totally hating either.

Knox lightly grasps my elbow, helping me into the cart. I bite back a whimper as his fingers brush down my arm. *What in the hell is wrong with me?* I've been around Betas all my life -the only Alphas I've really been around are my fathers- and I've never reacted to a Beta this way before.

We lock eyes, and my breath catches as I get lost in his stormy, gray eyes. His nostrils flare, and I curse myself because my perfume must be strong right now. But I just can't help it.

"Well..." His voice is thick with want. Fuck. I need to go to my apartment and lock myself behind its door. Alone. Because if I stay around him much longer, then I'm going to end up in a frenzy or in an early heat. And as much as I'm excited about the dicking of a lifetime, I don't want to lose my virginity to a man I just met. "Let's get you home. Tomorrow will be eventful, and you need your rest."

I nod, looking forward. He makes his way around the back of the cart and into the driver's seat. The ride to the

Omega compound is silent, but it doesn't bother me because as soon as we left the front of the school, Calling Wood opened up. Buildings all around light up the night sky. I soak in my surroundings. I have no idea what is what, but this place is so much bigger than I had imagined.

"So, this place, all these shops, they're just for the teachers and students?" I ask, looking at Knox.

"Yes. The people who run the shops all live outside the community. The only people allowed in here are the people who run them, the faculty, and the students. Calling Wood is like a mini town. It's meant to be a safe place for everyone to grow, thrive, and meet their mates. Everything you should need is within these walls. I'll show you around tomorrow, I'm sure there's a few places that will catch your interest."

Saying nothing, I look forward again, drifting into a comfortable silence until we pull up to a large stone gate, much like the main one. There's a sign next to a guard post that says 'Omega Compound'.

Knox parks the cart, then turns to look at me. "Well, this is your stop." He gives me a small smile.

"Do you... could you come in with me or...?" I ask, not quite ready to see him go.

"Umm..." He brings one of his large tattooed hands and scratches the back of his neck as he looks at the gate before looking back to me. "I could? It's really up to you. If you feel safer and more comfortable with me walking you to your place instead of one of these guards, I can do that."

"Do Beta guards hang out with their Omega? Like in their house?" *Sweet mother of god, Tia, way to sound like you're asking him to come over and fuck.* I blush at the words I just spoke and re-play them in my head.

He chuckles, deep and warm, his smile making me flush. "Well, some Omegas befriend their guards, some prefer it to be professional and only have them do what is required. You're in charge, Tia. We want whatever makes the Omega feel safe; that's our goal. You're also not a prisoner here, you're free to leave Calling Wood and come back whenever you want. We just prefer unmated Omegas not to be walking around alone. It's for your safety."

I nod. I like Knox more than just for the obvious reasons. Like he's fucking gorgeous, and he makes my pussy flutter, but he's also easy to listen to, and I find myself wanting to get to know him.

"I'd feel better if you were to come with me, for at least tonight."

His smile brightens. "Then I'm more than happy to accompany you." He gets out of the cart and starts walking around the front. My heart starts to pick up its pace as I track his every movement until he's standing right next to me. He holds out his hand for me, and I pray my palm isn't sweaty as I place it in his. His big hand engulfs mine, and I force myself to pay attention to each move I make so that I don't make a fool of myself.

But it's of no use. When I place my feet onto the foot step on the side and stand up, I slip. A startled cry almost slips from my lips but dies when strong arms catch me from face planting on the ground.

"Careful, Little Omega," his husky voice purrs, and there's no way he doesn't feel my full body shiver.

"Thank you," I whisper, blinking up as his smoldering gaze bores into mine. He helps me right myself but doesn't let me go. We stare into each other's eyes, our lips so close I can feel his warm breath mingle with mine. He smells amazing. Like a tropical smoothie, and I really want to take a long drink of him.

My body is screaming at me to close the gap, to press my lips to his and fuse our mouths together.

His hands tighten on my upper arms as if he's stopping himself from pulling me into him.

"You're welcome," he rumbles, brushing his lips against mine ever so softly before stepping back. I blink rapidly, trying to clear my brain from the lust fog, quickly looking away from him and down towards the ground. Wrong move, as my eyes move in that direction, they make a little pit stop at the massive bulge he's sporting. And I mean *massive*. My eyes widen at the sight. Dear god, who needs a knot when you have something that big to keep you satisfied?

You do, it's what your body craves. Needs. Was made for.

But that doesn't mean I can't enjoy some Beta beef.

Knox clears his throat, and his body disappears from my line of vision. Looking up, I see he's making his way towards the guard's booth.

My feet do as they are told and rush to catch up.

"Russ, this is my Omega, Octavia. But she prefers to be called Tia," Knox introduces me to a young gentleman who's stepped out of the booth.

"Nice to meet you, Tia. I'm Russ. I work the front gates almost every night, so if you ever need anything, please feel free to reach out to me. The front gate number should be by the phone in your apartment." He gives me a friendly smile.

"Or she could just call me," Knox grumbles, his words sounding a little defensive as he positions his body slightly in front of me. With the way he reacted just now, and with him calling me *his* Omega, my heart does a little happy dance.

"Of course. I'm here just in case." Russ nods at Knox and looks back at me. "You're in good hands with Mr. Hunter. He is one of the best."

With that, Russ opens the gate. Knox wraps an arm around my shoulder, guiding me through. I grin stupidly to myself, hoping he doesn't see just how happy I am right now.

"So, this is your little home. Until you're mated, of course. There's not much within the walls because we want to encourage Omegas to get out and mingle instead of staying cooped up. But it is set up to be comfortable. There's a walking trail with a little pond on the far side. We currently have fifty unmated Omegas attending the school from all over the world. Each apartment houses four people. Men on the east side, women on the west. Each place should have everything you need on top of anything you brought with you."

We come to a stop at the first apartment building. It's a square shape, two balconies on top and two decks on the bottom. On the side that I can see, there's a set of stairs leading up to the top apartment.

"All units have separate entry ways. They are also sound and scent proof. Yours is this bottom unit here," he informs, leading me to the only part that's not brightly lit up.

I pull the envelope from my purse with all the information Dean Benson gave me, and I slip my hand in to pull out a key on a key ring with a keychain that says Calling Wood.

"Well. If that's all you need, here's my number." He pulls a card from his back pocket and hands it to me. "Just call or text when you want to leave the Omega compound, and I'll be here right away."

"Thanks, Knox. For everything." I smile.

"Just doing my job." He smiles back.

"I'd like to think I could be more than just a job to you," I say. Knox's eyes widen slightly. The street lamp's glow shows me his handsome face, which is full of interest. "We're going to be together a lot. I'd like to be friends." *Yeah, friends, who fuck.* God, I really need to find my Alphas.

"Friends," he says slowly with a nod. "I could use a good friend," he says, giving me one of his signature cocky grins. I'd be a good friend, a *really* good friend.

Okay, I need to go inside now. This is all too much for my lady bits. *Get a hold of yourself, woman!*

"Goodnight, Knox. See you tomorrow." I quickly say before turning around, unlocking the door, and locking myself behind this closed door.

With my back against the door, I slide down to the floor and let out a breath of relief.

The amount of slick I've released tonight is enough to make a room full of Alphas feral if it wasn't for these scent blocking panties.

After getting myself under control, I pick myself up off the floor. The place is dark, only the moonlight casting a soft glow through the window to my left to see by. My eyes adjust enough for me to find the light switch beside the front door. Flicking it on, the room comes to life. I smile as I take in my new home.

Placing the keys, my phone, and the envelope on the counter, I start to explore. To my left is a nice sized kitchen. There's a stainless steel stove, fridge, and dishwasher. Plus a dual sink with enough counter and cupboard space for everything I might need.

Stepping further into the apartment, to my right is the living room. Everything is already furnished. We took a questionnaire on our preference of how we would like our place to be, and I'm excited I get to be out on my own. In a place that's just for me. I think it will be nice to have a little independence before I find my pack and start a new life with them. *If I'm lucky enough to find them, that is.* I really hope Calling Wood is the place that will make my dreams come true.

Running my fingertips against the back of the black leather couch, I take in the decor. It's just how I wanted it.

Slipping off my sandals, I sink my toes into the fuzzy white rug under the round black and white marble coffee table.

Tomorrow, I'll enjoy cuddling up on the couch and

watching a movie on the big, flat screen TV mounted to the wall over the electric fireplace. But right now, I need to wash up, change, and get a good night's rest.

I make my way to the other side of the living room and flick on the light switch that illuminates the little hallway. I look in the first door, turning on those lights as well. My eyes widen when I see the massive bathroom. On my right is a huge mirror above a porcelain sink and marble countertop. On it is everything a girl could need, apart from my makeup that I brought with me.

My eyes widen even more when I see the very modern walk-in shower. It has a waterfall shower head, and I can't wait to try it out. But not tonight. No, what's calling my name is the jacuzzi tub next to it.

"Come to mama," I groan as my feet carry me over the cold tile to the tub. I turn it on to fill it and grab some of the lavender bath salts off the counter.

Tossing in the salts, I get undressed and throw my dirty clothes into the hamper next to the toilet. Fully naked, I grin as I race into the kitchen to grab my phone before running back to the bathroom. I hit play on one of my playlists and turn the volume all the way up. *Ain't it Fun* by Paramore starts, and I'm suddenly in a much better mood. Singing along, I head out into the hall to the only other door. Opening it, I squeal as I take in my room.

It's not big, and I'm extremely happy about that. Big bedrooms give me anxiety if I'm in there alone. This room is perfect! It's practically a nest. There's a queen size bed covered in fuzzy blankets and pillows. The carpet is plush, softer than what's in the living room. There's also a vanity, dresser, and a bedside table. That's it. That's what I asked for, and it's just enough for me.

I spot my bag on top of the dresser, and I dart over to it. I unzip it, digging out a regular pair of panties and a big, baggy t-shirt that I love to sleep in. As I pull it out, something falls to the ground with a little thud. Bending over, I find my bullet vibrator. Biting my lip, I contemplate if I want to bring it in the tub with me.

After being around Knox for so long, I could use a little relief. I feel like this might be a consistent thing after spending any time around each other.

If this is how I am with a smokin' hot, tatted up Beta, what kind of state am I going to be in when I'm around Alphas? I might need to invest in some suppressants. I didn't want to take any and have it mess with my heat, but I don't want to be perfuming all over the place and causing issues if I'm already so easily affected.

Deciding that an orgasm would be the perfect way to relax after a long day, I clutch the bullet in my hand and go back to the bathroom.

Placing my clothes on the counter, I grab a big, fluffy towel from the rack next to the tub and place it on the ground, putting my little fun buddy on the edge. Turning off the water, I climb into the tub, groaning as the hot water covers my muscles.

Letting out a content sigh, it turns into a moan when I turn on the jets. The water pressure is perfect.

Wanting to get everything out of the way, I quickly wash my hair and body before really relaxing.

When I'm done, I grab the vibrator, sit back, and relax. I place my feet on the edge, opening my legs wide enough to allow myself room as the jets soothe my body. Turning it on, the buzzing echoes through the large room, but the sound quickly dies as I slip it into the water. Closing my eyes, I rest my head back and place the vibrator over my sensitive clit, and let out a startled moan at how overwhelming the feeling is.

I'm already so worked up that it doesn't take long until I start to feel the warmth in my lower belly. My breathing starts to come out in quick choppy pants as I feel the pressure building with every second.

I allow my mind to wander, picturing Knox tossing me onto my bed, getting down on his knees, and burying his face between my thighs as I whimper and beg, chanting his name. His thick, tattooed fingers slipping into my tight pussy and fucking me until I'm a shaking mess, all while feasting on my clit like it's his favorite snack.

Biting my lip, I brace myself for the orgasm that's right there. My legs shake, threatening to slip off the edge, but I'm determined to push past the intense pleasure.

With a few more circles of my clit, Knox's name slips past my lips as I scream out my release.

When I'm done riding the wave of my climax, I drop my feet into the water, my arms feeling like jelly.

I don't know how long I sit there for, eyes closed as my body recovers. But when I lift my hand up and open my eyes, I see my fingers are all wrinkly, which tells me it's time to get out.

Shutting off the jets, I pull the plug to drain and grab my towel, wrapping the big, fuzzy fabric around my body and tucking the edge in so that it doesn't fall off before getting out.

Grabbing a smaller towel for my hair, I dry it the best I can. I slip on my night shirt and panties before grabbing my phone and abandoning everything else left in the bathroom. The need for sleep is hitting me hard.

Turning the lights off in the rest of the house and double checking to make sure the door is locked, I head to my room. Opening the curtain, the moon light spills in, providing just enough light to be able to get around.

I grab my charger from my bag, plug my phone in, and switch on the playlist of my nighttime songs, then place it on the table.

Pulling some of the blankets back, I climb into the nest of the heavens. It doesn't take me long before I slip into a deep slumber. I dream the sweetest dreams of faceless men loving me, comforting me, praising me as they worship my body. *My Alphas. I don't know who you are, but I can't wait until we meet. I just hope I can be the Omega you always wanted.*

CHAPTER 4

OCTAVIA

I wake to a chime coming from my phone. Groaning as I stretch out my muscles, I blink my eyes open a couple times before rubbing the sleep from them. Rolling over, I grab my phone and open the lock screen.

It's nine a.m. Looking down, I see Knox's name, and my eyes widen. Crap, I'm supposed to be with him all day, and I am nowhere near ready to see him.

Clicking on his name, I open his text.

Knox: *Good morning, Omega. We have a busy day ahead of us, hope you slept well. On my way to pick you up.*

Shit, shit, shit! Flinging the blankets back, I throw my phone down on the bed and start scrambling to get ready.

Digging through my bag, I grab an emerald green sundress, a black bra, and some scent blocking panties because there's no way I can wear regular ones around Knox.

Replacing my sleep wear with my new outfit, I grab my makeup and sit down at the vanity.

"This is why I don't go to bed with wet hair." I groan as I look in the mirror and see my fiery red locks. My already wild curls are out of control. Knowing there's no hope for my hair, I start digging in my makeup bag for my eye liner. Just as I bring the tip to my eyelid, I hear a knock at the door.

No! He can't be here already! I'm not ready.

I just stare in the direction of my open door, my mouth slightly parted as my brain decides what the hell to do. When the knocking comes again, I jolt out of my little trance and race towards the door.

Unlocking it, I fling the door open and thank the gods that I took scent precautions because... *fuck me.* Knox stands there, looking like a tall, tattooed god.

His face is relaxed, but the longer I just stand without saying anything, the bigger his cocky smirk grows on his perfect face. "Good morning, Little Omega." *God, his voice is music to my pussy. Ears, I mean ears.*

"It's Tia." I blink up at him before shaking my head.

"I remember." His smirk takes over the entirety of his handsome face. *Of course, he knows you, dummy, you think he would forget overnight?*

"Right." I'm sure my cheeks are starting to match the color of my hair right about now.

Hair. *My hair.* My eyes widen as my hands fly to my hair. Shit, I probably look like some wild animal right now.

"You look... well rested," he says with a chuckle.

I clear my throat. "I am, actually." I give him a small smile, trying not to let the embarrassment get to me.

"Is the apartment to your liking? If there's anything you need or even want, just let me know, and I'll make sure you get it. I want to make sure you're comfortable and satisfied in your new home."

Oh, being satisfied was not the problem for me last night. Damn it. Just thinking about touching myself last night and his name slipping past my lips as I was filled with ecstasy has the blush that was starting to fade making its way back with vengeance.

Knox's eyes grow darker as his eyes watch me intently, his nose flaring. I bite my lip, shifting from foot to foot, willing my brain to say something, *do* something.

But when Knox leans down, the faint smell of mangos invades my nose and my brain short circuits. His cheek lightly brushes against mine as he whispers in my ear.

"You know, Little Omega..." His hot breath causes a shiver to wrack through my body, and I have to bite down hard on my lip to hold back the whimper threatening to escape. "You're going to make my job a lot more eventful if you keep smelling so fucking delicious." Squeezing my eyes shut, I will my knees not to buckle as slick soaks my panties. They clearly are *not* doing their job because he can smell it. And he *likes* it. I like that he likes it. *Fuck!*

"Sorry," I say, my voice barely a whisper.

He pulls back so that we're face to face. His tattooed hand gently tips my chin up, forcing me to look him in the eyes. "Don't you ever apologize for being you, for your body reacting naturally. Omega or not."

My eyes flick from his eyes to his plump lips as my breath quickens, and my pulse beats manically in my ears. We're so close, all I'd have to do is lean forward, just an inch, and his sinful lips would be locked with mine.

"But, I do have to admit," he says, pulling away from me as he stands tall again. He gives me a sexy as hell smile while his hand still lingers on my cheek. "I've never received such a reaction from another person before. It's quite an honor." He brushes his thumb lightly against my cheek, and when he pulls away, I almost cry out at the loss of his touch.

I stand there like an idiot, just blinking up at him, my hormones a wild mess. Seriously, if this isn't my body warning me that I'm going into heat soon, then this man is going to put me in a frenzy and cause it to come early.

His smile turns into a smirk like he knows exactly how he's affecting me, and he's enjoying every moment. "This is for you, sleeping beauty." He holds out a coffee cup and a brown bag.

I look down at it, then back to him. "Hold for a moment, please," I say, then slam the door in his face. Not taking any time to think about how rude I just was, I race back to my bedroom and quickly change into a fresh pair of scent blocking panties. I shove a few extra pairs into my purse before grabbing my phone and deciding to go as is for the day. From the look he was giving me, I don't think my lack of makeup or nicely styled hair bothers him much.

"Sorry about that," I say as I swing the door back open.

He looks down at me, amusement written all over his gorgeous face.

"No problem," he says, still holding out what he brought for me again.

"Thank you." I give him a beaming smile. "You didn't have to."

"I know. But I wanted to."

Opening the brown bag, I take out a chocolate croissant, my eyes widening with excitement. "I love these!" I say before sinking my teeth into the flaky goodness. "God," I moan, closing my eyes. "This is really friggin' good."

"Kitten, if you keep making sounds like that... I don't think it will be safe to take you anywhere," he growls. My eyes snap open, meeting Knox's with a look of pure hunger in his eyes.

"Right," I mumble around a mouthful. "Let's go." I put the rest of the croissant back into the bag and place it, along with the coffee, on the little bistro table on my little porch and lock up.

"So, where do we start?" I ask as we drive down the main road in a golf cart, looking around at Calling Wood. It's different in the daylight. Everything looks so bright and alive. People are walking around, laughing, and smiling.

"Well, I think the most important places first, then I'll take you on a tour of the school. If we have time, I'll show you some of my favorite spots too," he says, looking away from the road for a moment, giving me a wink.

Blushing, I bite my lip and look away. We drive a little longer, and Knox points out a few things; a park where they hold concerts at the gazebo and a community center that has a pool and other activities.

We stop in the middle of what seems to be the busiest spot I've seen so far.

"This is where most of the shops are," he informs me, parking the golf cart. He gets out and makes his way to my side before I even have a chance to turn around in my seat. I smile sweetly as I take his outstretched hand, trying to hold back the gasp that almost slips out at the feeling of his hand around mine. The contact sends another small jolt of electricity through me as he helps me down.

We walk down the sidewalk, and he points out places as we go. "That's the pharmacy. Over there are some clothing stores. An electronics store, were you can get anything from cell phones, to computers, to video games. We don't have a hospital here, but we do have a clinic that can do pretty much anything except major surgeries. We have a few convenience stores. One down there." He points to the end of the street. "And one back there." He turns around and points at the other end. My attention is on everything he's saying, wanting to make sure I'm observing everything he's showing me. And trying to get my mind off of what it might be like to be trapped under his thickly muscled body as he thrusts deep into me.

His attention is back on me, giving me a smirk and a raised brow.

"What are you thinking about, Kitten?" he asks, his words filled with mirth. "Do convenience stores turn you on?" His deep chuckle does nothing to help the situation.

"No," I huff, jutting out my chin. His smirk grows at my sass. "I was just thinking."

"About what?" he asks, stepping towards me.

"Nothing," I squeak as he towers over me.

"Mmhmm," he hums, that cocky smirk never leaving his face.

"Oh look, ice cream," I chirp, looking over to the shop on my right. Not bothering to wait for him, I dart into the store. A tiny bell chimes as I enter, and I shiver as the A/C hits my exposed arms.

It's a cute little place. It reminds me of something you might see in a fifties movie.

My gaze roams over the variety of flavors, each sounding better and better with every new one I see.

"I'll get a scoop of mint chocolate," I hear Knox tell the lady at the counter. "What would you like?"

My eyes lift to his. "You don't have to. I can pay for it myself. You already got me breakfast."

"And if you're alright with it, I'd like to get your dessert. And maybe dinner later?" There it is again. That sexy smile that has me wanting to melt into a puddle at his feet.

"Thanks." My voice is soft as I smile. Looking back at

the ice cream, I debate between coconut and cotton candy. "I'll get the coconut, please," I tell the lady.

"You know what? I'll take a scoop of coconut too," he says, changing his mind. Knox pays, and the lady hands us our ice cream. We move over to one of the red leather booths and sit on opposite sides.

"Why did you change your mind on the flavor of ice cream?" I ask as my eyes follow his tongue as he laps at his cone.

He licks his lips, staring at me for a moment before answering me with a heated look. "Since the moment I met you, all I've been able to smell is your sweet scent, Omega. Toasted coconut. I've been craving it ever since."

Sweet mother of god. *Naked grandmas!* Think of naked grandmas to distract your mind from making you gush like a fucking garden hose.

From the way his eyes grow hooded and his nostrils flare, I don't think it's working. Crossing my legs, I will my body to calm down. *How am I supposed to be around this man every day?* At this point, I might just lock myself up in my apartment and only come out for classes.

"Kitten," he growls. *Are we sure this man is a Beta?* This man seems more Alpha than Beta to me. And that nickname. *Why do I love it so much?* "Talk to me. Tell me about yourself. I want to know everything." I silently thank him for changing the subject.

We eat our ice cream, and I do exactly as he asks. I tell him all about my life growing up, my brother, and parents. The more we talk and laugh, the more I feel comfortable and confident around him. He's really easy to open up to and talk with. He tells me all about himself as well. His favorite color, food, activities. He likes to work out at the gym in the Beta compound or surf on the weekends. He said he was training to become a UFC fighter but had to switch career paths when he blew out his knee in a fight.

After we finish our ice cream, he takes me to the school and shows me where all my classes are going to be. This time I pay close attention to where the Dean's office is. He shows me the cafe and the library. The latter looks like it was plucked right out of *Beauty and the Beast*.

"Are you ready for your first day of classes tomorrow?" he asks as we stop outside my apartment door. The day went by way too fast, and I find myself sad to see him go. Thank god, the more we got to know each other, the less I was affected by every look he tossed my way. *Is it normal for Omegas to be this wet all the time?*

"Don't forget meeting with my first unmated pack." I force a smile. I've been excited at the idea of meeting my Alphas. But after meeting Knox, I can't help but feel like maybe I should hold off a little bit longer.

"Tia?" he asks, his face serious. "I know we just met. And I know you're looking for your Alphas... I don't know who they might be, but whoever they are, they'll be one lucky pack. But if it's something you want, I would like to be considered to be a part of that pack too. If your future Alphas accept me, that is."

"You want to be with me?" I ask, hope swelling in my heart at his words.

He gives me this adorable nervous look as he scratches the back of his neck. "I know this is fast, but that's kind of how things work in our world." He shrugs. He's right. All it takes is meeting your pack; one day, you're alone, and the next, you have a whole new life. "But I thought I'd shoot my shot before I lose my chance." When I say nothing, just stare at him in shock, he starts to panic. "I mean, if that's not what you want, and I totally misread the connection, then that's cool too."

Moving in close, I lean up on my tiptoes and cut his ramblings off with a kiss. It takes a moment for him to react, but when he does, he threads his fingers into my hair, holding my lips to his as he groans.

He pulls me to his body, pressing me against his hard length, making me whimper into his mouth. He kisses me tenderly but with so much passion as his tongue tangles with mine in a heated dance. I've never been kissed before, but I never dreamed it would be like this. This is everything, and I'm glad he's my first with at least one thing.

He ends the kiss by pulling back, both of us panting. His eyes are practically black in the moonlight as he looks at me like if he doesn't leave now, kissing won't be the only thing we do.

"Thank you, Kitten." His voice is a low rumble. His thumb brushes against my lower lip before moving away. "Thank you for giving me this chance. I promise you won't regret it. Now, go get some sleep, my Little Omega. Tomorrow is the start of your new life." He smiles before giving me one last, quick peck, leaving me wet and desperate for more of his touch.

Tonight, I fall asleep with the biggest smile on my face. Calling Wood was definitely the right choice. Now, the hunt for my Alphas begins. I just hope they accept Knox into the pack. Because as of right now, I don't think I could see my life without him.

CHAPTER 5

OCTAVIA

I woke up this morning feeling a mix of excitement and dread. What if I don't find my bond mates? What if I do, but they turn out to be total douche canoes?

Only one way to find out.

Turning off my hair straightener, I give myself a once over in the mirror and smile, nodding my head in approval. I'm not a morning person, and if I could have it my way, I would stay in bed snuggled up in a fort of blankets and pillows all day with a good book... or five. But I wanted to look nice on my first day, and this wild mane doesn't just tame itself.

My green eyes look more vibrant today, my smile extra wide as I think about Knox and that kiss. *God, that kiss.* I want more of that. *Need* more of that. More of *him.*

Shaking my head from turning to dirty thoughts, I stand

up and straighten out my dress. I picked out a white, short sleeve dress with a cute cherry blossom design and paired it with my black ballet flats. Grabbing the bottle of desensitizer, I spray myself down. With the way I've been perfuming these past few days, it's probably a good idea to mask my Omega pheromones the best I can. Being around all these Alphas for the next few weeks might start a riot if I don't. As much as I don't want to, I'll also be taking scent blockers to dull my own senses. Being around so many Alphas in close proximity would just be too much.

There's a knock at the door, causing the butterflies in my belly to do flips. At least I won't be alone on my first day. Knowing Knox is always going to be close by makes me feel a hell of a lot better about starting at this new school as well as meeting all the packs.

Not that the classes have me worried. All Omegas in their first year have to take basic home economics classes. There's cooking classes, childcare, how to sew and clean. Hell, there's even a sex ed class on the Alpha and Omega anatomy, how everything works, what it's used for, and how each person can please the other.

I took most of these classes in high school, but the information packet said it's because most Omegas don't choose to stay longer once they find their mates.

At least I'm able to take Art and Music History as well.

Thankfully, if I choose to stay beyond this year, I can start taking courses towards the degree I want. Calling Wood offers many different career options. The only things they don't offer are more elite classes that are required to become doctors and scientists. But that's okay because I want to become an elementary school teacher anyway.

I might not be ready for babies of my own, but I do love kids and would love to be able to teach young minds, to set them up for a wonderful future.

With one last look in the mirror, I grab my backpack, phone, and keys before making my way to the front door to greet Knox.

"Hi," I say as I open the door. A shy smile takes over my face as I remember that this man, this tall, sexy, tattooed Beta is all mine. Well, not officially, but he told me he wanted to see where this goes, so I guess we're... dating? *God, I don't know, how do I ask him something like that? It's only been a few days.*

"Hi, Kitten." Knox grins, an amused smile slipping over those sexy lips. "I can see the gears whirling in that pretty head of yours. What are you thinking?"

"Umm." I bite my lip as I step outside and lock the door behind me before looking at him again. "I was thinking about last night. The kiss..." His smile turns more predatory than playful now. "And what you said. How you wanted a chance at being mine."

"And what about that are you confused about?" he asks softly, reaching out to tuck a loose strand of hair behind my ear. His hand lingers as he cradles the side of my face, and my eyes flutter closed. I let out a little contented sigh, leaning into his touch. Blinking my eyes back open, I answer him.

"Are we... are we like, dating now?" *How high school did that just sound?*

He lets out this sexy chuckle that has me weak in the knees. "Is that what you want, Little Omega? Do you want us to be dating?"

"Do you?" I ask, feeling silly as I think maybe I've made a bigger deal about everything than it really is.

"Yes, Kitten, and so much more. But that will come with time. Just know that I am yours until you say otherwise. No other woman exists in my eyes but you." The hand cupping my face slides under my chin, tilting my face up so that he can bend down and place the sweetest kiss to my lips. I whimper as his tongue swipes across my bottom lip, asking for entrance that I gladly grant him.

His tongue slips in and over mine. I moan into his mouth as he pulls me flush against his body. I can feel every hard ridge of his body as I wrap my arms around his waist.

We kiss slow and deep for what feels like a lifetime before he breaks the kiss, putting his forehead to mine.

"Now, let's get you to school and find you some mates." He grins, kissing the tip of my nose before taking my bag from me. This man does wonderful things to my body, like turning me into a needy puddle of slick.

"That sounds so weird, right?" I giggle.

He holds out his arm, and I loop mine into his before we start heading towards the front gate of the Omega compound.

"We'll stop to grab some coffee and something to eat on the way," Knox says, helping me into the cart.

"Oh, I don't know if I can eat," I warn as he takes his spot in the driver's side and starts the engine.

"You have to eat *something*, Kitten. I'm not going to let you go hungry," he growls. "At least something light, it might calm your belly and nerves."

"Okay. Maybe a plain croissant this time?"

He smiles. "And some water."

We drive over to a little coffee shop, and Knox gets me my order before we head off in the direction of the school. I lean my head against his shoulder as I take in the beauty of this little town while my mind wanders. *Will today be the first day of my new life? Will my world get turned upside down in all the best ways?*

That day was, in fact, not the first day of the rest of my life. Two weeks have gone by now since my first day at Calling Wood. I've met with nine unmated packs, and I didn't click with any of them. Most of them just wanted me as a prize, to have an Omega because that's what they think all Alphas should have. They all talked over me, never really got to know me. And if I have to hear another Alpha tell me how sexy I'll look popping out babies after my next heat, I'll lose my freakin' mind. The ones who actually let me talk didn't seem to care about or agree with what I had to say.

When I would talk about my interests, they looked at me like I was crazy. Because apparently, an Omega who loves Harry Potter, reading for fun, and watching Sailor Moon is odd. Well... fuck being normal, normal is boring. And so were they. *All of them.* They would just drone on and on about sports or working or other things I didn't want to listen to. I'm all for supporting my Alphas in what they love, even if it's not something I really enjoy myself, but if they're not going to support me as well, then why should I care?

When I mentioned how I wanted to stay here and get my degree in teaching, they all laughed like I was telling some kind of joke. No one took me seriously.

However, I do like how the school has the program set up. We meet at lunch each day with a new pack. We get one hour to meet and get to know each other. After, if it's something the Omega wants to pursue, they can work something out outside of school hours.

Knox was ready to knock each one of them out. He was always nearby if I needed him, and I love how protective he is of me already. I always feel safe and wanted when he is around.

We have gotten to know each other really well, and I've quickly become dependent on him being around. He's pretty much with me twenty-four/seven from the moment I wake up and only leaves when I'm ready for sleep. I told him at this rate, he was gonna get sick of me. He told me he could never, then kissed me until I forgot how to talk. I want him so bad, I want him to be my first. But every time I try to bring it up, I clam up, and I can't help but think about my future Alphas. Is that something I should be giving to them?

I know it's stupid, this is my body, and Knox is just as much mine as any Alpha would be. Maybe I should stop overthinking it and just let things happen naturally when the time comes.

But at this point, if this last Alpha pack isn't the one, I am going to be going through my heat alone. I have thought of asking Knox to help me through it. Sure, he doesn't have a knot that my body would be aching desperately for, but it would be better than going through it alone and in pain.

"So, how did it go?" Knox asks me as we walk away from the table of Alphas I was just meeting with and out into the main hall of the school.

"Come here," I demand, pulling him into a little dark corner and wrapping my arms around his body, shoving my face into his chest. I take deep lungfuls of air, letting his mango scent take over my senses, replacing the smell of all the Alphas back there. "So good," I moan.

"Really?" He chuckles.

I look up at him towering over me. "Not them. No, they were terrible, just like all the others. Their Alpha pheromones were all wrong. It was giving me a headache. Yours, well... your smell is amazing." My voice comes out dreamy as I take another whiff of him.

"Now, now, Little Omega. If you keep feeling me up like that, then we're going to end up putting on a very exciting show for the school."

"I wouldn't mind," I mumble into his chest.

His chest rumbles with laughter as I relax into him, his arms tightening around me in the most perfect hug ever. "You still wanna go to the library?"

"Yeah. I need to grab a few textbooks for my Art History class."

"Then come on, Kitten. Let's get those, then we can go out to eat. Gotta feed my woman. When was the last time you ate?"

His woman. *Swoon.* "I just ate." I giggle. "Nothing much, but the smell of my strawberry yogurt helped block out their smells. Normally the alpha blockers work, but this group's pheromones were just too strong."

"Well, that's not real food. You *need* real food," he growls. *Fuck me.* I went the whole day without needing a spare pair of panties, that's a first. But now, yeah now, I'm horny as hell, with slick coating my inner thighs. He can smell it too, and he lets out another deep growl, not helping the situation at all.

"Come on, Kitten. Let's get going." He tucks me under his arm and starts to guide me towards the library.

I don't know if it's because of being around all these Alphas, my heat nearing, or just Knox being so damn irresistible, but I've been more needy and wanting lately. I'm like a cat in heat, most of the time, and can't help but always be touching Knox.

Tomorrow is my last meeting with the last unmated Alpha pack that signed up for the program. Dean Benson said that the school almost always has every unmated Alpha pack enrolled in the program, so they have a fair shot at wooing an Omega. That means if this last pack isn't my bond pack or even one I'd consider, I'm out of luck.

Honestly, I'm already starting to give up hope that there's even an Alpha pack out there meant for me, let alone a bond pack or a scent match, like my parents. Maybe I'm not meant to be with anyone but Knox. *Would that be so bad? Or would he always feel like he's not enough, that I'd always be wishing for more?*

CHAPTER 6

TRISTAN

"She's really pretty," Finn says, looking at the new Omega from across the room. He has his chin in his hand, his elbow resting against the table as he watches her with this dreamy look on his face.

"She looks miserable as fuck," Dom grumbles, shoving a fry in his mouth, glaring at the girl in question like she has somehow offended him.

"You would know all about being a miserable fucker, wouldn't you?" Sawyer laughs as he takes a seat next to us at the table.

It's been two weeks since the news of a new Omega started circling around the school. She signed up for the program to help meet an Alpha pack, and every weekday we all sit here and watch her reject one pack after the next. Not that I can blame her, most of the unmated packs are unmated for a reason. They really don't have much to offer.

"Fuck off," Dom growls, swinging his glare to our shaggy, blonde-haired, blue eyed pack mate.

"I still think we should have signed up this year," Finn says, not looking away from the Omega.

"Why? So we can be passed up like always? Hell, half the time, the Omega finds their mates before it's even our turn, or they take one look at us and rather have their heat by themselves. Face it, Finn, we're Alphas in every way other than where it counts. No fucking Omega wants us, and I'd rather not face that rejection again. It's been almost four years, and this is our last year. It's just us," Dom says.

"Whoa there, let's not drown ourselves with all that cheer and positivity," Sawyer says sarcastically, rolling his eyes.

Leaning back into my chair, I watch the Omega too. She's stunning. I haven't seen her up close yet, but her fiery red hair stands out a mile away. A part of me is kicking myself in the ass for not signing our pack up this year. But it's an all or nothing thing, and with Dom not up for it, I didn't want to sign us up without him on board. It wouldn't be fair to the Omega. And he has a point. There's only so much rejection one can take before it really starts to fuck with your head.

We are not your typical Alphas. Sure, we have the anatomy of one, but when you think of an Alpha, you think big and strong, able to protect an Omega from any harm. Someone who has an Alpha personality, someone dominant.

We've gotten a reputation of being the reject pack. The one no one wants. The faulty Alphas. And it's taken a toll on all of us.

Finn is quiet, quirky, and sometimes I wonder if the universe meant for him to be an Omega. Other Alphas love to point out how weak he is, calling him a pussy, a geek, all the hurtful things they can think of. His red hair, glasses, and love for suspenders just adds fuel to the flame for them.

Sawyer is a jokester. He never takes things too seriously, always trying to make light of any situation, and it might often seem like he's coming off too strong. He uses humor to mask his pain and feelings.

Dom would have to be the closest of us to give off the traditional Alpha vibes. He's tall, strong, and a broody fucker, with a beard that does nothing to hide his permanent scowl. But he's not what most women would call 'fit'. They've made fun of his weight because his muscles don't show like most Alphas. He doesn't have the rippling abs that women drool over. I'm not into men, not that there's anything wrong with that, but I've tried telling him he's an attractive guy. But it doesn't have the same effect that it would have coming from a woman.

And me? Well, I'm what people call the boy next door. Brown hair, gray eyes, lean body with a bit of muscle. Very average, or so I've been told. Put us all together, and well... it's not a pack most Omegas would be chomping at the bit for.

What pisses me off, though, is that I know each of us would love and care for our Omega like we should if we were ever just given the chance. Just because we don't look how society thinks an Alpha should doesn't mean we don't know how to be one.

We would love and spoil them. But it's been years, and Omegas are so rare that we've lost hope. Well, Finn is a hopeless romantic; he still believes that someday an Omega will find their way to us. And he is completely entranced by the one a few tables over.

Sometimes, I have hope too. But as time goes on, I have this empty feeling, a longing to love and care for an Omega. I know we all need one to complete our family, but we've come to believe Omegas don't want us.

"Finn, stop staring, people are gonna think you're creepy or some shit," Dom mutters.

Finn turns away, a sad look on his face as he looks down at his plate of food and starts to pick at it.

"You don't have to be such a dick to him," Sawyer says, frowning at Dom.

Dom watches Finn for a moment before letting out a sigh and rubbing his hand down his face. He looks at Finn again, his face softening. "Sorry, man. I didn't mean to be an asshole."

"Sure, you didn't," Sawyer snorts, and Dom flips him off.

"It's just... I hate seeing you look so sad. We've gotten our hopes up way too many times, only for them to be shattered time and time again. Is it even worth it? She's probably gonna pick this pack or the next one anyways. There's no point in longing over someone we don't have a fucking chance with."

I don't know about that. The way she looks, as if she wants to be anywhere but here, tells me this meeting is gonna go like all the rest. I've heard some Alphas in my class talk about how she passed them up, and there must be something wrong with her if she keeps turning Alphas down or how no one is good enough. I just see it as the girl knows what she wants and doesn't want to settle for anything less. That alone has my interest peaked way more than I'd like to admit.

The Omega, whose name I've found out is Octavia, looks behind her where her Beta guard stands watch. It's just a quick glance, but I can see how her shoulders relax, knowing he's still there, making sure nothing bad happens to her.

Knox is a good man. I don't know him very well, but from what I've heard and seen, he's a hard working man who takes his job seriously. Finn, however, knows him. He hasn't talked about him much, only telling us that their parents are close friends, meaning Finn and Knox spent a lot of time together growing up. With the way Finn would looks at Knox whenever he sees him, I know there is more to the story. But it's none of my business, and I'd never try to force any information out of him.

The way Knox looks at this Omega, though... she's not just a job to him, there's definitely more to their relationship. It's easy to see whenever they are together. Maybe that's why she's being so picky when it comes to choosing her Alphas. Not a lot of packs are understanding, let alone welcoming, of a Beta having a romantic relationship with their Omega. I would like to think we would be. But, on the other hand, I don't know how Finn would feel about having Knox around if she selected us. Good thing we don't have to find out.

"I still think there's an Omega out there for us," Finn whispers.

"Maybe. But I'm not going to hold my breath." Dom shrugs, going back to shoving food into his mouth.

"I need to stop by the library before my next class. I'll see you guys back at home."

They all say bye as I grab my bag. Taking one last look over my shoulder at the beauty that I wish more than anything I could have a chance with, I take off for the library.

Thank god that's over with. That assessment for my English class has been one that I've been dreading since it was assigned. With that out of the way, I can focus on my other classes.

Shutting my text book, I place it on the table in front of me and let out a tired sigh as I lean my head back against the couch, closing my eyes. And there she is, the mysterious Omega. Octavia. I really wish we signed up this year.

Trying not to let regretful decisions take over my

thoughts, I gather up my stuff and head to put the text books away.

As I'm walking to the back of the library, I catch the most delicious scent. Toasted coconuts. I groan as my cock hardens instantly. *What the fuck is that amazing smell?* My brain goes on autopilot, making me seek out the source. Rounding the corner, I collide with someone.

"Sorry!" a musical voice says, making my cock twitch. Looking down, I see the person I've bumped into is none other than the person who's been consuming my thoughts. The very Omega who I've been wishing we got a chance with. She's standing before me now, here in the flesh.

The coconut smell is stronger now, and as I stare at this wide-eyed Omega who's looking at me with a mixture of lust, confusion, and panic, I know it's coming from her. The Alpha in me is screaming *'mine'*. The need to scoop her up, hold her, love her, protect her, fuck her... is so damn strong. She's mine, I know this for sure. She's my scent match, my bond mate. *Is this really happening right now?*

Her whimpering brings me back to reality.

"It's okay, *Little Omega*. I'm not gonna hurt you," I say, my voice coming out soothing and deep. These feelings are new, the urges foreign to me. It's like I'm watching behind a two-way mirror while the Alpha part of me that's been trapped inside for so long takes control. Her pupils are blown wide, her nipples pebbling against her sky blue dress as she shifts from foot to foot like she's trying to rub her thighs together. Another smell makes its way into my senses, and I know it's her slick. And fuck if it doesn't mix well with her scent like the finest chocolate money could buy. I let out a low growl, and I can smell more slick leaving her sexy body. "Are you needy, Omega? Do you need help to take that ache away?"

She bites her lip, her chest heaving, but after a moment, she nods. "Please?" she questions in a needy whisper.

I don't know what comes over me next, but one moment my hands are on her shoulders, and the next, I have her pinned against the bookshelf. My arms wrap around her waist as I devour her mouth. I growl against her lips as she whimpers against mine. We kiss until our bodies fight for air.

"Please," she begs, and I don't like that. I don't like my Omega having to beg me for anything. She deserves everything she wants, when she wants it. Not wanting her to ask twice, I start to nibble at her neck, loving the groan that slips from her swollen lips.

Holding her close with one arm, I slip my free hand down her side, trailing down to the hem of her dress. Her body shivers in my hold. "Can I touch you, Omega? Can I take that ache away?" I ask, giving her an out if she really wants it. But I think we're both too far gone, our natural instincts taking over.

"Yes," she pants. "I need you."

I move back enough so that I can look into her emerald green eyes. She looks at me with lust and a desperate need she doesn't seem to quite understand.

We stare deep into each other's eyes as I slide my hand under her dress. Her eyes flutter closed as my fingertips graze her belly, just above the band of her panties.

Moving my hand to cup her core, I find that she's soaked right through the fabric. A moan mixed with a growl rumbles in my chest. "Is this for me? Are you dripping with slick for your Alpha?" I don't know where that came from. Maybe from the unshakeable knowledge that the universe fated us to be together, proven by the fact that she is my scent match. I haven't even introduced myself, but I already want to consume every inch of her body, lay her down on the floor, and claim her as my own.

She doesn't answer with words, but the intake of breath as I slip my hand into her panties and over her slick coated pussy tells me that this is all for me. The Alpha in me loves that.

Capturing her lips again, her hands come up behind my head. Her fingers tangling in my hair as she holds me in place, kissing me back with just as much urgency.

She moans into my mouth as I dip my fingers into her center before bringing them back out, rubbing her swollen clit. I do that for a bit until she's trembling in my arms before thrusting them back in. I pump my two fingers while using my thumb to play with her sensitive bundle of nerves.

"Oh," she breathes, breaking the kiss. "Oh, god." I can tell she's close. "Please. Don't stop."

"Never," I growl, feeling a gush of slick coat my fingers. "Cum for me, Little Omega. This orgasm is mine."

With a few more pumps, she breaks apart in my arms. Quickly, I kiss her again, swallowing the cries of her release as she cums all over my hand.

When she's had a second to recover, I remove my hand

and slip my fingers into my mouth, sucking them clean with the need to taste her. I moan, my eyes rolling into the back of my head. I've never tasted something so mouth-wateringly delicious.

"Tia, Kitten. How long does it take to find some books?" A deep voice pops our little lust bubble. Octavia's eyes go wide like she's just realizing what we did. She quickly turns her head just in time to see Knox come into view.

His eyes find Octavia's before looking at me. He knows what happened. His nostrils flair as he takes in the scent of slick, sex, and our pheromones mixed together.

A deep rumble sounds in his chest, one that's very *un*-Beta like. It triggers my own growl. I move to hold my Omega close, but she wiggles out of my arms, moving between Knox and me.

"Let's go," she says to Knox, looking up at him. He looks down at her, his face softening, seeing something I can't because her back is to me.

He gives her a nod as his arm wraps around her shoulder, and he starts to guide her away from me. I wanna scream and yell that she's mine, to pull her away from him. But I don't. I can't. I have no fucking idea what just happened, what is going on, or what to do about it. My mind is a big, confusing jumbled mess.

She looks at me over her shoulder one last time. Her eyes look lost, full of longing, but I can tell she feels the same. Unsure of what just happened.

Then she's gone, out of my view. I stand there, watching

the spot where she just was. Her slick still coats my tongue, drying on my hand. Fuck, I may never wash this hand again.

I didn't even get to make sure she was okay. To reassure her that everything will be alright. But will it? The feeling is like an itch that can't be satisfied.

I just got a girl off. Not just any girl. An Omega. *My* Omega. That's never happened before. What the fuck is going on, and how the hell do I explain this to the guys?

CHAPTER 7

OCTAVIA

I slept horribly. I tossed and turned all night, having an amazing dream of all my Alphas loving me, only for it to come crashing down when each one of the faceless men reject me and leave before being replaced by *him*.

I was not expecting for my trip to the library to end in me having one of the best, most intense orgasms brought on only by the freaking fingers of a complete stranger. And I sure as hell wasn't expecting it to be with my scent match Alpha.

The moment he bumped into me, with his hot apple cider scent invading my nose, I was a goner. It was like a switch inside of me was flipped, and I went full Omega. All I wanted him to do was kiss me, touch me, fuck me. To rub his scent all over me and make me his. My heart felt as if it were a puzzle and a piece of it clicked into place.

When his piercing, gray eyes locked with mine, the lust, the need within them had my knees threatening to buckle beneath me. And when he kissed me, my body hummed with approval. I was willing to let him do anything to me.

So when he asked if I needed help with the ache between my legs, I was more than happy to agree. I was ready to beg if needed.

I can still feel his fingers inside me, his growl vibrating in his chest, turning me into a puddle of slick. The look on his face as he sucked my slick from his fingers had me gushing, and a sense of pride that my slick brought him such pleasure filled me.

Then the moment Knox turned the corner, it was like a bucket of cold water was splashed over my body.

Knox *knew* what had just happened. I could see it by the look on his face. He was pissed, and I still don't know if it was at me or the nameless Alpha who rocked my world.

Leaving with Knox was hard. All I wanted in that moment was to cuddle with the Alpha stranger, to have him care for me, to listen to his sweet voice tell me all the things I wanted to hear.

But instead, I got taken home in silence. Knox wouldn't even look at me. He drove me home, gave me a quick kiss good night, and left.

When I got into bed, I let the tears fall. I've never felt more Omega than I did at that moment. All I wanted was to be surrounded by Alphas, my Alphas, but instead, it was just me.

I woke up in a cold sweat, reality hitting me all over

again. I whimper, remembering yesterday. Looking over at the clock, I see that I woke up fifteen minutes before my alarm is set to go off.

Sighing, I scrub my eyes, feeling like death. Dragging myself out of bed, I grab some fresh clothes; a pair of leggings, a t-shirt, and a hoodie. I don't feel like dressing up and looking pretty today.

What's the point when I'm going to be let down yet again? I have one last pack to meet with, and then that's it, I would have met with all the available Alphas here. And seeing how every other pack I met with was a total bust, I wasn't getting my hopes up with this one.

I scrub the gross feeling from my body as I take a nice, hot shower. I can't help but hope and pray that the mystery Alpha from yesterday is a part of the pack I'm meeting with.

Because if he's not, that means I'm destined to be bonded with an Alpha who already has a pack and an Omega. I don't want to be a homewrecker. I feel horrified at the possibility that he cheated on his Omega with me. If that's the case, scent match or not, I don't want anything to do with him. I'm not that kind of person, and I'm not looking to be forced into a pack as an inconvenience because of how our biology works.

When I'm done getting ready, I hear a knock at the door. My heart starts racing, my body prickling with nervous energy.

Is Knox still mad at me? I can't handle it if he is. He's quickly become such a big part of my life. I've fallen for him hard and fast, and if I lose him, I don't think I'll handle it very well.

Grabbing my bag and phone, I answer the door. His back is to me, and when he hears me, he turns around. He doesn't look much better than I do.

"Hi," he rasps, sounding anguished.

"Hi," I say softly.

"Ready?" is all he says, holding out a coffee and pastry like he does every morning.

"Yeah," I say, taking them from him. "Thanks."

"Of course." He gives me a weak smile. "Let's go."

He turns around, starting for the gate. I quickly lock up and race to catch up with him. He's pissed at me. I've lost him, I just know it. He's not his charming, sweet self anymore. It's like the man I've been with for the past two weeks is gone and replaced with a complete stranger.

We sit in that nerve wracking silence again as we head to school. I bite my lip, looking out of my side of the golf cart so Knox can't see the tears I'm holding back.

"Tia?" Knox asks as we park outside the school. His voice makes me jump as he suddenly breaks the silence. "Tia, look at me." His tone isn't demanding but soft.

I turn my head to look at him, and the distant eyes I saw this morning are gone, replaced with fire.

"Yes?" I croak, my emotions taking over.

"Fuck," he sighs, cupping my face. His thumb brushes against the corner of my eye, swiping away a fallen tear. "I'm so fucking sorry for being a dick. What I walked in on at the library had me freaking out. I was lost in my head, and it was fucked up of me to take it out on you."

"Are you mad at me?" I ask, feeling far more vulnerable than I want to be. "Do you hate me?"

"No," he says with more force. "I could never hate you, Kitten. What I feel for you is the complete opposite of hate... that's why I freaked. I'm not mad at you. You did nothing wrong."

I let out a harsh laugh. "Yeah, like I didn't let a total stranger finger fuck me in the library."

He blows out a breath. "Yeah, well... when you meet your scent match, there's nothing much you can do. Gotta love the dynamics of Alpha and Omegas."

"So much fun," I agree sarcastically.

"It can be. This isn't a bad thing, Tia. Finding your bonded mates, it's one in a million. What you and Tristan have, it's rare."

My eyes widen. "You know him?" I ask in disbelief.

"I know *of* him," he says, dropping his hand and sitting back in his seat.

"And let me guess, he's not a part of the pack that I'm meeting with at lunch."

He looks at me with pity filled eyes. "No, he's not."

Anger fills me, and before he can say another word, I'm out of the cart, storming towards the front doors.

"Tia, wait!" Knox calls, racing after me.

"I don't wanna talk about it anymore," I say as he makes it to my side.

"But-"

I shoot him a death glare.

"Alright. But we really should talk more about this later. There's more to his story that you really need to know," he insists.

Like how he just pretty much confirmed that the Alpha who's meant to be mine isn't available, no thanks. "Yeah, sure," I grumble as we get inside.

The morning felt like it was going on forever. I was so distracted that I burnt the cake we made in cooking class, stabbed myself with a needle a thousand times as I tried to make a purse in sewing class, and told the fake, crying baby to shut the hell up in my child development class. The looks of horror I got from the other Omegas were almost comical. I probably would have laughed if I wasn't in such a shitty mood.

When class is finally over, I head outside into the hall to meet Knox, where I know he's waiting for me. He's never far when I'm outside the Omega compound.

Two hands grab my arms, pushing me against the wall. The only warning I get before a set of lips meet mine is the subtle scent of mangos.

I moan as he kisses me like it's our last day on earth. He

presses his body to mine, and I whimper against his lips as I feel his hard cock against my belly.

"What was that for?" I ask, breathless, when he pulls back. He puts his forehead to mine.

"I forgot to tell you how much you mean to me and that I've been wanting to do that since last night. I was a grade A asshole for leaving you like that."

"Knox..." I say, reaching up to run my hands through his hair when he leans back to look at me. "I really, really like you. You mean the world to me. No matter what Alphas I end up with, you will be right there next to me. If they don't want you, they don't get me. Because giving you up would be like giving up a part of myself."

He looks at me like I'm the best thing that ever walked into his life, and my heart flutters. "You're so fucking amazing. You better watch out, Little Omega. I think I'm falling in love with you," he growls.

Fuck me, it's not the best time to be turned on, not right before going to meet with a pack of alphas.

"Would that be such a bad thing? Because I think I'm falling in love with you too."

His megawatt smile makes my heart sore. "Never a bad thing."

He kisses me again until I'm dizzy before escorting me to the lunch room. Time to meet with the last pack. Here goes nothing.

Walking into the cafeteria, I head over to the same table I've met all of the other Alphas at before. As I pass, a few packs that I've met with previously give me a once over, then look at the Alphas I'm about to meet with before talking in hushed tones.

"Hi," I say when I reach the table, interrupting their conversation. They all look up at me, and immediately, I wanna turn around and walk away. They all look at me like they are a pack of wolves, and I'm the little rabbit they want to devour. So far, this pack is giving me the worst vibes, and I haven't even sat down yet. *Goodie.*

"Sit," an Alpha with a shaved head and tattoos demands. My body jerks as it fights to obey the Alpha's command. Gritting my teeth, I take a seat in the chair next to him.

They all introduce themselves, and my heart drops when I realize none of them are Tristan. I know Knox said he wouldn't be in the pack, but a part of me still was holding on to a little bit of hope.

We make some minor chit chat before they all start talking as if I've already agreed to pick their pack. Talking about how many damn babies we're gonna have and how they can't wait for my first heat. *Yet another pack who doesn't see me as a person but as their fucking property.* I hope they know they just fucked up any chance they had with me. Not that they really had one to begin with because, like I've said before, I don't want just any pack, I want my scent match, bond mates. And even with all the de-scenting patches they use, I know none of them are.

Tristan is. But he has his own pack. And I'm left with having to go through my heat by myself because there's no way I'd ask any of the available packs to help me, even if it's just for my heat. The thought of them touching me sends a gross shiver through my body.

"God, what a bunch of losers." One of the Alphas, Jason, laughs, catching my attention. I look up from the game I was playing on my phone to pass the time of this meet and greet.

"Who?" I ask, brows furrowing.

"Them." He nods his head. Looking in that direction, I see who he's talking about. Two guys sit alone at a table.

"What's wrong with them?"

"How about everything?" the buzz cut one whose name is Marty says. "That's pack Ashwood. They're unmated and will probably stay that way for the rest of their miserable lives."

The other Alphas start to laugh, but my pulse starts to pick up. *Unmated. So this wasn't the last available pack here. But, if they are unmated, why are they not a part of the program?* So I ask these guys just that.

"They used to be when they first started, but every Omega they met passed them up for another pack, or the Omega didn't even bother meeting with them. So they gave up. It was for the best. There is only so much rejection someone can go through before it's just plain sad."

Their words start to boil my blood. *What a bunch of assholes!*

"What is so wrong with them that makes them not worthy of an Omega?" I ask, trying not to snap.

"Because they're not real Alphas," another Alpha, Nick, shrugs.

"Real Alphas?" I ask, raising a brow.

"Yeah, I mean, look at those two. One of them looks like he could break as easily as a twig, the other one is so cringy with all his stupid jokes, and don't get me started on the other two."

"So just because they're not big, strong, and growly, that means their not real Alphas?"

"Well, pretty much? What Omega wants Alphas who can't protect them and care for them?"

And I'm done. I can't take their bullshit anymore. I was only staying to be polite, already knowing I don't plan on accepting them as my pack, but after this? They don't even deserve my kindness.

Standing up, I grab my bag. "Where are you going?" Marty asks, a pissed off look taking over his face.

"Well, seeing how none of you seem to like people who are different, I see no fucking reason for me to stay. I'm not like every other Omega, so this wouldn't be a good fit. Also, you're all a bunch of uptight, judgmental dicks, and I don't waste my time with shitty people. I'd say it was nice to meet you all, but it really wasn't."

I don't give them time to respond and start heading over to the table where the two men sit huddled together talking. As soon as I get a few feet away from the table, a wonderful smell hits my nose, and I have to bite my lip to hold back a moan. Packs that are part of the program had to wear scent blocking patches so they don't overwhelm the Omega with their pheromones. But these Alphas were not a part of that, so they don't have anything blocking their pheromones, and my body reacts like it did with Tristan. Letting me know that these guys are also my scent match. The mix of cotton candy and bubble gum mix together making my mouth water. What odd scents for Alphas. But I already know this pack doesn't contain your 'typical' Alpha types, and that's why I want to get to know them so much more.

My heart soars with hope, and my pussy clenches with need. *Is this Tristan's pack?* God, I freaking hope so.

Taking a deep breath, I try to get myself under control and look up to see Knox watching me. He gives me a smile, and a knowing look, like he knew this might end up happening. He gives me an encouraging nod towards the guys.

Rounding the table, I pull out a chair and sit down. Both of their heads snap up to mine, eyes going wide in shock.

The one with the shaggy blonde hair stares at me for a moment, lips parted. I can't help the little smirk that takes over my lips. He turns to look at the other guy who has red hair and black framed glasses, who is also looking at me like he can't believe what he's seeing.

"Finn," the blonde one says, nudging the redhead. "Quick, pinch me."

That snaps Finn out of his little trance, and he turns his attention to his friend. "What?" he asks with a look of confusion.

"Pinch me," he insists.

"Sawyer, why on earth do you want me to do that?" Finn narrows his eyes, pushing his glasses up his nose as he looks at his friend like he's some alien.

"Because... the most gorgeous, sexiest Omega just sat

down at our table. So, I'm going to need you to pinch me to make sure it's not a dream."

I bite my lip, holding back a giggle at how serious Sawyer looks right now.

"No." Finn shakes his head.

"Do it."

"No." Finn refuses again.

"Do. It. Do it, do it, do- ouch!" Sawyer growls, glaring at his friend after Finn finally pinches him.

"You told me to!" Finn's eyes go wide with panic as he leans away from his friend.

Sawyer grumbles something under his breath while rubbing the spot on his arm before looking at me. His face goes from irritated to a beaming smile. "Oh good, it isn't a dream."

"Hi." I laugh."I'm Tia."

"We know," Finn says, his cheeks turning an adorable shade of pink. He clears his throat. "I mean, new Omega on campus, news spreads fast."

"So, not that we totally don't love the fact that you're here talking with us, but like... why are you?" Sawyer asks me, looking behind him at the table of Alphas I was just at.

"Because I wanted to introduce myself," I say. "I can leave if you want."

"No!" They both shout at the same time making me giggle again.

"I mean, no. It's totally fine that you're here. We want you here. Stay," Finn says.

"Okay." I smile. "As for the others, the program wasn't a good fit for me." I shrug.

"No? How come?" Sawyer asks.

"Umm, how do I put this nicely? They were all assholes. None of them wanted to get to know me for me and only saw me as an Omega they can claim and breed. As much as I want to find my own pack, that's not what I want." I nibble on my lip, and a growl slips out of Sawyer. His eyes widen as if the reaction surprised even him. I wiggle in my seat, holding in a whimper.

"Sorry," he says, his face masked with fury. "It just pisses me off that they would treat you like that. You're not property, you're a person who deserves the same respect as everyone, if not more."

I smile at that.

"God, that line is ridiculous," a gruff voice that sends a delicious shiver down my spine says as a mountain of a man takes a seat at the end of the table.

"It's because it's cake day," a familiar voice says. Looking up, I see Tristan take a seat at the table.

"Guys. We have a guest," Finn says.

Tristan looks around before locking eyes with mine. My cheeks blush as I remember what we did yesterday. He's here, a part of an unmated pack. I didn't fuck with someone's life. He's available, and he's mine... I hope.

"You," he breathes, his pupils dilating from shock to lust. "We meet again, Little Omega." His voice turns husky, and I can't help releasing slick.

All of their nostrils flare, and they all let out low grumbles before they realize what they're doing.

"What do you mean 'meet again'?" The mountain man grunts at Tristan and the other two look to him.

"Yesterday, I met Tia for the first time in the library," he says, looking at his friends, then to me. A slow smile takes over his face. "It was a very rewarding first meeting." He chuckles.

"How so?" The mountain man leans over, resting his arms on the table.

The smell of pine and fresh snow clouds my senses, and I whimper. His gaze flicks to me, his nostrils flaring, and his eyes widen as the realization hits him.

"Tia is my scent match," Tristan says, giving me a warm smile.

"She's what?!" Sawyer shouts, looking from Tristan to me.

"Don't worry, so are you guys," I say shyly, biting my lip.

"We are?" Finn asks, and I can't help but feel a burst of joy at the excited look on his face.

"Then how come we don't smell your pheromones?" Sawyer asks, brows furrowing.

"Because she's wearing scent blockers," mountain man says. "But I can smell her now. Like a tropical fucking paradise," he growls, but it sounds more out of anger than happiness.

"Dom, stop being such a dick," Sawyer snaps.

"So what, just like that we have an Omega? After all these years of no one fucking wanting us, one just falls from the fucking sky? Fuck this, I'm out of here." Dom pushes back out of his seat and storms off.

My lip wobbles as I watch him leave, my heart breaking at the idea of one of my Alphas rejecting me.

"Hey," Tristan says, getting up from his spot and moving over to sit next to me. He places a hand on my shoulder and thigh, soothing me. "Don't mind him, he'll come around. This is all just happening very fast. We weren't expecting it."

"Isn't that how this works, though?" I whisper. "Wouldn't it have been the same if I picked one of the other packs? I didn't know any of them either."

"Yeah." He smiles. "But the difference is, we weren't looking. We gave up a long time ago. It's why we weren't a part of the program. We didn't expect to be so lucky."

"Wait. So, is this really happening?" Sawyer asks.

"Well, I mean, I hope so?" I look between them. "That is, if you want to see where this goes. I can't deny the attraction I have towards you," I tell Tristan. He smiles, and my heart flutters. I look at the other two.

"I'd love to get to know you better," Finn says, his voice soft as he smiles shyly.

"Me too." Sawyer beams.

"Well then." Tristan chuckles. "Pack Ashwood would officially like to put in a bid to court you, Miss Lockheart."

It's crazy how just this morning, I had no hope in finding a pack that I liked, let alone a pack of Alphas that the universe made just for me. But I'm not going to second guess it. I know in my heart this is what's meant to happen, and I couldn't be any more excited, happy, and nervous.

"I accept," I say with a smile. Sawyer lets out a whoop, and Finn looks at me like I'm something precious. Then I remember. "But... there's something you should know."

"What's that?" Tristan asks, his hand caressing my thigh, and if he doesn't stop soon, I'm going to straddle his lap and dry hump him in the middle of the damn cafeteria.

"My... umm... my heat is set to come in about two weeks." I blush. Finn looks pale, Sawyer's eyes turn glazed, and Tristan lets out a low grumble. "Is that going to be a problem? If you want to wait until we know each other better, I can do this heat alone."

"No," Tristan growls. "You're ours now, and we would never let our Omega go through that alone. You should have your Alphas there to help you, please you, take care of you. It's fine. It just means we have two weeks to get to know each other." I look into his eyes, and all I want him to do is hold me, pet me, and tell me all the pretty words in the world. *Damn it.*

"Also, there's something else you should know if I'm going to join your pack," I say, looking behind Tristan and over to Knox. "Knox has to join as well."

They all turn to look over at Knox, who's standing against the back wall within hearing range. Knox's eyes look between the guys like he's sizing them up before landing on Finn. Finn whimpers as Knox's gaze turns intense. I look between the two of them, wondering what the hell that's all about. It's something I'll have to talk to Knox about.

"Finn, you okay?" Tristan asks his pack mate. Finn tears his eyes away from Knox to look at Tristan.

"Yeah," he says, his voice a little shaky. Finn looks to me. "You two are together?"

"Yes. Is that a problem? Because if you want me, you have to take him too. We're a package deal."

Finn says nothing for a moment as he looks back over to Knox, who is now standing on my other side.

"Yeah, Finn," Knox growls, but not out of anger or annoyance. No, it's a fucking lusty growl as he leans over the table, getting right into Finn's face. "Is it going to be a problem if I join your pack?"

"No," Finn breathes, his pupils dilating.

"Good." Knox leans back just as the bell rings.

"We gotta get to class, but we would love to get together this weekend if you're available," Tristan says, looking between Knox and Finn before looking at me.

"I'd love to. I was going to go to the beach, how about a picnic?"

"Sounds perfect," Tristan says.

I stand up, and Knox takes my bag for me. I give him a grateful smile as he wraps me under his arm.

"Before you go." Tristan stands and cups my face. He kisses me deep, making me whimper against his lips. "Until we meet again, Little Omega." His husky voice has my slick leaking and knees buckling. Knox lets out an amused chuckle doing nothing to help the situation at all as he holds me right to his side. "I'll work on Dominic, okay?"

"Okay." I nod. "Bye," I say, turning to everyone else. They all wave as I leave the room, looking sad to see me go.

"Knox," I say, stopping him once we get outside the front doors of the school.

"Yes, Kitten?"

"Did that just happen? Did I really just meet my pack, my bond mates?" I blink up at him, my mind in a haze of shock.

"Yes, Kitten, I believe you did. And you deserve it. They are good guys. Not your typical Alphas, but I know they will love and cherish you as much as I do."

"What's up with you and Finn?"

His face falls a little. "It's complicated."

I grin, raising a brow. "Really? Looks to me like the two of you were ready to throw down on the table and fuck."

He grins, chuckling. "I wish." Why is the idea of him and Finn so fucking hot? "Now, now, Kitten, don't cream your panties." He smirks, and I slap his arm with a laugh. "I'm bi. I knew Finn growing up. Our parents were friends. As we got older, I started getting feelings for him, but Finn isn't like most guys. He's shy, smart, and very quirky, all the things I liked about him. I started getting the feeling he liked me too. The night before he left to come here, we were hanging out, and I kissed him."

"You did?" I ask in surprise.

He nods. "I did. He freaked out, and I left. I don't think he was ready to admit what he felt for another guy, and I wasn't going to push it. He came here, and we didn't talk for a while. When I got a job here, we ran into each other a few times, but he had met his pack, and well... things have never been the same." He looks back at the school with a look of confliction.

"Well, I have a feeling that's all about to change. It's meant to be, you know." I smile, wrapping my arms around him. I'm not jealous of the idea of Knox and Finn together; no, quite the opposite. I wanna watch and join in. But I also just want everyone to be happy.

"Yeah? You think so, Kitten?" He nips the tip of my nose.

"Yup." I pull him down to my lips. His tongue slips into my mouth, and I whimper as he devours my mouth.

"Little Omega, if you keep making those noises and smelling so fucking tempting, I'm going to embarrass myself like a teenage boy," he growls, grinding his thick cock into my belly.

"I can help with that," I purr, really wanting to be of assistance.

"You're such a naughty kitten." He kisses me again, this time soft and tender.

"Then punish me," I breathe against his lips.

He pulls back. "Are you spiking?"

"Maybe." I shrug, not knowing what it would feel like. "All I know is I wanna rub all over you like a cat in heat." I giggle.

"Come on." He laughs. "Let's get you home. Big day tomorrow."

He guides me to the cart, and the whole way home, I'm a mix of horny and excited.

Knox says goodbye, properly this time, leaving me wanting to drag him into my house and toss him onto my bed. But he leaves me for the afternoon. I need a little alone time to wrap my head around today.

I fix myself some supper and watch tv until I start to feel tired. Crawling into my nest, I close my eyes and drift off to sleep. This time when I dream of the sexy, mystery Alphas, they all have faces. And there's a new person, a tattooed, growly beta. I've never felt more complete.

CHAPTER 8

DOMINIC

They're crazy. The whole lot of them are. They are fooled by the gorgeous Omega and too blind to see that it's all too good to be true.

Do they really think after years of being rejected by every Omega, male or female, that one would just drop into our laps?

"Seriously, man, why the fuck are you acting like this?" Sawyer growls as he storms into our house, the others following behind him. "I didn't think you would just be head over heels excited about this, but you almost made her cry, man. So not cool."

I shake my head, plopping down on the couch. "Don't you see it? She's only interested in us because we're her scent bonded. If it wasn't for that, she would see what everyone else sees, a pack of rejects."

"Do you really have to remind us?" Finn mutters, sitting down on the chair beside me. "I know we're not like all the other Alphas, but honestly, I don't want to be. I like being me, even if no one else does. And I don't think Tia is like that. She seems really sweet. I don't think she knew we were scent matched when she approached Sawyer and I, and she seemed shocked to see Tris there."

"Yeah, she did," Sawyer says, turning to our pack leader, who's leaning against the wall next to the doorway to the living room. "How do you know Tia? And why haven't you mentioned it before?"

Tristan sighs, pushing off against the wall. "It only happened yesterday. I was in the library, and when I went to put a book away, I caught the scent of toasted coconuts. It consumed me, and it was like something in my brain told me to find the source. I followed it, and bumped into the sweetest Little Omega." Tristan grins. "It was like I knew she was mine. I didn't get a chance to really think about anything else. She looked up at me with her wide, green eyes, and then I smelled her slick. All I wanted to do was please her, take care of her needs, and make her whine for me."

"Did you?" Sawyer asks.

"Yeah, I did. I asked her what she wanted, and she wanted me. So I gave her what she needed."

"Then what?" Finn asks, blinking as he listens with rapt interest.

"Then Knox came around the corner, and our little lust

bubble popped. The look on her face and how she wanted to get out of there fast broke my heart."

"Why?" I ask.

Tristan looks at me like I'm crazy. "Because... I just found my mate, my Omega, and she looked like she was ashamed of what we just did."

"She seemed just fine today." I roll my eyes. She probably just wants us because she rejected everyone else, and she realized she's left with nobody to help with her heat.

"Enough," Finn says. I narrow my eyes at his little outburst. He's never been this outspoken about anything. His eyes widen, realizing what he just did. "I'm sorry," he says as his cheeks heat. "It's just... I know we've all been hurt. I know we've been passed up over and over again and that we had just kind of given up hope, but I also know deep in my heart, Tia isn't anything like that. I can't explain it, but it's like my soul knows she's ours. She's meant for us. And I won't let any of us ruin this before it's even started."

Tristan gives our normally shy and awkward pack mate a proud smile. "I couldn't agree more." He turns to look at me. "Give her a chance before you write her off, thinking she's just like all the others. Get to know her, see it for yourself. Because what you're doing right now? Assuming she's something before actually getting to know her, it makes you the same as the people who took one look at us and judged us before knowing anything about us."

Fuck. He's right. But it's hard not to think this way. I'm not blind, I can see how fucking stunning she is. The moment I laid eyes on her for the first time, I wanted to charge across the room, pull her into my arms, and kiss her like she owned me.

I feel the pull, and when she locked eyes with me at the table... *fuck,* I almost got to my knees and begged her to be mine.

It's wrong of me to assume something about her with nothing to show for it. But what if she decides this isn't what she wants? That we're not what she wants? That she wants better than us. I don't think I could survive giving her a part of me only to have it ripped away.

"Let's spend some time with her at the beach, get to know her. I know you will feel differently about her by the end of the day."

I hope so. *Can she really be the one? The one to finally see us for who we are and not run away for something better?*

OCTAVIA

"You ready, Kitten?" Knox asks as he pulls me in for a hug. I wrap my arms around his waist, burying my face into his chest.

"I'm both excited and nervous," I murmur, rubbing my face against the soft fabric of his shirt. As much as I really want to get to know my Alphas, the idea of pulling Knox into the house and getting naked with him in my bed is starting to feel more and more like a better idea than going to the beach.

"Your heat is close, Little Omega," Knox's voice rumbles in his chest.

"I know." I sigh. "It's why I want to get to know them as soon as I can." I tilt my head up to look at him. "I was really worried, Knox. I thought I was going to have to go through my first heat alone. Because as much as the whole getting a temporary pack is a great option, it's not for me. I don't care if it's what my body is built for, that it will crave an Alpha, I don't want to sleep with someone just for the sake of sex. I want a connection, I want it to mean something."

"You know I would have been there for you, right?" he says, kissing my forehead. "I wouldn't have let you be in pain for days, suffering alone. I might not have the knot your body will crave, but I do have something else you might like, and I know how to use it too." His grin is one of pure sex, and fuck me, maybe going out so close to my heat isn't a good idea. His nostrils flair. "Good thing I'm coming with you. These guys might not be anything like those meat heads you met with, but they're still Alphas, and with you smelling so fucking tempting... Let's just hope they can control themselves."

"You're really okay with this? Me being with them, being their Omega?"

"Yeah, Kitten, I am. I'll admit, I was worried that if you picked one of the other packs, they wouldn't have been so accepting of me being part of the deal. But I'm glad you picked Pack Ashwood. They're good guys from what I've heard, and they deserve a chance at having an Omega."

"The Alphas I met with at lunch yesterday were assholes to them. Are they always treated like that?"

The smile Knox gives me is a sad one. "Unfortunately.

They're not what society thinks Alphas should be. So, people judge them for things they don't know, like, or understand."

Knowing people were so cruel to them fills me with a rage I'm not quite used to. "Well, they can all go fuck themselves because that's one of the things I think I'm going to love about them most." I smile up at Knox, and he gives me a real one this time, chuckling.

"I think it is, too. Thinking about it, you're the perfect match for them." He nips at my nose, making me shiver.

"And you're the perfect match for me and Finn." I bite my lip.

His brows raise. "Finn? You're really okay with *that*? If something happens between him and me? Not saying it will, because I don't know him like I used to."

"I'm okay with it, Knox. You're going to be a part of the pack too, and if you want Finn as well as me, then I'm happy for you. I just want you happy. Plus, Finn wants you. Trust me, you had him melting into a puddle of goo, just like you do with me."

"He did look ready to get down on his knees for me." Knox chuckles.

"Fuck, that would have been hot to watch," I breathe.

His eyes flash with fire. "Let's go before I drag you inside, Little Omega."

"Yes, please," I whimper. He growls, pulling me into a heated kiss before tossing me over his shoulder and spanking my ass, making me squeal.

"You're a little brat sometimes, you know that? I'm going

to enjoy fucking the sass right out of you."

I moan against his back. I don't know how much longer I can go without having Knox in every way I want him. I'm going to need to have that talk with him tomorrow.

The beach isn't very busy, thankfully, so it's not hard to spot my Alphas amongst the crowd. My Alphas, that's so weird to say. I know they said they want to court me, and I'm excited to see what they come up with, but I already know these guys aere meant to be mine. Dominic, however, might need some work, but whatever doubt he has about me, I'll show him I'm not like all the other Omegas who thought they were too good for these guys. I'm glad no one has picked them, or I would have never found them. I just hate that they had to face so much hurt to get to this point.

They look so out of place, sitting there awkwardly in the sand. I smile as I take them in. Finn is reading a book, Sawyer is playing with the sand, Tristan is observing the crowd, and Dominic sits in a beach chair with his arms crossed as he scowls at the people playing in the water.

"Hi," I say, giving them a little wave, a beaming smile spreading across my lips as I try and mask the nerves battling in my belly.

Like a magnet, they all look at me at the same time,

every one of their faces lighting up with a smile. Well, all but Dom's. He doesn't scowl at me like yesterday, just gives me a cautionary look. I'll take it as a win.

"Tia," Sawyer says cheerfully, jumping up from the sand, leaping over the towel to pick me up and swing me around. I laugh as we spin, loving the feeling of being in his arms.

He sets me back on my feet, but doesn't let go. We smile at each other, not saying anything. His eyes flick down to my lips, as if he's fighting with himself not to kiss me. So, not wanting him to think too much into it, I wrap my arms around his shoulders, tangling my hands into his sandy blonde hair before pulling his face down to mine.

He gives me a look of surprise before my lips meet his. He only hesitates for a moment before one of his hands slides from around my waist up and into my hair, holding me to him.

He gives me a little growl as his tongue licks my bottom lip. I whimper, opening for him. The kiss is slow and tender, and damn, it has me dripping for him.

"Kitten," Knox says, making me pull back from the kiss, panting and blinking as I remember where we are and who we're with.

"Sorry." I blush.

Sawyer shoots a glare at Knox, but he just grins back, raising a brow. "I don't mean to be a cockblocker, but we're in public... where there's unmated Alphas. Also, Tia is close to her heat, and anything could send her over the edge at this point, do you want that to happen right now?"

Sawyer's face softens as he looks down at me. "More of that when we're alone," he promises, and I lick my lips before biting the lower one, nodding in agreement.

His eyes flash with heat as he lets out another little growl.

"Hi, Tia," Tristan says, stepping between me and his pack mate.

"Hi," I grin up at him, giving him a hug. He gives me a lingering kiss on the side of my head before pulling back. I can see it in his eyes that he wants more, but he restrains himself.

"I'm glad we could do this," he says.

"Me too," I say, moving to sit on the blanket next to Finn. "What are you reading?" I ask him.

He blinks at me like he can't believe I'm sitting next to him. "Oh." He looks down at the book in his hand. "Umm…" His face heats up, and I can't help but smile at how adorable he is. "It's a romance."

Dom snorts. "Romance? You mean word porn."

Looking up, I see that Dom isn't even looking at us, his attention is on the water as he looks out at the vast ocean.

"You don't have to be so crass," Finn mutters, his face growing brighter than his fiery red hair as he pushes his glasses up his nose.

Word porn, huh? "What's it called?" I ask. Finn puts his bookmark in, closing the book, and hands it to me. Flipping it over, I grin when I read the title. *Omega's Obsession by Sarah Blue.*

"It's a reverse harem," he says, looking up at me through

his lashes.

"I know." I giggle, opening the book to skim through the pages. "It's one of my favorite reads."

"It is?" Finn asks in disbelief.

"You read porn?" Dom asks, and I look up to see him watching me this time.

I roll my eyes. "Look, I might be an Omega, but there's a lot of things I'm open to." I look down, flipping through the pages to find the spot in the book I'm looking for. "This is one of my favorite scenes," I tell him, showing him the part where the Alpha Dean gets on his knees for his Beta River and... well, go read the book and find out. Trust me, it's worth it.

Finn reads where I'm pointing, and I can't help but smirk as he squirms in his spot.

"I didn't get that far yet," he says, clearing his throat.

"What part?" Knox asks, crouching down behind us. Reaching between Finn and me, Knox takes the book from my hand.

"Umm." Finn goes to grab the book, but Knox chuckles and stands up. I observe both Finn and Knox as Knox reads the scene. The smirk on Knox's face slowly falls, turning into a lusty hunger.

"You like this?" Knox asks, looking down at Finn. I look over at Finn, biting my lip as I hear a whimper leave his lips. Knox crouches back down, bringing himself so close that he's only an inch above Finn. He gazes down at Finn with a predatory need. "Do you wanna get down on your knees for your Beta and suck his pierced cock? Because that's something I have in common with this River fellow." Knox grins, handing the book back to Finn. Finn takes it with shaking hands, and Knox stands up, not expecting an answer from Finn. "I'll be back, Kitten. Going to grab the chairs and cooler from the golf cart."

He holds his hand out to me, and I take it, letting him pull me up into his arms. "You're such a tease," I giggle, brushing my lips against his.

"You love it." He grins, giving me a kiss. "And now he knows I want him too. I'll talk to him about us when the time is right, but I opened a door without asking too much from him. I want you to establish something with your Alphas before I figure out what is going on between Finn and me."

"Don't be long," I tell him, hating when he's away from me.

"Back in a flash. Go talk to your Alphas." He gives me another kiss, this one hard and fast, leaving me panting and wet. "Be good while I'm gone," he says, giving me a wink before slapping my ass and taking off towards the cart.

With my heart racing, I turn back to the others, finding them all watching me with hungry, feral looks.

They can smell how turned on I am because I'm not wearing any scent blocking panties. I'm wearing my bikini, and they still have yet to make ones that work like the panties.

"Alright, who wants to go for a swim?" I say, my cheeks flushing. I need to cool off, or this is going to be one long, frustrating day.

CHAPTER 9

FINN

She pulls her dress off over her head, tossing it down onto the blanket next to me before taking off towards the water. I watch as she goes, my eyes taking in her smooth, creamy skin, stopping at her butt. I can't help it, she's stunning, and the way it bounces with each step, damn it.

I've found women attractive before, but no one has really caught my attention like Tia has. Not many girls thought I was good looking, being called geeky or nerdy way too many times, then being laughed at. But not Tia. She looks at me like she does the others, like she wants what she sees. I've smelled how she reacted to being around us. It's not something we're used to, it's still really hard to believe this is all real.

"Perfect, isn't she?" Knox's deep voice says as he takes a spot on the blanket. I jump at the sound of his voice, eyes shooting to him. His attention isn't on me but the breath-taking Omega. Looking back at Tia just as her feet meet the water, she lets out a squeal and a giggle that melts my heart and makes me smile.

"She is," I say softly as I watch Sawyer catch up to her, trying to will my dick to go down with being this close to Knox. They both start to laugh as they splash each other with water, confirming in my heart again that she's meant for us. I haven't seen Sawyer smile like that in a very long time. It's not like the fake ones that he puts on for the world. No, he is truly happy in this moment.

"So, how are you?" Knox asks, and when I turn back to him, he's watching me this time. I swallow hard under his intense stare. I haven't really talked to him in years. I miss him so much it hurts.

"Umm... good?" I tell him not really sure how to talk to him anymore.

We used to be best friends, hanging out all the time and telling each other everything. Until we didn't anymore.

As we got older, my feelings grew from friendship to something more, and it scared me. I wasn't afraid of being attracted to guys, more of this particular guy in question.

When he kissed me, I freaked. It's not that I didn't want it, but because knowing he was attracted to me as well set off a whole new set of worries. What if it was just sexual? What if he just wanted something physical and nothing more? It was easy to assume. I've never stopped being the dorky kid, but Knox? He grew into this gorgeous man that anyone would be lucky to share their time with.

I was set to go to Calling Wood just like my parents had. I didn't know what would happen when I got here. Would I meet an Omega that wouldn't allow me to be with him? Would she like him more than me? Would he find someone better while I was gone because I wasn't worth waiting for?

Every negative thing ran through my mind, so I ended things before they could start.

Worst mistake of my life. I not only lost my best friend, but also the man I fell hard for, and I didn't find the Omega I dreamed was meant for me.

Now, here we are, years later, and I missed a lifetime with him.

When Tia sat at our table the other day and said she couldn't be our Omega if Knox wasn't accepted too, I was thrilled and terrified all at the same time.

He's been at this school for years now, but our paths hardly ever crossed. And there he was, standing in front of me and with the Omega who was fated to be mine.

I was thrilled because I had them both in my grasp, but I was terrified that they wouldn't want me back. Or one would but the other wouldn't.

Now I'm sitting here, next to him, knowing both of them want me... right?

"Finn." Knox's deep voice snaps me out of my inner turmoil. "Stop over thinking."

"I'm not," I tell him. *Lie.*

He gives me a smirk making my cock twitch. Damn, he's so fine. "Don't lie to me, Finny, I know you better than you do, remember?" He moves so his full attention is on me.

"Here's the deal. You know I like you. I have for a long time. I know we have some shit to talk about and work through, but that can wait until you get to know our Omega. She comes first, always will. But... I need to know; do you feel something for me, more than friends? I know it's been awhile, but could something be there?"

My heart is pounding so hard I'm sure he can hear it. I look out at Tia, not knowing if she would be okay with any of this.

"She is," he answers me as if he read my mind.

"What?" I ask, turning back to him.

"Tia has already told me she's fine with something happening between us."

"Oh." I blink up at him. She really *is* perfect.

"Are you?" he asks, and I can't miss the hope in his eyes that he's trying to hide but failing at.

"Yes," I whisper, cursing at how hard I'm blushing right now.

His grin has me swooning hard. Sometimes I really do wonder if I was meant to be an Omega. "Good." He nods. "You always meant more to me, Finn. My feelings haven't changed towards you." He turns to look at Tia. "But her?" We watch as Sawyer spins Tia around, her feet skimming the top of the water before they both fall over, a wave crashing against them sending them both into a fit of laughter. "She's become my whole world. I want you a part of that, but never at the cost of her."

"I want her too," I tell him. "And if she's okay with it, then we can talk." I don't want to assume anything. We have a past, but we haven't been around each other in years.

"I know you do. I think your pack is perfect for her."

I laugh in disbelief. "I don't know if I'd go that far. What if we fail her? There's a reason why we've never found an Omega. No one wants us."

A firm grip on my hand brings my attention back to Knox. "I'm sorry you guys had to deal with all that bullshit these past few years. It's not right. But those Omegas? They missed out on something amazing. But think of it this way. If you found an Omega, you could have missed out on your chance with her."

"Guys," Tia says, jogging over to us dripping wet. "Look!" she says, pointing to the beach volleyball net that some of the beach workers are setting up for anyone to use. "Let's play!"

"You're on my team, Kitten," Knox says, giving my hand one more squeeze before getting up and throwing Tia over his shoulder, making her laugh as he takes her over to the net.

"I'm down to play," Sawyer says. "What about you?" he asks me. I look at Tia and Knox, and my eyes lock with hers. She gives me a beaming smile that makes me want to offer her the world at her feet. Knox is right. If we found an Omega before meeting Tia, we would have missed out on *our* Omega; the one we were meant to be with, and the idea of that fills me with an overwhelming need to protect and love my Omega. Something tells me all the years of hurt and pain may have just been worth it in the end. There is nothing we can do about the past now, and I won't let the past ruin my future.

Is there a part of me afraid that all of this is going to be a dream when I wake up tomorrow? Yes, but I'll enjoy it now while it lasts if that turns out to be the case.

"Yeah. I mean, I have no idea how to play, but why not."

OCTAVIA

I can't remember the last time I've had this much fun. I've laughed so hard and so much today that my cheeks hurt and my belly is cramping.

"Heads up!" Sawyer calls out as he launches the volley-ball over the net. I dive to hit it back over, landing on the ground when I do. It flies back to the other side, and I watch in horror as it sails past Finn, who misses it, and right into Dom's face.

I scramble up from the sand, my hands going to my gasping mouth in horror as I hear Dom curse, his hand covering his nose. My heart breaks as I see blood drip onto the sand at his feet.

"Fuck!" he curses.

"Shit," Sawyer says as Dom straightens up.

"You okay?" Tristan says, jogging over to Dom.

Finn, Sawyer, and Tristan check to see if he's okay while my eyes sting, and I bite the inside of my cheek really hard to try and stop myself from crying.

"Hey," Knox says, stepping into my line of sight, blocking me from seeing the others. "Kitten, look at me," he tells me, cupping my face so that my eyes meet his. "Baby girl," he sighs, his face softening. "Don't cry, it was an accident."

"But I hurt him," I say, my voice cracking. "What if I broke his nose? He already hates me as it is."

"Stop," Knox growls, having the same effect on me as it always does, the same as an Alpha growl does. "He does *not* hate you. He's just a broody man who has a lot of trust issues. He will come around. You're amazing, how could he not?" Knox leans in and kisses each corner of my eyes.

"Not now," I say, on the verge of crying. The idea of me hurting my Alpha makes me sick.

"What's wrong?" Tristan says as he comes over to us, stopping next to Knox. He sees the state I'm in, and he too growls. "Tia, love, what's wrong?"

"She's upset that she hurt Dom," Knox answers for me, and I'm grateful because if I talk, I think I'll cry.

"He's fine," Tristan says, his face softening as he pulls me into his arms. I wrap mine around his body, burying my nose into his chest and taking a deep breath. The smell of apple cider helps me calm down, and I relax in his embrace. "Just a little blood, nothing broken," he reassures me, rubbing his hand up and down my back.

"Come on, Kitten. You've had a long day. You wanna go home?" Knox asks, and Tristan holds me a little tighter like he doesn't want to let me go. I don't wanna go home yet. I wanna stay with them, my Alphas, a little longer. We've been having so much fun. Well, up until a few minutes ago.

"Stay, have some supper with us. The sun will be setting within the hour, and we can watch it together," Tristan says.

Moving my face to the side so I can see up into Knox's eyes, I give him a pout. He rolls his eyes but grins. "Fine. Anything you want, Little Omega." I turn my face back into Tristan's chest to hide my grin.

"Let's get you some water; it's hot, and I don't want you to pass out from heat stroke," Tristan says, and my heart feels so happy that my Alpha is taking care of me, that he cares so much about my well-being. I could get used to this.

Knox jogs ahead of us to our spot as Tristan wraps his arm around my shoulder. Knox grabs me a water bottle from the cooler and hands it to me. "Thanks," I say, giving him a soft smile.

"You're welcome, Kitten," he says, kissing the top of my head before moving to sit on the blanket. He starts to talk to Sawyer about something, and Tristan moves to sit next to Finn. Everyone falls into a steady flow of chatter while I just stand there a few feet from Dom, who's sitting in his beach chair with tissue shoved up his nose and an angry look on his face as he plays on his phone. It makes me wanna cry all over again, knowing I've ruined his mood.

I don't move to sit, needing this moment to myself, but I see the others look up at me to check if I'm okay.

After a few minutes, I turn to look out at the water, watching the seagulls on the beach. I'm trying to hold in my emotions, so many things flowing through my mind. *What if I fucked this up before we really had a chance?*

"Tia," a gruff voice has me spinning around to face

Dom. He's got a sandwich on his plate, and his phone is put away. "Come," he demands, nodding his head in a beckoning motion.

Biting my lip, I slowly move towards my injured Alpha, stopping right in front of him. We just stare at each other for a moment, and I'm waiting for him to bitch me out. But then he holds out his hand, and I just stare at it like an idiot.

Take it, Tia, take the man's hand!

With a shaky one of my own, I take his, and he pulls me down into his lap, wrapping one big arm around my waist, holding me in place. "Eat," he commands, holding up half of the sandwich in front of my face. "And stop worrying, I'm fine. I know you didn't mean to."

Fuck. Fuck, I'm gonna cry, but for totally different reasons.

I reach out to take the sandwich, but Dom moves it away. "Open," he instructs, and I preen at the fact that he wants to feed me. Looking over to the others, I see them all watching with looks of happy amusement. Unable to hold back a smile of my own, it breaks free. Dom can't see it, so I take a bite and do as I'm told, loving every moment of it.

He feeds me until I'm done with the whole sandwich. He doesn't make me move, so I snuggle into him, his woodsy smell wrapping around me like a blanket, and loving his warmth as the night starts to chill. He holds me close, although we don't speak as we watch the sunset, but I don't mind. This is more than I could have hoped for today, and I'm gonna enjoy it before I lose this when I have to go home.

I'm not sure when I fall asleep, but I wake up in my own bed, Knox tucking me in.

"Hey, Kitten," he says, kissing my lips softly. "I'm so glad you had fun today. Seeing you happy with your Alphas, it's all I wanna see from now on."

At the thought of them, my heart grows heavy. "Shhh," he says, brushing my cheek bone. "Soon. Soon you won't have to spend a day away from them."

With that thought in mind, my eyes drift closed again. And before I fully fall back to sleep, I feel the bed dip next to me as Knox pulls me into his arms. It's like he could feel that I didn't wanna be alone tonight, more so than any other night since I've been here.

In his hold, feeling loved and protected, I have a peaceful night's sleep.

One day at a time, Tia. Everything will be okay.

CHAPTER 10

KNOX

My life has never been more perfect than it is with my Omega in my arms. I never thought in a million years that I would find a woman who would want me, let alone this drop-dead gorgeous Omega. Sure, I know I'm not bad on the eyes, at least that's what I've been told, but normally they don't look past the built body and tattoos.

But Tia? My little Kitten, she wants me for me. I know she appreciates my body, but she also loves my mind. She trusts me, wants me, and cares for *me*.

And me? God, this woman. I fell in love with her the moment she got out of that car in front of the main gates of Calling Wood. Her fiery red hair, her stunning smile. I knew right away she wasn't a typical Omega, not that there was anything wrong with that. I just knew there was something... special about Tia.

I'm a Beta, an Omega has never looked at me like they would an Alpha, but she did. And always has. But it's not that she wanted me to be an Alpha. She just saw me as their equal, and for that I will always love her even more.

We hit it off fast. I was protective and entranced from the start. I'm so fucking happy I was given the chance to know her as more than just an Omega, a job. She's become my best friend. I didn't have a lot of them before her.

Growing up, I was a popular guy, a jock, and later became a pretty big name in the MMA world. But then I had my accident, and after I recovered as much as I could, I took this job. I needed something that wasn't behind a desk, making me feel useless. I needed a job of importance.

But until Tia, all the Omegas I'd been assigned to only saw me as a guard, someone meant to keep them safe until they met their pack, and then I moved on to the next.

When Tia asked me to walk her home and not just leave her at the gate that first night, I was already falling down a slippery path of hope, falling even farther when she said she wanted to be friends.

She was all I could think about, and getting to know her more the day I showed her around Calling Wood, made the all consuming thoughts worse. I knew once she met her Alphas they would see how amazing she is, loving and adoring her like she deserves. Jealousy surged through me. I knew I needed to take my chance and tell her how I felt before it was too late.

And god, when she said yes to giving me a chance, I was

gone. I tried to keep cool and not act like a lovesick fool, but it was really hard.

Watching her meet and pass on the unmated Alpha packs was hard to watch. Seeing her lose hope with each one hurt. I don't like seeing my Kitten upset.

Never did I think pack Ashwood would end up being her Alphas. But I'm glad they are. They might not be your typical Alphas, but they are good men. It's going to take a little time for Tia to break down each of their walls, but my little Kitten is determined. And I'll be right there beside her. She has everything she said she ever wanted. A bond match and good men, who -even though some still have to get used to finally having an Omega- are head over heels for my Omega. *Our* Omega.

I knew who they were, talked to a few of them over the years, but kept my distance because of him. *Finn.*

When Tia said she was okay if something were to happen between Finn and me, I fell for her all over again. She's so damn amazing and selfless. Omegas can be jealous or possessive, but I saw the look in her eye at the idea of Finn and me together.

I know I want him, just as much as I want Tia, but she comes first. I need her to know Finn loves and wants her before I start anything with him, just to be sure. She needs to know that she is the most important thing in all of our lives, and we live to please her, to put her needs first.

"Knox?" Tia's soft voice breaks through the inner thoughts distracting me from the movie we're currently watching. I don't even remember what it's called.

"Yes, Kitten," I murmur into the top of her hair, my arm that's wrapped around her pulling her closer to my body.

"Will you make love to me?" she says, her words almost a whisper as if she's afraid to speak them.

My mind goes blank for a moment. I just blink at the TV before looking down at her. She moves away from my body, angling herself so she can look me in the eyes.

"What?" *Are my ears playing tricks on me?*

"I want you to be my first," she says, a shy expression taking over her beautiful face as she bites her lower lip. Fuck, my cock hardens.

"Are... are you sure?" I'm not trying to get her to change her mind, but I don't want her to feel like she owes me anything because we're together.

She nods, moving to climb onto me, straddling my lap and placing her hands on my shoulders. "I've been saving myself for my Alphas, but as I get to know them, I can't help but worry about what it might do to the group. They are best friends, family, a pack. I don't want them thinking I favor one of them over the other by choosing one of them to be my first. Not only will it be my first time, it will be theirs too. I can be all of their firsts, but they can't all be mine."

After the day at the beach, her Alphas spent the past week getting to know her, spending time with her, and with me always close behind her. It was mostly suppers in the dining hall or walking her to her classes. She's making good progress with them and has gotten to know a lot about them. I even see Dom starting to soften up... maybe? Who knows, that man is gonna be the hardest nut to crack, but I know my Kitten can do it.

"So..." A slow grin takes over my lips. "You don't want to favor one over the other. Does that mean I'm your favorite then?" I tease, knowing she doesn't want one of us more than the others.

"No." She giggles, playfully slapping me on the shoulder. "I like you all the same. No one will have more space in my heart than anyone else. You're all my family, and I will love each of you the same. It's just, we already have this close connection. I trust you, I feel safe with you. And I really don't want my first time to be while I'm in heat. Both are known to be a nerve wracking experience but put them together... no, I don't want that. I want you to be who I give this to, with a clear mind so I can remember every moment of it."

"This is really what you want?" I ask, needing to know she's sure because there's no going back once we've made love.

"Yes." She nods, biting her lip again, and fuck me, I'm a goner. I'll say yes to anything her pretty, little Omega heart desires. "If... if that's what you want. If not... I-I understand."

"Do I want to make love to you? Tia, I can't think of anything else in this whole fucking world I'd rather do than to please the woman I'm madly in love with," I growl. Her eyes go wide, and she lets out a whimper that has my cock ready to go.

"You love me?" she asks, her words barely a whisper,

filled with shock.

"Yes, Little Omega. From the moment we met." Her beautiful green eyes shimmer with tears.

"I love you too," she says, her voice cracking with emotion.

Gripping her chin, I lightly guide her down so I can catch her lips with mine in a kiss. She whimpers again, and my cock twitches. I need her so fucking much.

Breaking the kiss, I slide my hands under her ass, her legs locking around me as I get up and carry her to the bedroom.

Placing her onto the bed, I step backwards, taking in the perfectly stunning Omega before me. Her pupils are blown wide, her lips parted as her breathing starts to pick up in anticipation of what I'm gonna do with her next.

A growl slips from my chest as I inhale her sweet, toasted coconut scent. "Look at you, Little Omega. Are you wet for me? Is your pussy dripping with slick, needing to be filled by my cock?"

"Yes," she whimpers, her thighs rubbing together, chasing the friction she desperately needs right now.

"I'm gonna make you feel so good, baby girl," I tell her, gripping the hem of my shirt and slowly pulling it off over my head, tossing it to the floor.

I can't help but smirk as I'm hit with another wave of her scent while her eyes take in my body, like she's memorizing every inch of my tattoos. And when she licks her lips as her eyes drop to the bulge in my pants, my cock twitches, loving the attention she's giving me.

She watches as I unbutton my jeans and pull them down, taking my boxers too. She sucks in a breath of surprise, and fuck, if I don't preen at her approval. My Little Omega loves my body.

Gripping my inked cock, I give it a few pumps, rubbing the pre cum over the piercing at the tip. "I want this bed drenched in your sweat and slick by the time I'm done with you. Do you think you can do that, Omega?"

"Yes." She nods her head frantically as I move to kneel on the bed.

"But first, I want to taste your cream, Kitten. I want it dripping down my chin as you scream my name while you cum."

"Knox," she whimpers.

"I know baby, I know. I've got you. I'm gonna make you feel so fucking good. My good, Little Omega."

She's still dressed, and that just won't do. Crawling, my cock bobbing with every move I make, I stop when I'm hovering over her. "I hope you didn't like this little sleep set very much. Don't worry, I'll buy you a new one."

Tia's brows pinch together in confusion, but she doesn't get long to wonder what I'm talking about because I sit up a little and grip the thin material of her top with both hands before ripping it in half, letting her perfect tits fall free.

She gasps, and I can smell the slick gushing out of her. She fucking loves the way I am with her. I'm going to have so much fun with her.

"Look at these perfect tits. I can't wait to fuck them," I growl, leaning down to suck her peaked nipple into my mouth. She lets out the sweetest cry as she arches, pushing her breasts into my face.

My cock throbs as she mewls and whimpers at my touch. After playing with one nipple, I give the other one the same attention.

"Knox," she whines. "Please."

"Shhh, Little Omega," I tell her, kissing my way down her belly. I want to kiss and suck every inch of her creamy skin, but not tonight. I can't make my Kitten wait any longer.

When I get to her shorts, I pull them down her thick thighs, my heart pounding because... fuck, I really hope she crushes me with them as I eat her like she's my last meal.

She's fully naked, and I waste no more time, needing to taste her sweet slick.

"You smell fucking amazing, Little Omega. I wonder if you taste just as sweet," I purr, parting her thighs, and when I see her dripping cunt, I growl, something snapping inside of me. I dive down, desperate for her on my tongue.

I groan like a dying man as I lap at her pussy, not wanting any of her slick to go to waste. But it's like a never ending river because every time I lap her up, she's gushing more as she whimpers and cries out my name. Her hands find my hair and she pulls, her nails scratching at my scalp. I fucking love the bite of pain, spurring me on.

"Knox, oh fuck, yes," she moans as I suck her clit into my mouth, nibbling slightly. I need to be inside her, my cock is aching, and fuck, I feel like I'm going to blow my load early from all the noises she's making.

I can tell she's close, the bed is already soaked under us,

and her legs are shaking. "Cum for me, Kitten. Give your Beta all your fucking cream," I growl into her pussy.

"Oh fuck," she whimpers, her thighs locking around my head in a death grip, and she holds me there, grinding her pussy on my face as she screams loud. I shiver at the sound. Her slick flows out, coating my tongue, and I do my best to lap up as much as I can.

"Such a good Omega," I praise her as she finally lets me come up for air. She blinks her eyes open, and they widen when she sees the state I'm in. Her little blush is adorable.

"Sorry. I... I didn't mean to be so rough," she whimpers, and nope, I will not let her think for a moment she did anything wrong.

I move, trapping her beneath me. "Never apologize, Kitten. I am yours, to do with as you please, and if you wanna drown me in your slick or crush me with your thighs... well, baby, I can't think of a better way to go."

"I don't know what came over me," she says, shying away.

"Tia," I say softly, cupping her cheek with my hand. "This is all new to you. But I promise you, no one will judge you for how you enjoy yourself in the moment. I love it a little rough anyways." I grin, brushing my lips against hers before giving her lower one a nip. She moans, wiggling underneath me. "Be as loud as you want. I never want you to hold back or be embarrassed. I can assure you anything you say or do will have us all ready to cum because of it."

"Knox," she giggles.

"I only speak the truth, Kitten." I kiss her for a while,

moving so that my body is pressed against hers. She wraps her arms around me, holding me close as we explore each other with our hands and tongues.

"I need you," she whimpers when we break apart, her eyes heavy lidded and filled with need.

"You ready, baby?" I ask. We already talked about condoms and contraceptives before. She knows I'm clean, I haven't been with anyone in a long time, and when an Omega gets here, they decide how they go about birth control. She chose to get an implant that can be taken out whenever she's ready for babies, because she wants to stay here and go to school.

"For you? Always." She smiles, and fuck, if my heart doesn't just melt for this girl.

Moving to get in position, I hold myself up with my left arm while gripping my cock with the other. She places her feet on the bed, knees bent a little and watches me, waiting.

"I love you, Tia," I tell her, needing her to know this will always be more about our connection then sex.

"I love you too, Knox." She cups my cheek, and I lean into her touch.

"I'm gonna make you feel so good, baby. It's gonna hurt for just a moment, but I promise you won't remember the pain. Only the feeling of your cunt strangling around my cock as you cum. I might not have a knot for you, Kitten, but I'm not a small guy, and I know how to use it." I wink, loving the huffed laugh and smile on her lips.

Rubbing the tip of my cock against her slit, I groan as I feel how wet with slick she is. I'm thankful she is because it will help me slide in a little easier, and hopefully be a little less painful. The idea of hurting her makes me sick, but I know it won't be much or for long.

"Touch yourself, Omega. Make yourself feel good while I enter you."

She whimpers but moves her hand between her legs, and when she lets out a little moan. Her eyes flutter close as I start to press into her. Fuck, she's tight.

Her eyes fly open again, and I can feel her panicking. "Shhh, Omega, shhh. That's it, baby. Touch yourself, play with that pretty, little clit. Look at you, taking me so good. Such a good girl." I soothe her as I press into her a little more. Her breathing picking up as her hand moves faster, little whimpers leaving her.

When I feel the tip of my cock hit something, I know it's her hymen, and this is the part that is gonna hurt the most. "Alright Kitten, I'm gonna give one final thrust, it's gonna hurt, but then I'll spend the rest of the night making you feel good, okay?"

She nods, licking her lips, her eyes still wild with need. She grips my shoulder with one hand, and continues to play with her clit with the other. Leaning over, I kiss her hard, devouring her as our tongues tangle together. Then I thrust forward, breaking that little piece of skin and filling her to the hilt. She lets out a squeal as her nails dig into my shoulder.

"Such a good girl. I'm all the way in, baby. Fuck, look at you taking my cock like the good little Omega you are," I praise her, peppering her face with kisses as I pet her sweat slicked hair. "I love you so fucking much, baby."

"I love you too," she whimpers. "But why do you have to be so fucking big?"

I let out a deep chuckle, kissing her lips again. "You're gonna thank me for my big cock later on, baby."

"So full of ourselves, aren't we?" she asks, rolling her eyes.

"More like you're full of me." I wiggle my eyebrows. "Ready for me to move?"

She nods, taking a deep breath. "It hurt a little, more pressure than anything. But it's just a dull ache now. I need you, please."

"You never have to ask, baby." I kiss her again. I'm so in love with this girl, I still can't help but think this is all a dream.

Moving back, I pull all the way out before slowly pushing back in. She tenses up again, but by the fourth thrust, she relaxes under me. "More," she whimpers. "Harder."

"You sure?" I ask, not wanting to hurt her.

"Fuck me, Knox. Make me cum," she breathes, arching into me.

With a growl, I start to pound into her, loving the cries of pleasure leaving her as the sound of our skin slapping together fills the room. She moans and whimpers, demanding more, and I give it to her. She cums soon after, clamping her pussy around me in a vice grip as she screams out her release. I have to bite the inside of my cheek to keep myself from cumming because, fuck me, it's a perfect sight. She coats my cock in slick, the wet sounds as I fuck her are so damn hot.

"More," she moans.

"My Little Omega, do you need to cum again?" I ask as I take in her tired body. She looks so sexy covered in slick and sweat. Her cheeks are flushed, and she can hardly keep her eyes open, but she wants more.

"Yes. You feel so good," she says, lifting her hips. Omegas are designed to go for days, cumming as many times as they want or need to. But that's normally when they are in heat. I know her heat is set to hit any day now, and I have a feeling that this may trigger her to start sooner than expected, but if my Omega wants me to fuck her some more, who am I to tell her no?

She whimpers when I pull out, reaching for me. "Shhh. It's okay, Kitten. I'm not done with you yet. Let's get you on your hands and knees, though."

I help her roll over and pull her ass up, growling as I take in the sight of her. "So fucking perfect." Bending over, I bite the round of her ass, getting a groan from her.

"This ass is mine, baby girl. You want me to take you here when you're in heat?" I ask, giving her cheeks a squeeze with both hands.

"Please," she moans into the pillow.

Thrusting my cock back into her, I groan at the feeling of filling her up again. "I'm gonna fill this pretty, little Omega pussy up with my cum. I wanna watch it drip from your cunt as it mixes with your slick."

"Yes," she whines, thrusting her ass into me. "Fuck me, Knox. I'm yours."

"Yes, you are," I growl, gripping a handful of her hair and pulling her up until she's flush against my chest. I hold her hip while the other hand slides up her chest between her breasts until it clasps around her neck. "Such a perfect and pretty Omega. You're a good girl, aren't you? Letting me fuck you so thoroughly."

"Knox," she moans.

Licking up the side of her face, I groan, loving the taste of her sweat. "I could just eat you up like the big, bad wolf, you know?"

"Then do it," she breathes. "Bite me, Knox. I want your mark."

All playfulness is gone as my heart threatens to beat out of my chest. Did I hear her right? "What...?"

"I want your mark, Knox. Make me yours officially. I'm your Omega."

"But..." Betas are hardly ever marked. Their bonds don't show up as strong, and most Alphas find them annoying to be within their heads. Betas aren't normally a part of the pack like Alpha and Omegas. They aren't known to be involved romantically or sexually very often, more of a best friend or sibling.

So her asking me to mark her skin, to leave a piece of me behind, to give part of her to me... fuck, I'm trying really hard not to cry right now. She will never understand how big of a deal this is, how much this fucking means to my heart and soul.

"Unless you don't want to. It's okay," she whispers, and fuck, I waited too long and now she thinks I don't want her.

"Kitten," I growl. "Don't ever think I don't want to make you mine. To mark you and show the whole fucking world you belong to me. I was just a little shocked, that's all." I kiss her hard, my hand flexing around her throat as she moans, melting into me. "I'm yours, and you are mine. And I want everyone to know it the second they see you. So if you want me to mark you, I'd be more than fucking honored to do so."

"Then do it," she breathes.

Fearing she might take it back, I kiss her shoulder before grazing my teeth against her skin where I kissed. She shivers, letting out a whine. Then I sink my canines into her, making her cry out as she cums around my cock again. I grunt, her blood hitting my tongue. Then I feel it all at once. Her fear that her Alphas won't accept her, that she's not good enough, but most of all, I feel an overwhelming feeling of love she has for me.

I lose it, the new sensations are fueling my body. After lapping at my mark, I push her back down onto the bed on all fours. Gripping her hips, I start to rut into her like crazy. She loves every moment of it, begging for more, screaming my name. I can't hold back anymore, and with one last thrust, I still, cumming inside her so fucking hard I almost pass out.

Jet after jet fills her core, coating her insides and marking her with my scent.

"Good girl," I breathe, bending over to kiss my new mate mark. "Now, all I need is your mark," I joke, not expecting her to want to make me hers. But when I fall to the bed, taking her with me to cuddle, she wiggles out of my arms to straddle my lap, my cum and her slick drip onto my belly. "What are you doing, Kitten?" I ask, my cock still hard even after cumming. She rocks her hips against my length, rubbing our releases together.

"Making you mine," she says, her voice sounding feral, her eyes growing hungry.

My eyes widen as she moves fast, leaning over and latching onto my neck. But when her little teeth break my skin, I moan loud and long as our souls click together.

The feeling is even more intense than before, and I find myself cumming again, covering my chest with streams of warm liquid.

"Fuck," I breathe. "You marked me."

"I did," she says, sitting back looking pretty proud of herself as she licks her lips. "Now, I am yours and you are mine."

"Forever." I grin. *How the fuck did I ever get so lucky?*

Feeling the need to care for my Omega, I try to clean her up, giving her a bath and changing the sheets, but she's not having any of that. We go for another round, then pass out in each other's arms, the mess becoming tomorrow's problem.

One thing I learned tonight for sure is that Tia has a sexual appetite and isn't afraid to show it. Especially after I told her to stop hiding it from me. If this is what she's like now, I hope those Alphas can handle her during her heat.

CHAPTER 11

OCTAVIA

My alarm goes off, and I'm seconds away from tossing my phone across the room. "Fuck off," I mutter, slapping my hand across the screen without opening my eyes until the thing shuts up.

Letting out an annoyed sigh, I roll onto my back and slowly open my eyes, blinking up at the ceiling.

I know I need to get ready for school, but my body feels heavy and sore like I've been hit by a bus. I really hope I'm not getting sick because that's the last thing I need right now with my heat coming up so soon. Who wants the flu while begging for knots?

Looking over at the empty side of the bed, I pout, wishing Knox was still next to me. He had to do a few things for the Dean last night, so he slept at his own place. I don't like it. I want him here, next to me. He's my mate, and I crave his touch.

Since the night we bonded, we've hardly spent any time away from each other. It's only been a few days, but they have been some of the best days of my life. And I can't wait until I get to feel this way with my Alphas.

Things have been going really well with them. Although, we haven't spent much time outside of the stolen moments at school. I always find myself excited when I do get to see them, even if it's only for a few seconds.

They have a few class projects that have been taking up a lot of their time, but Tristan told me yesterday that they are all done, and we should be able to spend more time together outside of school.

We haven't talked much about what they are going to do when it comes to my heat, and I'm starting to panic because every time I hint at it, one of them always changes the subject, casting glances at Tristan as if they're not sure what to say.

I really hope it's not going to be all on Knox to help me through it. As amazing as he is in bed, and lord knows he rocks my fucking world, I'm going to need a knot. I've thought about maybe ordering some special toys, like a dildo with a knot at the end, but knowing I have four amazing Alphas who have the real thing makes the idea of a fake dick do nothing for me.

School hasn't been as relaxed as it was when I first got to Calling Wood. Ever since word got around that Pack Ashwood asked to court me, and that they were my scent bonds, I've gotten nothing but dirty looks and whispers. I couldn't care less about what they think about me or who I choose to spend my life with. But what I don't like are all the jabs aimed at my Alphas.

The other students are quick to point out why they think Pack Ashwood doesn't belong, and I think it's all bullshit. Everything they seem to think is wrong about the guys are things I'm loving most about them.

Tristan gives off the 'boy next door vibes', and there's nothing wrong with that because he's sweet and caring. He's also super protective and attentive. I find myself blushing every time he looks at me, remembering just how Alpha he can be when he wants to be. Tristan is always making sure I have everything I need. For example, at lunch, he always brings me food and something to drink, not letting me leave until I've had a good amount of each. I've even caught Knox smirking over at me with approval at how my Alpha is taking care of me.

If caring is the one word that perfectly describes Tristan, then Sawyer's is silly. He loves to joke around and never fails to make me laugh. It's always some random joke, a funny comment, or sometimes when I catch him looking, he'll wiggle his eyebrows while giving me this sexy crooked grin that has me perfuming like crazy. But I can tell he uses humor when he feels out of place or awkward. The way he jokes around with me and the guys versus how he jokes with his classmates is very different. Although, I understand what it's like to go overboard when feeling put on the spot or trying to fill in the awkward silence. I tend to blabber on when my nerves get the better of me.

While Sawyer is more like me and easy to relate to, on the opposite side of the spectrum there is Finn. Finn is my soft one, my quiet Alpha. He has a very unique sense of style. I haven't had many conversations with Finn yet. He still seems pretty shy, and I don't want to make him uncomfortable. I can only hope he gets used to my bubbly personality soon because I'm finding it hard to hold myself back from talking all the time. But then there are times when I'll spend my free period in the library, -because it's nice to just get out of the house and read on the comfortable couches they have there- and I almost always find Finn there too. We silently take out our smutty books and read side by side, occasionally looking over and giving the other a small smile. I love it. His love for reading dirty books along with him being one of the sweetest men I've ever met is way more important than him being big and strong or being the take charge type. He's like the Yin to my Yang. He's quiet, I'm loud. He's shy, I'm bubbly. And I think we level each other out. I like him just the way he is, even though I can't wait to open him up a little more and really get to know him, better than I do now.

And Dom. My poor Dom. I see the way he watches everyone with a scowl. I know the fat shaming jokes the students make hurt him. It makes me want to hug him and tell him everything is alright. When he's not looking, I can't help but look at him like a sad puppy, knowing how much this pains him. I've heard other Omegas whisper, wondering how I could want to be with Dom, because according to them, someone who isn't all muscles is unattractive. I shut that shit down fast and told them that I think Dom is sexy as hell, and who doesn't love a little extra to cuddle with? Not that we've done any cuddling... yet. I'm still working on him. Besides a few short conversations with me, he hasn't tried to get to know me like the others have, but at least he's not giving me death glares like he wishes I'd go away anymore. The day on the beach was the one and only time he's given me any physical interaction. I miss his touch; I crave it.

I think all those Omegas are blind because Dom, as well as all the rest of them, are sexy as hell in my eyes. I love the variety of body shapes I get to explore and love on when we decide to finally take the next step. I'm big on seeing what's on the inside and not fixating on outer appearance. Although, like I said, I think they're all gorgeous. It's been hard to keep from showing them just how good-looking I find them with all the perfuming I've been doing. But I think they like it, even if they have hard-ons every time I do.

They've all been pretty good about not pointing out that I'm always turned on. They know I'm going to start my heat any day now, and there's not much I can do. And there's only so much that my scent blocking panties can do.

Groaning, I sit up, my hands flying to my head. *Why do I feel like I'm hungover without getting to enjoy the drinking part beforehand?*

Dragging myself out of bed, I go to the bathroom and grab some painkillers from the medicine cabinet, filling a glass with tap water before downing the pills.

"Sweet lord," I mutter, taking a look at myself in the mirror. I look like I haven't slept in weeks, and my body feels like I went a few rounds with a MMA fighter.

Turning away from the stranger in the mirror, I strip out of my PJs and turn on the shower. The hot water seems to help, but not much. After only being able to manage a quick shower, I get out, dry off, and throw on some sweatpants. I also toss on one of Knox's t-shirts and hoodies that he's left behind.

Bringing the collar up to my nose, I inhale the mango scent, making me feel a little better.

There's a knock on my door, and my mood perks up a little, knowing it's Knox.

With a little more energy, I go to the door and pull it open.

"Hi there, Kitten," he says, holding out a coffee and a little brown bag.

"Hold please," I say, taking them from him and placing them on the counter inside my apartment before grabbing him by the dress shirt of his uniform and pulling him inside my place. I throw him against the wall, and he lets out a grunt.

"Is my Kitten feeling a little feisty today?" He chuckles, but it turns into a groan as I smash my lips to his. We kiss deep and slow for a few moments before I pull back panting, wrapping my arms around his body, burying my nose into his chest.

His large arms envelop me, holding me tight to his body.

Inhaling his scent, I sag into his chest, letting out a contented sigh. "Better."

"Tia, baby, are you okay?" he mumbles into my hair, kissing the top of my head.

"I just missed you, need you." I hold him tighter. "You're not allowed to be without me again. You're mine now. My mate. Mine. Never leave me." I feel bad about how moody I've been the past few days. One moment I'll be laughing, the next I'll snap at one of them for looking at me funny. They've been good about it, making sure not to say anything because they know it's not me, just the crazy pre-heat hormones. But because Knox is with me pretty much all day, he gets the brunt of my mood swings.

He chuckles, and my lower belly heats, my perfume hitting us like a freight train. "Are you spiking?" he asks, pulling me away from his body so he can look me over. I whine, not wanting to move.

"I don't know." I shrug.

"How do you feel?" he asks, his face full of concern.

"Like I've been run over by a bus," I deadpan.

His brows pinch as he brings his hand up and places it on my forehead. "You're a little warm, but nothing too bad." His eyes flick around my face and down my body before coming back to my eyes. "Maybe you should stay home today."

"Nooo," I whine, pouting like a child. "We're making cupcakes in cooking class, and you know how much I love those. Please don't make me stay home," I beg, giving him puppy dog eyes. I've been eating like crazy too, my body knowing I'm going to need all the nutrition I can get with all the physical activities I'll be doing soon. The guys will have to make sure I'm being taken care of while I'm in heat because I'll be too sex crazed to think about anything other than cocks, cum, and knots. The joys of heats and being in a frenzy.

"Fine," he sighs. "But I'm gonna be on you like flies on shit today. Just in case."

"Oh, look at you, a regular romantic with that line. Come on, mate, keep speaking your pretty words," I snort.

He raises a brow, a smile twitching at his lips. "I love you, my odd Little Omega."

"Damn right you do." I smile, jutting out my chin. "And I love you."

Knox growls, pulling me back into his arms and kissing me hard until I'm boneless in his arms, whimpering against his lips. "I will never get tired of hearing you say that," he murmurs against my lips before pulling down the hoodie and licking his bonding mark on my shoulder, making me moan.

He kisses me again, hard before I have to push him back a little. "Knox, I'm three seconds away from pulling you into my room and making you do dirty things to me," I breathe against his tempting lips.

"Fuck," he groans. "Come on, Kitten, let's get you to school."

I pout as I grab my bag, slip on some flip-flops, and follow after him. I was hoping he would agree to my idea.

Oh well, maybe my day will be a little better now that I have Knox with me.

My day, in fact, has *not* gotten better. If anything, it's been going rapidly downhill. Everything and everyone has been annoying me. I've snapped at a few of my teachers, and when someone commented on seeing Finn in bright orange suspenders, saying how stupid he looked, I almost punched her in the face.

Now, I'm sitting in Art class, wishing I'd stayed home. The guys weren't at lunch which put me in an even pissier mood because all I wanted was to be surrounded by my Alphas. I feel bad for being a miserable bitch towards Knox, but he's been so good about everything. It makes me love him even more.

"Miss Lockheart. Are you alright?" the teacher asks.

My head is resting on the cool desk, my belly is in knots, and I think I'm burning up. I wanna cry because the pain is getting worse by the minute. *Why does my skin feel so itchy?* It's like I'm burning from the inside out, and I want to just claw it all off.

She tries to talk to me again, but I can't concentrate on her over the blood pounding in my ears. The other Omegas whisper and gasp, the word 'heat' being passed around. I hear their chairs scraping against the floor as they move away from me. Probably not wanting to get another Omega's perfume on them for their Alphas to smell.

"Tia, Kitten." Knox's voice breaks through the buzz. "Baby, you're burning up. We need to get you to your Alphas."

"It hurts," I whimper, clutching my belly, the pain becoming so unbearable that I let out a cry.

"Fuck," Knox curses. "Come on, baby, I've got you." Knox pulls my desk away from me, making me hunch over in a ball. I start to cry as he picks me up. Squeezing my eyes shut, willing the pain to go away, I clutch onto Knox like he's my saving grace.

"Tristan," Knox says. Prying my eyes open, I see Knox with his cell phone against his ear. I want to reach up to brush away the worried look on his face and tell him everything is okay. I don't like seeing him upset, but I can't move. Everything hurts. "Are you at your new place?... Good, I'm bringing Tia to you... Yes, she's in heat."

Am I? I thought being in heat was supposed to be this mind-blowing experience. The only thing I'm experiencing is severe pain.

"I don't give a fuck, make a choice and be ready. Tell the others because you're her Alphas, and at least one of you needs to help her through this. There's only so much I can do. I don't have a knot, and she's going to need one."

I can hear Tristan's frantic voice on the other end, and I whimper at my Alpha's voice. "Put me on speaker," I manage to pant out as Knox runs with me down some stairs.

Cracking my eyes open, I see Knox approaching the golf cart. He climbs into it while also shifting me to his lap, not letting me go.

"You're on," Knox says as he puts his phone in the holder and starts the cart up.

"Tia, love, are you there?" Tristan's voice causes another wave of pain to crash into me. I need him, his touch. I need all of their touches.

"Alpha," I sob in response.

"Fuck. Shhh, Little Omega. You're going to be okay. You will be here soon, and I'll make the pain go away."

"Please," I cry out again. "It hurts so bad."

"Shhh, Baby, you're doing so good," Knox says, rubbing my back in an attempt to soothe me.

"Breathe, Omega. Breathe through the pain," Tristan coaches.

"She's not giving birth for fuck's sake," Knox growls.

"Well, sorry! This is all new to me," Tristan snaps back.

"Stop," I cry. "No fighting." I hate hearing them upset because of me.

"Sorry, Kitten," Knox says, kissing the top of my head. "We're almost there, Tristan, be ready," he tells him before shutting off the phone.

This is it. My first heat. I really hope it gets better than this, because right now, all I feel is fear and pain.

DOMINIC

She's always on my mind. She's the first thing I think about when I wake up and the last thing I think about when I go to sleep.

It's becoming harder and harder to pretend I don't want her. Because I do. I want to hold her, touch her, kiss her, taste her. Hell, I wanna fucking consume her. I want to pin her down and fuck her until she's creaming on my cock with her slick while crying out my name. I wanna tell her how good of a girl she is while she takes my knot.

But instead, I've been keeping her at arm's length. I haven't been rude, the idea of making her sad kills me. I really fucking hate how fucked up my past has made me. The mean words from others, being passed up on so many occasions by Omegas, making me feel like I'll never be good enough. My parents are Alphas, we're a top ranking family in our society, but they never miss the chance to tell me how I'm wasting my life with this pack.

With all of that bullshit in my life, it's hard to believe that this gorgeous, red-headed, feisty Omega wants me. Although, I can't deny the looks she gives me. Like I'm a juicy steak she wants to take a bite out of. *Is she blind?* Because I can't understand why she would look at me like that.

The others, sure. Finn is shy in an adorable way. Sawyer is cute and funny, while Tristan is good-looking and attentive. But me? Not so much. At least, that's what Omegas and other Alphas love to remind me of.

"Oh, thank god you're home," Tristan says, bursting through the door of our new pack house. We moved in here the other day, knowing Tia was going to be going into heat soon and would need to be in a pack house for her safety.

Her nest is almost ready. The plan was that she'd come over tonight and tomorrow, we would take her shopping to pick out everything she needs for her to feel comfortable and ready.

I have a blanket that's been with me since I was a young child. It's blue and soft, and I think it would be perfect for a nest. I just hope she likes it and doesn't think I'm stupid for offering it to her. *God, maybe it is stupid.* She won't want some old blanket. Maybe I'll just keep it to myself.

"What's going on?" Finn asks, setting his book down on the coffee table.

"Knox called, Tia started her heat."

"What?" Sawyer shouts, stepping out of the bathroom with a towel around his waist and a worried look on his face.

"What are we going to do?" Finn asks. We've been talking a lot about what would happen, but our pack leader Tristan never made the final decision.

"I'm going to help her with her heat this time with Knox," Tristan says with a look that means no arguments.

"Are you crazy?" I growl. "You can't handle her heat by yourself! You've never even had sex before."

"And neither have any of you. Look, do I want to lose my virginity like this? Not really in the heat of the moment... no, but I can't imagine another woman to have this moment with. She's our Omega, and she needs an Alpha. I'm pack leader, and it's my job to make the hard decisions. I know how much it means to you guys to have finally found our Omega. This moment should be special for you all. I want you guys to have the time with Tia to show her how much she means to you, to enjoy things and take it slow. I'll have that with her *after* her heat. But you guys are sitting this one out. Then you can be with her like this when the time is right and before her next heat."

"So we just sit here and wait?" Finn asks, scratching the back of his head. "I don't want to just be useless."

"You guys can get us food, water, anything she might need outside the nest."

"Are you sure?" Sawyer asks.

"No. But this is what we're going to do. I won't be alone, I'll have Knox."

Thank god for Knox. Lucky bastard got to mate her before anyone else. But he deserves it. He's a good guy, and it's a pretty big honor for a Beta to not only get marked by an Omega but to be able to give them their mark as well.

Well, looks like we're in for one hell of a few days. "I'll make some calls," I grumble. "Let the school know we won't be in for classes."

"You guys can go. You don't have to wait around here," Tristan says.

I scoff. "What kind of Alphas would we be if we just leave while our Omega is in heat? We might not be able to help her out this time, much to my disagreement, but we're not going to abandon you."

The Alpha in me wants to be there for her, care for her,

please her, and I really want to rip Tristan's head off for denying us that. But he does have a point. I want to get to know her better before taking such a big step with her. That is, if she's even attracted to me enough to *want* to have sex with me. Maybe, we can do it in complete darkness, then she won't have to see me. Or I can just please her with my clothes on, and she won't ever have to see me naked.

"Thanks, man." Tristan blows out a breath, running a hand through his hair.

"Everything will be okay," I tell him.

"I hope so. Fuck, I'm terrified that I'm going to let her down."

"She's gonna be so out of it, all you need to worry about is knotting her and pleasing her. You got this."

"Yeah. You're right." He nods, taking off into the bathroom.

I really hope I am.

CHAPTER 12

TRISTAN

I'm freaking out. I think I'm gonna puke.

"Get a hold of yourself, man!" Dom says, grabbing my shoulders and giving them a little shake.

"Right, shit, sorry. Fuck," I breathe. It's a lot to take in. Tia is in heat, and she needs me. But hell, I'm about to have sex for the first time. I don't want to fail her. Good thing Knox is going to be there too, or we would have one pissed off and in pain Omega.

There's pounding at the door, making my head snap over as Finn rushes to answer it. Knox pushes his way inside with a whimpering Tia in his arms.

Her perfume hits me hard, and we all let out strangled groans, her slick more potent than ever before. My cock hardens in an instant, straining against my dress pants.

"Where's the nest?" Knox demands, his eyes hard.

Fuck, the nest.

"It's not ready yet," I say, my stomach dropping as I point down the hall towards the room. I've already let her down.

"Why the fuck not?!" he barks, his lips pealing back in a snarl.

"Hey, don't fucking yell at him. We were going to all go shopping together after school, remember?!" Dom growls, but he keeps his distance, his eyes landing on Tia when she whimpers louder. "Shit, sorry," he says, looking at her with hopeless eyes.

"Fuck, alright. Grab every blanket and pillow you can find, and bring it to her nest," Knox says, carrying Tia towards the room that's meant to be her nest.

"Alpha," she cries out in a desperate plea, and my heart breaks as I let out a growl.

I want to go to her, but Knox slams the door behind him. "Guys, go into your room, grab your bed sets and any blankets you can find. She's gonna want your scents to calm her if she can't have you."

"Alright." Finn nods, rushing to his room.

"Got it," Sawyer says, doing the same.

"I don't have any blankets to give her," Dom says, his brows pinching. "I only sleep with a sheet. I get too hot at night."

"Sheets will do," I tell him, leaving him standing there as I go into my room. I rip off my comforter, gathering it in my arms, and snatch the fuzzy blanket off the chair in the corner of my room. Bringing them to the door of the nest, I set them down on the floor, moving to the closet to grab any spare ones we have. I stop dead in my tracks when I hear the sweetest moan. Knox must be doing what he can to take the pain away. My cock twitches, needing to get in there and help.

Shaking my head, I grit my teeth with a low rumble in my chest and force my feet to move away from my tempting Omega and grab everything from the hall closet.

"This is all I have," Finn says, stopping next to her room with a pile of blankets.

"Same," Sawyer says with his own blankets.

Dom steps up, holding out his sheet. "I feel fucking useless," he grumbles. I got to say, I'm pretty proud at how far Dom has come since meeting Tia. He went from hating the idea of having an Omega, in fear of getting hurt, to wanting to believe this is real; that she's ours. She is, and he will see that for himself soon.

"This will have to be good enough for now. Maybe one of you can go out and get some stuff from the store? We already have some fairy lights that Finn picked up to set up in there, but that's about it other than the bed," I remind them. The houses all come with basic nest set-ups. Darker colored walls with a king-size, pillow top bed that's set on the floor over fuzzy carpeting. There's a closet that can open up, with a dresser and desk tucked inside, but the doors close completely to blend in with the walls to give the appearance of a smaller room.

"Help me bring these in?" I ask, bending over to grab some blankets. Just as I open the door, Tia lets out a cry of pleasure. My eyes lock on her. She's naked, Knox's head between her thighs as her back arches off the bed.

Holy shit, she's so fucking gorgeous, her creamy skin on display as her red hair fans out around her. Her breasts are plump, her belly soft, and her thighs thick. She's a goddess, and I can't believe she's mine, ours.

"Fuck," Sawyer whispers. Finn whimpers and Dom lets out a low growl. Her toasted coconut scent fills the room, and I almost cum in my fucking pants.

Tia's head turns to the side, looking right at us. She reaches out an arm. "Alphas," her word a simple plea.

My brain kicks back on, and I bring the blankets to the bed, taking the ones from the others as well.

When I do, they give Tia one last look, their eyes desperate for her. "She'll be fine."

"Let us know if you need anything," Dom says before turning and leaving, Sawyer follows him. Finn looks over at Knox who lifts his head from between Tia's legs, licking his lips. I can smell how turned on he is at the sight of the two of them. With a whine, Finn turns and leaves with the others. I close the door before going to the bed where my Omega waits.

Tia is looking at the closed door like she's gonna cry. *Shit.* "Hey, love," I say, getting down on the bed. Her eyes turn to me, tears swimming within them.

"They left?" her voice cracks.

"They want to be here. So fucking much. But..." *How do I tell her this?*

"Kitten," Knox says. I look at him, and he gives me a

nod like he seems to understand what's going on here. Tia turns her attention to her Beta. "The guys have never been with a woman before. This is all new to them. They want to be with you so bad, but Tristan wants them to wait until they can really show you how much you mean to them."

"They want me?" Tia asks me, her eyes filled with hope.

"Of course they do." I give her a smile. "So much. You're ours, Tia, and we plan on spending the rest of our lives showing you just how much we care for you, how much we want you. Thank you, love, for giving us what we've always wanted but never seemed to be blessed with. Thank you for choosing us."

"Alpha," she whines as she moves into a ball.

"Shit," Knox says. "She's not in a full frenzy right now, but she's getting there. Help me make this nest, so she can get settled with your scents. You can help her feel good, take some time to please her before she needs your knot."

I nod, and he moves Tia over a little, telling her how much he loves her and how good she's doing. We toss the blankets onto the bed, leaving it in a messy pile before Knox puts Tia in the middle.

She buries her face into the blankets, her body relaxing a little.

"Look," I tell Knox as he stands up and starts taking his clothes off. "I hope this isn't too much to ask, and let me know if I'm over stepping but... I don't... I don't know what I'm doing."

Knox tosses his shirt into her nest, giving her extra items

with his scent, and looks at me. "You need me to take control? Are you okay with me telling you what to do?"

"I know I'm the Alpha, and I'm sure some of this will be instinct, but yeah, I'm gonna need some help."

"No problem, man. We're a pack. I got you," he says, clapping his hand on my shoulder.

"Someone better get the fuck over here and make me cum, or I'm gonna lose my fucking mind," Tia growls from her nest. My eyes widen as they snap over to a very pissed off, horny Omega. She's sitting up on her elbows, giving us a death glare.

I've never heard her talk like that before. I know it's the hormones, and she's had a few snappy moments the past few days, but *wow*. Why is it kind of hot?

"Yes, Kitten," Knox chuckles, taking his pants off until he's fully naked.

"Now, you," Tia says as I continue to stare at her like an idiot.

"Right," I mumble, my cheeks heating as I start to undress. When I'm fully naked, Tia moans, her hand sliding to her slick covered pussy.

"You're so fucking hot," she moans, slipping her fingers into her folds. My cock twitches at her approval, a growl rumbling in my chest. The sound makes her whimper, her fingers dipping inside herself. Looks like Tia turns into a dirty, little Omega when she's in heat. I've never wanted to be dominated so much in my life as I do right now.

Kneeling on the bed, I crawl over to her, needing to touch her. "Hi." I smile nervously down at her.

"Hi," she smiles back. "Thank you," she says.

"For what?" I ask.

"For being my Alpha, for letting me be your first."

"You're mine, Little Omega. I never want anyone else for the rest of my life," I growl, swallowing her whimper as my lips crash to hers. Her hands slide into my hair, pulling as she sucks my tongue into her mouth. I move until my body is covering hers, pressing my body weight into her. She wraps her legs around me, thrusting her hips so that my cock slides through her slick and over her swollen clit. *Fuck, that feels amazing!*

We kiss with a hungry fever as my hands roam her body. "Need to taste you," I pant out, her perfume making me dizzy with need.

"Eat me, Alpha," she moans. "Then fuck me like the needy little Omega I am."

"Fuck," I groan.

"Hot, isn't it?" Knox grunts, watching us with his hand wrapped around his cock, stroking it lazily. "I love when she's sweet and shy, her cheeks blush so perfectly. But that mouth," he groans. "I love when she's naughty too." He looks to Tia. "You're a naughty little Omega."

"Eat my pussy, Alpha," she moans, pushing my shoulder, trying to guide me where she wants me.

Don't have to ask me twice. I shuffle down until my face is hovering over her soaked pussy, her slick already coating the bed. Looking up at her, I see her watching me with heavy lidded eyes. She's starting her frenzy, and I feel like this might be the last moment I get her with a clear mind.

"Don't think too much into it. Let your instincts take over. She will let you know what she likes," Knox says.

"Knox," she whimpers. "I wanna taste you too."

Knox moves until his dick is next to her face. "Lick it," Knox demands. Tia's tongue flicks out, licking the bead of pre-cum off the tip. He hisses, moving to grip her hair. "Suck my cock, Little Omega. Let me feed you my cum." She moans at his words, muffled by his cock as he guides it into her mouth. She starts to suck him off like her life depends on it, and it's turning me on.

Looking back down at her pussy, I dip lower. Taking a deep inhale, I almost black out at how fucking amazing she smells. And just like that, the Alpha in me takes over. I grip her ass cheeks, lifting her pussy to my face and give her a long lick. She moans around Knox's cock, and once that toasted coconut with a hint of chocolate hits my tongue, I feast on her like a starving man.

Growling into her cunt, I lap up her slick as more and more gushes out. She writhes on the bed, gagging as Knox fucks her mouth. Her hips buck while I suck on her clit a few times before thrusting my tongue into her tight hole. And when I thrust two fingers in, she screams around Knox's cock, cumming hard as he does too, groaning loudly.

Digging my fingers roughly into her ass, I get every last drop of her release. She tastes like fucking heaven, and I need more. But my cock is also throbbing, and I need to be inside her, need to fuck her until I know her.

"So fucking perfect," Knox praises her as he pulls out of

her mouth. She gives him a blissed out smile as her eyes start to flutter close.

"Get some sleep, Omega," I tell her, crawling up next to her, kissing her on the cheek. She hums, snuggling into the blankets and blindly reaches for me.

I move so that I can wrap my arm around her waist, and Knox does the same to her other side. We both lay there as Tia falls into a deep sleep.

"I'm going to try my best to help you out, but I'm not an Alpha. I can't cum as much as you can. I mean, I can go for a while, last long enough for her to cum a few times, but I'll need breaks to recharge. I think we can get her through this heat if we work together, but it won't be easy."

I nod. "The guys want to be here, but they've been waiting for this day for a really long time. I want them to get to know Tia on their own. See how amazing she is and give her a special time they both can remember. They will be ready by her next heat."

"What about you? Don't you want that with her too?" He asks, rubbing Tia's thigh.

"I do, and I still plan on wooing her." I grin, my body buzzing from the smell of her slick, my cock still aching to be touched. "But she needs an Alpha, and I'm more than happy to be her first. To be what she needs in this moment. As much as it hurt not to have an Omega want us until her, it hit the others in a harder way."

Knox and I go quiet, both of us slipping into a sleep, knowing when we wake up, it's gonna be a lot more intense than just now.

Knox has been doing amazing at keeping her happy with sex while I explore her body in other ways like tasting her sweet pussy over and over again. I will never get tired of hearing her cry out my name as she gushes slick on my tongue. But I know she's getting restless, and soon she will be begging for my knot.

We've been in the nest for most of the night now, and my cock is desperate for release, but I thank Knox for letting me ease into the act of sex. After giving Tia another two orgasms, we've all gone back to sleep.

I'm awakened again by one of the best feelings in the world. I moan as I feel something wet and warm around my cock. Leaning up on my elbows, I look down to see my pretty, Little Omega swallowing down my dick like a pro.

"Fuck," I breathe. This is the first time that anyone other than myself has touched me there. And seeing my Omega, her eyes heavy lidded with lust, moaning as she slurps me down is fucking hot.

"Need you," she whines after letting go of my hard cock with a pop. I can't hold it off anymore, I need to take care of my Omega.

"Come here, love," I tell her, reaching for her. She scrambles up my body until her breasts are crushed to my chest and lips locked with mine. I roll us over so that I'm on top of her, thrusting my hips, so my cock rubs against her slick pussy.

"Knot," she begs. "I need your knot, please."

"I know, love. Shhh. I'm gonna knot you, Little Omega. Do you wanna gush around your Alpha's cock like a good Omega? You wanna please your Alpha, don't you?"

Her green eyes shine bright from the praise and lust. "Yes," she whines. "So bad." She lifts her hips towards me.

My cock is ready for her, my knot already swollen and heavy. *Fuck, I just hope I don't cum the moment I enter her.*

She starts to whine and whimper, so I soothe her, kissing and sucking her neck as I line my cock up with her opening. This is it.

Tia locks her legs around me, growing impatient with me. The move forces my cock inside her, and I let out a strangled groan as I feel her tight, soaked core wrap around my cock.

"Fuck," I choke. "Fuck, you feel amazing."

"Fuck me, move!"

"She's not herself right now," Knox's sleepy voice takes over. "She's gonna feel bad when she realizes she rushed you, but right now, you need to fuck her before she gets pissed or feels rejected."

Tia starts to move her hips, whining while clawing at my back. Dammit, I'm really failing at this Alpha thing.

"Stop thinking and just feel," Knox says.

I nod, gripping Tia's hip. I pull out before thrusting back in. My eyes roll into the back of my head, and I groan at how amazing she feels. "That's it, such a good Omega," I praise her through gritted teeth as I start to pick up the pace. She moans, running her hands up her chest to play with her tits. Her eyes are closed as she plucks and pulls at her nipples.

She's liking what I'm doing, so I stop thinking and just feel, letting my natural Alpha instincts take over.

Moving so that I'm on my knees, I grab her thighs and push her knees closer to her head. Looking down, I watch my cock thrust in and out of her slick pussy, and it twitches at the sight. "So fucking perfect," I murmur to myself. My knot is swollen, ready to be locked in place, but I'm not done with her.

The more I watch us joined together, hearing her crying out in pleasure, the harder I go until I'm rutting into her.

"Yes!" she screams. "Fuck, yes. More, harder!"

I pound into her, growling as I grit my teeth, feeling my knot bump against her opening.

"That's right, Omega, take my Alpha cock. Fuck, look at it stretch you. Your cunt swallows me so good."

"Knot me," she whimpers as she thrashes around on the bed.

It's time, and with a few more hard thrusts, I feel my knot pushing forward. Her cunt stretches around it until it pops into place, locking inside of her.

It's unlike anything I've ever felt before. Euphoria fills me to my very core, and I roar as I start to cum, sending stream after stream of cum inside her. Tia's eyes roll back into her head as she arches her back, screaming as her orgasm takes over. Her pussy locks around me, milking me of every drop I'm willing to give her, her slick gushing around my cock.

She looks perfect right now. I wish I could savor this moment forever.

It feels like we're cumming for hours, and Knox has to pet her hair as her body continues to twitch out her orgasm.

"Look at you, Kitten. You're taking your Alpha's cock so fucking good, isn't she?" he asks, looking at me.

"Such a good girl," I growl, moving until I'm covering her body with mine. She kisses me, and it's messy and hot, making me moan.

"Fuck. I can't stop cumming," I grunt when Tia moves her hips, sending her into a mini orgasm as more cum shoots deep inside her.

"Mmmhh," Tia hums. "That was fucking amazing."

"Yeah, it was, love." I kiss her neck, holding her to me. "Wrap your legs around me, Omega. I'm gonna move us so you're laying on top of me."

She does as I ask the best she can, and I roll us, settling her on top of me.

"You should be locked together for a bit, get some sleep because she's gonna be ready to go again soon. After another knotting and a nap, I say we give her a bath," Knox says, brushing damp hair out of Tia's face. I nod, rubbing my hand up and down her back, soothing her and kissing the top of her head.

"Tia, baby, you need to drink," Knox says, getting up and grabbing a bottle of water from the small cooler in the corner.

"No," she mumbles into my chest. "Sleep."

"Yes, baby. You can sleep, but I need you to drink a little," Knox pleads.

"No," she whines, and Knox looks at me for help.

Right. Omegas tend to listen to an Alpha's command. Normally, I don't like to demand anything from her but during heat, if it's what's best for her... I know what I have to do. Sometimes it takes a strong hand to get stubborn Omegas who only have sex or sleep on their mind to allow us to care for them properly.

"Omega," I say, my voice rumbling in my chest. "You need to drink." She moves her head up, looking me in the eyes. I give her a stern look. She pouts but opens her mouth for the straw Knox put in the bottle. She takes a few deep sips before moving her face to my neck and inhaling deeply. She sighs, relaxing into my body, and I smile into her hair, loving that I have her this close. "Good girl," I tell her, kissing her head and petting her hair back.

She preens at my praise, and a purr starts up in my chest. Well, that's new.

It doesn't take long until she's fast asleep, but any time she moves, I grit my teeth at the feeling of more cum filling her.

"No matter how much she asks, don't mark her," Knox warns me as he moves to put on his sweatpants.

"I know," I grumble back. As much as I want to mark her, make her mine, I won't do it while she's in a haze.

"I'm going to grab something to eat for us and use the bathroom, she should be out for at least an hour."

When he leaves the nest, I relax back into the pillows, wrapping my arms tighter around Tia. I'm not gonna lie, it's only the first day and Knox is doing most of the work, like the good mate he is, but this heat is gonna drain us all. Although, there is nowhere else I'd rather be. This is something I've wanted for a very long time, and I still feel like I'm going to wake up to all this being some sort of wild dream. If this is a dream, I'm going to enjoy every moment before it's over.

We don't deserve Tia, but we plan on spending every day showing her just how much we want her, need her, and thanking her for choosing us.

CHAPTER 13

SAWYER

I don't know how much more my poor dick can take. It's been two days of pure hell. Hearing her cries of pleasure as she climaxes, mixed with the smell of her intoxicating perfume and slick has us almost going feral.

At first we locked ourselves in our rooms, jacking off to relieve some of the pain and pressure, but no matter how many times I cum, my cock won't stay the fuck down.

I haven't seen Tristan or Knox leave the nest, but I know they've come out for food and to use the bathroom at some point. When they brought her out of her nest to use the bathroom next to it, the other guys and I had to leave and take a walk, careful to stay away from other people so they wouldn't catch our Omega's scent. The idea of anyone except us smelling her sweet aroma of her heat has a growl threatening to escape me every time.

We're just getting back from one of our walks, Finn and Dom looking just as miserable as I am, when we see Tristan stumbling out of the bedroom where Tia's nest is.

"You okay?" I ask, taking in the state of him. He's only in boxers, looking like he got mauled by an animal. There's scratch marks all over his body with hickeys on his neck and collar bone. His hair is all over the place, and dark circles line his eyes.

"She's asleep," he rasps out. "I can't do this on my own again," he groans, rubbing his face with both hands. "You guys need to spend some time with her before her next heat. As amazing and mind-blowing being with her is, and trust me, it fucking is, I feel like my dick is gonna fall off. How much cum can one body have?" he says in disbelief.

I snort, shaking my head. A part of me envies him. I want to be with her, to fuck her, knot her, care for her, and make her feel good. And even though I was a little pissed about him kicking us out of this heat, he has good intentions. I do want to have my own time with her, to take her on the date that I've all planned out and make it a special moment. Tris and Finn are more of the romantics, but there's something about Tia that just makes me want to spoil her. That's what Alphas are supposed to do, right? Spoil their Omega, and she's *my* Omega.

It still sounds so surreal to say that. For years we were nothing but a second thought, brushed to the side for bigger and better Alphas. And much like the others, I lost hope we would ever find an Omega who would finally want us.

But a fucking miracle happened because we did, and I'll

never take her for granted. I plan on showing her everyday just how glad I am that she's mine, ours.

She's even better than I hoped. She's funny, smart, sweet, and caring. And my favorite thing about her is she sees me for *me*. She laughs at my jokes, not to be nice, but because she genuinely thinks I'm funny. I don't feel like I have to try so hard when I'm around her. Before her, the only ones I could truly be myself around were the guys.

Seeing her bright smile and hearing her musical laugh while knowing I'm the one who was the cause of that, makes me proud, makes me feel good.

I know I'm an Alpha, but I've never truly felt like one until Tia came into our lives. She makes me feel a little less broken, a little less out of place.

"We were ready to help, but you're the one who said you were going to do this on your own," Dom grumbles, his nostrils flaring as he gets a whiff of Tris. The scent hits me too, and I groan, adjusting my now hard again cock.

"I know. And I'm not complaining or regretting my decision. I'm just saying, this is a one time only kind of thing," Tristan says, moving past us to get to the kitchen. We follow him, watching as he grabs a bottle of water from the fridge and downs it in four gulps. "Fuck, that feels good."

"How is she?" Finn asks, moving to take a seat at the kitchen island, his face full of concern.

"She's doing well. We've been working together to keep the pain away and fulfill her needs. I've gone into a rut a few times, but she seems to love that."

"Lucky bastard," I mutter, getting a smirk from him, and I just roll my eyes.

"Is she eating, drinking?" Finn asks.

"Kind of. Knox got her to take a few bites of food when she had lucid moments. But we care more about getting her to drink. It's taken some Alpha coercing. She's a stubborn little thing," he chuckles, taking a bite of a banana.

"Really?" Dom asks, leaning against the wall next to me.

"Oh, yeah." Tristan grins. "And fuck, the mouth on her when she's in heat? It's like a whole new Omega."

"What do you mean?" Finn asks, brows pinching as he pushes his glasses up his nose.

"She dirty talks more than an Alpha." Tristan chuckles as Finn's cheeks heat. "It's fucking sexy as hell, and I feel like she's gonna want to take control sometimes in the bedroom. At least during her heat."

Finn clears his throat. "I wouldn't mind that," he says, shifting in his seat.

"Oh, we know," Dom teases. "I can just see it now. You, between Knox and Tia as they tell you all the things you can do to be a good little Alpha."

Finn says nothing, his face turning bright red, telling us he would very much like that.

"You know, you could have told us about your feelings for Knox before," I tell Finn, taking a seat next to him.

"I wish I did," he sighs. "I know you guys would have been supportive. But I was afraid."

"Of what?" Dom asks, moving to stand next to Tristan.

"Of him rejecting me. Me reading into everything

wrong and ruining our friendship by asking him what the kiss we shared way back then meant." He puts his chin in his hands, leaning against the counter with a sad look. "But I lost him anyway."

"You have him back now," Tristan says.

"Have you guys talked yet?" Dom asks.

"Kind of. He said something to me that day at the beach."

"And?" I ask.

"He said he wanted something with me too. He still sees me as more than a friend, and he wants to explore what we have. But he said he wants me to get to know Tia better, make her number one before anything can really happen."

"Smart man. And it just proves how amazing Tia is. She's meant for us," Tristan says.

"I never lost hope we would find our Omega." Finn smiles.

"I mean, I did sometimes, but I'm glad I didn't write it off. The moment she sat down at our table, I knew our whole world shifted, for the better." I say.

"What about you, Dom?" Tristan asks.

Dom glares at him. "I'm done being an asshole if that's what you're asking."

"Well, that's good to know." Tristan laughs. "But not quite. I know you have a hard time trusting people, but Dom, she's not like the others."

"I know," he growls. "I know, but it's not as easy as you want it to be! You three might not be what everyone expects Alphas to be like, but at least you're all good-looking."

"Don't start," I warn him, not wanting him to think his feelings aren't valid but also not wanting him to go down this spiral again. "Do you see how she looks at you? Dom, half the time I think she's seconds away from crawling into your lap and grinding on you like a cat in heat."

Dom turns his eyes to mine, shooting that glare in my direction now.

"Hey." I raise my hands. "All I'm saying is spend time with the girl before you assume things."

"Guys," Knox says, stepping into the kitchen. Before I can turn to him, I see Finn shoot to his feet, a deep blush finding its way back to his cheeks. I snicker and look at Knox, my eyes going wide. He looks worse than Tristan.

I whistle. "Damn, Beta. What happened to you? The little Omega kick your ass?"

"Haha," Knox says with a blank look. "At least I'm worshipping the most stunning woman on the planet, who is rocking my world every hour on the hour. How about you?" He quirks a brow.

"Shut up," I grumble.

"Thought so," he laughs, then turns his attention to Dom. "You, I need something more from you."

"What?" Dom asks, brows furrowing.

"That sheet you gave for the nest, it's not enough. She's whining for your scent, won't let me touch her until her nest is perfect, and a pissy Omega during her heat is not something we want."

"Oh," Dom says. "I don't have anything else."

"Really? Nothing at all?" Knox growls.

"Well..." Dom says, then lets out a defeated sigh. He moves past Knox and into the hall, heading towards his room. I follow after Knox and wait with him outside Dom's door. He comes out a moment later holding up a tattered blanket. "I have this."

"Perfect," Knox says.

"You sure? It's just a stupid, old blanket," Dom mutters.

Knox rolls his eyes and grabs the blanket, heading back to the nest. Dom and I follow him. Knox opens the door, going inside. The door starts to close, but I stop it, leaving it open just a crack, and seeing Tia almost in tears as she moves around on the bed like she's trying to get comfortable. My heart hurts to see her so unhappy.

"Kitten," Knox says, kneeling down on the bed and holding out Dom's blanket. "Here, baby."

Tia looks up at Knox, then at the blanket in his hand and takes it from him, bringing it to her nose. She takes a deep inhale, and it's an instant shift in her mood. She lets out a happy content sigh, snuggling her face into the blanket. "Dom," she says, her voice dreamy.

Closing the door, unable to handle the smell anymore because my cock is gonna burst the moment it brushes against anything, I look at Dom. He's staring at the closed door, a look of shock on his face like he can't believe his scent means so much to her.

"Don't be so surprised, big guy. The girl looks at you like she wants you to be her everything. You're her Alpha now. All you need to do is see it for yourself."

Dom looks down at me. "Do you think... do you think she will want me when she sees me? I mean, *really* sees me?"

Fuck, seeing my best friend, someone who's like my brother, look so broken hurts. I know he struggles with his weight, and he's not fat like everyone so fucking rudely likes to whisper about him. He's just big boned with some extra parts to love. Parts that Tia *will* love. I just know it.

"Yeah, man. I think she's gonna look at you like she looks at all of us. With love, and like she wants to ride you like a pony." I pat his arm and grin when I get a laugh out of him.

"Come on, let's get out of here before I nut in my pants," he says, turning just as Tia lets out a lusty moan.

Fuck. "I hear you, man." *I'm right there with you.*

KNOX

"Hey," I say, nodding my head to Finn as I crack open a bottle of water and take a drink. I'm tired and sore, but fuck is it ever worth it. I gave Tia Dom's blanket, ate her out until she gushed all over my face, then when she fell back asleep, Tristan came back in to cuddle her while I came out here to get something to eat and drink.

I'm doing my best to help Tia through her heat, and I think the teamwork Tristan and I have is working, but this can't be an all the time thing.

You wouldn't know it by getting to know Tia outside her heat that she would be such a vixen but... *holy shit*, she's so feisty, and the dirty talk makes my cock hard again just thinking about it. So I force myself not to because it needs a break.

"How's everything going?" he asks, trying not to stare at the claw marks and hickeys covering me. I fucking love them, being marked by her, claimed by her... *fuck.*

"It's going well. But I'll be glad when you and the others will be a part of it." I smirk, loving the way he blushes so easily.

"Me too," he tells me, clearing his throat. "I mean, I'm nervous because Tia is gorgeous, and well, I'm... me." He forces a laugh, looking down at his own water bottle as he picks at the label.

"You're what?" I ask, walking towards him until I have him boxed in against the island. "Cute? Sexy? Kind, caring, and sweet? Stop me when you find something Tia wouldn't love about you, because trust me, there's nothing," I growl down at him, loving the way his pupils dilate.

His breathing grows heavy, and I can smell his arousal, making a cocky smirk twitch onto my lips. I love how I affect him. I love how he looks at me like I'm a god, because I feel the same fucking way. He will never understand how sexy I think he is, how much I crave him. Finn could never top me, it's not who he is, I just know it. So the idea of seeing this Alpha, my Alpha, on his knees before me, begging for my cock, begging to please me, it's a power trip.

"Knox." The way he breathes my name makes me groan.

"I miss you," I tell him, my gaze flicking from his eyes to his lips and back up.

"I miss you too." He swallows hard.

"Go on a date with our Omega, get to know her, fall in love with her like I have. Then, it's my turn," I tell him, my lips hovering just over his.

"Okay," he whimpers. I growl, unable to hold myself back any longer. I need to taste his lips. I kiss him hard, my hand sliding into his curly, red hair to hold him in place.

His hands go to my chest as he moans into my mouth. My tongue slips between his lips and over his. It's slow, lazy, and oh so fucking perfect.

When I pull back, his eyes are almost black. Glancing down, I see his cock pressing against his pants. "There's a small taste of our little Omega and what's to come," I taunt him. He licks his lips, and a small moan slips out. "How's she taste?"

"Divine," he breathes out.

"Trust me, it only gets better." I grin. Grabbing the strap of his suspenders, I pull it a bit and let it snap back in place, making him jump. "Later, Finny. Think of me while you take care of that," I say, looking down to his cock.

He looks down before his eyes quickly snap back to mine, and there's that blush again. "You're fucking adorably sexy." I chuckle before turning around, heading back to my Omega, licking my lips and savoring the taste of both pieces of my heart. I plan on tasting him as he spills from my Kitten's pussy.

When I get back to the nest, I find Tristan groaning as he's balls deep in Tia. *Well, I should say knot deep, right?*

"Look at you," I say, taking my pants off. "You look so perfect right now."

Tia smiles, reaching for me. I take her hand, kissing her palm before taking her lips. She moans in my mouth and gives me a curious look when we break apart.

"I gave our sexy, fiery Alpha a kiss. I couldn't resist giving him a taste of you," I tell her.

Her eyes flash with need as she lets out a whimper.

"Fuck," Tristan groans into her neck. "Love, you're squeezing my cock so tight," he says, but it doesn't sound like he minds much.

"How are you feeling?" I ask her, brushing the sweaty hair from her face.

"Better. I think the worst of it is over." She gives me a sweet smile.

"Really? Already?" I ask. Heats are normally four to five days long, sometimes more depending on the omega.

She nods. "I still feel needy." She blushes. "My body still wants your touch, but it's not a burning need. My doctor told me when I got the birth control implant that it can shorten my heats."

"Ahh." I nod, kissing her swollen, puffy lips. "Well, how about a shower, maybe some food?"

"I'd like that." She smiles, and turns to Tristan as he moves his face from her neck to kiss the tip of her nose, her eyes filling with tears. "Thank you," her voice cracks.

His brows pitch. "What for?" he asks.

"For being here for me. For helping me through my heat." She turns to me. "Both of you." She takes my hand in hers before turning back to Tristan. "I was so worried I'd be alone, but you guys made it amazing. Well, at least what I can remember." She giggles, and the sound of the Tia that I've grown to love makes me smile big.

"You're my Omega, Tia. I would do anything for you," he tells her, kissing her softly. "But you're not just my Omega, you're so much more than that."

"You mean so much to me already. The idea of not having you, any of you, scares me," she admits.

"You don't have to worry about that," he tells her. "We're yours, Tia, forever. And we're all excited to get to know you better, to fall in love and start our lives with you. We don't care where life takes us, as long as it's with you."

"I feel the same way," she tells him. "But god, you guys must be exhausted." She blushes. "I'm... sorry... for ummm... how I was during my heat," her cheeks brighten again.

"Don't be." I grin. "It was fucking hot," I tell her, looking down at the scratch marks on my chest.

"I agree." Tristan chuckles. "I love all sides of you, love."

"Same for you." She grins up at him. "And I don't know if this counts for anything, but Alpha," she purrs, running her hands down his arms. "For a virgin, you sure knew how to use that cock."

Tristan growls as he rolls his hips, getting a moan out of Tia.

Tia sucks me off so perfectly as Tristan works her into another orgasm with his knot. We sit and talk after like this is totally normal, and it's perfect. This is something I've been craving in my life; a family, someone to love. I just didn't know it until I had it.

When Tristan's knot deflates, he pulls out of her, and a gush of cum mixed with slick follows.

"Wow," she says, but it comes out more breathy than surprised. "That's a lot."

"Yeah." Tristan chuckles as he grabs a towel and cleans her up the best he can, enough to get her to the bathroom. "I'm surprised I even had that much left in me."

She stares at it, then at his cock, biting her lip.

"Does my Kitten like what she sees?" I ask with a grin, and she nods, shrugging with no shame.

"I like you guys filling me up," she says softly.

"Next time, we'll be sure to paint you with our cum too."

She whimpers, loving the idea. *Ah, my little vixen, you're too perfect for us.*

CHAPTER 14

OCTAVIA

Three days. Three days of being in a haze of cocks, knots, orgasms, and sleep. I'm not sure what I expected my heat to be like, but it wasn't that. No, it was so much better than I could imagine, and I know it's only going to get better when the others join me next time.

I craved all my Alphas, but I understand now why Tristan decided for them to sit this one out. I get to have my first times with each guy be perfect, where I'd remember it always. Tristan is right; I wouldn't want the guys to be overpowered by my heat, and for me to be so out of it that I couldn't make sure I give them what they want, what they need.

A part of me feels bad Tristan's first time was during my first heat. But last night when we cuddled before falling asleep, after the final wave of my heat ended, he told me it was amazing, and he doesn't regret it. I do plan on giving him a day with just the two of us so we can have our moment to take our time and just enjoy each other, take things slow, and explore our bodies as one.

There are a few things I learned about myself during my heat. I have no filter and say anything and everything that's on my mind with no shame. Knox has nothing on me when it comes to dirty talk, and I'm honestly surprised I said half the things I did. But Knox and Tristan seemed to love it, so I don't feel too embarrassed.

Right now, my body is hot; not because of my heat but from the two sexy men I'm sandwiched between.

Blinking my eyes open, I smile as I look at Tris and Knox. Poor guys must be exhausted. I knew heats could be intense, but from what I remember, I was sex crazed; desperate for their touch, their cocks, and their cum.

Cum, that's another thing I learned about myself. I guess I have a cum and breeding kink, -as long as I don't actually end up pregnant, at least not right now- I can get behind it.

I'm starving, but knowing they need their rest and not wanting to wake them up, I slowly and carefully crawl out from between them, climbing out of my nest.

Looking down, I see I'm still naked, so I search for something to wear. I find a black band tee, but it's not Knox or Tristan's. Bringing it up to my nose, I inhale and grin when I smell Dom's woodsy scent. I'm not sure when this got here, but I'm wearing it. I slip it on and giggle. I hope Dom didn't want this back because it fits like a nightgown, and it's mine now.

Frowning when I find no clean panties to wear, I shrug and leave the room. The shirt stops above my knees, so as long as I don't bend over, I should be good.

Quietly closing the door behind me, I take a moment to stretch, a small groan slipping past my lips. I never knew it was possible to feel so satisfied but sore at the same time.

Heading down the hall, I make a beeline for the kitchen. *What time is it anyway?*

When I get to the living room, I see the sun is shining through the big bay window. But the house seems quiet, so it must be early.

Walking into the kitchen, I look at the time on the stove clock to see its six am.

Not wanting to make any ruckus with pots and pans, I look in the fridge for something to eat. "Yessss," I groan, eyes lighting up when it lands on a pizza box.

Wiggling my butt in a happy dance, I grab it and place it on the counter, opening it to see what kind. Plain with extra cheese, yum.

Getting a plate out of the cupboard, I take two slices out and put them in the microwave, setting it to one minute. I stand there, watching the timer count down, and right before it's about to make that annoying beeping, I stop it and take it out.

Because I'm hungry and have no patience, I take a bite of the hot, cheesy goodness, hissing as it burns my tongue, doing that silly huff and blow thing to help cool it down before chewing the rest and swallowing. *So fucking good.*

Just as I'm halfway done with my second piece, Dom walks into the kitchen, rubbing his eyes as he moves over to the fridge and grabs a water bottle. He looks half asleep and doesn't seem to notice me as he brings the bottle to his lips, tipping his head back and downing it.

He's only in his boxers, his morning wood proudly on display. I'm so glad there's a piece of pizza in my mouth, because a whimper threatens to slip out as I take in the sight of him. He's so hot. He's got tattoos like Knox, but not as many. A few on his arms, and some on his upper chest. He's got a little bit of hair on his pecs and a trail down his belly right to the band of his boxers.

He's like a sexy teddy bear, and it's taking everything in me not to jump him and grind myself on him. Damn it! My lady bits need to relax and stop acting like we didn't just have days of mind-blowing, soul consuming sex.

Yes, but not with him. We want him.

"Morning." His gruff voice has my eyes snapping up to his, getting caught ogling him. He quirks a brow as I just blink at him like a fucking idiot, a piece of pizza still hanging from my mouth.

"Morning," I mumble around it, eyes flashing with horror. I blush, taking a bite, and quickly chew before swallowing hard.

I wanna die of embarrassment, but the little grin he's giving me has me perfuming. *Really, Tia, you have no chill.*

He clears his throat, his nostrils flaring as he smells how

turned on I am. When he looks down, seeing that he's half naked, his eyes flick back to mine, panic taking over.

My heart hurts at how self-conscious he is of his body. I wish he could see how sexy he is.

The need to make my Alpha feel better hits me hard, so I do the first thing I can think of. "Here," I say, taking his shirt off of me and handing it to him. "It's yours anyway. But I'd like it back later." I grin.

He doesn't take it, He lets out a growl, but not in anger. No, this one's full of hunger as his eyes trail over my body.

Oh fuck. I just stripped naked without even realizing it. My brain frizzes out on me, and I panic, dropping the shirt and turning to get the hell out of here.

But just as I'm leaving the room, I bump into Sawyer. "Hey there, pretty girl," he says, then his eyes go wide when he sees I'm wearing nothing.

With a squeak, I slip past him and sprint back towards my nest, past a stunned Finn who's standing in the bathroom doorway in his flannel PJs with a toothbrush hanging out of his mouth as he gapes at me in shock.

Groaning, I look away. I slide to a stop at my nest door, ripping it open, and slamming it closed behind me.

"Ummm, Kitten?" Knox asks, his voice full of humor. My eyes widen, and I spin around to see Knox and Tristan looking at me with amused grins.

"Don't," I say, pointing my finger at the two of them. "Just... Don't." I try to sound as serious as I can.

They both burst out laughing, and I growl, jumping into the nest on top of them.

"Sorry, love, but what the heck happened?" Tristan laughs.

I groan as I bury my face into the blanket, the woodsy scent making me think of Dom's heart stopping stare.

"I went out to get food," I mumble into the blanket.

"And forgot to put on clothes?" Knox asks, trying to hold back another laugh.

"No, I put on one of Dom's shirts that I found. Also, why was it in here?" I ask, peeking up at Tristan.

"He felt bad that he didn't have much to offer for your nest, so he gave me the shirt he was wearing to add." That explains why his scent was so strong. He did offer me enough with the blanket he added to the nest. It's what I cuddled with the most. That blanket is also mine now.

"Oh, well anyway, I put it on and went out to the kitchen to eat. Dom came in, saw me, realized he was only in his boxers and started to freak because I was seeing him like that. Hating to see him feel so out of place and without thinking, I gave him the shirt to cover up with. I don't want him thinking that I didn't enjoy seeing him like that because, fuck..." I bite my lip, and the guys let out low growls as they smell my perfume, not helping the situation at all.

"And that left you the naked one?" Tristan asks.

"I wasn't thinking," I huff, hiding my face again.

"Don't be so embarrassed, Little Omega," Tristan says, running his hand down my spine and over my ass, giving it a squeeze. "You just made his day a whole hell of a lot better." He chuckles. *Damn it! I'm still naked.*

Tia, only hours ago their cocks were deep inside you, filling you with their cum, don't be shy now.

"And at least he was the only one to see you," Knox says, but the smile in his tone tells me he knows damn well that's bullshit.

"Yeah, sure. Not like I bumped into Sawyer on my way out, and streaked past poor Finn as I ran by the bathroom."

The two of them are silent again before bursting out into another fit of laughter.

"I hate you both," I grumble. But that's a total lie.

It's been a few days since my heat ended, and things between pack Ashwood and I have completely changed.

Normally, when a pack is courting an Omega, the Omega stays living in the Omega compound until their first heat. Because they've already moved into pack housing, and I have a nest and room at their new place, on top of the fact they are my scent matches and are meant to be mine, I'm moving in with them.

Also, because they have not mated me yet, and the only person I am mated to is a Beta, Knox is staying on as my guard on top of being my bonded.

I don't think any Alpha would try anything with me, but Knox doesn't want to take a chance.

"I wish you could move in too," I pout as we take the last box of my things out of the back of Knox's truck. Thankfully, I was able to take everything the school furnished my apartment with because my room here has nothing in it. My nest is set, but I don't want to be in there, unless it's for my heat.

"Why can't he?" Tristan asks, holding one of my boxes in his arms.

"Really?" Knox asks, looking at Tristan with an unsure look. "Is there even any room? There's only six rooms, and two of them are for Tia."

I'm about to tell him that I'd give up my room and stay in the nest if it means having him close, but Finn speaks first. "You can room with me." We all turn to Finn, his cheeks turning pink. "I mean, my room is big enough to fit another bed in there. I don't mind sharing."

I bite my lips, trying to hold back a grin. I love how cute he is, and it's adorable how flustered he gets around Knox. I groan to myself remembering when Knox kissed me after kissing him, the taste of him on my tongue a faint memory. I want to taste him myself, but I haven't had the chance just yet. But I will, soon.

"Problem solved. You're part of the pack now, and you're one of Tia's mates. If it makes our Little Omega happy, then that's all that matters," Tristan says.

"Thank you," I squeal, jumping into Tristan's arms, making him drop the box. Good thing it's only blankets. He chuckles, catching me and hugs me tight. When he places me on my feet, he looks down at me with so much emotion, I melt into him.

"Anything for you, love," he says, his voice low and sensual, making my pussy clench, slick wetting my panties. "Fuck, I love how responsive you are with us," he murmurs against my lips before kissing me hard. I whimper, feeling my knees turn into jelly.

"Where do you want this box of dildos?!" Sawyer yells from the front door. My eyes fly open as I break the kiss, looking at him in horror. He has a smirk on his face, but it falls when he sees Knox storming over to him, bitching him out. Sawyer screams like a girl before taking off back into the house with the box.

I burst into giggles, and Tristan shakes his head. "You know, Little Omega, you're gonna shake up our lives, in all the best ways. I can't fucking wait." He kisses me again before taking his box into the house, leaving me alone with Finn.

"Thank you," I tell him, giving him a soft smile.

"For what?" he asks, pushing his glasses up his nose. I step into him, loving how his breath hitches.

"For offering to share your space with Knox. I need to be near all of you. The idea of being away from any of you makes me feel sick," I tell him.

"I'd do anything for you, Tia," he tells me.

My heart warms at his words, feeling so full that I could burst. "I believe you. And I would do the same."

"Really?" he asks, brows pulling together. Alright, I'm ready to track down every Omega who's turned my guys down and give them a good ol' bitch slap because fuck, people have done them dirty.

"Of course," I tell him, wrapping my arms around his neck. He wraps his around my back, pulling me closer to him. I try not to whimper as his hard length digs into my belly, not wanting to make him feel awkward or embarrassed. I think it's hot. Whether he's hard for me or Knox, it doesn't matter.

"We don't deserve you," he tells me, and my heart goes from being full to hurting for my Alpha.

"Finn, there's something I'm going to need you to do for me," I tell him.

"Anything," he's quick to respond.

"I'm going to need you to stop thinking like that. Those thoughts aren't welcome anymore. I want *you*. I *need* you. And right now, I like you all a lot, but I know I'm gonna fall in love with you hard and fast. It's just how it's going to be, so I need you to know this: you *do* deserve me, every inch of me, my heart and soul. And if anyone ever tells you otherwise, send them my way, and I'll tell them how wrong they are real fast."

His eyes water, and mine do the same. "I promise, I won't let you regret picking us as your pack," he says, his voice cracking. "You are everything we ever wanted."

"And you're everything I could have ever asked for and more." I give him a teary eyed smile.

"You're perfect, you know that? How many Omegas would share their mate with their Alpha?"

"Well, I'm not sure if you knew this, but I have a secret."

I giggle. "I'm not like every other Omega. Life is short. I say fuck it all and do what makes you happy. Knox makes me happy, you guys make me happy. But you also make him happy, so let's just be one big, happy family."

"I like that idea." He chuckles, and damn do I love hearing that sound from my quiet, shy Alpha.

"Finn," I say his name as I look up at him with need.

He swallows hard. "Yes?"

"Kiss me?" I ask, my heart pounding out of my chest, hoping he doesn't say no.

He hesitates a moment, but not because he doesn't want to, but because of the lack of confidence in himself. Although, I think he sees the want in my eyes, the need for his lips on mine because it only takes a second for him to lean down, sealing his lips to mine.

I whimper at the rush of heat filling my belly from his kiss. He growls at the sound, and, fuck me, if hearing my nerdy man growl like the Alpha he is doesn't have me gushing, then I don't know what would.

Parting my lips for him, I let his tongue slip into my mouth, caressing mine. He backs us up against the truck, pinning me against it. His leg slips between my thighs, and I start to shamelessly grind against it, my clit aching with need.

He growls again, the kiss growing more intense, making my head swim. I need his knot, I need him to fuck me here against the truck. I don't give a shit who sees.

"You guys wanna order pizza?" Dom's voice has Finn jumping back, startled.

We're both breathing heavily as he looks at me with wide eyes, and there's that blush.

"Well, hello there." I grin. "Don't sell yourself so short when it comes to your Alpha instincts because that... was all Alpha, Finn." I lean up, kissing my bruised lips against his cheek.

I leave him standing there with a bulge in his pants and a dopey smile on his face. I wanna offer to take care of it, but he's not quite ready for that.

Heading towards Dom, I try to not let his heated look make me trip over my own two feet. "Pizza sounds perfect." I stop in front of him and smile. The way he's looking at me is much like the way he was when I stupidly took his shirt off, leaving me stark naked. The same shirt that ended up on my bed with the blanket he gave me for my heat. My new *favorite* blanket, by the way.

"You're gonna be trouble, aren't you, Little One?" he rumbles, making my skin pebble. I keep the smile on my face, not letting him know he's affecting me just as much as Finn. Although, by the way his nostrils are flaring, he can smell it.

"You ain't seen nothing yet." I grin, giving him a wink before slipping past him, needing some alone time to get my thoughts in order.

"I can't fucking wait," he growls, so low I don't think I was supposed to hear him, but I do, making me walk faster.

CHAPTER 15

OCTAVIA

The first night at the new place is different. After they helped me set everything up, each of them taking every chance they could to at least brush their fingers over me, they left me alone for the rest of the night.

I think they thought that I wanted alone time after being around them so much over the past few days as well as my heat, but I didn't really enjoy it.

Spending almost every free moment with Knox outside of school and with them inside of school, I've gotten used to always having someone with me. Being on my own is too... quiet and kinda lonely.

But I knew they were tired and busy helping rearrange Finn's room to make space for Knox.

So I'm surprised when I wake up to find myself surrounded by every single one of them.

Biting my lip to hold back an excited squeal. I slowly sit up, careful not to wake them. Knox is sleeping in the far corner of the massive bed, giving my Alphas a chance to be near me. Tristan is on my left and Dominic is on my right with Finn by my feet and Sawyer between my legs, using my belly as a pillow. They look funny, like they were playing Twister and all fell at the same time. Legs and arms tossed over each other. Not sure how they can sleep like that, but it fills my heart with so much joy knowing that they all wanted to be next to me.

"Morning, Little One," Dom grumbles quietly as he turns his head to squint at me.

"Hi," I say softly, giving him a smile.

He sits up a little, looking at the others around me and grins, shaking his head.

"Come," he says, swinging his feet off the side of the bed and stands up. He's in a t-shirt and PJ pants, but his morning wood is not trying to hide, and it takes everything in me not to whimper because fuck, I really want his knot right now. "Come," he says again, more of a growl this time. He doesn't wait for me to get up, bending over and scooping me up into his big, strong arms like I weigh nothing. Sawyer grumbles in protest as his head falls down to the bed, but he doesn't wake. I let out a small squeak as my arms fly up to wrap around his neck.

He's quiet as he carries me out of my room and down the hall. I can't take my eyes off the side of his face, trying to resist the urge to tuck my face into his neck and get a lung full of his woodsy Alpha scent. So, instead, I lay my head against his chest and press my nose against his shirt, sighing as his smell settles something in my soul.

He growls softly, sending a shiver through my body. "You know, Little One, when you act like this, it's hard for me to keep thinking you're gonna turn out to be this shallow Omega and leave us."

My heart sinks at the thought of him still having the fear that I'm gonna reject them like all the others. "Then stop thinking like that," I say, my hand tracing the design on his shirt as we walk through the living room and into the kitchen.

He sets me down on the counter, and before he can move away, I grab him by the shirt. Pulling him down towards me, I bring his face closer to mine so that we're eye to eye. "Listen, and listen good, Dominic. I'm not like all of those selfish bitches who allowed their own shallow needs to pass up some of the best men to ever walk this earth. And as much as it hurts to know how shitty you've been treated, I'm glad they didn't pick you. Because if they did, *I* wouldn't have you. But I do now, so you're *mine*, all of you. And I'm not going *anywhere*. The sooner you get that through your sexy head, the sooner we can start our new life together. A life I know could be fucking amazing if you just gave me a chance." My eyes are watering now, and I'm breathing heavily, trying not to cry. I just need him to know, to understand. "You don't like the way people judge you at first glance? Well, the same goes for me. I'm my own person, Dom, just take the time to get to know me and you will see that. Please."

His eyes soften, and before I can think another thought, his lips are on mine. I moan as he fists a handful of my hair, tugging on the long, messy strands as he fucking devours my mouth.

He steps closer between my legs so that his cock grinds against my dripping pussy. I whimper as I lock my legs around his waist, not wanting him to move. He moves from my mouth, leaving me gasping for air as he kisses down my jaw. With a sharp tug of my hair, he pulls my head to the side, his nose trailing up my neck. He takes a deep breath, letting out a growl in appreciation. "You smell so fucking good, Little One." He licks up the side of my neck before biting the soft flesh, but not enough to break skin. "I'm gonna mark you right here someday soon, Omega. You have no idea how long I've waited for you. And if you mean what you just said, well... I'm sorry, but I don't think I'll be letting you go either."

I moan as he pulls off the shirt that I stole from Tristan's room, exposing my breasts. He growls again as his eyes zero in on my hardened nipples. "Fuck," he says, both of his large hands moving to cup my breasts. "I wanna cum all over these." Another moan echoes throughout the room as he leans over and sucks one into his mouth.

Grabbing a handful of his hair, I hold him to me as I rub against him, my clit needing the friction.

I suck in a breath as he bites down on my nipple, playing with it between his teeth before letting go with a pop. The cool air against my wet skin makes me whimper as he moves to my other breast to do the same.

It's all too much; the things he's doing to my body as he sucks on my flesh, playing with the other nipple, and his cock rubbing against my pussy. Add in his orgasmic scent, and I'm a fucking goner.

Squeezing my eyes shut, I can't hold back and shatter in his arms, biting his shoulder to smother my scream as I climax, slick soaking my panties.

"What a pretty sound, Little Omega. Do you think you can make it again while I'm knot deep inside you?" he growls as he straightens up.

Biting my lower lip, I nod, unable to form any words, my mind still spinning as I try to get my breathing under control.

His nostrils flare as he takes in the scent of my slick. His hands slide up my thighs, stopping at the waistband of my panties. Without breaking eye contact, he grabs them and pulls them off me, leaving my ass on the cold marble of the counter, completely naked before him. This time my face doesn't heat up in embarrassment. No, it heats from how fucking turned on I am.

He doesn't look at my body though, still keeping eye contact as he brings my black, slick drenched panties up to his face. He takes a deep inhale, his eyes rolling into the back of his head as he groans in pleasure, making more slick gush onto the counter top. *God, this is not sanitary at all.*

When his eyes open, they're full of pure fire; a hungry need. My heart is pounding in my chest, this whole thing is so hot.

When his tongue comes out, licking up the crotch of my

panties, getting a good amount of slick on it, he growls. My eyes widen at his action as he puts the part that covers my pussy into his mouth, sucking the rest of the slick off. I think I'm about to pass out with how my mind is spinning. *Is this really happening?*

"Like the finest dessert ever created," he rumbles. "And it's all *mine*."

He takes my panties, tucking them into the waistband of his pants, hiding them with his shirt before grabbing the shirt I was wearing before and slipping it back over my head to cover me up before going over to the fridge.

I just sit there blinking at him, acting like that didn't just happen. *Did it? Am I still sleeping and dreaming right now?*

"How do you like your eggs?" he asks, setting the carton of eggs and butter down on the counter before grabbing a pan from the rack on the wall.

"Ummm..." I say, shaking my head to clear my mind. "Well." I laugh. "You might think I'm silly."

He side eyes me with a smirk as he puts the pan on the stove. "Try me," he says, turning on the burner.

"I don't like the yoke. So, I only eat the egg whites. Three eggs, crispy on the edges with salt and pepper."

He nods. "Then that's how I'll make them. Also, not silly at all."

I sit there silently, watching while he makes me breakfast, smiling softly. I watch his arms flex as he cracks the eggs into a bowl, then scoops out the yoke into another bowl. I wonder how his arms would look as he tossed me around my nest.

"What are you gonna do with those?" I ask, referring to the yokes he sets to the side.

"Save them for Sawyer's omelette. He has one every morning. No need to waste." He shrugs.

I put that bit of information away for later.

"Alright, all done," he says, plating the fried eggs. It smells amazing. When I reach for the plate, he pulls it back, cocking a brow at me. I raise one back as he grabs a fork and breaks a piece off, then holds it out for me to eat.

I grin, taking the bite and moaning, eyes closing at the taste. "Yum."

He growls, holding out another piece when I swallow the one in my mouth. He feeds me the rest of it, and by the time I'm done, the others are entering the kitchen.

"There you two are," Tristan says, looking all sexy and sleep rumpled.

"We were wondering where you two went off to." Knox grins, giving me a knowing look. I stick my tongue out at him in response, which only makes him grin wider. I love how much he supports my Alphas and me being together.

"Why does it smell like eggs and coconuts? That's an odd combination," Sawyer says, coming over to me and giving me a kiss. "Morning, pretty girl," he says, and I smile up at him.

"Morning."

"Coffee anyone?" Finn says, putting on a pot of coffee. The guys all mutter in agreement.

"Don't worry, Kitten, I'll get you your usual on the way

to school." Knox says, seeing my pout as the smell of coffee fills the room.

I perk up at that. "My hero," I say, batting my lashes at him, getting a chuckle.

"Anything for you, Little Omega," he rumbles, pulling me in for a kiss.

"I'm going to shower and get ready for school," Dom says as he puts the pan in the sink.

"You're not going to have anything to eat?" Tristan asks him as he grabs some fruit and yogurt from the fridge.

"I already had a snack. It will hold me over until I can have a full meal," Dom says, looking right at me with eyes full of filthy promises that I want him to keep so badly.

"Really?" Sawyer asks. "What did you have?" He looks at Dom, brows furrowed, then over to me. It takes a moment before his eyes light up with understanding. "Ohhhh."

"Alright," I say, hopping off the counter. "I'm going to go get ready for school too."

"Hey, Dom. I think you left a bit of your snack behind on the counter," Tristan says, and I look over at him eyeing up the puddle of slick on the counter, then at me with knowing eyes and a smile full of heated mirth.

These guys are going to be the death of me. Dom chuckles as I rush past them and out of the kitchen, setting the rest of them off.

I'm almost to my room, when I'm pulled to a stop, my back meeting the wall.

"I'm sorry for being an asshole," Dom says, looking down at me as he crowds into me.

"You weren't an asshole," I tell him. I wasn't mad about anything that happened this morning.

"Not back there. The first time we met. I was a fucking dick. There..." He closes his eyes and takes a deep breath. "There's a lot I need to work through when it comes to myself. But I want you, Tia. I want you to be our Omega. And I'm sorry if I had you feeling, even for a second, that you weren't worthy of being part of our lives, because you are. It was meant to be filled by you. I'm starting to see that now. Just, give me time, okay?"

"Okay," I tell him.

He kisses me. This time it's a lot softer and sweeter, a lot like the teddy bear I know he can be. "Go get ready for school," he rumbles. I nod as he takes a step back. And when I turn to leave, I yelp as his hand comes across my ass. I look at him in shock, but he just grins, disappearing into the bathroom.

If this is just the start of my day, I wonder what the rest of it is going to be like.

After getting dressed, I meet up in the living room with all my guys so we can all head to school together. I can't keep the smile off my face as we all walk through the front doors of the school together.

One hand is laced with Tristan's while Sawyer has his arm thrown around my shoulder as Dom and Finn walk next to their pack mates, Knox close behind us all.

Sawyer kisses the top of my head, and Tristan brings my hand up to his lips, kissing it before giving me a toothy smile that's full of pure happiness.

I feel so full of joy, I think I might burst.

The guys walk me to my first class, Art History, stopping at the classroom door.

"Are you up for doing something tonight?' Tristan asks, wrapping his arms around my waist and pulling me to him. I smile and lace my hands behind his head, playing with the strands of hair. He lets out a purr, closing his eyes.

"With you guys, I'm up for anything," I tell him.

His eyes open again, and he grins down at me. "Good, because as of tonight, the courting begins," he says, leaning down to kiss my cheek.

"What are we doing tonight?" I ask, excitement filling me.

"That's a surprise, Little One," Dom says, leaning in to kiss the side of my head.

"No fun," I pout, and Sawyer laughs.

"Now, pretty girl, you be a good Little Omega, and let your Alphas spoil you. And if you're a good girl, maybe you will get a treat." He grins wickedly, making me blush. Sawyer and Finn are the only ones I haven't done anything with besides kissing, and I'm excited to explore our growing relationship.

"Promises, promises," I tease back, loving the spark of

heat in his eyes. He lets out a playful growl, gripping my chin with his hand and giving me an overly dramatic kiss on the lips that still has me going weak in the knees. I giggle as he winks.

"Later, pretty girl."

"Bye," I call back.

"I gotta get to class, but I can't wait for tonight," Finn says, his cheeks turning a pale pink shade as he pushes his glasses up his nose.

Moving out of Tristan's hold, I step close to Finn, his breath hitching when I enter his personal space. "When we get back from whatever you sneaky Alphas have planned, do you wanna cuddle and read before bed?" I ask, my fingers gliding up and down one of the straps of his black suspenders. He's wearing a deep red dress shirt with black slacks, dress shoes, and a bow tie. He looks sexy and cute. I just wanna fit him in my pocket and take him everywhere with me.

"Of... of course," he says, looking a little surprised. He shouldn't, because I love spending time with him. I'm eager to get him out of his shell and show him he doesn't have to keep quiet because he thinks people aren't going to be interested in his hobbies or the things he likes.

"Good," I say, beaming up at him. "I've missed our reading dates." It's been about a week or so since our last one.

His eyes dart between mine, and I see the need he has to kiss me, but he hesitates. Not wanting him to think too much into it, I grab both straps of his suspenders and lean up on my tiptoes to kiss him. He lets out a little moan before care-fully sliding his fingers into my hair and kissing me softly and sweetly. My lower belly ignites into a needy burn, getting a growl from my remaining Alphas as well as my Beta.

When I pull away, Finn clears his throat, his cheeks blazing as he adjusts himself in his slacks.

"Go, before you're late," I tell him, biting the inside of my cheek to hold back my smile.

"I might need a minute," he mumbles, and Knox lets out a deep husky chuckle that does nothing to help poor Finn. He snaps his eyes over to Knox who's grinning at him like he's a little bunny that the hungry wolf wants to devour. With a whimper, Finn turns back to me, gives me a quick kiss on the cheek and a fast goodbye before taking off down the hall.

"You love to get him going, don't you," I scold Knox playfully.

"Oh, you love it too, and are just as guilty," he smirks. I just grin, rolling my eyes.

"See you at lunch, Love." Tristan gives me a possessive kiss before taking off to his own class, leaving Dom and me.

"You know, Little One. I'm going to love spending the day with the taste of you on my tongue," he growls, cupping my cheek. My eyes widen with understanding, thinking about this morning. *Did he brush his teeth after? Or did he have another taste?* I shiver at the idea. "I see your mind trying to piece things together. Let me answer your ques-tion," he says, pushing me against the wall, blocking me from the view of anyone who might walk by. I look up at him with excitement as he slips his hand under my skirt and into the front of my panties. I gasp as he dips two thick fingers into my pussy, gathering slick before pulling his hand free. He brings his fingers to his mouth and sucks them clean with a growl that makes my pussy throb, never taking his eyes off me.

I give myself a pat on the back for wearing a pair of scent blocking panties today because I don't think I've ever needed them as badly as I do right now.

"So fucking mouth watering," he growls before crashing his lips to mine. I moan, tasting myself on his tongue as he kisses me fast and dirty, leaving me a wet, panting mess. "I'll need more of that later. Have a good day, Little Omega. Be a good girl for me."

He turns, leaving down the hall, and I watch him go, eyes wide and momentarily stunned.

"You look so fucking sexy when you're turned on," Knox says, taking Dom's place. I blink up at him. "But I kind of like his idea."

"What idea?" I say, letting out a moaned gasp as Knox bends down, kissing my neck as he too slips his hands down into my panties, doing the same thing Dom just did and growling as he licks his fingers clean.

"Yeah, he's right; fucking mouth watering."

"Knox." I gape at him in shock, but also loving what he did, what both of them did.

"Run along to class, Kitten. You don't wanna be late." He grins.

The bell rings, and I curse, grabbing my bag from his shoulder while giving him a slight glare. I spin around to go into the classroom, and Knox slaps my ass, making me let out a small squeak as I walk into the room.

Heads turn my way, and I want the ground to swallow me whole right now.

I've been out of school for a week, and I'm sure everyone knows it's not because I was sick.

"I wonder if they were even able to get her off, or was she suffering her whole heat?" one of the Omegas whispers as I take a seat in one of the empty chairs.

"Can you smell her? She smells like sex," another scoffs. Normally, I'd be embarrassed, but right now, I'm starting to get pissed off.

"She had to have faked it, or had a lot of toys to help her. Poor thing probably had to work overtime to try and make sure her alphas didn't feel completely useless," another one giggles. "Do you think they even knew how to use their dicks?"

That's it! That's fucking it! I can handle the whispers and snide remarks about me not being your typical Omega, or them wondering why I don't want to start a family and have babies, because I'm sure the Alphas I rejected spread that around like wildfire, but fuck with my Alphas? Yeah, not happening.

"Not that it's any of your business," I say, turning in my seat. "But no, I didn't need toys because not only do my Alphas have massive cocks with knots that make me black the fuck out from cumming so hard, but I have a Beta with a dick the size of my forearm. So trust me when I say, they know exactly how to use what they were born with. No need to pity me or my Alphas because they rocked my world, and I rocked theirs. So, with all due respect, kindly fuck off and worry about your own Alphas because mine are just fucking fine. *Really* fine," I tell her, smiling sweetly as I flip them off.

They gasp at my outburst, and I grab my bag to move into another chair, far from those judgmental bitches. *God, I'm so glad I'm nothing like them.*

Muttering in annoyance, I ignore the glares from my teacher as she goes about starting her lesson.

"Don't mind them," someone whispers. Looking over, I see a pretty, little, blonde Omega. She smiles softly at me, and I find myself smiling back. There's something different about her. "They're all selfish assholes who only care about big dicks and bigger wallets."

I grin. "I had a feeling," I whisper back.

"Not all of us are like them. I know I'm not."

"Same," I tell her.

"I'm Everlee by the way," she says. I've heard that name before. Then it clicks.

My eyes widen and so does my smile. "Your Ivy's Omega."

"I am," she says proudly.

"Shit. I'm such a shitty best friend," I groan, putting my head to the desk. "I've been here for a month now and still haven't seen her."

"It's okay." Everlee giggles. "She knows you've had stuff

of your own going on. But now that you had your first heat and you've met your Alphas, I think she's gonna demand you get together."

"And we will, how about this weekend? I'll call her to set something up."

"I know she will love that," she smiles.

The teacher clears her throat, glaring at us. We giggle but spend the rest of the class focused on our work.

I didn't come here looking for friends. Omegas don't often get along with other Omegas; mostly due to the protectiveness we have towards our Alphas and the fact that most Alphas don't let their Omegas go too far without them.

But I just know Everlee isn't like the others, same as me. And she's my best friend's Omega, of course I'm gonna be besties with her. I already know I'm going to love her.

My first few weeks at Calling Wood haven't been the best outside of my guys, but I think that's about to change.

CHAPTER 16

OCTAVIA

The next few classes went a lot better. Turns out, Everlee is in all of my classes, and I didn't even realize it. I haven't really tried to get to know any of the girls here, and I guess that was a little rude on my part. But now I have a new friend, and it makes getting through some of these boring classes a little easier.

She's new here too, only getting here a few months before me, so she has to take all the same classes for her first year before she can start taking the classes she needs to become a vet tech. I did a happy dance inside knowing that I'll have friends here for the next few years.

As much as I love being around my guys... at some point I'm going to need some me time or girl time. So having my best friend and new friend here with me will be amazing.

"I'll have Ivy text you to set something up," Everlee says, giving me a bright smile.

"Thank you! I plan on apologizing for being a crappy friend until she's ready to shake me."

"Who's going to shake you?" Knox asks as he steps up next to me. "Hi," he says, smiling down at Everlee.

"Hi," she says. "I'm Everlee, Tia's best friend, Ivy's Omega."

"Oh," Knox says, looking down at me, then back to her. "Well, it's nice to meet you, Everlee." He smiles, then looks down at me. "Ready for lunch, Kitten? The guys are gonna come hunt you down if we're not there soon."

Rolling my eyes, I smile. "Yes." I look back to Everlee. "See you tomorrow!"

"Bye!" Everlee says. Someone calls her name from behind her, and she spins around, letting out an excited giggle before taking off down the hall to launch herself into a very big and tall man's arms. He helps her onto his back, and she looks at me again, waving one more time before they take off around the corner. That must be one of her Alphas.

"And I thought *you* were a tiny, little thing. She's almost the size of a pixie."

"I know." I laugh. "And I love it. She's too cute."

"Look at you making friends. Come on, Little Omega. You only had eggs for breakfast, and you need to eat. Plus, they're serving tacos today."

"Oh, tacos! Sold, let's go," I tell him.

"Want a piggyback ride too?" he asks with a smirk.

"Maaaaybe," I say playfully, batting my eyelashes.

"Hop on, Kitten," he says, crouching down.

I giggle and climb on. "Onward to the hall of the dining!" I cheer, and he barks out a laugh.

"Anything for my Queen."

After lunch, school went by far too slow for my liking. The guys told me they were leaving last period to get a few things done for tonight, while I had to sit in class and wish I was with them.

The bell rings, and I'm out of my seat, running for the door within seconds.

"Where's the fire?" Knox chuckles as I grab his hand and start tugging him towards the exit.

"Tonight is date night, and I wanna look my best!"

"You always look your best, Kitten. You could wear a brown paper sack and we would all bow at your feet," he says, pulling me to a stop and tucking me under his arm.

I blush, smiling as I tuck my face into his side. I love him.

The whole ride home, I talked Knox's ear off about the book Finn and I are reading. When we get to the house, I see the guys' golf cart in the driveway. And a thrill of excitement fills me as our cart shuts off.

Leaning over, I quickly give Knox a kiss on the cheek before hopping out and rushing to the door.

When I get inside, the place is quiet. Looking around, I can't find anyone.

"They're probably getting ready," Knox says, coming up behind me. I jump a little but settle when he wraps his arms around me. I sigh, leaning my head back against his chest. My eyes close as I revel in the sensation of his touch. "Remember, Little Omega." He kisses my neck, making me moan softly. "This is their first date. All of them. So go easy on them."

"I will," I say. "We could just sit at home and watch a movie for all I care. It doesn't matter to me because as long as I'm with them, it will be perfect."

"You're perfect for them, Kitten. Perfect for me. I love you, my mate."

I love it when he calls me that. "I love you too, my mate," I say, spinning in his arms. He cups my cheeks, kissing me deeply. My lips part for him so his tongue can caress mine, which sends a tingle through my body right to my clit and makes my pussy spasm while slick coats my panties.

His nostrils flare as he looks at me with need. "I'll take care of that later, Little One," he growls, making my knees go weak. "Now, go take a shower and get ready," he says, spinning me around and giving me a nudge towards my bathroom.

The house is a nice size, everything on the ground level, but as much as I like it, I can't wait until we leave and buy a nicer family home with our own backyard and a pool.

Although, I do like my room. It has a little more inside of it than my nest does, and the guys helped me decorate it just how I had it back in my apartment. I also have my own bathroom. Well, it's the same one that's attached to my nest, so both rooms have access to it. It has a big shower and tub, bigger than the one I had in my old place.

When I get inside, I strip out of my clothes and grab a clean towel from the rack. Turning on the shower, I groan as the warm water hits my skin. I clean quickly, but I'm thorough because you never know what might happen while we're out. Or any time really. One thing I love about my guys, at least from what I've seen with Dom and Knox, is that they aren't afraid to show me just how much they want me. I love it. If they wanted to fuck me against a wall or bend me over and take me, I wouldn't say no. I can't say no when it comes to them, not that I'd want to. I want to be fresh and clean for anytime they're near, just in case, but I don't think they would really care.

When I'm happy with everything, I shut off the water and step out, grabbing my towel and wrapping it around my body, tucking it in at the top.

The mirror is steamed up, so I wipe it away to look at myself. For the first time in a long time, I feel sexy just how I am. I was sweaty with no makeup, hair a mess during my heat, but I remember flashes of when Tristan or Knox looking at me like I was the most beautiful girl in the world.

Knowing that they like me just how I am settles something inside me that I didn't know I needed reassuring. The guys aren't the only ones who think they have something wrong with them.

It took a long time for me to be okay with my body. I'm not what one might call skinny. I'm not a 'big' girl, -although if I was, I'd still be a fucking bombshell because all women are goddesses- but I have thicker thighs, my belly isn't flat, my butt and boobs are big and round. After a battle with an eating disorder when I was younger, I got the help I needed, and thankfully, now I can look in the mirror and see myself as the gorgeous woman I am. But sometimes, I get those moments of self doubt, more so after I got to Calling Wood. Knox doesn't know about my past, none of them do, but I plan on telling them. If they open up to me, I will with them. I don't want secrets between us.

Giving myself a smile, I leave the bathroom and head into my room. When I notice the stuff on the bed, I gasp, tears stinging my eyes. Slowly, I walk over to see what was left for me.

Laying across the bed is one of the most stunning emerald dresses I've ever seen. It has the style of a sundress, my favorite thing to wear, but looks so much more elegant and formal. Next to it are a pair of ruby red heels and what looks like three jewelry boxes.

On top of the dress is a note, and I pick it up to read it.

HELLO, *my Love, my Little Omega. Wear this dress for me so we can show the world just how stunning you are, how blessed we are to call you ours. But don't think it's the dress that will make you breathtaking, you do that all on your own. - Tristan*

MY EYES BLUR as a tear slips free and drops onto the paper. Not wanting to ruin it, I fold it back up and place it on my dresser.

My heart feels like it's going to burst as I pick up the note tucked into one of the heels.

KITTEN, *wear these with the dress Tristan picked out. I wanna look down and imagine just how sexy you would be in nothing other than these heels as you lock me in place between your mouthwatering thighs. - Knox*

MY BODY FLUSHES with arousal as I read who signed it..

Biting my lip, I add his note with Tristan's.

Next, I grab the boxes. The first one is a long rectangle, and when I open it, I find a gorgeous white gold chain with a teardrop pendant. It has an emerald in the middle with little diamonds around it.

· · ·

I GOT *this for you because it reminded me of your eyes. The eyes I can happily get lost in for hours without ever wanting to find my way out. Thank you for choosing us. Enjoy some pretty bling for a Pretty Girl. - Sawyer.*

I LOVE IT. The next box holds a pair of earrings that match the necklace.

THIS IS *all new to me. I honestly have no idea what to get a woman, let alone one as enchanting as you. So, I saw what the others were getting you and thought these earrings were perfect. I hope. Thank you for being the ray of sunshine we all need. Our lives have been cloudy and gray until you entered them and lit everything up. You've done more for us than you will ever know. - Finn.*

ANOTHER TEAR FALLS, and I wipe my eyes. I need to stop crying or they're going to be red and puffy.

Grabbing the last box, I open it to find a diamond bracelet with a matching anklet.

. . .

I KNOW *nothing about any of this. But I saw these and thought of you. They're dainty, perfect, and I bet the ankle bracelet would look good on my shoulder as I lock my knot deep inside your pussy. Can't wait to see if I'm right, Little One. - Dominic.*

WELL, the tears are gone, but now I have slick running down my leg. Fuck, these guys are all so different from one another. They're perfect for me.

Taking the towel wrapped around me, I wipe myself off and throw it into the dirty laundry basket.

I put on a bra and scent blocking panties, knowing that these guys are going to work me up at some point tonight. Then I move on to hair and makeup. I do all the basics like foundation and concealer with a bit of blush, but for my eyes, I don't use any eyeshadow, just some wing liner and mascara. Topping it off with some blood-red lipstick, I work on my hair. First, I straighten it so it's tamed, then curl it. It's a bitch to do because have you ever tried curling hair after straightening it? Let's just say it takes a while.

When I'm done, I put my dress and shoes on before a sudden knock at the door has me spinning around.

"Need any help, kitten?" Knox adds.

"Please," I answer back.

He opens the door, and I almost gasp at the heat that fills his eyes the moment his eyes land on me. He lets out a growl, sounding more Alpha than Beta, like he always does.

"Fuck me, Kitten. Let's just stay home. I wanna make you scream my name. But don't take anything off," he says, his voice husky.

I'm not the only one looking good. He looks so sexy right now. He's wearing black dress pants and a black dress shirt that's rolled up to his elbows, showing off the ink on his forearms.

"Okay," I breathe, really liking that idea.

He chuckles. "As much as I want to take myself up on my suggestion, there are four really excited but nervous Alphas waiting for their Omega down the hall."

That has nervous butterflies erupting in my belly. "Help me put this on?" I ask, holding out the bracelet. I already put everything else on, but working a clasp one handed is a bitch of a task.

He takes the box as I hold out my wrist for him. His fingers brush my skin, making me shiver before he clips it on. Bringing my hand to his lips, he kisses my wrist. "Breathtaking like always, Little Omega. Ready to go out there and give those Alphas a hard on for the rest of the night?"

I can't help but giggle. "Let's go."

Taking a deep breath as I step out into the hallway, I can hear the others talking quietly, but when I step into the living room they all go quiet, turning their eyes to me.

"Fuck me," Dom growls.

"No thanks, I'd rather it be her," Sawyer breathes, making a smile twitch at the corner of my lips.

"You look amazing, Tia," Finn says in awe, and I blush, matching the one he has on his cheeks.

"What about me?" Knox says, stepping up behind me. He's joking, but Finn doesn't know that, or doesn't catch on.

"You look hot." Finn shudders, taking in Knox. Knox growls, clearly liking how Finn is looking at him.

"As do you, Finny," Knox growls, getting a whimper out of him.

"We can't go," Tristan says, making all of us turn to look at him in confusion.

"Why not?" Dom asks.

"Because! I don't know how to fight. I'd get my ass kicked."

"What the hell does fighting have to do with anything?" Sawyer asks, looking at his pack leader like he grew a second head.

"If we go out, a fight is going to break out. There's no way Alphas aren't going to be ogling our girl, looking as radiant as she does. I can't just sit there and let them do that to our Omega. Hence, the fight I will most likely lose," Tristan says, sounding very serious right now.

We all stand there quietly for a moment. Then suddenly I giggle, Finn snorts out a laugh, Sawyer is cackling, while Dom and Knox roar in laughter.

Tristan is mumbling, his cheeks heating as I walk over to him. "You sure do know how to make a girl feel sexy," I tell him, wrapping my arms around his neck. The heels give me a little height, so I don't have to go too far to kiss him on the cheek, leaving a perfect red lip print behind.

"Well, you are. You're sexy, hot, beautiful, gorgeous, and everything else," Tristan says, giving me a shy smile.

"Don't worry, Tris. If someone starts something, I'm sure we can handle it," Knox says.

"Look, I'm an Alpha, I know this but... I will most definitely lose in a fight," Finn says, looking at us in panic.

"I'd kill anyone who put their hands on you," Knox growls. "Both of you." *Why are his words so fucking hot?* I don't think he would actually kill anyone, but he *would* kick their asses.

"No one is fighting anyone," I say, laughing as I step back.

"Let's go, our reservation is at six," Knox says.

"Wait!" Finn says, making us all stop as we head towards the door. "We forgot the flowers."

"Right," Dom says, looking down at his hand. I didn't even see them at first, too distracted by how handsome they all looked in their fancy cloths. But each of them has a single red rose in their hand.

"For you," Dom says, holding it out to me.

"Thank you," I say, those butterflies fluttering around in my belly for a whole new reason. He kisses my check before stepping to the side.

They each give me their rose and a kiss. When they are done, I smell the bundle of pretty flowers before putting them in the vase Knox holds out for me. He takes them to my room before joining us again.

I look around at all my guys and wonder what I ever did to deserve them. I'm one lucky Omega.

OCTAVIA

We don't take the golf carts to the restaurant because the one we're going to isn't located in Calling Wood. So, the guys called a limo. *A freaking limo!* When it pulls up, I shamelessly let out an excited squeal. I looked and felt amazing, and the limo was the cherry on top.

"After you, Little Omega," Sawyer says, holding his hand out. I smile up at him and place my hand in his, loving the feeling I get whenever I touch any of them.

"Why thank you, Alpha," I tease, but he seems to like me calling him that because he lets out a growl in approval. There's a flash of surprise in his eyes at his own reaction.

Sawyer and Finn always seem a bit shocked when they growl or purr like an Alpha does. It's not something I think they're used to, and with me being their Omega, I bring it out in them. Natural instincts kicking in.

Dom is always growly, so there's no change for him. Tristan is pack leader, and the most Alpha of them all. Some people just don't see it when they first look at him.

We all get into the limo and leave the community. I haven't been outside of Calling Wood since I arrived, so it's going to be nice to not have to be around everyone who knows my pack and me; to avoid the judgmental stares and whispers.

The limo is quiet, everyone looks around at each other, wondering what to say or do. My eyes roam over my Alphas, taking in each of their outfits of choice for tonight.

None of them are wearing their suit jackets since it's too hot down here in California. So, Tristan is in navy blue pants and dress shirt with a black tie. Sawyer is wearing a classic white shirt, black pants. Finn is wearing black pants and a red and black striped shirt, but Dom is the one who stands out the most. He's in beige dress pants and a plaid button up. He looks like a sexy lumberjack that I'd like to crawl up onto and ride his *log*.

At that thought, the whole car erupts in low growls as my perfume fills the space. My cheeks heat, and I look up. "Oh, look, a sunroof," I say, pressing the button to open it and standing up, popping my head outside.

The guys all protest below me, but I feel a rush of joy as I look around. The sun is starting to set, casting beautiful shades of yellows, oranges, and pinks across the sky. We're driving alongside the ocean, and I can see boats out at sea, birds flying over.

The wind is cool, perfect, as it hits my face. My curls are probably going to be ruined, but right now, I can't find it in me to care.

"Pretty Girl," Sawyer says, popping his head up next to me. "You have the guys in a tizzy down there."

"I'm sorry, but look," I say, not taking my eyes off the water, a big smile on my face. "It's so pretty."

"Yeah, you are," he says, making my eyes snap to his. He has a soft smile on his lips that has my heart melting. His eyes glance down at my lips, and before he can say or do anything else, I grab the back of his head and kiss him.

He moans, getting a whimper from me as my belly flutters. Curses erupt below us, and I giggle against his lips as he chuckles.

"I'll never get sick of the taste of your lips and the musical sound of your laughter."

I blush, biting my lip and ducking down, not wanting my Alphas to worry any longer.

The drive isn't long, and before I know it, we're stopping outside the restaurant.

"This place is so cute!" I say in awe as we get out of the limo. It's a nice brick building that has a wrap-around porch with an outside seating area underneath fairy lights. There's live music coming from inside, and the vibe is relaxed yet classy. A part of me is really happy they brought me here and not some fancy place where I'd be too worried about saying or doing the wrong thing.

My heart beats a little faster, knowing they know me well enough to bring me to a place that suits me.

"I've been wanting to come here for a while. I thought you might like the place?" Tristan says, looking at me with slight nerves.

"I love it," I tell him, wrapping my arms around his body and smiling up at him.

"I'm glad," he says with a slight growl, making me shiver as he takes my lips with his.

"I'm starving," Dom grumbles, making me chuckle.

"Me too," I tell him.

"Then what are we waiting for?" he says, taking my hand in his. "We have an Omega to feed."

We enter through the front door and are greeted by a

pretty, blonde Beta. "Hi. Welcome to Harmony's. Do you have a reservation?"

"Hello. Yes, under Ashwood," Tristan says, wrapping his arm around me.

"Alright, table for six?"

"Please. And outside in the back with a waterfront view, please. I requested it in advance."

The woman looks at her computer for a moment, then nods. "I see you have." She grabs some menus before giving us a bright smile.

We follow her outside and around to the back. There's only one other table with people back here, and I'm glad we'll have some privacy. Sawyer pulls out a chair for me, and I thank him with a smile before sitting down. He sits next to me with Finn on my other side. Knox sits next to him, then Dom and Tristan, until we're all seated around the circular table.

"Here are your menus. Is there anything I can get you to drink to start?"

My eyes go wide when I'm hit with the realization that I can now drink. "I'll have a pina colada please," I ask her. "And a water." The guys look at me with small grins, and I grin back.

Tristan, Dom, and Knox order beer while Finn orders an iced tea and Sawyer orders a rum and coke with a pitcher of water for the table.

When she turns to leave, she casts a lingering look at Knox that bothers me. Knox is a very attractive man, and I know he turns heads, but I don't like the look she gave him.

He didn't seem to notice, just looking at me with a tilt to his head. I give him a smile, trying to brush the feeling off. *It was just a look, Tia, nothing more.*

"Since when do you drink, Love?" Tristan asks.

"Since tonight," I tell him. "So, I'm not sure how I'll react. Be ready, just in case," I tease.

"Ready for what?" Knox asks with a grin.

"Well, it could go a few different ways. I could be a lightweight, and you could end up holding my hair back while I puke, or maybe it will make me horny, and I'll end up keeping you up all night."

They all growl, liking the idea of that. My cheeks flush because I was joking... kinda.

We all make light conversion as we look over our menus. I'm stuck between a very yummy looking shrimp dish or a chicken and salsa dish. I go with the chicken because seafood with alcohol doesn't sound good to me.

"Alright, here are your drinks," the waitress says, setting the tray down, giving everyone what they asked for. "Are we ready to order?"

I ask for the chicken first, then the guys give her their picks, most of the guys get the steak, while Finn gets spaghetti.

As she picks up all the menus, she goes out of her way to brush her hand along Knox's arm. His eyes snap up to hers in slight shock, but she just gives him a sexy, little grin.

A growl rumbles, and for a moment I'm wondering what Alpha of mine is seeing this and getting pissed off in my honor. Then I realize it's me. *Well, that's new.*

The Beta woman looks back at me in surprise before taking off.

"Is my little Kitten jealous? As hot as it is, you have nothing to worry about, Little Omega. I'm all yours."

I know this. He has my mark, and I have his, but seeing another woman touching him... it makes me uneasy.

Giving him a smile, I nod, not wanting to talk about it. I'm not used to feeling this way, but when it comes to my guys, I find myself being very protective. I take a sip of my drink to distract myself, and it's really good. I'm going to have to stop myself from having more than one because I can see myself easily drinking these like they're juice.

The guys fall into easy conversation, and I enjoy just sitting here and listening. Sometimes they ask me something or I ask them, getting to know each other a little bit more. We will get into more personal details when I have my one on one time with each of them. For now I just enjoy being out with my new family.

"What are you smiling about, Pretty Girl?" Sawyer whispers into my ear. I jump a little, being pulled out of my head. I shiver, and move to cross my legs because of the effect he's having on my body, but he puts his hand on my thigh, keeping me from closing them.

I suck in a breath, trying not to draw attention to myself. Biting the inside of my cheek, I keep my eyes on the guys as they talk and joke. Finn and Dom are mostly quiet but involved in their conversation.

Sawyer lets out a little chuckle, like he knows what he's doing to me, before joining the conversation once again.

Back and forth, his thumb brushes the sensitive skin of my thigh as he inches up towards my core.

My heart starts to pound in my chest, my body feeling like it's slowly burning to ash, a fire growing below, and fuck me, I'm surprised the others haven't smelt me perfuming like a department store as my pretty, black panties get destroyed by my slick.

When his fingers brush my clit, it takes everything in me to hold back the whimper caught in my throat. We're in public, and I don't want to draw attention to myself. I should tell him to stop, but I don't want him to. I'm loving his touch, my pussy craving the relief he's teasing me with.

"Let's play a game, Pretty Girl. I wanna see how long you can keep quiet. Can you do that for me?" Sawyer asks, his voice low and husky.

I can't speak; it will give me away, so I give him a sharp nod. Taking a deep breath through my nose, I will myself not to pass out from the sexual tension building like a fucking volcano.

"Good girl," he praises, and I can't help it, a little whimper slips out. Knox glances at me, and I swear I see the smallest quirk of his lips. But he goes back to talking to Dom, I think about his time as a UFC fighter, but I can't concentrate worth shit right now.

Sawyer's fingers start to rub my sensitive bundle of nerves, and the feeling of pressure on my aching clit has me biting down on my cheek so hard that I can taste blood as I hold in the moan sitting on the tip of my tongue. The ember in my belly is quick to become a full on burning inferno. I'm close already, the build up getting me all worked up. Also, these guys have no issue revving my engine.

"You're doing so good, Pretty Girl. But I can see you starting to break. Just a little longer, then I want you to cum for me. Let your Alphas, and that Beta of yours, hear your sweet cries as you cum by my hand."

Fuck. He's not helping!

He starts to add more pressure, going a little faster. I'm trying to stay still in my seat, trying to keep my whimpers and whines to myself. But I can't, I just fucking can't anymore. This man has my mind spinning and my pussy humming.

Just as I'm about to cum, the waitress brings us our food. Sawyer doesn't stop as she places everything down. And just as she turns to leave, I fucking explode. Squeezing my eyes shut. I cum, hard, choking out a sob that has the whole table stopping their conversation and snapping their attention to me.

When I'm finally able to open my eyes, it's to see a table of very hungry men. But not for the food before them, no their hunger is for me.

"Fuck's sake, Sawyer!" Dom growls. "Now, I'm fucking hard as stone."

Sawyer just laughs and leans over to kiss my cheek. "Such a good Little Omega we have. I love how much she craves our touch. I needed to hear those sweet sounds again. It's been too long."

"And now the poor waitress is going to be scarred for

life," I groan. But a part of me is glad she heard. She should know these are my men, including Knox.

"Really, Sawyer?" Tristan glares at him.

"What?!" Sawyer chuckles. "Dinner," he says, pointing to the food. "And a show." He looks to me. "Although, I'd rather have you for dinner." He gives me a wolfish grin.

Okay, I need to put an end to this now, or I'll be wet all night. "Eat," I tell him, giving him a playful glare.

"Fine," he sighs. "Yes, ma'am."

I giggle and dig into my meal. When I get the first bite in my mouth, I moan, my eyes rolling into the back of my head. "So good."

Growls break out all around the table again, and my eyes snap open. "I'm just eating!" I protest, trying to hide my smile.

"Yeah, I wish I was eating," Knox mumbles, taking a bite of his steak.

I stick my tongue out at him and, lightning fast, he leans over the table and is in my face, biting my tongue.

My eyes widen, and I let out a whimper of surprise. "Watch what you do with that tongue, Kitten," he tells me, sitting back down looking proud of himself. "Next time, I'll do much worse." He winks, and I flush. This is going to be one long supper.

Tonight was perfect. I enjoyed talking and laughing with my pack. Experiencing what my life is going to be like from now on, and knowing there's still so much to learn, has me excited for the future. The food was delicious, the service was good. Well, that was after we got our food because we ended up with a new waiter. *I wonder if it was because of me?*

Now we're getting ready to leave. Knox went inside to pay, and I'm using the bathroom quickly before we go, with my sweet Finn outside waiting for me.

I'm quick to pee, glad the dress wasn't a pain to deal with. After washing my hands, I meet Finn outside.

"Ready to go, Sunshine?" he asks with a bright smile. I grin, nodding my head. I go to take his hand when his smile drops, and he looks behind me, his eyes going wide.

"Hey there, Sweet Thing," a gruff voice says, making the hair on my neck stand up and an uneasy feeling fill my body.

I spin, looking up at a big mountain of an Alpha. "Hi," I say, forcing a smile, trying to be polite.

"What's an Omega like you doing out here all alone?" he asks.

Alone? Does he not see Finn right behind me? Asshole much?

"I'm not alone. I have my Alpha here with me," I say, shifting to the side so I can point to Finn. I look to my sweet Alpha, who looks stunned, eyes wide as he swallows hard. *Poor love.*

"Him?" the Alpha asshole snorts. "He's an Alpha?" The guy makes it sound like I told the funniest joke that he ever heard. "Beta maybe, Omega for sure, but Alpha? Nah."

"Yes, he's an Alpha, *my* Alpha. Now, if you don't mind, we gotta go," I say through gritted teeth. My heart is pounding, my anger taking over the fear that I had before. As I turn to leave, the fucker grabs my arm. I'm about to chew him out, but Finn surprises me. A growl I've never heard him make before leaves his mouth.

He puffs up his chest, new-found confidence taking over. "Let my Omega go!" he says in a shaky warning.

"Or what?" the Alpha growls.

"Or I'll kick your fucking ass," Dom growls, stepping up behind Finn. I can see Finn's shoulders relax now that backup is here, but I'm still so proud of my Alpha for defending me when I knew he was afraid. It was fucking hot.

The Alpha looks at my guys, then scoffs letting me go. "You're not worth it anyways." *Ouch. Well, fuck you too, buddy!*

"Are you okay?" Finn asks, looking me over for injuries.

"I'm okay. Thanks to you," I tell him, stepping close and wrapping my arms around his neck.

"Me? I-I did nothing," Finn stutters. "I was useless." He frowns, looking upset.

"No. You were so fucking hot," I say in a breathy tone, then pull him down to kiss me. He whimpers, and I love it. "Thank you."

"I will always do what I can to protect you, Sunshine," he tells me. "I just wish I was better at it."

"I think you did good, man." Dom claps him on the shoulder. "I bet if I didn't show up, you would have taken a swing."

"I would have," Finn says. "I really would!" he says, eyes

narrowing at my smile. I'm not smiling because I think what he's saying is silly, but because I'm just really happy with this confidence he's found. "I might be a pussy, but if you were truly in danger, I would do everything in my power to help."

"I know you would, baby," I tell him, brushing my thumb against his cheek. "And I love you for it. Also, take that back." I growl softly. "You are not a pussy. You are my sweet, sexy alpha, but not a pussy."

His eyes widen, and he blushes.

"Come on you two, let's get your Beta and go home."

We follow Dominic out to the lobby, finding Knox getting the receipt. "What's this?" he asks, looking at the piece of paper.

"It's my number, call me sometime. I think we would have fun together," she giggles.

Nope, nope. Hell. Fucking. No. No! Beta bitch.

A rage I've never felt before takes over me. With a growl I'm still not used to, I charge towards them, the little bit of alcohol I consumed hyping me up, and Dom and Finn start cursing from behind me.

"Do you mind?" I snap at the waitress from earlier. *Of course, it's her.*

"I'm sorry, what?" she asks, looking at me with bitch eyes.

"This!" I snatch the paper from Knox while he just stands there, letting me take the lead.

"I gave the hot Beta my number. What do you care?" she snarks.

"This hot Beta is *my* fucking Beta," I say, stepping up to her, hating that she's got a good few inches on me. I'd still take her. I could pull a few of those hair extensions out and leave some nail marks. *Try me, bitch.*

"Yours?" she snorts. "He's a Beta. You're an Omega. I get he might be a part of your pack, but let the poor guy date."

"Not only is he my Beta." I step up to Knox, not missing the massive smile on his face. He's fucking loving this. *Good, I hope he sees how much I love his ass.* Pulling down the collar of his dress shirt, I point to his mate mark on his neck. "He's my mate!"

Her eyes widen, but she doesn't say or do anything. I step up to her again. "So take your number," I say, crumbling it into a ball. "And shove it up your ass."

"Why you little-" the girl starts, but she doesn't get to finish because Knox is throwing me over his shoulder and carrying me out of the restaurant.

"Put me down!" I shout, smacking his really toned ass. "Let me at her!"

"Down, Kitten," he says, putting me on my feet. "Retract those claws for me."

"But," I pout.

"Or keep them out and use them on me," he says, giving me a heated look. "Because that was the hottest thing I've ever seen." He pushes me against the limo, my Alphas standing and watching, not saying anything as Knox grinds his cock against me. It's hard, and I whimper, slick soaking my pussy. "Seeing you claim me like that. Fuck, Little Omega, you feel how hard I am right now?"

"Knox," I breathe, really wanting to fuck him right now.

"We're going to get into that limo, Kitten," he growls. "And you're gonna ride my cock all the way home while your Alphas watch. Because I need you, *right now*," he growls.

CHAPTER 17

KNOX

My cock is so damn hard. And all I can think about is my Kitten riding me like the fucking queen she is.

Watching her go all possessive on that Beta waitress's ass was one of the sexiest things I've ever seen.

The moment the woman started getting flirty, I ignored her. I have my Omega, my love, my heart, and soul. No other woman exists in my eyes. So she never stood a chance. And I know Tia knows I would never do anything to hurt her. She knows how I feel about her. I make sure to tell her all the time, every day. I'm not ashamed to tell her how much she owns me.

But fuck, hearing her claim me and show off my mate mark was a gift. She will never know how much it means to me that she's so proud of me, a Beta, as her mate. I'm so damn lucky to call her mine.

We stumble into the limo, our lips fused together, not wanting to break apart. My ass finds the seat, and I pull her down on top of me. "I need your cock inside me, now," she says in a desperate plea as she pants before her lips are back on mine. She grinds herself against my cock, and I can feel her slick soaking my slacks already. She's drenched, soaked right through her panties.

"Yes, Kitten," I growl against her lips.

The others climb into the back, but say nothing as I make quick work of my pants, freeing my cock. It's hot and heavy in my palm, ready to be swallowed whole by this breathtaking Omega above me.

She rips her lips away from mine, a determined look swirling in her eyes, which are full of heat and need. She gathers up her dress, moving it out of the way as she raises herself up.

Moving my cock so that it's just below the heat of her core and pulling her panties to the side, I give her a devilish smirk. "Your throne is ready and waiting, my Queen. Why don't you come and take a seat where you belong?"

She whimpers, one hand holding her dress and the other bracing herself on my shoulder as I move her panties to the side. With one last look as she bites that sexy, plump bottom lip, she impales herself on my cock.

We both moan; the feeling of her pussy wrapped around my cock making my head spin.

"That's it, Kitten. Ride me, baby, take your pleasure. I'm yours to use however you please," I encourage her. I would do anything for this girl, and I mean *anything*.

She starts to ride me, both hands on my shoulders now. With every roll of her hips, she whimpers and whines. She looks so fucking beautiful right now. Her lips are parted as little gasps slip past every time my cock hits her sweet spot.

Her slick is coating my thighs, the smell filling the back of the limo as we drive home.

When she closes her eyes, getting lost in her pleasure, I look over at the Alphas. Tristan has his cock out and in his hand, watching his Omega ride me. His movements are slow as he tries to outlast the show we're putting on. Dom is palming his cock through his pants, his brows furrowed as he enjoys himself too.

Sawyer is watching with a heavy lidded look, heat blazing as he jacks himself off at a little bit of a faster pace than his pack leader.

Then I turn to Finn, the closest one to me and Tia. He's not touching himself, but I can see his cock straining against his pants as he watches with wide eyes. He's biting his full lower lip as he tries to hold himself back from whatever it is he wants to do.

"Touch yourself," I command, groaning as Tia picks up the pace. My hands find her hips, and I help her keep a steady rhythm.

"What?" he chokes out, his eyes flicking from her to me.

"I can see how much you're loving this. Your cock is begging to be freed. So free it. Pleasure yourself as your Omega fucks your Beta."

"Are... are you sure?" he asks, looking at Tia with a pinched brow.

"She won't mind. Isn't that right, Little Omega? Do you want your Alpha to touch himself as he watches you fucking own me?"

Tia's eyes open, and she looks to Finn, nodding her head. "Please," she moans. Finn hesitates, still not sure.

"Isn't she a good girl, Finn? Look at her riding me so perfectly," I growl.

"Such a good girl," Finn says breathlessly.

Tia whimpers, her movements starting to get choppy, her pussy fluttering around my cock. Tucking her face into my neck, she bites down on our mating mark, making me moan as she screams out her release. Slick gushes down my cock making an absolute mess out of this limo.

"I'm not done with you, Kitten," I growl as she slumps against me, panting like she just ran a marathon.

Without taking my cock out of her, I flip her so that she's laying on the seat. With one knee on the seat and the other on the floor, I move her legs so they are draped over my shoulders and start to pound into her.

I move her dress so that her Alphas can see my cock thrusting in and out of their Omega's cunt. "Look at her, Finn. Do you see how well she takes my cock?" I growl, loving the whimpers that I get from both of them.

Finn watches where Tia and I are joined together with rapt attention and, with shaky hands, he works on his pants until he can free his cock.

I growl as I watch him wrap his hand around his thick shaft. He's fucking huge. Who knew my shy little Alpha had such a fat cock and an even fatter knot? A fat cock I want him to choke me with as I bring him to the brink of insanity. A cock that I want to watch get knotted in my Kitten while I fuck his tight ass.

The image has me thrusting into Tia harder. Her cries fill the limo, and when I start to rub her clit, she clamps around me, her pussy gripping me with everything she has. She screams out her second orgasm, coating me with even more of her slick.

Finn moves his hand faster, his eyes flicking from me, to Tia, to where my cock is pounding into her pussy.

The combination of that image in my head, the sight of the man I love touching himself to me fucking his Omega, and the fact that Tia whimpers so sweetly, is my undoing.

Locking eyes with Tia, I give her one more hard thrust before roaring as I cum hard into my Omega's pussy, filling her with my cum.

Finn lets out a choked noise, and then he's cumming. Ropes of cum shoot out and over his hand, getting his suit dirty with his seed.

The others let out sounds of their own releases, but I pay them no mind as I watch my man come down from his high. His chest is heaving, and his cheeks heat, turning a pretty red color.

"Hand," I growl, and he blinks at me with confusion. "Give me your hand, Finn." He holds out his clean hand, but I shake my head, clicking my tongue. "Not that one, Finny, the other one." He looks down at his cum covered hand that's still wrapped around his sinfully hard cock, and his eyes widen. "Finn," I say in warning. If he says no, I won't push him. I can tell he enjoyed himself, but this is all new to him, and I don't want him to feel uncomfortable.

I let out a low rumble of approval when he lets go of his dick, letting it fall into the puddle of cum below, and holds out his hand for me.

I can see Tia watching out of the corner of my eyes, biting her lip as I reach out and grab Finn's wrist. He swallows hard as I bring his hand to my mouth and slowly start to lick his hand clean.

He tastes amazing, his salty flavor quickly becomes an addiction, like my Kitten's slick. Fuck, I can't wait to eat my Little Omega's sweet pussy as it drips my Alpha's cum.

Finn whimpers as Tia moans, her pussy gripping my cock again as she has another orgasm just from the sight of me licking Finn's cum.

"All clean," I say, licking my lips.

"Don't kill me, I'm just the messenger, but guys, we're home," Sawyer says.

Finn and I break our little stare off, and I look around to see the limo has stopped and the others are gone. Glancing over my shoulder, I see Sawyer grinning wickedly at the three of us.

"That was pretty fucking hot though," Sawyer laughs. "I'm not into guys, but I'm down to watch. I think I'm gonna love pack life." He takes off, leaving us alone again.

Finn tucks himself back into his pants as I pull out of Tia, cum and slick flowing out of her and onto the seat.

"Umm," Finn says, looking down at the mess he made of himself.

"Go get cleaned up. I'll bring sleeping beauty into the house," I chuckle, looking down at Tia who is now fast asleep below me.

"Knox," Finn says, and I look up at him. "Thank you."

"For what?" I ask.

"I'm new to all of this, and there's a lot of things I wanna do, but I'm too shy or awkward to voice it. Just now, you saw the need in me and helped me take that step. Tia's been doing the same thing, bringing me out of my shell and showing me that I don't have to be afraid of what I want. So, thank you."

"Finn, we're gonna always be there for you no matter what you need. I'm excited to explore what we have, and I know Tia is too. But Finn," I tell him, giving him a heated look. "The moment you take that big step with Tia, your ass is *mine*," I growl.

He whimpers and nods his head, swallowing hard. "Yes, Sir."

"Good boy," I praise. "Now, go get cleaned up."

He nods again, and gets out of the limo.

Looking down at my Kitten, I grin and move her dress back into place.

Scooping her up, I carry her out of the limo and up into the house. Tristan is coming out of the bathroom, and he smiles down at our Omega with so much love.

"Call the limo company and have the car cleaned right

away. By a Beta. I don't want any Alphas smelling our girl's slick," I tell him.

"Good idea." He nods, then kisses Tia's cheek before taking off down the hall.

I take Tia into her room and carefully take off her dress, shoes, and jewelry. She doesn't stir once, too exhausted from today.

Cleaning her the best I can with a wet cloth, I tuck her into bed after putting on one of my shirts and a pair of my clean boxers.

There's a knock at the door as I settle in next to her.

"Come in," I say quietly.

Finn pokes his head through the door and looks at the two of us. "Can I sleep with you guys?" he asks, and my heart swells.

"Of course. I'd love that, and I know she would too."

He steps inside and closes the door behind him. He's already dressed in his Iron Man PJs, and I smile to myself at how adorable he is.

Taking off his glasses, he places them on the bedside table before getting into bed on Tia's other side.

"Finn," I say after we lay there in silence for a bit.

"Yeah?" he whispers back.

"I want you to know, I've always been in love with you. And I'm sorry if you ever thought I'd never want you back."

He says nothing for a moment, then takes my hand that's resting on Tia's belly and laces his fingers with mine.

"I wish I was brave enough to say something back then.

And I'm mad at myself now because if it wasn't for Tia, I don't think I'd ever have the courage to say anything."

"Don't be mad. This was how it was supposed to happen. Tia is the missing piece to our puzzle. Now that we have her, we can be whole. We can be the picture perfect family we were always meant to be."

CHAPTER 18

OCTAVIA

Chewing on my lower lip, I look at my swimsuit options laid out on the bed. I have three weeks to get to know my Alphas before my next heat. I know Sawyer, Finn, and Dominic all have special dates planned for me with the intention to get to know me better and well... lose their virginity.

It might be unconventional, but I'm excited. I want them, all of them, all the time. I'll never understand how they kept getting passed up by Omegas, because they are amazing men. But they're mine now, and I've never been so happy.

I think it's sweet that they each want our first time to be special and not to get lost in the crazy haze of my heat. I still feel bad for how it happened with Tristan, even though he told me he wouldn't have it any other way. I still plan on having some one-on-one time with him. That way we can take it slow and enjoy each other.

Sawyer hasn't told me anything about today's adventure, only saying I need to bring a swimsuit.

"I think you should go with the black one," Knox says, coming up behind me and wrapping his arms around me. I smile and lean my head to the side, letting out a little moan as he kisses his mate mark.

"You think?" I ask, looking at the strapless, black bikini. "My boobs might fall out." I laugh.

"And you think that would be an issue for him?" Knox teases with a low chuckle.

"I guess not." If at the end of the night we will be having sex, then I don't think he will be taking me somewhere where there will be a bunch of other people around. So if one or both of the girls happen to fall out, it wouldn't be the end of the world. "Alright, black one it is."

"He's gonna cum in his pants just at the sight of you, Kitten," Knox growls, spinning me around, sliding his hand into my hair at the back of my head. He grips it lightly before kissing me in a dirty, frantic way. "Can't help but tease him a little." Knox grins as we break apart. My heart is pounding in my chest, and I'm very close to pushing him onto this bed to take care of what he just caused. "Your scent is going to drive him wild."

"You're mean." I giggle. Knox just shrugs, smirk still in place.

He leaves me to finish getting ready, and I pick out a black sundress with white flowers. I finish off the look by piling my hair on top of my head in a cute messy bun. If we're going swimming, I don't wanna spend a lot of time on my hair and makeup, just for it to get ruined. But I also don't wanna go with no effort.

After swiping on a few coats of waterproof mascara, I put the suit in a cute tote bag and grab a towel along with some sunscreen because, you know, redhead problems.

Making sure I have everything, I meet Sawyer by the front door. He looks sexy with his shaggy, blonde hair all messy. I wanna run my fingers through it and just play with it for hours. He's wearing a pair of blue board shorts and a white drop armhole tank top, his arm muscles on full display.

"Like what you see, Pretty Girl?" Sawyer grins and starts to flex, making a show of it. I giggle as I step towards him.

"Always," I tell him, leaning up onto my tippy-toes to kiss him.

"You look beautiful, Little Omega," he growls against my lips, sending a shiver through my body.

"Thank you," I breathe out.

"Are you ready to go?" he asks, grabbing a wicker basket from the floor next to him.

"Yup!"

We leave the house and climb into the golf cart, my belly flipping with excited energy. Just as Sawyer puts the key in the engine, he turns to me. "I should probably ask, do you get sea sick?"

It's a good thing my answer to Sawyer's question was 'no' because as we pull into the dock, I realize we're going out on a boat today.

"So, you up for a boat ride?" Sawyer asks with a smile, but I can see the nervous gleam in his eyes.

"Yes! That sounds exciting."

"Oh, thank god," he breathes out, running his hand through his hair. "I was worried you would say no."

"I love the water. Plus, I've been on a few boats with my parents before, and I loved it."

"Then let me show you to mine," he says, getting out of the cart and grabbing the basket from the back before coming to my side to help me out. I thank him, grabbing my bag, and we walk down to the dock, hand in hand.

Sawyer leads me down the dock, past some jet skis and small speed boats until we stop before a yacht. It's not as big as the massive ones all the way at the end, but it's fairly large and looks pretty new too.

"This is my baby. A Bavaria R55. Got her for my birthday this year," Sawyer says.

"This is yours?" I gape at him.

"Yeah..." he looks at me nervously, scratching the back of his head. "My parents are kind of..."

"Rich?" I giggle.

"Is that going to be a problem?" he asks, his eyes going wide.

"No, silly. I wanna be with you for *you*, not what you can or can't give me."

"Really?" he asks, looking surprised.

"Sawyer," I scold him. "I love *everything* about you. You make me laugh, you care for me, you're sweet, and so much more. I'm so happy to be here with you today so I can get to know a lot more about you."

"Me too," he says, his shoulders relaxing as he gives me a soft smile.

"So, what's her name?" I ask, checking out the boat.

"Name?" he asks, stepping onto the boat.

"Yeah, don't all captains name their boats?" I ask, taking his hand as he holds it out for me, helping me up and onto the deck.

"Oh. I haven't named her," he says, looking at the boat for a second. "But I think I'll call it the Pretty Girl, what do you think?" he asks me, grinning.

I blush and smile. "I think it's perfect."

"Me too," he agrees. We head up the little stairs and into the main part of the boat.

"Wow," I say in awe as I take in the interior of the ship. When we first get up to the bridge, there's a little seating area. Just past that, we step into a mini kitchenette, and next to that is another seating area with a much cozier feel.

"So this is the main part of the cabin. The controls are in here." He points to the two chairs and a panel of buttons with a screen. "And a second area up on the fly deck. Down below are the bedrooms and bathrooms."

"How many people does it sleep?" I ask.

"Umm," he thinks. "Well, there's two bigger beds that would sleep two each and some singles that would also sleep two... so six?"

That's enough room for all of us. "I think we should all come and spend a weekend here sometime," I tell him, thinking that it would be a fun time with the pack.

"Anything for you, Pretty Girl," he says, then places the basket on top of the table in front of one of the sofas before moving to sit in one of the driver's seats. "Let's get out onto the water first, then this date can *really* begin."

I sit next to him, looking out at the water as he starts up the engine. Once we're free of the harbor, Sawyer speeds us up. A little thrill goes through me at the feeling. I look over to Sawyer, who's grinning.

When we get so far that we can't see any land, Sawyer anchors the boat and turns to me.

"So, what do you wanna do? Eat, talk, or swim first?"

"Swim!" I say excitedly. "We can talk while we eat after."

"Sounds good to me, Pretty Girl. I'll go get us set up on the fly deck with some drinks while you get changed," he says, kissing my cheek before taking off upstairs.

Grabbing my bag, I go down the little steps, and my eyes fly wide open. *Wow, you wouldn't think all this would be here, but it's really nice.*

I decide to do a little exploring before I change. Straight

ahead from the bottom of the stairs is one of the rooms. The interior is really nice and modern with a bed that can fit two and a little bathroom. Moving to the door next to it, there's another room that has two single beds; it also has it's own bathroom. Then off to the right of the bottom of the stairs is what looks to be the master.

It has a bigger bed and more space with a much larger, nicer bathroom. Claiming this bed as ours, I put my bag down on it and get dressed. I leave my clothes here but grab the sunscreen and a towel before joining Sawyer on the fly deck.

"Woah," I say, looking out at the endless water. "Stunning."

"Yes. You. Are," Sawyer says. I look and find him watching me with a heated stare, making me feel very sexy at the moment.

"Stop looking at me like that." I giggle playfully. I love it, but I'm about to start dripping slick here soon if he doesn't stop.

"Sorry, Little Omega. It's hard not to appreciate my girl," he growls. *His girl.* I love it. "Drink?" he asks, holding out some sparkling apple juice. "We can have real drinks later if you want, but it's not safe to drink and swim. I'd hate for anything to happen to you."

"You're too sweet," I say, taking it from him and thanking him.

I take a few sips before setting the cup down on the table behind me, turning back around just in time to see him pull off his shirt, distracting me as I stand there with the sunscreen in my hand, that I was about to put on, ready to put some on. "Want some help with that?" he asks.

"What?" I blink, making him chuckle.

"The sunscreen, Pretty Girl."

"Oh." I hold it out to him. "Please?"

I hold out my arms and legs for him to spray before doing a little spin for him to get my back side. His hands find my ass cheeks, and he starts to massage them, squeezing the flesh.

"Umm, Sawyer." I giggle. "It's spray on sunscreen, you don't need to rub it in."

"Can't be too sure, Pretty Girl."

When he stands up, I turn to face him. "Maybe I should do these too," he gives me a wicked grin before he starts to do the same thing he did to my ass to my tits. My nipples harden, and I have no doubt that he can see them through the fabric.

My core is aching, and I can feel the slick at my entrance ready to make an appearance, so I step back. "All done," I tell him, going down the few steps to the side of the boat so I can jump off the side. I really need to cool down.

SAWYER

I'm jumping into the water right after her because I'm so fucking hard right now, it would be hard to miss. As much as I'm aching to be knotted deep inside her, I want to actually use this time to get to know my mate, my Omega, before we get to the intimate stuff.

Tia already owns my heart, and I've already fallen hard for her. I'd tell her that I love her, but I don't want to scare her off.

On the other hand, that's how it is in our world. Growing up, my parents taught me that when you find your Omega, you fall hard and fast. And if they are your scent bond? Well, that just hits you in a whole different way.

My soul knows she's my forever. I'm already head over heels for this girl. I'd do anything she asked me to do. I've been dying to get her alone, to have her all to myself, since the moment she sat at our table.

I knew my time would come, and with how different Tia's situation was, I knew it had to go this way.

Now, it's my time with my Little Omega, and I plan to use it wisely.

When my body hits the water, I curse, sending air bubbles to the surface. Fuck, this is cold, but at least my dick isn't an issue anymore.

I suck in a lung full of air when I surface and wipe the water from my eyes, finding a sexy Tia, now sitting on the edge of the boat.

"The water is so cold," she says with a big smile, her teeth chattering.

"You gotta stay in and let your body adjust to the temperature, silly girl," I say, swimming between her legs. "But I have something you might enjoy."

Kissing the inside of her thigh, I smirk at her little gasp before moving next to her and pulling myself out of the water.

Grabbing what I'm looking for out of storage, I move to the side of the boat and strap it on. Then I press the button on the side as an inflatable water slide unfurls and expands.

"No way!" Tia says, sounding giddy. I love that I can make her happy. "Is it safe?"

"Let me see," I smirk before moving to sit at the top. Pushing off, I let myself slide down. I shout as I speed down it, hitting the water. When I come back up, I give her a thumbs up. "I think it works fine."

She hurries over to get on it, and with her hands in the air she screams happily all the way down.

"Okay, that was fun!" she giggles, water dripping down her face. She's so fucking sexy.

"It was." I swim over to her, pulling her close to me. She wraps her body around me as I kick to keep us floating.

"I'm glad we get this time together, Sawyer." She smiles, playing with the wet strands of hair at the back of my head.

"Me too, Little Omega." I kiss her, licking the water off her lips, and my cock hardens again at her little moans. "Play first, then eat. After that, I'm going to have my dessert."

"What about me?" she asks in a husky tone.

"You can have whatever you want, Little Omega," I growl, taking her lips again before dunking her with a laugh and swimming to the boat.

"Hey!" she shouts from behind me, making me laugh harder. "You're gonna pay for that."

"I can't wait, Pretty Girl. Punish me like the naughty boy I am." I grin down at her from the edge of the boat.

She glares at me before swimming towards me.

We spend the next half hour in the water. Sometimes we're on the slide and other times I'm tossing her into the water. Hearing her laughter and seeing the smile that lights up her face fills my heart with so much joy, especially knowing that I was the one who did that.

"I'm starving," she announces, wrapping a towel around her yummy body.

"Me too," I growl.

"For food!" she giggles.

"Call it whatever you want, baby. You can be my meal any time, any day."

She blushes, and quickly moves to the front of the boat, where I have a blanket and the basket of food set out on the sun deck.

"Alright Alpha, what did you pack to feed your Omega?" she asks, crossing her legs as she bounces with excitement.

"Well." I chuckle. "I packed some sandwiches and some meat and cheese. Then for dessert, we have chocolate covered strawberries. But later I plan on making us a nice, *real* meal, then we can settle down for the night."

"Yummy! I love chocolate covered strawberries, but what do you mean for the night? Are we sleeping here? I didn't bring a change of clothes."

"Oh, Pretty Girl." I grin wickedly. "What makes you think you're going to need clothes?"

"Oh." She blushes so beautifully. I love how easily we get to her.

"Are you okay with spending the night? We don't have to if you want to go home." I want her to myself, all night long because I know once tomorrow hits, she will be spending time with the others until each of them has had their own time with her. So, I want every moment I can get with my sweet, little Omega.

Also, this will be my first time having sex, and I know once I'm inside her perfect pussy, I'm never going to want to leave.

"No, I want to." She smiles. "I want us to have the best night."

"And we will," I tell her, taking her hand and kissing the top. Her belly lets out a growl, and I chuckle. "Now, let's get some food in you."

We sit and eat, laughing and talking, getting to know each other.

"You don't have to answer, but have you been with anyone before? I know you were a virgin until Knox, but did you ever have, like a boyfriend or something before?"

"Ahh..." She laughs. "I had crushes, but no. I never had a boyfriend. I don't think any boy saw me that way," she says, her voice goes soft as she looks down at her towel, picking at it.

"Why on earth do you think no one would have seen you like that? Tia, you're fucking gorgeous."

"Thanks." She gives me a small smile, but my heart breaks because I can see something is bugging her. "I know that now, but back then? It took me a while to believe it."

"Why? If you don't mind me asking."

She sighs, but holds my stare. "I know I'm not what most Omegas look like. I have thicker thighs, bigger boobs, and my belly isn't what some would call 'flat'. Now, I love my body, I feel sexy and free, and when you guys look at me like I'm everything in the world you could have asked for, it settles this broken piece inside of me."

I don't like where this conversation is going, but I stay quiet and listen.

"When I was growing up, people liked to constantly point out my flaws," she says, getting a little growl of anger from me, but she keeps going. "I was told that there was no way I was going to be an Omega like my mom, because Omegas don't look like me. Then at one point, because there was only so much I could take, I started eating less. Eventually, it got to the point where I was..." She looks down, a look of shame taking over her face. "I was starving myself. I thought I was fat and ugly, and no one would ever want me."

"Hey," I rumble furiously, lifting her chin so that she can look me in the eye. Her's are filled with tears, and fuck, I never wanna see her like this again. "It doesn't matter what you look like, you will always be a fucking goddess, do you understand me? Everything about you is perfect in our eyes. You never need to change anything about yourself unless it's what *YOU* want."

She nods, giving me a small smile. "I know that now, but thank you for saying that. It helps," she says, continuing with her story. "My mom found me one day passed out on the bathroom floor. She rushed me to the hospital, and from there, I got all the help I needed. It was a long process, but I'm better now."

Fuck, I wanna scream and yell at every person who told her she wasn't perfect the way she was. None of those guys who looked at her funny would have deserved her anyways. We're gonna treat her like the queen she is and remind her everyday just how stunning she is. Not just her body, which is smoking hot, but her personality too. I love everything about her.

"I'm sorry people were assholes and you felt that you were anything but perfect," I tell her, not knowing what else to say.

"Thank you. But that's in the past. I know my worth now, and you guys are amazing at reminding me every time you look at me." I respond with a heated stare and a low growl, making her squirm. "What about you? Did you have any girlfriends before?"

"Yes, I have," I tell her, sucking in a breath. "Well, kind of. Nothing serious, but when I was a teenager, I dated a few girls. I've kissed and done... other things." It's my turn to blush when her eyebrows rise to her hair line in surprise. "But we never went all the way. I wanted to wait until I was with the person I loved. And when I came out as an Alpha, that turned into wanting to wait for the Omega I loved."

"And did you?" she asks, her words low.

"Did I what?" I ask, shifting closer so that we're sitting right in front of each other.

"Wait for the Omega you love?"

I cup her cheek, loving how her pupils expand as I

feather my lips across hers. She whimpers, her perfume filling the air, and I repress a groan so I can answer her. "Yeah, I did, Little Omega."

I kiss her, pulling her into my lap so she's straddling me. She slides her fingers into my hair, holding my mouth to hers as our tongues dance together. She starts to grind on me, seeking friction before pulling back from the kiss, out of breath.

"I love you, Sawyer. I know we've only known each other a month, but I feel it in my heart. I love all of you so much."

My eyes bore into her emerald green ones, seeing the truth within them. "Fuck, Pretty Girl," I growl. "I love you too, with all my heart."

I kiss her again, my heart pounding out of my chest. For the first time in my life, I feel seen. I feel loved. I feel like it's okay to be myself and that I don't have to hide.

We shift so that I'm on top of her, settling between her legs. "I can smell how wet you are, Little Omega. You're soaked, and it's all for me, isn't it."

"Yes," she moans as I grind my cock against her pussy.

"Well, I can't let your sweet gift go to waste, now can I?" I rumble, pulling the towel off her to reveal her perfect body. "Mine," I growl again before moving down so that my face is hovering over her pussy. "Fuck, you smell so sweet, Little Omega."

"Taste me then; see for yourself," she breathes, watching me with hooded eyes. My Omega needs me, and this is what I've been waiting for my whole life. For *her*.

"Don't mind if I do." I chuckle as I sit up and pull off her bikini bottoms. Sitting on my knees, I grab her thighs and part them, opening her wide for me. A growl rumbles in my chest as I see how wet she is, slick dripping from her core.

I haven't done this to a girl in a very long time. But never have I wanted to devour someone as much as I want to with my Little Omega. "This pussy is mine."

"Yours," she whines, trying to wiggle, but my hands are holding her wide open for me. I lean forward, and lap up her juices. My cock throbs at her taste, like toasted coconuts with a hint of chocolate. It's perfect for my sweet tooth, and it's now officially my favorite flavor.

My Alpha instincts take over, something I've never felt so strongly until Tia came along.

Sliding my hands down and under her ass, I hold her up to start feasting on her perfect pussy, licking up all the slick she gives me.

"Sawyer," she whimpers.

"I know, baby," I murmur into her pussy before sucking her clit into my mouth, eliciting a cry from her sweet lips. "Cum for me like a good Omega, and I'll give you my knot."

Like the good girl she is, she does as she's told while I lap and suck her for a few more moments. She rewards me with a fountain of slick. I hurry to lick it all up, not wanting to waste anything.

"Alpha..." she whines, reaching for me. "I need your knot."

"I know, Pretty Girl." I move, covering my body with hers. "But we forgot about the strawberries."

She glares at me, making me chuckle as I remove her top. A growl slips from my chest as I take in her plump breasts, her nipples pebbled tightly. She whimpers again, any anger she was holding against me is gone as she gives me a needy look. Reaching over to the basket, I find the container and open it, taking one out and bringing it to her nipple.

She sucks in a gasp at the contact, of the coolness of the hardened chocolate. I watch as the heat of her breast melts the chocolate, coating her nipple.

Moving it away, I suck her nipple into my mouth, swirling my tongue around, making sure to get every last bit.

"Oh, fuck," she moans, arching her back and pressing her breast into my mouth. Grinning against her flesh, I do the same thing to the other nipple, licking the chocolate from my lips before cleaning that one too.

"Bite," I tell her, holding the strawberry against her lips.

She blinks her eyes open before parting her lips. She bites down, the juices dripping down the side of her mouth. I lick it off, cleaning her up before taking a bite of the berry myself.

"So good. But not as good as you, Pretty Girl."

She swallows, and I take her lips again. We kiss as I shimmy out of my shorts, letting my cock bob free. Gripping it, I give it a few strokes, placing it at her slick entrance.

Just as I'm about to press in, I pause.

"What's wrong?" she asks me, breaking the kiss. She brushes my hair back, away from my face.

"I don't want to disappoint you," I admit, feeling nervous all of a sudden. I was doing so good until this point.

"You won't." She smiles. "Take your time, do what feels right. No pressure, baby. We have all the time in the world." We really don't, though. I know she's aching for my knot. She's an Omega, and that's what they love, but I love her all the more for putting her needs aside to make me feel better.

"Just don't laugh at me if I don't know what I'm doing," I joke, trying to cover up my fear, but she sees past it and right into my soul.

"You're thinking too much. We're here to learn and explore together. I don't expect you to be an expert at sex, Sawyer. This is your first time, and I just want you to have a *good* time. It's gonna feel amazing to me no matter what happens because you're my Alpha, and I know you won't let me go unsatisfied. You already made me cum once." She grins, making some of my nerves wash away. "I have no doubt you will again."

She grips my cock, giving it a squeeze before rubbing the tip through her slick folds. "You feel that? It's all because of *you*. I want *you*, not just your knot or your cock, but you. We could just cuddle, and being in your arms would be enough to make me drenched."

"You really know how to say the right words at the perfect time, don't you?"

She just grins and shrugs, placing the tip back to her entrance before wrapping her legs around my ass and using the heel of her foot to push me forward.

I let her, loving how her eyes widen, and her lips part as I start to fill her with my cock.

I groan, biting the inside of my cheek. She's perfect. So wet and tight; so warm around my cock.

"Sawyer," she moans. "Fuck, Alpha, you feel so good."

"God, Pretty Girl," I growl, looking down as I watch her cunt swallowing me whole. "So fucking perfect. Look at you taking my cock like a good little Omega."

"More," she moans once I'm all the way in.

Bracing my forearms next to her head, I shift so I'm able to move my hips. Pulling out, I thrust all the way back in, stopping just as my knot hits her entrance. She whimpers, moaning that it feels so good. So I keep going, thrusting in and out of her slowly at first, and just as before, my Alpha instincts take over. I'm no longer in fear, like the little, virgin boy I was moments before, as the need to rut into my Omega like the Alpha I was born to be consumes me. *I'm* her Alpha.

CHAPTER 19

OCTAVIA

It's like something inside him snapped. I could see the fear of failing me as my Alpha at first, but once he was inside me, it seemed to disappear, his Alpha instincts taking over.

Sawyer pounds into me, making my body hum in pleasure. I don't know why he was so worried, because he's doing a fan-fucking-tastic job right now.

My slick is gushing out around his cock with every thrust. My body is needy and on fire for his touch, his cock, but most of all, his knot. Being with him feels right, feels *perfect*. I love this man, there's no way I couldn't.

Gone is the silly man who makes me laugh, replaced by the alpha who has my mind spinning, pleasure coursing through my body. I want him to take his time until he feels ready, but I need his knot now. I'm ready to sob and beg for it.

"Alpha," I whine. "Knot. I need it."

"You want my knot, Pretty Girl?" he growls as the sound of our skin slapping together fills the room.

"Yes!" I moan.

"You're gonna take it and love it," he grunts. I gasp as I feel the pressure of his knot forcing its way inside me. With a pop, it's in place, making me cry out in pleasure, my orgasm hitting me like a tidal wave. I scream his name, my pussy gripping his cock while I demand he pumps every drop of cum deep inside me until it's pouring out the sides. I arch my back, my body locking up as I twitch and writhe beneath him.

"Fuck!" Sawyer roars as he holds me tightly, thrusting his hips just the tiniest bit as his cock jerks wildly inside me. Stream after stream of cum coats my inner walls.

"Alpha," I whine, the orgasm going on longer than I'm used to. It's all too much and not enough at the same time. This is the first time I've been knotted outside of my heat, the haze making my awareness of everything fuzzy. But now, my mind is clear, and it's a lot more intense than I remember.

"Hey," Sawyer pants as he moves to stroke my face in a soothing motion. I look at him with panicked eyes as another orgasm takes over. "Shhh. You're okay, Little Omega. I've got you. You're doing so good, Pretty Girl, taking my knot so perfectly. You feel so fucking good, stretched around me. Do you feel that? My cum is dripping from your pretty cunt, mixing with your slick. Fuck, it's the hottest thing I've ever seen."

He keeps soothing me, grounding me in this moment. I breathe through the sensations, and he stops moving, allowing me a little break from the intense amount of pleasure.

"You're okay." He peppers my face with kisses until my heartbeat slows to a normal rhythm, the panic ebbing away with each brush of his lips. "There's my girl." He smiles down at me, and my heart swells with so much love.

"Mark me," I tell him, knowing deep in my soul that I'm his, and he is mine.

"What?" he asks, his eyes going wide. But I mean it. I'm not in a heat haze, I know what I'm saying.

"Mark me, bite me. Make me your Omega officially, Sawyer. I love you, and you love me. I'm yours forever."

"Really?" his eyes start to tear up, like he can't believe someone really wants him in this way, reminding me of just how much I hate all those omegas who fucked my guys over. "Are you sure?"

"With my whole heart," I tell him, smiling up at him.

He kisses me, making me melt into his arms. Once I'm breathless again, he breaks away and starts to kiss down my jaw. "I promise to love you," kiss. "I promise to care for you," kiss. "You will never want or need for anything with us around." Kiss, kiss, kiss. "You are mine, Little Omega, and I'm yours." His lips find the spot he wants on my neck, and he sucks before biting down, marking me as his.

I gasp, my eyes rolling back into my head as I arch into him. The gasp turns into a loud moan as my inner walls grip his cock again, cumming harder than before. A whole new feeling takes over me, like another piece of my heart and soul is clicking into place.

"I can feel you," he groans after kissing and licking his mark. "I can feel what you're feeling."

"Pure bliss," I sigh, blinking up at him with a dopey smile. "Like everything is right in the world."

"I still can't believe I just did that," he says with the biggest, proudest smile on his face. "I'm *officially* your Alpha."

"You were always my Alpha, Sawyer," I tell him, wiping the blood from the corner of his mouth. "This was just a way for me to show that off when you're not around." It means way more than that, though. More than words can describe. And to show him just how much he is mine, I slide my hand into his hair, gripping it hard and pulling him down to me. My mouth latches on to his neck, and I bite down hard, getting a loud groan from him as his cock pulses more cum inside me. I feel so full of his seed, it leaves me with this drunk feeling. *Cum drunk, it's a thing.*

"Fuck, Little Omega," Sawyer growls as I lick his mate mark clean. "I didn't expect you to mark me back."

"Why not?" I give his mark a little nip, making him moan. "I need the world to know I'm yours too." It's not uncommon for Omegas to mark their Alphas, but the more they are connected, the more there is going on inside your head within the pack. The connection becomes stronger with each mark, and it can be a lot when everyone is in the same room, often becoming too much for the Omega. But I don't care. There was never a group of Alphas more deserving of an Omega mark than my guys.

"I love you, Pretty Girl." Sawyer smiles down at me like I gave him the whole world.

"I love you too, Alpha. So, how was your first time?" I giggle.

"There are no words to describe how amazing it was. Better than how I've imagined it all these years. I wanna live inside this pussy," he growls, nipping my lips.

We kiss lazily for a little while, waiting for his knot to deflate, before we hear an engine of another boat. A few moments later, a little speed boat pulls up next to us.

"US Coast Guard!" someone calls out. "Anyone aboard this boat?"

We break our kiss, looking at each other with wide eyes. Fuck, fuck, fuck. We're butt ass naked in the middle of the ocean.

"What do we do!" I hiss.

"Fuck." Sawyer pulls out, a gush of cum and slick following after. I don't even get to enjoy the feeling as he throws a towel over me. He stands, looking around frantically to find something to cover himself up with.

Holding the towel over my body, I sit up on one of my arms watching him. He finds something and puts it over his junk before moving to the side of the boat to where the coast guard is.

"Hey there. Everything is good! Just having a date with my Omega," he calls out to the man.

"I'm glad to hear everything is fine. We saw that the boat

was lacking life and wanted to double check, to see if anyone was in danger."

"Nope, all good here. Right, Tia, baby?"

"All good!" I call back, trying not to giggle as I stare at Sawyer's toned, tan ass.

"Alright then, we'll leave you to it. And son..." the guy says.

"Yeah?" Sawyer asks.

"That's a life-buoy you have covering your manhood there, meaning it's not covering all that much."

I burst into giggles as Sawyer's head snaps down as he realizes his dick is on full display through the hole. I saw what he grabbed, but I didn't get a chance to say anything.

"Fuck." Sawyer crouches down. "Sorry."

The man chuckles and says his goodbyes. Sawyer looks over at me.

"What are you laughing at, Little Omega?" he growls playfully.

"You," I wheeze.

"Oh, I'll give you something to laugh about." He launches himself at me, making me giggle harder.

We get dressed, moving into the little living room to snuggle up to watch a movie. After that, we do a little fishing, and I manage to catch us part of our supper. I'm so proud, and he takes a ton of photos to show the guys.

After we eat, we move down into the bedroom, where Sawyer rocks my world again and again, late into the night.

It's perfect, and I never want this time to end. But I remind myself, it's only the beginning.

CHAPTER 20

OCTAVIA

When we wake up in the morning, Sawyer puts me in an amazing mood by giving me his knot and telling me I'm his good little Omega.

After we shower, we clean up the boat before heading back to land. I have a big smile on my face the whole drive home, and by the time we get to the house my belly is hurting from laughing so much.

The guys are all in the living room looking like *'Night of the Living Dead'* zombies as they get ready for school. I'm probably going to crash at some point today, but I'm still buzzed from the high of everything.

"Well, don't you two look all bright-eyed and bushy tailed," Dom grumbles, his brown hair all messy on the top of his head.

"Oh, hush now, Mr. Grumpy Alpha." I giggle, reaching

up to ruffle his hair. He grabs my wrist, bringing it down and over my belly before pushing me against the wall. I gasp, my smile slipping as I stare up at him in shock.

"I didn't sleep well knowing you weren't safe in this house, in my arms. I don't like you being away from me for long periods of time. So, you're gonna go get dressed in fresh clothes, and I'm gonna drive you to school today. And when you come home from your little girly date with your bestie and her Omega, you're gonna cuddle with me and watch a movie. Do you understand, Little Omega?" he growls, and with all the sex I had in the past twelve hours, I shouldn't be this wet.

Whimpering, I nod. He kisses me, making me moan before biting my lip. "Good girl, now go." He gives me a slap on the ass, making me suck in a sharp breath.

I scurry off to my room and do as I'm told, finding myself loving this more than I thought I would.

When I come out, the guys are now all dressed and ready to go.

"Hey, Dom," Sawyer says, tilting his head to the side. "Do I have something on my neck? It's a little sore."

"Fuck off," Dom growls. "It's your mate mark. We get it. Lucky bastard."

"Yeah, it is," Sawyer says smugly, looking at me with heated eyes. "Damn well better believe I'm showing this baby off." He winks, making me smile and blush.

"Whatever," Dom grumbles.

"You're gonna get yours soon too," I tell Dom. I want to mark him like I did with Sawyer, but he left himself as the last one for a date. I know it's because he's insecure about his body, and I'll give him the time he needs. Although, I won't let him get lost in his head for too long, and if I have to remind him of how sexy he is, I will.

Dom gives me a look that is a mix of need and worry, and I hate seeing him like that.

I say an official hi and bye to the others, giving them each a kiss before moving back to Dom, taking his hand in mine and pulling him to the door.

"Knox is going to meet us at the front doors. Can we stop in for coffee and something to eat before we go to the school? We didn't get a chance before coming home."

"Of course, Little One," Dom says, picking me up and placing me on the seat of the golf cart before buckling me in.

"You know, we don't normally use the belts," I tell him. He looks at me with an angry glower.

"Well, then remind me to kick Knox's ass. I'm not risking my Omega for anything."

I melt inside as he moves to take the driver's seat. I apologize to Knox in my head through our bond for throwing him under the bus, and he sends me a confused feeling, but I just send a loving one back.

From the moment we left to the moment we get to school, Dom is touching me, whether it's his arm around my shoulder while we get coffee or his hand on my knee while we drive. I fucking love it, seeing my grumpy Alpha be all sweet for his Omega. I can see him slowly growing, and it makes me happy.

The day at school goes by slowly, but I get to see my

guys at lunch and even sit next to Everlee in all the classes I have with her.

When the day is done, I go to meet up with Ivy. Tristan demands that Knox keeps an eye on me, especially with me being around strange Alphas. But he has nothing to worry about, my bestie would never hurt me, and I know Ivy would protect me. We've been best friends since birth. Despite the age difference and what we are, that will never change.

"Ivy!" I scream as I see her coming out of her pack house. She gives me a beaming smile, and Everlee steps out from behind her with an even bigger smile as she watches me bolt over to her Alpha, throwing myself into Ivy's open arms.

"Ugh, I missed you, bitch!" she laughs into my hair.

When I step back, I look behind her to see two big men. One has longish, blonde hair, and the other has a similar hairstyle, but it's jet black. They gape at their pack mate. Yeah, Alphas don't talk to Omegas the way Ivy just did with me. But that's how we are. Alpha and Omega doesn't change who we are or our friendship.

"Oh, close your mouth." Ivy laughs, rolling her eyes.

"But..." the one with blonde hair, whose name is Calix, says.

"This is my main bitch, Tia, remember? Don't think anything has changed just because I turned out to be an Alpha and she's an Omega," she tells them, then turns to me. "Tia, you remember my stepbrother Calix, and Carter, his best friend?" Ivy smiles up at them, and they give her one back, filled with so much love.

"Nice to see you again, Tia," Carter says, giving me a polite smile.

"Ivy and Everlee never shut up about you," Calix chuckles.

"Whatever," Ivy snorts.

"Because she's amazing!" Everlee says. "And I need a good friend. I love you three, but I need a break from all this Alpha energy sometimes." They all give her playful growls, making her giggle as she looks at me. "See what I mean?"

"I don't know that feeling yet." I smile. "I've just found my Alphas, and they're all I wanna be around."

"Hey, what about me?!" Knox says from behind me.

"And you too, of course," I tease, getting up on my tippy-toes to kiss him.

"So, you're the Beta guard?" Ivy questions, eyeing Knox up like a protective best friend.

"Yes," I say. "Ivy, Knox. Knox, Ivy."

"It's nice to meet my Omega's besties, but I'm also her mate," Knox states, not missing the chance to show off his mate mark.

Ivy's brows shoot up, her eyes flicking to mine. "Nice." She nods her head. "Not a bad choice, either."

Ivy's Alphas growl from behind her. "Oh, relax," Ivy scolds them. "You two are enough Alpha for me. And even though Knox here isn't an Alpha, I'm guessing he gives off Alpha energy." She looks back to me, and I nod with a smile. "Also, girl code. I'd never try to take my bestie's man."

"With all due respect, you're a beautiful woman, but I only have eyes for my Kitten here," he says, pulling me into his arms.

I look up at him with a big smile. "I love you," I whisper.

"I love you too, Little Omega," he growls.

"Alright. Enough big dick energy. Come on," Ivy says, turning to toss Everlee over her shoulder, which makes Everlee giggle as Ivy slaps her ass. Ivy reaches out, grabbing my hand and pulling me towards her. "Us girls have a lot to gossip about and you better fucking believe it's about all your men."

"Be good, Poison Ivy," Calix says.

"Never!" she shouts back as she takes me deeper into the house towards her room. Fuck, did I ever miss her.

"You're kidding me, right?" Ivy snorts out a laugh as I tell her about the last pack I rejected before finding my guys.

"Nope. Like fuck I would want to be with people who were so fucking rude, and they were all bullies. Enough to make my vagina cough dust. No thanks." I laugh.

"Then what happened?" Everlee asks.

"I felt the pull to go meet these guys for myself. I took one whiff of their scents and knew they were mine." I smile, remembering that day that set everything into motion.

I tell them about Tristan in the library and everything that's happened since that moment. Yes, in detail, because Ivy and I are pretty open with each other.

Everlee just sits there and listens, seeing how much Ivy and I needed this little reunion.

"I still can't believe you're mated to your brother and his best friend." I giggle.

"Stepbrother," she growls playfully.

Calix came into Ivy's life when she was around fourteen. Her mother is an Omega too. She had a whole pack and life already, but when you find your scent match, none of that matters. If you both want to have a life together, you make it work. And she did. But Calix's dad had him. He was an only child, and his mother was a Beta who left years prior, leaving him to be a single dad. They moved in with Ivy, and the two of them never really formed a sibling bond.

I used to think he was cute, but I could tell Ivy was into him. She never admitted it to me, but she knew I knew. And when Carter started coming by, my girl was done for. But the poor girl never said anything, though.

So when she called me up a few months after getting here and told me she found the Omega she wanted to be with, I was beyond happy for her. Then she told me that the Omega was also scent bound to Calix and Carter. At first, they formed a pack, but my sneaky new bestie saw what was there between her Alphas and eventually got them to break. They all admitted their feelings and became mates. Ivy might not be scent matched to Everlee but she still loves her just as fiercely. The way she looks at her is the same way my guys look at me.

"Still, I'm happy for you babe," I tell her, then look to Everlee. "So, how is she with you? Is she like bestie vibes or is she all sexy Alpha?" I giggle.

"Both." Everlee smiles up at her Alpha. "Most of the time we're like best friends, but where it counts she takes control." Everlee blushes, and Ivy growls.

"Don't let this sweet face fool you," Ivy says, wrapping her arm around Everlee's shoulder, pulling her close as she kisses the top of her head. "She's small as a pixie, but she's all sass."

"Am not!" Everlee says, sticking her tongue out at Ivy.

"Oh, yeah?" Ivy says, raising a brow. "You're just proving my point, Tinker Bell."

Everlee rolls her eyes, and I can't help but grin at the two of them. "Okay, I can be a bit of a brat. But you three wouldn't change me for the world."

"No, we wouldn't. We love you just the way you are."

My heart swells at how in love they look, but then I see my best friend happy and remember my brother back at home pining for Ivy, knowing he can never have her.

"So..." Ivy says, bringing the conversation back to me. "Tell me all about your Alphas. You landed yourself the untouchable pack."

"They are amazing. And it pisses me off that they are seen as outcasts here." I frown. "There's nothing wrong with them."

"Don't have to tell me that, babe. I'm a female Alpha,

I've had to deal with my fair share of shit here too. It's not fair, just because we don't fit into the perfect, little mold we've been taught about, doesn't mean we're any less of a person because of it. Female Alphas are rare and few between, but don't think my size is a disadvantage. You know how many knees I took out in combat class?" she grins wickedly.

"Ivy likes to go all ninja on the guys and spider monkey their asses when they least expect it." Everlee giggles.

"Hey." Ivy shrugs. "It keeps them on their toes." She wiggles her eyebrows, making us giggle.

We spend the next hour just sitting on Ivy's bed, talking about our guys, school, and life. I'm so glad to have Ivy here and that her Omega and I click so well. It makes it a lot easier being in her life. I would never give up on my best friend, but if I needed to step back to make her Omega feel comfortable, I would have. I'm just so fucking happy I don't have to.

"So, how long until your next heat?"

"About three weeks." I sigh.

"Well, then it's two down, two to go." She grins.

"Ivy," I laugh.

"Well, it's true! What do you have planned for the others?"

"The fair is this weekend, so the guys want to take me."

"Oh, shit." Ivy's eyes go wide.

"I know." I groan, covering my face.

"What's wrong?" Everlee asks.

"Tia hates rides. They make her feel sick. And she is terrified of heights."

"Oh, no." Everlee looks at me. "What are you going to do? I mean, they normally have games and stuff, you could just do that."

"I could, but you didn't see their faces when Knox brought it up. They all looked so excited to go. It was so cute. Well, Dom just grumbled about how those places are just made to rip you off with overpriced prizes and food, but yeah." I laugh.

"So you're just going to what, go on the rides and pray you don't freak out?" Ivy asks.

"Pretty much." I laugh.

"Girl, you must love these guys. I had to bribe you just to ride the carousel with me back home." Ivy laughs.

"I do. I really, really do," I admit to her. "Anyway, Sunday, Tristan and I are going to have our date because we didn't get the chance to have one before he helped me through my last heat. Then next weekend we're going back home so the guys can meet my parents and Spencer. After that, I'm not too sure, but I know the guys will think of something."

At the mention of my brother's name, the smile slips from Ivy's face.

"How's he doing?" she asks, her voice a lot lower than before. Everlee is watching her Alpha's change in mood with curious eyes.

"He's doing good." I force a smile. It's not a lie really, from my understanding he seems to be, overall, pretty happy. He's been hanging out with his friends a lot since I left, keeping himself busy. We text a lot and talk on the phone every now and then.

"That's good." She nods. "So, an Omega, eh?" Her eyes look almost longingly, and the slight elevation in Everlee's brow tells me she saw it too.

"Yup." I laugh. "Glad I got out of there before I hit my heat. It would have been a bloodbath with more than one Omega who's hit their heat cycle."

"Who's Spencer?" Everlee asks.

"My little brother," I tell her with a small smile.

"He's gonna be coming here then, if he's an Omega?"

"Yup, in about two years. He's turning nineteen this weekend, actually. So it's a perfect time to see my family."

"Tell him I said happy birthday," Ivy says, chewing on her lower lip.

"I will." I give her a sympathetic smile. She knows I know she had a thing for my brother. Sometimes I wonder if she should have been the Omega with a harem of men.

"We should still be here when he comes! Maybe we can all be besties." Everlee grins. But I see something behind those baby blue eyes. This one is a handful, I just know it.

"Maybe."

Hanging out with Ivy and Everlee was a lot of fun and something I didn't know I needed. As much as I love being around the guys, it was nice to get a break from all their yummy smells. Now, any time I smell cotton candy, bubble gum, or mango I get all horny and depending on where I am, it's uncomfortable. Thankfully, Tristan and Dom's scents aren't common everyday smells.

When I get home, the guys are all growly because I smell like other Alphas, and it's cute how they all stripped me and put me in the shower. They're going to have to get used to at least Ivy and her pack, because we come as a package deal.

I have no interest in my bestie like that, and despite the once upon a time attraction to Calix, way back when, I have no attraction to them now in any way.

After my shower, Dom wraps me up in a big, fluffy towel and brings me to his room, placing me in the center of his big, king sized bed. I snuggle into his sheets, inhaling his woodsy scent. We don't make it far into the movie before I fall asleep with my head on his chest.

The next morning, I'm a big ball of nervous energy.

"Ready to go?" Knox calls out from the hallway.

I look at myself in the mirror, giving myself one last look. I'm dressed in denim shorts with a cute, flowy, tan tank top. My hair is down in tamed beach curls, and I add a dark nude lip to go with my natural makeup.

Taking a deep breath, I head to the front door to meet my guys, praying I don't puke on one of them tonight.

"Yup!" I give them the best 'fake' smile I can muster.

"I'm so excited!" Sawyer says. "They're going to have the slingshot this year. It launches you high into the sky, I can't wait to shit my pants." He cackles.

"Eww," Finn says, giving his best friend a grossed-out look. "I will not be going on that ride with you then." Finn pushes his glasses up his nose and steps away from Sawyer, making me giggle.

"You can sit with me on the ferris wheel, Finny," Knox says, snaking an arm around Finn's waist and pulling him close. "I've always wanted to kiss someone at the top."

Finn's eyes are wide as he blinks rapidly at Knox, swallowing hard. Knox gives him a slow grin. "You like the idea of that, don't you, sweet boy? You want my lips on yours, don't you?"

Okay, I need to leave now, before my panties are flooded, and I end up begging Knox to take me into the back room to do dirty things to me and Finn.

"I'm ready! Whose car are we taking?" I ask, looking around.

"How about you ride in my truck with me?" Dom says, stepping up to me.

"Tristan and I can take the car with Finn and Knox," Sawyer says.

"Actually, if we're not all going in the same vehicle..." Knox says, turning to Finn. "How about you and I take my bike?"

"Bike?!" Finn's eyes go wide. "You mean as in motorbike? Like the death trap on two wheels? No. No, no, no." Finn shakes his head.

"Have you ever ridden on one?" Knox chuckles, reaching up to trace Finn's bottom lip. Finn closes his eyes and shakes his head. "There's nothing like being on the open road with the wind against your body. It's freeing, Finny. Let me free you. You know I wouldn't ever put you in danger, right?"

Finn's eyes flutter open. "I know," he says softly.

"If you really don't want to, we can go with the others," Knox says.

"Can we go for a test ride? Like around the housing complex?" Finn asks.

"Of course." Knox agrees with a smile, then leans in and places a soft kiss on Finn's lips.

But it's not enough for Finn. Finn whimpers, grabbing a hold of Knox's shirt to pull him in closer. Knox growls, gripping the back of Finn's head to deepen the kiss.

Tristan whispers in my ear, telling me that he and the others are going to go to the parking garage to grab the vehicles. I just mindlessly nod my head, too entranced by my Alpha and Beta in a sexy embrace.

Knox pushes Finn against the wall, putting his leg between Finn's. Finn moans as he starts to grind his cock against Knox's legs, and Knox devours Finn's mouth.

Too late to save my panties now, they are already coated with slick. I'll have to change before we go. But the way Finn is going, he may need to change as well.

"That's it, Finny," Knox growls as he kisses down Finn's neck, his hands sliding down to cover Finn's ass. "Grind that big, fat, Alpha cock against me. Use me, baby, cum like a good boy." Knox starts to suck on Finn's neck, and I'm over here a few feet away, clit throbbing as I bite my lip, holding back my whimpers and moans while watching the two of them. I don't want to ruin the moment.

"Knox," Finn whines, his eyes squeezed shut as his hips move frantically. Knox grabs Finn's ass, using it to help Finn grind against him.

"Shhh, Alpha. I know what you need. Just cum for me. You will feel so much better."

My heart is pounding, pussy aching as Finn rests his head against Knox's shoulder and lets out a cry of pleasure as his body starts to twitch in our sexy, tattooed Beta's arms.

"That's it," Knox purrs. "Fuck, I can feel your cock pulsing against my leg."

Finn is breathing heavily now, and when he lifts his head to look up at Knox, his face turns scarlet. "Ummm," he starts, "I need to change."

"Yeah, you do," Knox says, smug as fuck. "I'd offer to help you clean up, if that's something you'd want." He winks, making Finn blush harder.

They both seem to, only now, remember that I'm here and turn to look at me. "Oh, Tia." Finn's eyes go wide. "I'm so sorry! I..." He looks at Knox, then me, and starts to panic.

"It's okay, Finn," I say, stepping up to my shy Alpha. "I told you, I'm okay with you and Knox being together. I know you both want to be with me just as much as each other."

"You really are amazing, Sunshine." Finn smiles adorably.

"Helps when I have amazing people." I shrug. "Also, you

two? Hot as fuck, and I very much want to watch you two fuck during my heat." I grin, biting my lip as Finn makes this choked sound, and Knox chuckles deeply.

Finn lets out a squeak before pushing past Knox and racing down the hall to his room.

"I love that you like to watch the two of us," Knox says, pulling me into his arms, moving me into the same spot Finn was just in against the wall. "But do you really think we would get you all hot and I wouldn't help you take care of it?" Knox kneels before me, my eyes widening as they follow him down. He puts his nose against the crotch of my shorts, and inhales deeply. "I can smell your slick, Kitten. If I can't help Finn clean up, then I wanna help you."

He unbuttons my shorts and rips them down taking my panties with them. "Knox," I gasp as he tosses them to the side.

"No need for those, Little Omega. Lean back against the wall, palms against the wall too," he instructs me, and I do as I'm told. Then I let out another gasp as he takes one leg then the other and places them over his shoulders, shoving his face against my pussy. He wastes no time licking me clean.

I whimper when he sucks my clit into his mouth, tongue flicking back and forth. "That's it, baby," Knox says as I moan out his name. "Cum for me, give me all that sweet slick, coat my tongue, and give me the honor of pleasuring this pretty pussy. Cum on my tongue, Kitten."

One of my hands flies into his hair, and I grab a hand full, tugging hard. I want to grind myself against his face, but I don't want to fall. As if Knox can read my mind, both of his hands slide up my body, hooking underneath my armpits to hold me up against the wall. My hips start to rock, and it doesn't take long before I feel that burn in my lower belly expanding.

But it's the whimper from the hallway that has me tipping over the edge. I look over to find Finn watching, his cock thick in his new, clean pants as he takes his turn to watch.

I scream out Finn's name, making his eyes go wide as I cum hard on Knox's face. He chuckles against my pussy before lapping up more of my slick. The vibration makes me gush more for him, for them.

When I'm done, heart pounding and out of breath, Knox lowers me to the ground on shaky legs.

"Now it's your turn to go get changed, Kitten," Knox says, pressing a kiss to my lips and giving me a taste of my slick before pulling me away from the wall. He spins me in the direction of the hall and gives me a little push before slapping my ass, making me yelp. Finn steps out of the way as I race down the hall, trying not to fall because my legs are practically jelly.

And Knox, the smug asshole, just laughs, real proud of what he's done. Something tells me this night is going to be a rollercoaster ride. And I don't even like rollercoasters.

CHAPTER 21

DOMINIC

I'm not really sure what exactly the naughty Beta, our horny little Omega, and their Alpha got up to while the other two and I went to get our vehicles, but the smell of toasted coconut is filling my truck and making my cock hard.

"You know, Little One, you're gonna make it really difficult to walk around the fairgrounds with a raging hard on," I growl lightly. Her gaze snaps to me, her cheeks flushing a pretty pink.

"You can smell me?" she whispers.

"Yes, Little Omega, and it's making it hard for me to be a respectable Alpha, right now."

"I changed," she says, looking down at a different pair of shorts.

"But you didn't shower," I tell her. "Don't worry, Little One. With your scent blocking panties, you should be fine to anyone else. We're just so used to your sweet smell, it's hard to miss," I explain, putting my hand on her knee. I don't try anything, not wanting to make it worse, I just give her knee a squeeze before taking her hand in mine. Without taking my eyes off the road, I bring her hand up to my lips to give it a soft kiss before setting it on the seat between us.

I can see her sweet smile out of the corner of my eye, making my heart swell.

With each passing day, I fall harder for my Omega; the fear of rejection slowly leaving my mind, body, and soul.

Her mate marking Sawyer, someone officially in my pack, was the biggest relief. I know she's an amazing woman. She's kind, caring, and loving. But there was always a part of me that kept thinking she would wake up one day and think there's better out there for her than us.

Seeing her start to make my pack hers, fills me with joy, but also, with worry. *Like, what if she marks all of them except me? What if she wants my whole pack, but is fine without me?*

Then I see the way she looks at me when she thinks I don't know she's looking; like some love sick girl, and it penetrates the walls I've built up around me.

I'm not gonna deny her, push her away, or miss out on anything. She's mine, and I'll make sure she doesn't feel unwanted by me, because it's anything but true.

A little part in the back of my mind will always try to tell me this isn't real, that she's gonna leave, but I'm gonna do my best to shut it the fuck down.

We ride in silence with me being a man of few words,

but she doesn't seem to mind. That's another thing I love about her. She's never once tried to change me or my brothers. Her personality fits with each of our individual ones.

Lately, I've had this overwhelming need to protect her, to keep her in my sights, so having her gone for a whole day and night with Sawyer sucked. I was pacing the house wondering if she was safe, if she would come back to us. I hated not being able to make sure no harm came to her.

And when she went with her Alpha friend, I wanted to glue myself to her hip and go with her. Even though Knox was with her, I was still moody about it. At least until she came home and did exactly what I told her I wanted to do when she got back. She got into bed with me and didn't even make it very far into the movie before she passed out on my chest. I wanted to stay like that forever, her wrapped in my arms, warm, and safe.

I know that even though she's my Omega, she's not mine to control or own. I can keep her safe while she lives her life the way she chooses to without taking control. I mean, I'm at least gonna try.

But I need her with me today because Tris is taking her out tomorrow, so I need as much time with my Little One as I can get. I should feel bad for stealing time away from the others, but I'm just making up for the time I missed out on in the beginning when I was too fucking stubborn and in my own head. Another thing I love about her, she doesn't hold that against me and never thrown it in my face.

And the fact that when Sawyer was being a prick about his mate mark, she told my grumpy ass that she plans on giving me one too just proves my point. It took everything in me not to get on my knees and beg for her to do it right then and there. She wants me for *me*. She doesn't know I come from money; technically, we all do. It's not something we've really kept from her, but it hasn't really come up in conversation either. I mean, Sawyer was outed when he took her on his boat, but the fact she wanted all of us for who we are and not what we can give her is yet another thing that makes her so much better than all the other Omegas who looked down on us.

We sit in silence for the entire ride out of Calling Wood and into the next town over where the fair is being held. I can't keep my hand off her, needing to feel her, even if it's just the brush of my fingers against her creamy smooth skin. Who knew, me, a grumpy bastard who hated the world, would turn into a big ol' teddy bear for an Omega.

When we get there, I look at how packed it is and start to mutter under my breath.

"Hey," Tia says, brushing her thumb against the back of my hand. "Are you okay?" Her eyes are filled with concern, and I love that she catches the shift in my mood and cares enough to ask.

"I'm not a big fan of people," I tell her, looking at all the happy families, laughing and smiling as they leave their cars, heading towards the entrance.

"We don't have to go in if you don't want to," she tells me.

"What about the others?" I question, watching as Tristan pulls up next to us. The guys get out of the car, both laughing at something, pure happiness shining on their faces. I don't want to be a downer on their fun and hold them back.

"Wanna know a secret?" she asks. I look over to her, and she has that cute blush on her face again.

"I wanna know anything and everything about you, Little One," I rumble out.

She bites her lip before continuing. "I like the fair. But only for the games and food. I... I get sick from most of the rides they have. And I'm *deathly* afraid of heights."

My eyes widen at this new information. "But you seemed just as excited as the others about coming here."

"I didn't wanna ruin the fun," she admits, just like me.

I nod my head, my mind working to see what we can do about this. "How about this? We let the boys run wild, ride whatever they want. You pick any ride you feel comfortable going on and we'll all go on those together as a pack. Then while they are busy, we play games and win you some stuffies."

Her shoulders relax, telling me I said the right thing. "Yeah, I think I can handle that." She smiles up at me, making my cold heart melt just a little bit more.

"If you're ever afraid, just hold onto me. I'll never let you fall, Little One," I growl, loving the shiver that takes over her body.

The rev of a bike has us both looking out Tia's window. "Looks like everyone is here."

We get out of the car just as Finn gets off the back of

Knox's bike. He takes off his helmet, a massive smile on his face.

"Oh my god!" he laughs. "That was frigging amazing!"

"I knew you would have fun, Finny. Sometimes you just gotta let loose and trust the ones who love you." Knox grins as he tucks his helmet under his arm.

Finn's smile doesn't fall, but his eyes do widen. "I love you," he tells Knox. "Thank you for having patience with me, this is all so new."

"I love you too, Finn," Knox growls. "And I'd wait a lifetime for you."

"As adorable and sexy as the two of you are together, and trust me the sight of you two on a bike does nothing to help some of the dirty things floating around in my mind, buuuut we're in a family friendly place, so I'm gonna need less heated looks and about five feet between you two for a while," Tia says, stepping up to Finn. "Alpha," she purrs. "I think I may need you two to wear these again sometime," she says, pulling at the leather jacket Finn is wearing.

"Anything for you, Kitten," Knox growls, stepping closer.

"Stop!" she holds out a hand with a laugh. "I mean it! Family friendly."

Knox chuckles, and Finn blushes as Sawyer walks over to him. They start talking about the bike ride while Tristan heads off to buy our tickets.

"Alright my sexy lumberjack, ready to have fun?" Tia smiles up at me.

"Lumberjack?" I ask, brows furrowing.

She smirks, raising a brow. "Plaid shirt, jeans, and hiking boots," she says, looking and pointing at each item as she says it.

"Ahh." I laugh. "I think I could be your sexy lumberjack."

"Good. Now, let's go have some fun... I hope."

OCTAVIA

It's adorable to see Finn, Sawyer, and Tristan as excited as kids in a candy store. For the past hour, they've been running around going from ride to ride while Dom and Knox stuck with me.

We've played a few games and gotten something to eat. So far, I've agreed to go on one ride, and it was one of those slides you go down while sitting on a carpet. It wasn't very high, probably because I think it was meant to be a little kid's ride. Oh well, I had fun and watching my Alphas go down was hilarious, especially when Knox and Dom went down. The stink eye Dom shot the worker who tried to help push him down almost made me pee myself.

But he kept his word and agreed to go on any ride I wanted.

"So, Tia. Are you having fun? You haven't gone on many rides," Tristan asks as he takes a bite of a hot dog we just got from one of the vendors.

"Haven't found anything I've really been interested in." I shrug, taking a bite of my pizza.

"Sunshine," Finn says, getting my attention. "Do you

like going on rides?" The way he's watching me right now tells me he's about to call my bluff. He knows something is up.

So I take a deep breath and sigh. "No," I say, cringing. "Not really."

Tristan's hot dog pauses mid air, and he looks at me with wide eyes. "What? Really? Then how come you agreed to come here when I brought it up?"

"I saw how excited you and the others were at the idea, and I didn't want to be a Debbie Downer."

"Love," Tristan growls. "Don't force yourself to do things you don't like or don't feel comfortable with just to please your Alphas."

"And why not?" I ask, raising a brow as I lean back in my chair, crossing my arms. "You would do it for me." He starts to protest, but I stop him. "Don't even try to deny it, Tristan. I know damn well you all would do any silly or crazy thing I wanted to do if it was something I was excited over or loved. So why can't I do the same thing for you guys?"

"It's not the same. If you don't like rides, we don't want you going on any that would make you feel uneasy."

"And I didn't," I point out. "You guys have had fun going on rides together, right?"

"Yes."

"And none of them were with me, other than the slide, right?"

"Yes," he sighs, seeing my point.

"And I have been having fun," I tell him. "Dom won me

the monkey, you won me the teddy, and Knox won me the black cat."

"Finn and I still have to win you something before we leave, by the way," Sawyer pipes up.

"And I can't wait to see what game you kick ass at or what prize you pick for me," I tell him, giving him a smile before kissing him on the cheek.

"Alright, fine. But as long as you're not miserable," Tristan grumbles.

"I'm not," I laugh. "I'm having a good time. Mostly just because I'm with my guys."

We eat our food before walking around the fairgrounds some more as we scope out what rides we want to go on or games we want to play.

I can't help but giggle watching my tall, sexy men holding the prizes they won for me.

"What about this one?" Finn says, pointing to the strong man game.

"Are you sure, man?" Sawyer asks.

"Yes, why not?" Finn looks at his friend confused.

"Alright." Sawyer puts his hands up. "Go for it, man."

Finn steps up to the Alpha who's running the booth and hands him the money. The Alpha looks at Finn and snorts out a laugh. "You're kidding me right? You wanna play *this* game?"

"Yes," Finn says, sounding annoyed, and I'm starting to get annoyed for him. "It's why I gave you the money."

The Alpha looks Finn up and down, then to the rest of us behind him. "Why don't you get that tall, tattooed one to take a swing at it, or even the beefy one? Might have a better chance at getting that sexy little Omega a prize. Although, I don't think that's gonna help you win her over."

My guys all growl, ready to defend their pack mate when Finn handles it himself. Finn grabs the hammer from the man sharply and juts his chin out. "I can do this myself. I don't need any help or anyone taking my place. And for your information, I don't need help getting the pretty little Omega because I already have her. That's my girl, my Omega, so if you don't mind, see that sloth behind you? Yeah, I'm about to win that for MY Omega," he growls, making me so fucking hot, I whimper.

Finn raises the hammer and brings it down hard, making the little metal thing shoot up and hit the bell hard. Finn tosses the hammer down on the ground next to the gaping Alpha's feet. "I'll be taking that," Finn says, grabbing one of the sloths from the stand and bringing it over to me.

"For you, Sunshine," Finn beams at me. My pupils are blown, my breathing is harsher than I'd like, and I'm almost positive people nearby can smell my perfume.

I take the sloth from him and partially moan. "Thank you."

Finn is spun around fast, Knox gripping the back of his head and smashing his lips to Finn's. He kisses him hard and dirty, getting a few gasps from people who pass by.

"That was the hottest fucking thing I've ever seen," Knox growls against Finn's lips. "Seeing you not only defend our Omega, but claim her and defend yourself... damn, Finny, confidence looks so hot on you."

Finn swallows hard, and Dom clears his throat.

"As our Little Omega said before, family friendly place, remember?"

"Right," Knox says, nodding his head, then gives Finn a smirk. "Later, babe." He winks at Finn before coming over to me. "Come on, Kitten. I can smell your cream from here, and I don't want anyone else to." He pulls me down the path, making me laugh as the others trail behind us.

We found a few more rides that didn't make me wanna puke just by looking at them before playing some more games. Sawyer won me this life sized bag of cotton candy, and I can feel the sugar rush just by looking at it.

"I can just see the sore belly now," Knox sighs.

"We can hold her hair back while she pukes," Finn adds, making Knox snort a laugh.

"Oh, come on. It won't be that bad. It's not like I'm gonna eat it all in one sitting." I roll my eyes as the others lead me into another line. "And be nice, or I won't share." I stick my tongue out at them, making them laugh and me smile.

But it drops when I see what line we're in. The Ferris wheel. Fuck.

"I saved the best for last," Tristan says with a big smile. "I love riding the Ferris wheel. It was one of my favorite things to do as a kid."

This is my worst nightmare right now. I do something stupid and look up to the top of the ride and feel my stomach drop.

"Little One," Dom says, stepping up behind me, wrapping his arms around me. "You can say no. You can always say no."

I could. I want to so badly, but the excited looks on their faces make it extremely hard to do that. I avoided a lot of rides today, and didn't go on a lot of the ones they were excited for.

But this is our last ride before we go home. *Do I sit this one out like all the others, or suck it up?*

Then I remember back earlier when Finn overcame his shyness and didn't let that Alpha make a fool out of him.

If he could do that, then I can overcome my fear of heights, at least for tonight... right?

"Hold me?" I ask, not just meaning right now, but when we get on the ride.

"Always, Little One. But don't ever expect for me to let you go," he purrs.

I never want him to.

The line moves way too fast for my liking, and before we know it, we're next. "You three," he says, pointing to Finn, Sawyer and Knox. "On one side. The rest on the other, to even out the weight."

Letting out a small sigh of relief that I'm sitting with Dom, I grasp his hand and squeeze it with a death grip as we step onto the ride.

I close my eyes, focusing on my breathing and pretending that my feet are flat on the ground.

I'm sandwiched between Tristan and Dom, and it helps me a little bit. That is until the ride starts to move, making me grip Dom's hand harder. "Hey there, Little

One. Shhh. It's okay. I have you, nothing is going to happen. Breathe."

I nod my head, forcing myself to suck in a breath.

"Kitten, are you okay?" Knox asks.

"Yes," I say quickly on a breath.

"No, you're not," Tristan growls, making my hand shoot out to grip his thigh in surprise. He grunts as I dig my nails into him as the ride jerks a little.

"Kitten," Knox says softly as if not to frighten me. "Are you afraid of heights?"

"Yes," I whimper. "*Really* fucking terrified."

"Then why on earth did you come on this?" Knox asks. "Fuck. How did we not see this? We should have skipped this ride."

"Let's see if we can get the worker's attention and get off," Tristan says.

"No!" I say. Forcing my eyes open. "No. No, we're on here now. Let's just enjoy it."

Sawyer snorts. "Pretty Girl, you look like you are enjoying this as much as you would getting your nails ripped off."

"And thank you very much for putting that image in my head," I grumble, shuddering at the idea.

But then my eyes look out to my right to see the stunning sunset. "Wow," I breathe. Where my line of sight is, I can't see the ground, only the water reflecting the pinks, oranges, reds, and even a bit of purple. "Okay, this makes it worth the pounding of my heart," I say. "I'm too afraid to move, so can one of you take a photo of this?"

After I get a good look of the horizon, I shut my eyes again as the ride does its few loops around after everyone's gotten on.

Thankfully, the little circles Dom and Tristan are rubbing on my thighs help distract me, and I even sneak a peak when Finn and Knox share a really sweet kiss at the top. And I can't help but get one of my own from the two Alphas sandwiching me. But of course, that leads to Sawyer grumbling about being left out.

"Want a kiss too?" Finn jokes, making Knox growl.

"Chill, dude. I'm not gonna steal your man," Sawyer says. "The only dick I'd be interested in is if it's attached to our Omega." Sawyer grins. I know he's joking... I think, but the look on my face has his expression turning to worry. "I don't like that look, Pretty Girl."

"What?" I say innocently as the ride stops. "You don't wanna be fucked by my cock?"

There could not have been a worse time to say those words because just as they leave my mouth, a family with three kids step up to take our place on the ride.

My guys all burst out laughing while my face heats up like an inferno.

They are damn lucky I love them.

CHAPTER 22

TRISTAN

Today is my day alone with Tia. I've asked the guys if they minded if we came back to the house for our alone time, and other than Sawyer joking about them most likely being hard all night, listening to the two of us, they were fine with it.

Tia has been on the go non-stop since getting to Calling Wood. Two weeks of nothing but stress while trying to find her Alphas before her heat, along with trying to get to know us as much as she could before going into heat.

Then having only Knox and me to help her through it when our little vixen is, clearly, going to need all five of us from now on.

After her heat, between school and her time with us, she hasn't really had time to just breathe.

So, today for our date, because I really don't care what

we do as long as we're together, I planned something more laid back.

"Tristan?" Tia's musical voice breaks me out of my own thoughts as I finish getting ready.

"In here, Love," I call back, grabbing a t-shirt from my dresser.

"Are you sure I can wear anything? I don't wanna clash with..." her words trail off. I smirk when I see her standing in my doorway, her eyes slowly eating up my body. I'm shirtless, and by the way my Omega is perfuming right now, she likes what she sees. I almost hate to put my shirt on and lose that look on her face.

"Little Omega," I growl playfully, and her eyes snap up from my abs to my eyes.

"I'm sorry, what was I saying?" she asks with a blush.

"I don't know, Love." I chuckle. "Something about clashing?" I ask, putting my shirt on. She gives me a little pout, making me chuckle again. "You have nothing to worry about, Little Omega. You look perfect," I tell her, taking in her outfit. She's in a black top with a black and white layered skirt. The front stops just above her knees, while the back flows closer to her feet. "And I love that you wore your hair down," I tell her, stepping closer. She sucks in a breath as I crowd her space. "Gives me something to grab onto while you're on your knees, begging for my knot."

I'm slammed with the smell of toasted coconuts, and I curse myself for my playful game. Because now my cock is as hard as a fucking rock, and my knot is aching to be deep inside her.

"Tease," she pouts, not at all mad about it.

"Yeah, I didn't think that one through," I groan, making her laugh.

"Come on, Alpha, let's get out of here before I say 'to hell with the date, let's fuck'," she says, grabbing my hand and pulling me out of the room.

"My, my, Little Omega, that mouth is gonna get you into trouble." I chuckle as I follow after my feisty little red head.

She looks over her shoulder, giving me a smile that does nothing to help with the situation down below. "Then punish me, Alpha," she purrs.

We get into the golf cart, and Tia tells me about her classes. She hates that she has to do the mandatory Omega classes and can't wait until she can start the proper courses to become a kindergarten teacher, next year.

I love that she likes kids. We all want them, but we'll support her choice to wait. She wants to do something with her life that isn't just being our Omega or a mother, and there's nothing wrong with that.

We plan on being there and helping her with anything she needs.

Tia brings up the fair, telling me she's glad she got photo booth photos with everyone. The mention of the fair has me feeling instantly guilty. I didn't know she didn't like rides or was afraid of heights. If I did, I never would have brought up the idea, and I hate that she forced herself to go to please us. I'm just glad she didn't make herself go on any rides she didn't want to. Well, other than the Ferris Wheel. When I saw how terrified she was up there, I wanted to pull her into my arms and make everything alright. But that would have just made everything much worse.

We'll be making sure that anything else we have planned is something she wants to do. If not, it's not important enough.

"So, what's the plan for today?" she asks as I park the golf cart downtown.

"I was thinking we'd just have a chill day. Walk around town, grab a bite to eat, then maybe a nice walk on the beach at sunset before going home and snuggling up in my bed to watch a movie."

"Or... we can skip the movie and you can give me your knot," she grins up at me as she wraps her arms around my chest.

"You naughty Little Omega," I growl, nipping her lip.

"Yes. Knotty," she giggles, making me smile. "I'm sorry, but you've had your knot inside of me, so you know how mind-blowing it is."

"I do remember that." I brush some hair out of her face, my thumb lingering on her cheek. "It's the best feeling in the world, Love, being locked inside you. I never wanted to leave."

She sighs as I kiss her softly, leaning into my touch.

"I didn't realize how intense it was until I was with Sawyer." She blushes. "It doesn't hurt, but god the orgasms are never ending."

"Don't worry, Love. I'll make sure you love every moment," I tell her.

We head into a little cafe to get Tia her coffee and

chocolate croissant before browsing the stores.

"Oh, I need this!" she gasps, her hand running up and down a pink fuzzy blanket. "It's so soft."

"Then let's get it. It would be perfect for your nest," I tell her, grabbing it and a few more in different colors. "We can all sleep with one and make sure they have our scent before your next heat."

"You're too good to me." She smiles.

"There's no such thing, Little Omega. There's nothing in this world we wouldn't at least try to give you."

Her eyes glass over, making my heart race. I'm afraid I said something wrong when she buries her face into my chest, hugging me tightly. "I love you, Tristan."

My eyes go wide as I stand there, stunned. "Really?" I ask like an idiot.

She giggles and looks up at me, eyes wet. "Yes, silly. How could I not? You guys might not see yourself as the perfect Alphas, but to me, you are."

"The same goes for you, Tia. You're perfect for us. And knowing we've been lucky enough to end up with you makes all those years waiting for an Omega worth it."

I can't even remember what it felt like to be alone, to not be wanted or accepted anymore. Because since the moment Tia came into our lives, it's like it's been her life's mission to make sure we all feel validated, to feel loved. Like we are worthy of everything life has to offer.

Who knew just walking around shopping could be so much fun? I don't think I've smiled and laughed so much in my life, and the next few hours go by way too fast for my liking. Just holding my girl's hand, having her close, hearing her laugh, and seeing her smile; it's the best.

"You full?" I chuckle as she puts her fork down on her plate with a groan. I wanted to take her out to eat before we headed down to the beach, and she picked this new, little bistro by the water.

"Yes," she sighs. "But I don't think I can move. You might have to roll me out of here."

"Nah, I'll just carry you everywhere you need to go."

"Then I'll miss the walk on the beach!" she gasps playfully. "Okay, scratch that, just give me five, maybe ten minutes, and I'll be good to go."

"Take as long as you want, Love," I tell her.

She sits there with her eyes closed, and I can't help but watch her. She's so beautiful.

She ended up telling the rest of us what she told Sawyer, about her past eating disorder. It hurt my heart to know she felt, even just for a second, that she was anything other than a fucking goddess.

But seeing her like this, not giving a fuck anymore about what anyone else thinks, knowing her worth, and letting us remind her; it's so damn sexy.

"Alright," Tia says, opening her eyes. "I'm good."

"You sure?" I ask with a grin.

"I might walk like a little, old granny, but yes." She giggles.

"Hottest old granny I ever did see." I wink.

"You thinking of old ladies, Alpha?" she jokes.

"Come on, you little brat," I growl playfully, standing up

and tossing a hundred dollar bill on the table before holding out my hand for her.

"Me?" she gasps, holding her hand to her chest. "A brat? Never!"

OCTAVIA

Today was just what I needed. My life has been going like a train without brakes since the moment I got to Calling Wood. I hardly ever have time to just take the day slow.

I'm not really complaining because most of those times have been spent with my guys, and anything that involves them I love.

Just being with my Alpha, walking around and doing such mundane things made me smile because it was like a glimpse into our future. A future I can't wait to build with each and every one of my guys.

Now, we're walking on the beach hand in hand, barefoot in the sand as we listen to the waves crash against the shore and watching the sun set.

"Rocky!" someone shouts from behind us. We both turn around to see a man and woman running in our direction. But not at us, at the little chihuahua in front of them.

I'm about to say 'awe, cute dog' when Tristan lets out a curse before he starts to run off down the beach, leaving me standing there with my mouth gaping.

The dog chases after him, yapping his little head off, tail going a mile a minute. Tristan screams for help, and that snaps me out of it.

I start to run with the dog's owners after my Alpha who is screaming like a little girl as he climbs up a massive boulder. He takes the sandals in his hand and starts tossing them at the dog. *What the hell is going on?*

"What the fuck are you doing?" the man shouts as we reach the dog and Tristan.

"Trying to get that little monster away from me!" he shouts back. His eyes wide with fear.

"He wasn't after you. Well, not until you started to run, and he thought you wanted to play," the woman huffs out, picking the dog up into her arms. It starts to bark and lick her face like crazy.

"Tristan. Are you okay?" I ask as the couple starts to walk away, muttering about the crazy Alpha.

"He really was gonna get me," Tristan says, watching them leave.

"I believe you. Wanna come down now?" I ask once they're out of sight.

Tristan slides down, and when he realizes what just happened, his face turns bright red.

"So, what was all that about?" I ask, holding back my giggle.

"I hate those little rat dogs," he growls. "They're little demons. My Nana had one, and every time we went to visit, it would nip at my heels and corner me. Any time I tried to get past, it would bite me."

"Baby, how old were you?" I ask, raising a brow.

"Ummm... six?"

"Alright. So traumatized by small dogs. Got it." I nod.

"How about big dogs?"

"Oh, they're fine," he says, waving it off like it's no big deal. "I love them."

"Okay, then." I laugh.

"Tia."

"Yes, Tris?" I really shouldn't want to laugh, to burst out into giggles. He was *really* afraid.

"Did I really just scream like a girl in a cheesy horror movie?" he grins, telling me he's starting to see just how funny it was.

"Like one who would follow the scary noise," I giggle.

"Alright. Fine, laugh it up. Then we never speak of this again," he chuckles, and I start to laugh.

Turning around I start to run. "Oh no! Look, there's a seagull after me." I mock being in distress.

"You little shit!" Tristan growls as he starts to chase after me, making me laugh harder.

"Shower, then get that naughty ass in my bed," Tristan growls as soon as we get past the front door, sending a thrill throughout my body.

"Oh, someone's in trouble," Sawyer says when he steps into the living room. I shoot him a wicked grin before taking off down the hall to do as my Alpha told me to do.

Tristan isn't as dominant in his everyday life as Knox and Dom are, but something tells me his Alpha is gonna come out in the bedroom.

I don't think I've taken a shower so fast in my life. My body is ready for him, excitement and need coursing through my veins. I don't even care that I'm going to need to shower again after this.

I dry my hair off the best I can, and wrap the towel around myself. When I leave my room, Knox and Finn are coming out of the room they share. *I really need to ask him how that's coming along.*

"Have fun, Kitten," he grins.

"I will," I sing-song. When I open Tristan's bedroom door, I hear his shower still going. Turning around, I look at Finn and Knox. With hooded eyes, I take a step back, open my towel, and let it drop to the floor. Finn's eyes go wide as he lets out a whimper. Knox growls, giving me a predatory look before he starts to stalk towards me. But I just slowly close the door, getting a louder growl from Knox.

"Teasing your mates, Love?" Tristan asks from behind me.

I spin around, my playful mood all gone as I take him in. His brown hair is still wet, hanging to his shoulders. I watch as some water droplets run down his chest, stopping at the delicious V that I very much want to trace with my tongue. "Little Omega, I asked you a question."

"Maybe," I say, my eyes meeting his again.

"Now, that's not nice, is it?" he growls, walking towards me slowly.

"N-no," I stutter but not in fear. No, I am so fucking turned on right now, I can feel my slick running down my thigh. I bet if I looked down there would be a little puddle at my feet.

"Then I think you deserve to be punished, don't you think?" he asks, stopping right in front of me. I have to crane my neck to see his face.

"Yes," I agree, the word leaving my lips like a prayer.

"I don't want you to be quiet, Little Omega. I want you to let every sound of pleasure that you even think of holding back out. I want the whole fucking house to know what we're doing and who's doing it to you."

"Yes, Alpha."

"Good girl," he praises, making me preen at his approval. He sits on the edge of the bed, patting his knee. "Lay down." I practically trip over my feet to obey. "Two swats should be enough. One for laughing at me on the beach, and one for teasing your mates."

Laying across his lap, my heart pounds hard in my chest. I try to rub my thighs together, needing the friction for some release, but Tristan brings his hand down in a sharp but not hard slap. "Naughty, Omega. This is meant to be a punishment, not a reward."

Sorry, Alpha, but I know you can smell how much I'm enjoying this.

He rubs away the sting before his hand glides lower. Two fingers dip into my dripping cunt, and I moan at the feeling of his long, thick fingers inside me.

"Fuck me, Little Omega. You're dripping for me," he

growls, sending another gush of slick into his hand. I can't see him, but I can hear the deep rumble of approval in his chest as he sucks his fingers clean. "This is all I'll be tasting of you tonight, Little Omega. Because it'll be you who is tasting me. You, who will be taking my cock deep between those pretty, little lips until you're gasping for breath."

"Please," I moan.

His hand comes down two more times in quick succession, making me cry out his name. Once he's done soothing the pain away, he lifts me up.

"On your knees, Omega," he commands, and I drop to my knees. I don't care, I couldn't even stand, my body buzzing with need. "Take my towel off," he instructs next. With shaky hands and eyes full of lust, I grab the towel, untucking it and pulling it so that it pools around him.

His cock stands hard and proud, pre cum already weeping from the tip. I wanna taste it, clean it off him before working him over for more. But I don't. I look up at Tristan, hoping he sees the look in my eyes and gives me what I want. All I want to do is please my Alpha.

"Lick," is all he says, and I'm diving forward. Wrapping my hand around his cock, I hold it still while my tongue flicks out, cleaning his tip. I moan at his flavor. Not too salty or bitter. Almost kind of sweet.

"Fuck," Tristan grunts. "You look so perfect on your knees for your Alpha." He grips the back of my hair with one hand and grabs the base of his cock with the other. "Now, suck."

"Yes, Alpha," is all I can say before he pushes the tip

between my lips, and once it's in my mouth, he shoves me down. He groans, tossing his head back in pleasure. I gag a little, my eyes starting to water before he pulls my head back. I gasp for air before he does it again.

I lick and suck as my head bobs up and down on his shaft, loving the grunts, growls, and groans leaving his lips. I'm preening at the fact that I'm pleasing my Alpha so well.

"Yeah," he moans as I drag my teeth lightly up his cock before sucking him back down. "Fuck, just like that. Look at you, Omega. You're such a good girl. You suck your Alpha's cock so perfectly."

I want his cum, need to taste it on my tongue, swallow it down. So I grab his knot, giving it a squeeze as I grip his cock with the other hand and start to jerk him off as I suck his dick like my life depends on it.

"Oh, shit!" he growls. "I'm gonna cum soon if you keep doing that."

I pull back, releasing his cock with a pop. "Give me your cum. It's mine," I plead. I'm so fucking horny that the idea of him giving me his cum, in any way that he chooses, has a puddle of slick pooling below me.

He stands up with a growl, making me look up at him with wide, lust filled eyes. "You want this?" he asks as he starts to jerk off. I whimper and nod. "Tongue out, Little Omega."

I do as I'm told sitting back on my knees, sticking my tongue out. I wait like a good little Omega as he grips his knot. With a strained look, his breathing picks up. I know he's gonna cum any second now, and my body hums in anticipation.

I know the moment it happens because his mouth parts in a silent gasp before he lets out a loud, long grunt.

He works his cock hard, sending streams of hot cum all over me. Some hits my tongue, but most of it makes its way onto my cheeks and chest. "Fuck," he pants, milking himself of the last few drops. "God, you look so beautiful covered in my cum."

I groan, closing my mouth and swallowing the cum on my tongue before using my thumb to collect some from my face and licking that clean too.

"I love it," I purr, rubbing his cum all over my breasts, massaging his scent into my skin.

The dominating look in his eyes is gone as he looks at me in awe, that boy next door vibe shining bright again.

"Now, I want it in me," I tell him, getting off my knees. I stand before him, stepping closer as he steps back, swallowing hard with wide eyes. Gone is the sweet little Omega they love to call me, and in her place is a sex crazed vixen. I put my hands on his chest, pushing him back on the bed. "I wanna ride this big, fat, Alpha cock until you're locked inside me, pumping all your cum deep into me," I purr, moving to straddle his lap.

"Fuck... Tia," he says my name like a prayer.

He watches me as I grab his still hard cock, thanking the universe for the never ending stiffy Alphas can sometimes have, and line it up with my dripping core.

"Feel that?" I ask, rubbing the tip against my slick. "It's all for you, Alpha."

His eyes roll back as I sink all the way down on his cock, stopping just at his knot. I gasp as he fills me, and I don't wait for my body to adjust to his size; I need to feel him move inside of me now.

Balancing myself on his chest, I start to rock my hips, riding his cock. "So good," he moans, watching my swaying breasts like they are pendulums set out to hypnotize him. And the way his eyes are glassed over, I think I'm doing a good job. I feel powerful as I use my sexy Alpha for my pleasure, while he loves every moment of it.

"It is so good," I praise him, loving the way his eyes light up. "Your cock fills me so good, Alpha," I whimper as I find a good angle, hitting the perfect spot. "Fuck, I can feel my slick coating your belly."

"You're so wet," he says, tucking some of my long, red locks behind my ear.

"For you, Alpha. All for you." The burn in my belly starts to grow, but I'm starting to get tired from working my hips over, so I look to my Alpha for help. "I'm so close," I whine. "Help me fuck you, Alpha. Grab my hips and help me, please?"

He growls, gripping my hips and starts to rock me back and forth at a faster pace, helping that burn build higher and higher. "Yes," I call out. "Yes, yes, yes. Like that, don't stop."

"Never," he grunts as I dig my nails into his chest, squeezing my eyes shut.

Just as my orgasm is about to take over, Tristan thrusts

up inside me. I scream his name, my eyes flying open, cumming hard as he locks his knot inside of me.

He roars as he cums again, cock jerking harshly inside me as it fills me up just how I wanted.

Gasping from too much pleasure, Tristan holds my twitching body tight to him, wrapping his arms around me as our never ending climax continues.

When I'm finally able to move my head, I tuck my face into his neck, biting him and marking him officially as my mate. He moans loudly, his grip tightening on me as he cums again, making me feel deliciously full.

"I love you, Tia," Tristan says, sighing out my name like I just rocked his world. Because, well, I guess I just did. *Go me!*

"I love you too, Tristan," I whisper, too tired to talk.

"Sleep, my love," Tristan purrs, running his fingers up and down my back in a soothing motion. "Because when you wake up, I'm gonna take this sweet pussy again and again. All night long," he growls.

And as an Alpha who doesn't want to disappoint his Omega, he's true to his word. He works me over all night until I can't move, can't speak, can't keep my eyes open. He bites me, marking me as his Omega. Another piece of my heart finding its way home.

Part of me feels bad for my other guys who have to hear us for hours on end, and part of me hopes they're in their rooms touching themselves to my cries of pleasure. An omega can get used to this life. Never ending knots and orgasms. Sign me up and lock me down!

CHAPTER 23

OCTAVIA

The next week goes by way too fast, our time being spent mostly on school work. The guys are doubling down on theirs too because with Dom and me going away this weekend, wherever it is that Dom plans on taking me for our time together, and my heat coming up, there's not going to be a lot of time to do any school work they need to get done.

Finn is very adamant on getting a head start on class assignments to get them out of the way so that his complete focus can be me for the week I'm in heat. I love how dedicated he is. It's how they all are.

They all have something they want to pursue once we graduate. Finn wants to open up a comic book shop. It's something he's very passionate about and loves to talk about. One time he got carried away, telling me all about Marvel and DC comics, and after an hour of just him talking, he looked so ashamed of himself. He said that he shouldn't have bored me with things I didn't care about.

I surprised him back by telling him I loved hearing about everything he knew and how I've even watched some of the movies. He got so excited that he kept going, and I fell in love with him even more.

Sawyer wants to work for his parents. They own a fashion magazine, and he wants to become a photographer for them. I had no idea that he was even into photography and could take photos, but he showed me his portfolio, and he's amazing. Some were really stunning photos. There's a lot that people miss when it comes to Sawyer, only seeing a goofy side and thinking that he doesn't take anything seriously. He's also really smart in math, which will help me out a lot because I'm shit at it, and it's something I'll need to take next year. I don't think my Alpha will mind helping me out. I mean, being my tutor will come with some very enjoyable benefits.

Tristan just wants to be a dad. And I love that about him. He says he will find things to do to keep himself busy until I'm done with school and we start having children of our own, but when we do, he wants to be the one to stay at home and help raise them, so I don't have to give up my job. It's another reason out of so many that makes Tristan an amazing man.

As for Dominic, he doesn't know what he wants to do, and that's okay. He has tons of time to decide, and if he ever picks something that he has to go back to school for again, I'll support him.

Then there's Knox, he wants to stay in the security business. He's been talking about opening up his own security firm and hiring men in similar situations as him, unable to do what they love due to an injury but still fully capable of doing the job.

I love these guys, and I can't see my life without them in it. They're mine, and I can't wait for my parents to meet them tonight.

With it being Friday, we're leaving early to drive home for the weekend. Spencer is turning nineteen, and even though we can't take him drinking just yet, we do plan on going out to celebrate.

We're going to be staying in a hotel because I think it would be too many Alphas and Omegas in one house together. Even though it'll only be for a short time, and I trust my mom and dads, I don't want to risk it.

Also, I can't be intimate with my men in my parent's house with my parents there. That would be too weird.

"Do we have everything we need?" Finn asks as he eyes up everyone's bags.

"We're only going for two nights, Finny. I think we will survive." Knox chuckles.

"I know, but it's better to be safe than sorry." Finn blushes, pushing his glasses up his nose.

"I'm all packed with everything I think I'll need. And if I need anything like extra clothes or something, I still have most of my stuff at my parents house," I tell him with a smile.

"And our parents only live in the next town over. If we need something, we can get it there," Knox adds.

"Alright..." Finn says, not sounding too convinced.

"I'm excited," I tell them, bouncing on the balls of my feet. "I know my parents are going to love you."

"I hope so," Sawyer says. "I've never been liked by any girl's parents before."

"Whose parents have you met?" Dom asks him with a frown.

"No one's that's why none of them have liked me before," Sawyer says like he's making complete sense, getting a slap upside the head from Dom. I giggle and shake my head, turning to Finn.

"And I can't wait for the comic book convention. I ordered something to wear and had it shipped to my parents." I grin, biting my lower lip.

"You did?" Finn's eyes go wide. "Like, you're gonna cosplay?"

"Aren't you?" I ask him, stepping forward and grabbing ahold of his suspenders. I love playing with them and watching his hard swallows as he watches me. Much like he's doing right now, his Adam's apple bobbing.

"I wasn't going to," he says softly. "Not until Knox convinced me."

"Why not?" I ask. "Isn't that what you normally do when you go to these events?"

"Yes..." he blushes. "But I didn't think you would want to be seen with me like that."

"Finneas Ashwood!" I growl. "I love you just the way

you are. Don't you even think about hiding your true self from me. I want you, *all* of you."

"You love me?" he asks in disbelief.

"Yes. I do." My face softens. "So much."

"I-I love you too, Tia." He gives me the biggest, goofiest grin that melts me into a puddle at his feet.

"So, you gonna go as Catwoman or something?" Sawyer asks. "Because if that's happening, I wanna come to this nerd fest too. You in a tight, leather outfit? Fuck yes."

"No," Knox tells him. "This is their time, their date. You will just have to hope and pray our little Omega is nice enough to play dress up for you some other time."

"Fine," Sawyer mutters. "But if you're not going as Catwoman, I'm buying you that costume anyway."

I giggle, shaking my head. "No, it's not Catwoman," I tell him then turn back to Finn. "But... I think you're gonna be one happy Alpha," I tell him, leaning up to kiss him. He moans against my lips, pulling me close to him.

"As hot as the two of you are to watch, and even hotter when you confess your love to each other, we really need to get going if we're going to have time to get checked in and see your parents before we go out with Spencer," Knox says.

"Right." I nod. "So, who am I going with?"

"With Sawyer and me," Tristan says. "If that's okay?"

"Of course," I tell him with a smile.

"I'm gonna go in Knox's truck with Finn and Knox," Dom says, then looks at the two men in question. "So, keep your hands to yourself, please. I don't need to smell how turned on you guys are while being stuck in a small space with the both of you," he grumbles. "Bad enough it's all I smell around here. Now, my Little One? I don't mind smelling her when she's turned on, at least she smells amazing."

"I can't make promises if I don't know I can keep them," Knox grins, teasing my grumpy Alpha. "And I don't know, I think Finn smells delicious when he's turned on, don't you Kitten?"

"I do," I say with a blush. "But like you said, we need to go," I add quickly, not wanting to get turned on by thinking about how my guys smell.

I go to bend over and grab my bag, but Dom snatches it from me. I look up at him with a glare and go to the other one only to have Knox grab that one. I shoot my glare at him next, but he just smirks.

"Here," Dom says, handing me my purse before heading out of the house, Knox following after him. The others snicker, and I stick my tongue out at them, making them laugh harder. Damn Alphas should know well enough by now that I can do shit for myself.

But it's in their nature to care for their Omega, and if they want to carry my bags, it's not something I'm going to argue with them about.

The guys get the bags loaded up, and I kiss Dom, Knox, and Finn goodbye before getting in the front passenger's seat with Tristan.

"Can you teach me how to drive?" I ask Tristan.

He looks over at me with his brows raised. "You don't know how to drive?"

"Well, I can drive a golf cart, snowmobile, and ATV but not a car," I tell them. "I walked most places back home or one of my dads took me. I never felt the need to learn. But it's handy to know, so..." I shrug.

"For sure." Tristan smiles. "I'd love to. We can start next week."

Giving him a smile back, I lean in and kiss his cheek before buckling myself up.

"Alright. Now, here's the real question. What are we listening to for car music? Because I can't do metal, country, or classic. Oldies are okay depending on the song, but I'd much rather listen to 90's or early 2000's," Sawyer says, sticking his head between the two seats with a big grin on his face.

"Well, you're in luck," I tell him, hooking my phone up to Tristan's car. "That's pretty much what all of my music is."

The car ride was a lot of fun. We rolled down the windows, allowing the ocean breeze in as we belted out every song that came on. By the time we got to my parent's house, we're just getting done singing *Hollaback Girl* by Gwen Stefani. I was far too out of breath for my liking, but it was so worth it.

"You know, I learned how to spell banana from that song," I tell them as Tristan shuts off the music.

"Same!" Sawyer says with a grin.

There's a knock at my door that makes me jump, but when I turn around, I see Spencer standing there with a big smile on his face.

I scramble to undo my seatbelt as he steps back. Throwing my door open, I launch myself into his arms. "Spencer!" I laugh.

"Hey, big sis." He chuckles. "I missed you. I also forgot how small you are."

Spencer sets me down, and I take a good look at him. He looks the same to me. Although he has the personality of an Omega -sweet, loving, caring, and shy- he doesn't look how most male Omegas do.

He looks a lot like a Beta man, and he's often been mistaken as one since he emerged as an Omega. If it wasn't for his scent, people wouldn't think anything different by just looking at him.

He's tall, six feet with wavy, brown hair. It's grown a bit since I've seen him last. He looks like a regular 'gym bro'. He said he doesn't want to be some weak, little Omega, and trust me, he doesn't look like one.

"Yeah, we'll just say I'm fun size." I laugh.

"Yes, you are, Kitten," Knox says with a chuckle, getting out of his truck with Finn and Dom following behind him. Tristan and Sawyer get out of the car, and all my guys step behind me, guarding my back.

Spencer's face splits into an amused grin. "A whole entourage, I see."

Rolling my eyes, I crack a smile. "Spencer, meet my pack. These are my Alphas Tristan, Sawyer, Dominic, and Finn," I say, pointing to each of my guys.

"Nice to meet you guys. I've heard a lot about you," Spencer says, then turns to Knox. "Then that must make you the Beta-bodyguard-turned-mate," Spencer says before I get a chance to introduce Knox.

"I am," Knox says with a nod.

"Well, little sister, I must admit, these weren't the Alphas I was expecting to see," Spencer says, looking down at me.

"What the fuck does that mean?" Dom growls from behind me, making me stiffen. The guys don't use their Alpha bark or growl in any negative way that sets me on edge, but Dom's tone has me a little uneasy.

But Spencer isn't bothered by the Alpha before him. "It means, I'm fucking relieved my big sister didn't bring home a pack of douche bags who only care about knocking her up and wearing her like an accessory. Unless looks can be deceiving and you're all a bunch of assholes?"

"No," Finn says. "I don't think any of us could ever be mean to Tia."

Biting my lips to keep myself from smiling, I look up at my brother, whose eyes are still on my guys.

"Then this little brother approves," Spencer says. "Nice to meet you, and welcome to the family."

Turning around, I see all my guys have shocked and confused looks on their faces before they all collectively accept that my brother likes them all before even having a conversation with them. Spencer is pretty good at getting a read on people within seconds of meeting them. It's something we have in common.

"Come on in. Mom is pacing the floor waiting for you to get here." Spencer laughs.

I groan. "I feel so bad. I tell her I'll come and visit all the time, but I've been so busy with everything, I haven't had a chance."

"She understands," my bio dad, Jim, says, stepping out onto the front porch. He's legit a Viking of a man. Long blonde hair and built like a mountain.

"Daddy!" I shout, pushing past my brother to run into his arms.

"Hey, Princess," he says with a groan, hugging me tight.

"Did I hear my Tia Bear's out there?" my other dad, Robert, says from within the house, Russell stepping up next to him with a big smile.

My eyes water because they were gone for work when I left, and I didn't get a chance to say goodbye.

My dad puts me down, and I rush over to them, getting a group hug.

"It's so good to see you, Cupcake. We've missed you," Russell says.

"I missed you guys too."

"Tia! How come no one told me Tia was here?" my mother asks, rushing down the stairs. Stepping back from the hug, I see her stop at the end of the stairs, her eyes welling with tears. "My sweet girl."

She rushes over to me, crushing me in a hug that is surprisingly strong.

"Hi, Mom," I sigh, taking a deep breath of her calming scent. Man, have I ever missed this, missed her.

"Look at you," my mom says, taking a step back to hold me at arm's length. "Oh, you're just glowing."

"So, are they going to just stand outside all day?" Russell chuckles.

I giggle as I see all my guys standing in the driveway looking awkward as hell. Rushing to the door, I wave them in. "Come on, guys, get your butts inside." I look at Spencer, who is just watching everything from the foyer. "You know you could have invited them in." I narrow my eyes at my little brother.

"Yeah, I could have, but they aren't my guests." He grins.

"Asshole," I mutter.

"Brat," he says back.

"Pretty sure we're the only ones allowed to call her that now," Knox says in a smug as fuck tone. I blush, shooting wide eyes in his direction, making him chuckle.

"Alright, Cupcake, who do we have here?" Russell asks.

One by one I introduce everyone to my dads and mom. My mom loves them already. I can tell by the smile on her face that looks permanently there.

"So you got lucky too, eh?" Russell asks Knox once we all make our way into the main parts of the house. Finn and Sawyer went to help my mom with supper while Dom and Tristan went on a house tour with the other Alphas.

"I did," Knox says, wrapping his arm around my shoulder and looking down at me with so much love and pride my heart could burst. "I'm the luckiest man alive for Tia to even give me the time of day, let alone make me her mate."

"Good answer," my dad chuckles. "It's one of the things

I love most about my girls. They don't see what we are, Beta, Alpha, Omega. They love us for what's in our hearts and how hard we love them back."

"Tia's the best. She took those boys who've been rejected for years and saw every good thing they had to offer from the moment she laid eyes on them," Knox says.

"Guys." I blush. "I'm right here."

They chuckle as my mom comes over to me. "Oh, Tia. Your Alphas are just the sweetest! That Finn is just a little cutie pie."

"That I do have to agree with," Knox says.

My mom looks up at him with a head tilt. "Finn isn't just my Alpha romantically. He's Knox's too," I tell them.

"Oh! That's wonderful," my mom beams. "But that poor boy. You two are gonna give him a run for his money," she says, shaking her head with a smile before kissing my dad on the cheek and going upstairs.

Knox and I give each other a look that says she's a lot more accurate than she realizes.

"So, you're drinking tonight?" Spencer asks as we step in line for the bar we're going to tonight for my brother's birthday.

"Yes, I am," I tell him. "I plan on having fun. And if I'm

gonna go up and sing tonight, I'm gonna need some liquid courage."

"You can sing?" Sawyer asks.

Spencer snorts. "Hell no, she can't. She sounds like a dying whale."

My face heats in embarrassment and anger. "Fuck off, Spencer, I'm not that bad. I'm better than you."

"You wish, big sis." He grins.

"Remind me why I wanted to come hang out with my little brother?" I grumble as Tristan wraps me in his arms, bringing my back to his front.

"Because you love me. And it's my nineteenth birthday."

"You're lucky I do."

After supper, the guys and I went back to the hotel to drop our stuff off and check into our rooms. Then we got ready before coming back to pick up my brother.

My dads took the opportunity to pull me aside and tell me something that has me worried about my little brother. Apparently, he's been drinking with friends and coming home drunk. The few times that my dads confronted him about it, he always gave the same answer. It's about Ivy, how he doesn't want to go to Calling Wood because then he will be forced to see the woman he loves be with another Omega.

My heart broke when they told me that. They said it was just a young love crush, and once he gets to school and finds a pack of his own, he'll get over it. But they don't understand how Omega hearts work. When we fall, we fall hard. And it's not just for anyone.

So, I told my guys not to offer Spencer anything to drink

and to keep an eye on him. I didn't tell them why, just said that even though it's his birthday, he's still underage, and it's not a lie.

I don't like keeping things from my guys, but this doesn't have anything to do with them, and it's not my business to tell.

We all wait in line, talking amongst each other. I try not to talk too much about school, because anytime I mention Calling Wood, Spencer gets this far away, sad look. So we talk about his life, his friends, his school.

"ID please," the Alpha at the door says, not even bothering to look at us. He blindly takes them and scans them. When he gets to mine, he does a double take that has my Alphas growling before he checks the rest of them. When he gets to my brother, he gives it an even more heated look that has me growling.

The Alpha's eyes shoot up, and he quickly gives Spencer's ID back before waving us inside.

"Chill out, big sis. Don't worry. I'm not interested in any of these Alphas."

When we get inside, the place isn't too packed, but my guys step up to me and Spencer, making sure one of them is by our sides. My heart warms that their first instinct is to protect us, even though my brother is bigger than them all except Dom and Knox.

The bar is broken up in two sections. One is the restaurant part and one is more of a bar with pool tables. We find a table on the bar side next to the stage. Spencer, Finn,

Sawyer, and I all sit down while the others go over to the bar.

"Are you going to sing?" I ask Sawyer.

"Heck yeah." He grins. "It's the perfect chance to sere-nade my Omega." He wiggles his eyebrows making me giggle.

Spencer makes a gagging noise. "So corny. Stop being so cute, you're making us single Omegas feel bad."

"Don't worry, dude, you will find your pack. Only two years left before your life really starts."

Spencer doesn't say anything. My eyes catch his, and he gives me a forced smile. "Let's have fun tonight. We can rate the other people singing."

"What if they're bad? Wouldn't that hurt their feelings?" Sawyer asks, raising a brow. "That's not like you, Pretty Girl."

I roll my eyes. "Not like that. We used to come here with friends once I turned eighteen. I'd bring Spencer along. We would all come on mic night and cheer for everyone who sang, no matter how good or bad they were, and throw out random numbers. It always made them smile, and you could see their nerves settle." I grin.

"Remember that one little, old lady? She got way too confident and almost took off her top," Spencer snickers.

"No way," Sawyer says, eyes going wide before he bursts out laughing. "I hope she's back tonight."

The guys come back with drinks for all of us and a soda for my brother. "Sorry, man," Knox says.

"Oh well. Only two more years, right?"

We spend the next hour drinking and talking, falling into easy conversation that has us all smiling and laughing. It's nice to just go out and relax with my guys.

Finn and Knox have been flirting with each other and sending me glances while the others have been finding any excuse to touch me.

Karaoke starts up, and we wait until I'm three drinks in and feeling tipsy. We were the biggest cheerleaders for each person who went up. I loved when they smiled, their voices becoming more confident. And that little, old lady... turns out she *is* here.

"That's her!" Spencer says with a laugh.

"Really?" Sawyer grins.

The lady gets up and starts singing *Single Ladies* by Beyoncé. We cheer, and my silly Alpha gets up there with her and starts doing the dance. We're all cracking up, but I love the smile on the lady's face, pure joy.

"Alright, give it up for the young lady!" Sawyer says into the mic. "Now, I'll be gracing you all with a performance of my own!"

A new song starts to play, and a big grin splits my face when the song *I'm Too Sexy by Right Said Fred* starts playing. "No way." I laugh. "He's not gonna, is he?"

"Oh, he totally is." Tristan chuckles.

Sawyer starts to sing, getting right into the song. We're all laughing when Sawyer makes his way over to me, singing his heart out and dancing on the spot. My face hurts from laughing so hard. He turns around, and when it says '*I shake my little tush*', he starts to twerk his butt in my face.

"Stop!" I gasp, trying to catch my breath. "I can't breathe!" I laugh.

When the song is over and Sawyer gives the mic to the next person before hopping off the stage and walking over to us. "What did you think, Pretty Girl?"

"America's Got Talent material for sure." I giggle.

"Yes!" He fist pumps. "I knew it."

CHAPTER 24

OCTAVIA

Okay, so I might be a little tipsy. No, that's a lie. I'm *very* tipsy. But I'm feeling good, loving the night, and I'm brave enough to get up on the stage now. Sawyer and Tristan got up there. Their song choice was a little less silly but still fun. I didn't know the song, but they did pretty good.

We cheered some more strangers on, getting some of the other audience members to start hyping people up too.

"Come on!" I grab Spencer's hand and pull at it as I stand. "You wanna get me up there, now is your one and only chance."

"Oh this is gonna be good." Dom chuckles.

"You got this, Kitten!" Knox shouts as Spencer and I head to the stage. I turn to blow him a kiss and almost face-plant in the process.

"I'm good," I call back when I see my guys start to stand. Once we're on stage, Spencer looks at me.

"So, what song do you wanna sing?" Spencer asks. I think for a moment before giving him a grin that has him saying, "Oh boy, what?" I find the song and show him. He chuckles. "Alright, you wanna be Beyoncé or Lady Gaga?"

"Ah, you can do Queen B, I don't wanna butcher her part," I say.

"Good idea," he chuckles.

The song starts, and Spencer and I get right into it. I'm bad, so bad, but I don't even care. My guys are cheering me on like I'm the best they've ever seen. They're calling out my name, giving me catcalls and whistles, and I love every moment of it.

When we're done and get back to the table, I'm out of breath. "I think one more drink and then we should head back to the hotel."

They all agree, nodding their heads when Finn tosses his drink back, finishing it all in one mouthful. My eyes widen as I watch him stand up and dust himself off.

"What are you up to Finny? You okay?" Knox asks.

Finn nods. "I'm gonna sing."

"You are?" Knox asks, brows jumping to his hair line.

"Being here with you guys, watching you have fun and not give a crap about what others think... I want that. I don't normally care what people think about me, but I don't ever put myself out there, avoiding things that would have people turn and stare. So tonight, I'm gonna take a page from your book and try something new," he says, looking at me with determined eyes.

I get up and kiss his cheek. "You've got this, Alpha."

He gives me a small smile before heading over to the stage. I sit down in Knox's lap. He wraps his arms around me, holding me tight as we wait to see what song Finn picks.

Finn grabs the mic with shaky hands, taking it off the stand and bringing it closer to his face. He's not looking at us, but focusing on the far wall.

He takes a deep breath as the song starts. At first, I don't recognize the song, but as he starts to sing the first few words, my heart starts to pick up and my eyes start to water. A small sob slips out of me.

"What's wrong?" Knox asks, his voice filled with concern.

"Just listen," I say back, getting myself under control. Finn picked *Love Me More by Sam Smith*. I've heard this song a few times, and fuck if it doesn't hit you in the feels.

And Finn? He sings like an angel. I'm entranced by him, his voice, and the lyrics of the song. With each word, my heart breaks for the past him and heals for the new man he's become. The way he looks at me and Knox when he's finally able to look our way, it has tears streaming down my face. I want to find every person who's ever looked at him wrong, said a mean word to him, or hurt my sweet Alpha and beat their asses.

When the song gets to the part where it says, '*lately, it's not hurting like things used to*', I sob again as Knox holds me tighter. I can feel Knox's heart beating like a drum, wild in his chest.

When the song ends, the whole room is quiet for a few seconds. Finn looks panicked, vulnerability masking his face. Then the whole room breaks out into cheers. The sound is deafening as people stand and clap.

Finn walks back to us with red eyes. Knox sets me on my feet before pulling Finn into his arms. Knox kisses him hard, and watching how much love is put into that kiss makes my heart swell.

"I'm so fucking proud of you," Knox says, putting his forehead to Finn's.

"Thank you," Finn whispers.

"I love you," Knox says.

"I love you too." Finn turns to look at me. "And I love you too, Sunshine."

"You were amazing, Alpha," I tell him as I wrap my arms around him. He holds me tight, putting his face into my hair and taking a deep breath of my scent before letting out a sigh.

We sit and have a few more drinks, the whole group hyped up by Finn's performance.

"Alright. I think it's really time we go," Dom says.

"Noooo," I slur, my tipsy turning to drunk.

"Yes, Little One," Dom growls, making me pout. "You have your date with Finn tomorrow, and you need as much sleep as you can get. I wouldn't be surprised if you're hungover first thing in the morning."

"Boooo." I throw my napkin at him, and his eyes flash.

"Alright, you've chosen to be a bratty little Omega, I see," he growls.

"Ohhhh, Sis is gonna get it," Spencer says.

"Fuck you," I tell him, flipping him off. Well, trying to, but I end up showing him my pinky instead.

"I'll be right back," Finn says, getting up. "I'm just gonna go pay our tab."

A few of the guys go to the bathroom while we wait. They try to get me to go, but I'm drunk as a skunk, and I just feel like being a pain in the ass right now.

"What is taking him so long?" I sigh dramatically, making Knox laugh and Dom shake his head with a smirk. "I need to go find my sexy, nerdy Alpha," I declare, moving to stand up.

I get a head rush and spin a little bit. Tristan shoots up from his chair to steady me. "Thanks, sexy pants," I purr.

"You're welcome, love." He smiles, looking amused by my state.

"You know, me and you, we should fuck when we get back to the hotel. I need a knot," I tell him, a little too loudly.

Spencer makes a gagging noise. "Fuck, sis, I do not need to hear about your sex life," he shutters.

"Oh, relax." I wave my hand at him. "Someday, you're gonna be taking knots up the ass."

"Tia!" Knox barks out a laugh.

"So it's not just when she's in heat that she has a dirty mouth," Tristan says with a chuckle.

"You should live in here." I tap on my head. "There's so

much stuff that would blow your mind." I nod. "Just like I could blow your cock." I giggle.

"Alright. Let's find our boy before Kitten starts doing things that get us locked up," Knox says, and the whole table stands.

"You're no fun," I pout, but I do want to find Finn. Looking around, I squint my eyes trying to find him around the room. And when my eyes lock on him at the bar, I see red.

"Little One?" Dom asks with caution, eyes following my gaze. "Fuck," he hisses. Fuck is right. Meaning, I'm about to fuck up a bitch for touching my Alpha.

I push past Tristan and stumble my way over, my guys at my back cursing up a storm.

As I get closer, I see him talking a mile a minute. She doesn't seem to care about what he has to say, just pets his fucking arm. And my poor, sweet Finn doesn't even notice this bartender is flirting with him. "Your voice is so sexy," she purrs. "You should sing for me sometime. Like a private show."

I'll give her a fucking private show with my fist... in her face. They don't see me as I stop behind Finn.

"Oh." He stops talking. "N-o, I can't do that," he stutters out his words.

"Why not? I'm not an Omega, but I can be one for the night if you like, Alpha."

"No." He shakes his head. "I don't need you to pretend you're an Omega. I have an Omega."

"Really?" she asks, sounding a little surprised, and that pisses me off.

"Yes," Finn says, a dreamy sound to his voice. "She's so beautiful and funny. She has a heart of gold and is so accepting. I love her, a lot. She's the reason why I got up and sang tonight."

My shitty mood is gone, and I'm about to be a sobbing, drunk bitch because my Alpha is so damn amazing. I'll have to make sure I rock his world extra hard to remind him how much I love him tomorrow.

But we're here, and now there's no way I can just grab my Alpha's hand and tug him away like this didn't happen.

"Well, here's your receipt," she tells him, and she starts to hand him the piece of paper. "My number is at the top, just in case."

"I'll take that." I snatch it out of her hands. "What is up with Beta bitches giving my men their numbers? God, woman, have some self-respect. He told you he was taken, and you have the balls to *still* give him your number," I tisk. "Who hurt you, boo?"

She sneers at me, and that earns her a growl. But not by my other guys, no, by Finn.

"Don't get mad at her. She's speaking the truth. I told you I have an Omega, and it's very rude to disregard my relationship status," he says, wrapping his arm around me. "I thought you were a nice lady, but clearly, I need to learn to read people better."

With that, we turn and leave the Beta bitch gaping back at us like a fish out of water.

"Okay, that was hot," Knox growls as we join the rest of our group from where they were watching this play out a few feet behind us.

"Yeah, we were." I giggle, looking up at Finn, who still has me tucked under his arm. He's blushing, but he gives me a smile and a kiss on the lips.

"I'm sorry she was so rude. I hope you know I would never do that to you," he says with a slightly panicked look in his eyes.

"I know," I tell him. "I know you love me and Knox and only us. We trust you."

"With our lives," Knox adds.

They manage to get me in the car without me face planting over my heels. We drop my brother off, making sure he gets into the house safely before heading back to the hotel we're staying at.

"I'm fine," I mutter as Dom carries me like a baby.

"Yeah, sure, Little One. Let's just forget you almost face planted a moment ago." He chuckles.

"Don't laugh at me. It's hard to walk in heels. You try it!" I growl, and the rest of them laugh too. "Traitors," I mutter.

"She's cute when she's drunk," Sawyer says. I just glare at him.

"Get a good night's sleep, Kitten," Knox says, giving me a kiss on the cheek.

"See you in the morning, Sunshine. I can't wait to spend the day with you," Finn says, doing the same thing.

"Where are you two going?"

"Finn and I are gonna share a room," Knox says, giving Finn a look that screams sex, making Finn blush.

"Hey, you better leave him a sweet, virgin boy. He's mine!" I warn. Finn looks at me with wide eyes.

"Don't worry, Little Omega." Knox chuckles. "I'll leave him a virgin. But can't count on the sweet part."

Dom takes me away from my sexy lovers. "But I wanted to watch," I whine.

"I'm sure there's lots of watching in the future. For right now, we need to get you into bed," Tristan says.

"There better be." I sigh.

They laugh again. *What is so funny tonight?*

The moment we get into the hotel room, I feel my stomach lurch.

"Oh no," I say, slapping a hand over my mouth. "Put me down."

"Tia?" Dom asks.

"Put me down," I demand, slapping at his arm.

He does, and I beeline for the bathroom, making it just in time before I heave up everything from tonight.

Someone grabs my hair and holds it out of the way for me while someone else rubs my back.

"Go," I groan. "You don't need to see this."

Tristan snorts. "Like we would just leave our Omega like this? You're cute."

Dom brings me a cold cloth, wiping down my face before I get sick again. When I'm done, he offers me some water. I take a few sips before they help me into bed. They give me something for my headache and tuck me in.

I'm lucky to call them mine, but tomorrow... yeah, I don't think I'm going to enjoy the after effects of drinking. I might need to rethink doing this again in the future.

KNOX

"Are you mad at me?" Finn asks as I shut and lock the door behind us.

"No. Why would I be?" I ask him. He moves to sit on the bed, looking tired and a little sad.

"I didn't even know she was flirting with me. It didn't kick in until she was asking me to be alone with her," he says, pushing his glasses up his nose. "I thought she was just being nice because of my singing."

"Well, you're fucking amazing at singing," I tell him. And fuck is he ever. His voice is sexy and powerful and, god, I wanna hear him sing every song in the world to me and my Kitten.

"Thanks," he says with a blush.

"As for the girl at the bar, don't blame yourself. We don't," I tell him, taking off my shirt. His eyes widen, trailing all over my chest, taking in my tattoos as I walk towards him. Stepping up between his parted legs, I look down at him, cupping his face. "You didn't do anything wrong. You said all the right things."

"I love you both so much," he tells me, his eyes shining bright with emotion. "I don't want anyone else but the two of you."

"We know," I soothe him, brushing my thumb across his

cheek before leaning forward and taking his soft lips with mine. He moans, and I growl, my tongue slipping in and over his.

I kiss him to show him just how much he means to me as I grab the hem of his Batman shirt. Breaking the kiss, I pull it up and over his head. He watches me with wide eyes, but I see the trust that I'm not going to push anything tonight. He wants to save himself for Tia, and I'm fine with that.

"Knox," he whimpers as I push him back on the bed.

"I just want to help you relax," I tell him, unbuttoning his pants and pulling them down, boxers and all. His cock springs free, and I groan as I take him in. He's got thousands of freckles covering his body, and I wanna lick them all. "We're not going to have sex. But can I touch you?" I ask, moving to hover over him bracing myself on my hands next to his head.

"Yes," he breathes.

Capturing his lips again, I glide my hand down his body, loving the whole body shiver he gives me. I growl in approval as I find his throbbing cock. When I wrap my hand around his hot shaft, giving it a little squeeze, he bucks into my hand with a gasp. "Knox!"

"Shhhh," I soothe him. I start to slowly work my hand up and down his cock, loving the little whimpers and whines from my Alpha. I'm still hovering above him, kissing him as I put all my weight on my one arm. I want that gap between us so I can watch him cum. "Let your worries slip away. No one is mad at you, Finny. We trust you, we love you. No one is going anywhere. You're ours, and we're never letting you go."

The emotion in his eyes is almost my undoing. I know he has a lot of concerns considering everything he and the others had to go through because of the judgmental assholes of this world.

He closes his eyes when he sees that I mean everything I just said. "That's it," I tell him, giving his cock a tighter squeeze.

"I don't wanna sound like a loser right now, but I don't know how much longer I'm gonna last," he says, moaning as I move my hand a little faster.

"You're not a loser," I growl. "This is your first time having someone touch your cock who isn't you. This is new for you, and I'm not gonna judge you on how long you can last. Hell, half the time I'm ready to nut in my pants by just looking at my Kitten or you, Finny. I would never judge. Also, you're an Alpha." I give him a devilish grin, brushing my fingers against his knot, making him grunt and moan. "You're meant to cum and cum and cum."

"Damn it, Knox. Your hand feels so good," he groans, his body locking up as his cock starts to jerk in my hand, sending streams of cum out to coat his belly. My own cock is painfully hard in my jeans, and I want nothing more than to bury it in his tight ass, but I shut that thought down because this is about him, not me.

"You cum so perfectly, Finny," I purr as he lays there panting, out of breath as he finishes cumming. Letting go of his cock, I bring my hand up to my mouth and lick the cum off. "Fuck," I moan. "You taste so fucking good. I need more."

"Knox," he gasps as I move down a little to lick up the mess he's made on his belly.

"Oh, my sweet, sweet man." I chuckle. "Just you wait. Once our girl has you tomorrow, a door will be opened to a whole new world for us."

"I can't wait," he says, his eyes wide with excitement. I love it, my shy man is eager to explore with us.

"Come on, let's get showered, then we can get you ready for bed. You have a long day with our Little Omega tomorrow, and I know she's excited."

"Okay," he says, taking my clean hand as I help him up. I strip out of my pants before we even get to the bathroom, and I smirk as I feel my Finny's eyes on my ass. Something tells me my shy Alpha isn't as sweet as my Kitten thinks.

FINN

Today has been one long day. From meeting Tia's parents to going to the bar, now this? It's a lot more than I'm used to. But I have to admit that I had fun. Getting out of my comfort zone was terrifying but seeing my Sunshine up there not caring at all about what people thought and truly just loving her life, I wanted to see what that was like.

Singing in front of people for the first time, I almost puked, but the looks on Tia and Knox's faces was worth it. It was a song I always enjoyed because it had a deeper meaning to my life, maybe even to the other Alphas.

Tia and Knox have gotten me out of the little bubble that I've put myself in. Even though years of being rejected left a piece of me broken, it's been healed from the moment these two came into my life. And although I tend not to care too much about what people think because it's my life, and I like what I like, I don't usually go out of my way to put myself into social situations.

And tonight was a huge leap. Since Tia came into my life, I've done more sexually without having sex than I ever have. They bring out this part in me that is excited to explore my sexuality with them. Seeing how much they want me, how attracted they are to me, it makes me feel sexy and wanted.

Having Knox touch me like he did back on the bed, it was heaven. I never want to have to be the one to touch myself again. I need one of them to from now on because I know it will never be the same.

I don't think I've ever cum so quickly, and I would feel embarrassed about it, but the way Knox looked at me as he licked my cum clean, it made me ready to go again.

But I want to wait until tomorrow with Tia. That doesn't mean I can't help him with the massive, hard cock he has digging into my ass cheeks as he scrubs my hair.

The man is a god, his body is ripped enough to stop traffic and being here, naked in the shower with him, I can't get my mind off getting on my knees and worshiping his cock.

"Knox," I say his name, breaking the silence.

"Yes, Finny," he murmurs as he tips my head back into the water to rinse me clean.

"Remember back at the beach? The book I was reading?" My heart is pounding as I bite my lip, my nerves fluttering in my belly.

"Yes," he growls, making my knees go weak.

"Was it true you wanted to play out that scene?" I ask, turning in his arms.

"I wanna do everything and anything with you, Finn," he says, his eyes full of heat and need.

Without breaking eye contact, I take a deep breath and slowly get down on my knees. His chest rumbles with a low growl as I take his cock with my shaky hand.

"Finn," he hisses as I grasp his heavy cock.

My eyes go to his dick and they widen. Holy hell, he really is big, and every inch of his cock is tattooed with a piercing at the tip.

"So, I'm gonna be real right now." I chuckle nervously. "This will be our own version because I have no idea what I'm doing."

"Want me to guide you through it?" he asks, his voice gravely as he brushes the wet hair from my face.

"Please," I say on a whisper.

"Be a good Alpha and jerk me off. Grip me tight," he growls.

I do as he asks, working my hand up and down, loving the primal groan that he gives in response.

"Yes. Just like that," he pants. "Now, lick the tip. It's

dripping for you, and we wouldn't want to waste it now, do we?"

"No," I whimper. Leaning forward, I lick the tip and his piercing. His taste explodes on my tongue, making me crave more.

"Now take me into that hot mouth of yours, Alpha. I wanna see you gag on my cock," he purrs. My own cock jerks in response, and I'm quick to do as I'm told.

Wrapping my lips around the head of his cock, my tongue plays with his piercing.

"That's it. Now take me all the way." He groans. Taking a deep breath, I lean forward, going until his tip hits the back of my throat. He grabs a handful of my hair and holds me there until I start to gag a little.

"Look at you. An Alpha on his knees for me. Fucking perfection, you are, *my* Alpha," he says, before tugging at my hair to pull me all the way off his cock.

I gasp for air as spit drips down my chin. "You want this?" he asks.

"Yes," I moan.

"I'm gonna make you gag on my cock, Finn. And you're going to love it, aren't you?"

"Please," I beg.

"Grab the base of my cock with one hand. It's to stop me from taking you too far," he tells me, and I do it. "Now, are you ready?"

"Yes," I breathe.

"Good boy." He grins. "Now open up and take Daddy Knox nice and deep." I whimper at his dirty talk, loving every word. Opening my mouth, I take him back in. "Slap my leg if it's too much, okay?"

I hum around his cock as I give him a little nod. I'm not in control of this blow job, but I'm more than okay with that.

He starts to fuck my mouth, using me for his pleasure. But the way he looks at me... he's in awe, in love with me, and damn, it makes my eyes water. Or maybe it's from the fact I'm gagging on his cock.

The sounds coming from him has my own cock throbbing. I want to touch myself as I pleasure him, and it's like he can see that need on my face.

"Touch that perfect Alpha cock, Finn. Jerk yourself off while I fuck your face," he growls.

Rushing to grab my cock, I start to pleasure myself a little more roughly than I normally do. I wish it was Tia's hands on me, but I need relief, this is all so much but so perfect.

My heart is pounding, my body shaking, and I can't look away as Knox thrusts into my mouth over and over, his own chest heaving as his leg muscles tighten.

"Fuck!" he says, holding me still again. My hand keeps him from going too deep but enough to get that thrill. "I'm gonna cum, Finn. And I want you to swallow every fucking last drop like a good boy," he growls.

I moan around his cock, trying to ready myself to swallow him. But when he starts to cum, letting out this guttural groan as he empties himself down my throat, I struggle to swallow his cum. Some leaks out, there's just too much.

My own release finds me, and I cum hard, sending jets of cum down the drain, mixing in with the water from the shower.

I gasp as he pulls free.

"Missed some, Finny," he purrs, gathering the cum from my chin with his thumb and pushing it into my mouth. "Better."

He helps me to my feet before pulling me into his arms and kissing me hard.

"I fucking love you." He chuckles. "You did so good, baby."

It's like reality comes rushing back, and I find myself shy again, like I didn't just give my first blow job that had my balls ready to explode.

"I love you too," I whisper.

"You're cute, you know. Getting all shy on me. Fuck." He chuckles again. "Come on Alpha, let's get you to bed."

We get out and dry off before getting into bed. He pulls me to his chest, sighing as he tucks his face into my hair.

This is how we've been sleeping the past week since I finally got the courage to crawl into his bed, needing to be with him. I hated having him so close and not being in his arms.

Tia found us the other morning and slipped into bed with us. I asked her if she was mad, but she smiled sweetly, and said she's anything but.

I fall asleep feeling like I'm on cloud nine, knowing tomorrow is going to be even better.

CHAPTER 25

OCTAVIA

"Make it stop," I moan, rolling over into a warm body.

"Make what stop?" Sawyer's gravely voice answers.

"My head from spinning," I mumble into his chest.

He chuckles, wrapping his arms around me, kissing the top of my head. "Does our Little Omega have her first hangover?"

"Whatever it is, I'd like to give it back," I grumble, not liking this feeling at all.

"Sorry, Love, no can do. But we can help the best we can," Tristan says from my other side. He snuggles into my back, kissing my neck. I'm in heaven. Apple Cider and Cotton Candy fill my nose, and I sigh.

"Here, Little One." Dom's husky voice has me opening my eyes to see him standing by the bed with a glass of water in one hand and some white pills in the other. "Take these.

One will help with your headache, and the other will help your nausea."

Groaning, I slowly sit up. "Thank you, Alpha," I tell him, loving the way he sighs. "And thank you for taking care of me last night." I blush, avoiding eye contact as I take the water and pills from Dom.

"You have nothing to be embarrassed about," Tristan says as I down the pills with a mouthful of water, shivering as they go down.

"It was your first time *really* drinking. And you looked like you had fun. That's all that matters. I know I did," Sawyer says, sitting up. He pushes the hair off my shoulder and places a soft kiss there.

"I did have fun." I smile, remembering how much I laughed last night. Then I remember what happened right before we left. "Until the bartender hit on my Alpha," I grumble.

Dom chuckles. "You have nothing to worry about, Little Omega. You have all of your Alphas wrapped around your little finger. We don't want anyone but you, Little One."

"Even after having to deal with my pukey ass last night?" I laugh.

"Yes," Tristan says. "You're sexy, even when you sound like a dying cat."

"Frig off." I laugh, giving his shoulder a little shove.

"Don't worry, Pretty Girl, we still love you," Sawyer says.

My eyes find Dom, searching for any truth to that in his eyes. We haven't said those words to each other yet. I want to, so damn bad, but I can still see he's struggling with a lot within himself. I think he knows I'm here to stay, and I make sure to show him just how much I want to be with him. I don't want to say something so life changing and have him freak out. What if I say the words and he thinks I'm only saying them just because he thinks I think it's what he wants to hear?

The look in his eyes makes me suck in a soft breath. They're swimming with so much emotion, and I know one of them is love. But he has this vulnerable look on his face, telling me he isn't ready.

"I know," I respond to Sawyer, but keep my eyes on Dom's as I give him a soft smile. "I love you guys too." I didn't say it directly to him, leaving it to him to take it however he feels comfortable with.

"Alright, Love. You need to get up and get ready. I'm sure you're gonna wanna shower?" he says it like a question.

Looking away from Dom, I turn to him. "Hell yes, I want to shower." I laugh. "I feel like I've run a marathon, and I probably smell like I did too."

Sawyer gives me a sniff. "Yeah, I think a shower is a good idea, Pretty Girl." But I look over to him, seeing his playful smile. I glare at him.

"Bad Alpha." I stick my tongue out at him and get off the bed.

"I'm sorry, Pretty Girl!" he shouts after me. "You smell amazing. Like daisies and sunsets."

I giggle and lock myself in the bathroom. As much as I'd

love one of my Alphas to come in here and give me a helping hand, I have another Alpha who's waiting for me.

After a shower and brushing my teeth, I start to feel like my old self. The meds kicked in, and the only thing I need now is something in my belly and some coffee to help me get through the day.

Wrapping a towel around myself, I leave the bathroom to find three of my Alphas sitting in the little living room in our suite.

"Nice look," Sawyer teases. "Who are you supposed to be?"

"Haha." I grin rolling my eyes. "But speaking of..." I rush over to my bag and take out the costume for today. "So. I actually ordered something different, but when Knox found out what Finn was going as, I just had to match."

"Well, show us, Little One," Dom says.

"Can't yet." I wiggle my eyebrows at him. "I wanna get my hair and make up done first. Help with the whole look."

"Fine," Sawyer pouts. "But can you at least tell us who you were originally going to go as?"

"Poison Ivy," I tell him. All three of them groan, making me giggle. "Don't worry. I'll wear it for you guys one day." I wink.

"You better, Little One," Dom growls, making my body flush.

Alright, get ready before you drop this towel and get on your knees for your Alphas because now is not the time. Right? But I mean, isn't there always time for knots?

I shake my head, getting my mind out of my dirty

thoughts. But by the smirk on my guys' faces, they can smell me anyway.

"I have to get ready," I squeak out, grabbing my makeup bag and hair stuff before rushing back into the bathroom.

"Why do we have to wait to see?" Sawyer whines. "Show us!"

"Drama King, I tell you." I giggle. "Just wait!"

"Fine," he mutters as the four of us go next door. After I got my hair and makeup done, I put a robe on to keep my outfit a surprise for when Finn sees it.

We stop at the door and knock. "Well, hello Kitten," Knox purrs when he sees me after opening the door. I gasp as he pulls me inside quickly before pushing me against the wall. He tucks his face into my neck as he holds me close to his body. "I'd kiss you, but I don't want to ruin your pretty makeup," he says, licking up the side of my neck. "So this will have to do." He finds his mark, giving it a suck and making me moan.

"Alright, Beta," Dom growls. "We don't need our cocks getting hard right before she leaves. That just makes us a group of guys with boners alone in a room."

"Yeah, that doesn't sound as fun if our Little Omega isn't there naked too," Sawyer snickers.

I grin up at Knox when he pulls away from my neck. "Did you keep my Alpha intact?"

"Don't worry, he's yours to have in all the best ways," he chuckles. "But our Alpha is a very willing man. I don't think he would have a problem at all if you wanted to take control of tonight."

"Aww, man," I pout. "I missed some good stuff, didn't I?"

"Don't worry, Kitten. I'll make sure we do a little repeat while you're in heat and have all your holes filled." The look he gives me is pure sex.

"Oh, hey guys," Finn says, snapping me out of my horny little bubble. Only it fills right back up when I see him in his outfit. He's got a tight Superman outfit on, and it's hugging him in all the right places.

"Look at you." I whistle, making him blush as he pushes his glasses up his nose. "And those give you a little Clark Kent vibe too."

"You like?" he asks. "It's not too much, is it?"

"Not at all. It's perfect for what I'm wearing."

"What *are* you wearing?" he asks, brows pinching as he takes in my robe.

Moving in front of him, I grab the belt of the robe and open it, letting it drop to the ground. Finn's eyes widen as he takes in my outfit. They're full of heat, but they also light up with excitement too.

"No way!" he laughs. "We're matching!"

The smile that takes over his face makes me so damn happy that I changed my outfit. The guys are muttering behind me how it's not fair Finn gets me all to himself in this outfit, but I think it's more than fair.

"So, Superman, what are you gonna do with your Super-girl?" I ask him, stepping closer.

He gulps as my hands roam over his muscles. "Take her to the comic book convention and show her off to the world," he says.

"I can't wait."

"So, I was thinking we stay a few hours and meet some people. I have some comic books I wanna get signed. Take some photos and get a few items. Then we can go back to my parents' house. They're working late, so we can just hang out there for a little bit," Finn says as we both sit in the back seat of Knox's car.

Neither Finn nor I have our driver's license. He said he's way too paranoid to be in control of such a big and dangerous thing. So Knox is our driver for the day.

"I'll drop you guys off at the event and hang out in town. Then I'll bring you guys to Finn's parents before I go and visit my own."

"Sounds good," I agree. "I'd love to meet your parents too before we leave."

"Don't worry, Kitten, we can stop by tomorrow before we head out."

When we get to the convention, we each give Knox a kiss before he drives off.

"Ready, Superman?" I ask, holding my hand out for his.

"Ready, Supergirl." He grins, lacing his fingers with mine.

When we walk in, the place is packed. There are people walking around, but there's also a lot who are lined up for different booths.

"Now, don't judge me too hard," he says, grabbing something out of his bag. "They cost me a pretty penny, but I wanted to see as much as I could today because the three day pass just wasn't an option. So, I bought these." He puts a lanyard over my head. "This is an all access pass. We still have to wait in line a little bit, but it's going to be nowhere near as long as some of the others."

"Cool," I tell him, kind of happy because as much as I'm excited to be here, I hate waiting in lines.

We spend the next hour meeting actors, voice actors, and seeing a bunch of other things related to all the superheroes Finn loves. I don't know much about who they are, just who they represent, but I don't care. The look of pure joy and excitement on Finn's face is worth every moment.

I've never seen him so open, so relaxed outside our house. But being here, I've seen him talk to tons of strangers, proudly introducing me as his Omega.

"So. Your partner's the fan?" someone asks me. I look over to see a big, beefy man of an Alpha.

"Yup." I laugh. "What gave it away?"

"The look of pure love on your face as you watch him talking to that group of people. My Omega is the little one with pink hair," he says, smiling wide when his eyes land on her. "She loves this kind of stuff. And I come to these things because I love her. And watching her get excited over it makes me happy."

I smile, too, watching Finn toss his head back and laugh as another person says something. "Mine's the Superman with the glasses," I say.

"Omega?" he asks, tilting his head to the side.

"Nope. My sexy, nerdy Alpha."

"Well, he's one lucky Alpha," he chuckles.

"And she's one lucky Omega," I counter. "I'm here for the same reason. And honestly, I'm loving it. I'm having a lot of fun and learning a lot of new things."

"Same," he says.

We stand there in silence as we watch our lovers enjoy themselves for a little while longer before Finn comes over. "Look!" he says, his eyes wide with a massive smile on his face. "I got one of the voice actors from the old Batman cartoons to sign one of my comics."

"That's amazing!" I say.

"Are you bored?" he asks, his face dropping. "God, you totally are. Here I am geeking out like crazy, and I keep dragging you around to everything."

"Hey!" I tell him, reaching up to cup his face. "I want to be here. I'm having fun! And also, do you have any idea how happy it makes me to see the Alpha I love feeling so comfortable and truly enjoying himself? It's pretty hot."

His eyes widen before a huge smile spreads across his face. He grabs me and pulls me into his arms. "I love you, Tia. And it means so much to me that you came today. You see me for me, and there is not an ounce of judgment. You make me feel things that I can't put into words. All I know is that it's something I want to feel forever. Thank you for loving me, for me."

My eyes start to water. "I love you too, Finn. Every part of you. I love learning about new things with you, hearing about all your hobbies, and anything else you enjoy."

He pulls me into a kiss, and I melt into his arms. "I don't deserve you," he says. "But I'm so damn lucky you're mine. Mine forever."

"Forever."

After that we take some fun photos with a bunch of strangers, doing silly poses, and I love every moment of it.

Five hours later and two bags filled to the brim, we call Knox to come pick us up.

"Well, look at you two," Knox chuckles as he opens the trunk. He takes the bags from Finn, giving him a kiss on the cheek before Finn gets inside the car. "Was it fun, Kitten?"

"It was. But the best part was the smile on our Alpha's face the whole time."

"Good." He grins. "Now, make that smile slip from his face as he moans your name while you take his knot inside that tight pussy."

"Knox," I choke out. "Your mouth is gonna get you in trouble."

"And that's a problem how?" he chuckles.

"You're bad," I laugh, shaking my head.

Leaning in close, he hovers against my ear. "He wasn't complaining about how dirty my mouth was when I was licking his cum off his abs last night," he purrs. *Sweet mother of god.* I'm five seconds away from taking him in the backseat of this car, people around us be damned. Fucker chuckles as my face heats, and a little whimper escapes me.

He walks away, the cocky Beta he is. I take a moment to collect myself before I fill the car up with my perfume.

"What were you two talking about?" Finn asks as I slide in next to him.

"Just getting our girl all ready for you tonight," Knox says, grinning in the rearview mirror.

"What?" Finn asks, looking at me confused.

"Nothing," I tell him. "Knox is just being Knox."

The man in question chuckles as we pull out of the parking lot.

We pull up to a nice house with a white picket fence. I love it already. "Tell your mom and dad I say hi, and I hope to see them soon," Knox says as he helps Finn bring the bags in.

"I will. I know they are gonna be thrilled when I tell them about us." He blushes.

"Mine too." Knox smiles.

Knox says goodbye and Finn brings us into the house. "So, here it is," he says, scratching the back of his head. "Home sweet home. Sorry, it's nothing fancy."

"Who cares about fancy? I love it. It's so homey, and it makes me feel safe," I tell him as I take in the living room.

"Yeah?" he asks. "We have money, but my mom doesn't like to use it to buy unnecessary things. She loves to give to charities and help people in need. My dad doesn't care as long as she's happy." Finn's dad is an Alpha, and his mom is a Beta, but the way he talks about how his parents are together, it's like he treats her like a queen. How it should be.

"I really can't wait to meet them now," I tell him.

"They are gonna love you." He smiles. "Wanna see my room?" he asks, getting shy.

"Umm, *yes!*" I laugh.

He grins, shaking his head as he takes my hand and leads me upstairs.

"So. It hasn't changed since I was like, maybe sixteen. Even then, not by much," he tells me before opening one of the doors. Flicking on his lights, I gasp.

His room is decked out. One side is all gaming gear that includes a big TV with every gaming console you can imagine and a desk with a complex computer setup.

"I used to really be into gaming," he tells me. "It's something I wish I could do more, but the guys don't really game, and I'm pretty busy with school."

"Well, you're going to have to game with me then," I tell him.

"You game?" he asks in shock.

"Well, not really." I laugh. "But I love Mario 64, and any game on the Nintendo 64."

"That, I have." He grins. "I'll bring it back with us."

I look around the rest of his room taking in the bookshelves of comics, the posters covering the walls, but the thing that has me giggling is the Spiderman bed set.

"Do you think Spiderman would be mad if Supergirl deflowered Superman on top of him?" I ask, turning to Finn. His eyes widen, looking from me to the bed, then back to me.

"You wanna make love on my bed?" he asks.

"We can wait until we go back to the hotel room," I tell him, taking a step closer to him, loving how his breath hitches, and he swallows hard. "But you said your parents won't be home for hours. Let me make your teenage dreams come true." I grin up at him. I wrap my arms around his neck, pushing my body against his. I can feel how hard he is, how much he wants me.

"Sixteen-year-old Finn would be cumming in his pants right about now," Finn says, making me giggle.

"Well, good thing you're an Alpha now. Even if you do cum sooner than you would like, which is nothing to be ashamed of if you do, it's your first time. It just so happens that you've got like a supercharged dick, like the Energizer Bunny. You can keep going and going."

"Tia!" He barks out a laugh. "Knox is right. You really are a dirty little Omega."

"Only for my Alphas." I giggle again. My lips find his, and he lets out a moan as he grips my hips, holding me close to him.

"I need you," he whimpers. I love how different he is from the others. I love when my men take control, and I love doing exactly what they tell me to do. But having Finn ready to do what I say, seeing the pure need for me in his eyes? It's a powerful feeling.

FINN

This is really happening right now. I have my Sunshine in my arms, and I'm about to have sex, for the first time... in my teenage bedroom.

Never in a million years would I think I'd ever have someone so gorgeously breathtaking in my room, let alone, in my bed.

I did dream of Knox in here with me, laying in bed while we talked, kissing him until it led to something more.

But it wasn't meant to happen that way. We had to wait until our Little Omega came into our lives to make it right, to really start living.

I kiss her with fervent need. I've never been so turned on in my life. The need to be inside her, to knot her until I can't think straight, is so strong.

I'm glad we waited and didn't rush things. I needed this time with her, for her to see the real me, right down to the bones, to make sure she wouldn't run.

She didn't. She's seen the real me and loves me anyway.

"Let's get this off of you," she says, out of breath as we break the kiss. She moves to my back, finding the zipper to my Superman outfit.

I close my eyes, taking a few deep breaths, trying to will my heart to slow down before I pass out. It would be just my luck to pass out before I even get the chance to be inside her.

She unzips me all the way before coming back to my front. I stand there, slightly shaking, as I let her take the lead. She gives me a smile that makes my heart beat faster for a whole new reason. Her hands slide over my shoulder and down my arms, taking the material with her.

She crouches down, and when she gets to my boxers under the costume, she grabs the waistband, pulling them down too.

My breath catches in my throat as I watch her, unable to look away. My length springs free, slapping me in the belly.

"Well, Mr. Superman," she purrs, looking up at me. There's a change in her demeanor now. Gone is the sweet little Omega, replaced with a very hungry one. And it's looking like I'm on the menu. "Your Supergirl is gonna take good care of you."

Damn. I really don't wanna embarrass myself, but seeing her like this, hearing her role play for me, it's so sexy; she's so sexy.

"O-kay," I stutter out, not really able to say much more.

Her small, dainty hands wrap around my cock, and I let out an embarrassing groan. She doesn't break eye contact as she looks up at me with her bright, green eyes. Her tongue flicks out, licking the pre-cum off the tip, making my knees almost buckle.

Lifting my shaft up, she licks the underside. I grit my teeth as my cock jumps at the feeling of her hot, wet tongue.

"Oh, Sunshine," I moan as she licks around my knot. "Your mouth is like magic and you haven't even taken me in yet."

She beams up at me, giving my cock one last lick before taking me fully into her mouth. I gasp as she starts to work me over, my hands fisting at my sides because I have no idea what to do with them.

My breathing starts to pick up, and my legs start to shake. "Sunshine, as much as I love the feeling of being inside your mouth, I'm not gonna last if you keep going like this," I pant out.

And what does my Little Omega do? She grips my ass cheeks as she starts to bob her head faster, gagging a little as the tip of my cock hits the back of her throat. The sound mixed with the lust in her eyes makes my knot throb.

"Shit, shit, shit," I pant out. "Tia, I'm... fuck..." The feeling of my balls tightening, my knot pulsing, has my brain short-circuiting on me. "Tia," I moan her name loudly as my release takes over me. My cock jerks violently in her mouth as it sends jet after jet of cum down her throat. She swallows everything, even a part of my damn dick as she does it.

My orgasm is so powerful that my hand flings out,

grasping onto the edge of the desk to keep myself from collapsing.

I'm breathing heavily, and my head is spinning as Tia gets off her knees, standing up to cup my face.

"You good, Alpha?" she asks, giving me a sweet smile.

"Good?" I ask her, letting out a little laugh. "I'm more than good, Sunshine. But damn, are you sure you're not a witch too? Because what your mouth just did to me has to be some kind of witchcraft."

Her laugh is so carefree and sexy that I can't help but smile. "Well then, Alpha, let me work a little bit more of my voodoo on you. Let's move this to the bed because I need you inside me."

She takes off her Supergirl outfit and stands before me in only her underwear and bra. "I love that look in your eyes, Finn," she says as she puts her hands behind her back to unclasp her bra. "It makes me feel wanted, needed, and sexy."

I blush as my eyes zero in on her plump breasts as they fall free. "You are," I croak out. "All of those and so much more."

CHAPTER 26

OCTAVIA

My poor, sweet Alpha looks like a nervous wreck as I move to the bed and lay down naked. He hasn't moved from where I just sucked him so good; he came like a hose.

Every time I taste one of my guys, I get a high from their cum. Not as bad as it was when I was in heat, but it's still pretty strong.

And now, I want it in me, him in me as we both cum together for the first time.

"Come," I say, holding out my hand. "I don't bite." I grin. "Yet."

He looks at my hand and takes a deep breath before nodding. He walks over to me slowly, then crawls onto the bed. "You look so perfect right now, Sunshine. Naked on my Spiderman sheets with your hair fanned out on my pillow."

I giggle. "I love you," I tell him.

He smiles. "I love you too." I part my legs, allowing him room between them. He looks down at my dripping pussy and gulps. "I wanna taste you so bad. But I don't have any clue on what to do," he says in a shaky voice.

"It's okay. We can explore other things another time," I tell him softly, sliding my hand down and dipping my fingers into my wet core. I bring them back full of slick and hold them out to him. "But here's a taste to tide you over."

He whimpers, his cock going rock hard again. I grin as he leans forward and sucks them into his mouth. His eyes roll back as he laps at my fingers.

"Now I know why Knox looks like he's on cloud nine every time he tastes you. It's heaven, Sunshine."

"Kiss," I tell him, beckoning him closer with the same finger he just sucked clean.

He fumbles his way closer, apologizing as he moves. He takes his glasses off and sets them on the table next to us. I giggle, then sigh when his body is over mine and our lips meet.

We lay like this for a little while, kissing sweetly, hands exploring until he starts to thrust his cock against my slick folds. He needs me just as much as I need him.

"Are you ready?" I ask him when we pull apart. My lips tingle from all the kissing, and his are red and swollen.

"Kinda," he says with a small smile.

"Just take your time." I cup his cheek. "It doesn't matter how this goes, it will be perfect because it's with you."

He closes his eyes, leaning into my touch before kissing my palm and nodding.

We kiss again, and he moves his hand between us as I open wider for him. He takes his cock and pushes forward, trying to find my entrance. "Wrong hole," I squeak as I feel the tip of his cock moving against my tight ring.

"Oh shit. Fuck, I'm sorry, Sunshine," he says, his eyes going wide, and he looks so embarrassed.

"Hey." I kiss him again. "It's fine. They are kind of close together, and it's pretty slippery down there." I giggle.

"I'm such a loser," he sighs in defeat, hanging his head in shame. "I can't even get my dick inside you! Some Alpha I am."

"Finn," I growl. "Do not talk about yourself that way. You are not a loser! This is all new to you, and I don't expect you to know everything."

"But–" He groans as I reach between us and grab his cock, gripping it hard. I guide it to my entrance, and wrap my legs around him, pressing the heels of my feet into his ass cheeks to push him forward.

"Oh shit. Oh, oh god," he moans as I shove him inside me.

"Alpha," I moan as his thick cock stretches me.

"Sunshine," he groans. "You feel so good."

"Need you," I growl.

"Take me?" he asks with pleading eyes. I can see he's still so afraid of messing this up.

"Roll," I tell him, and he hugs me close, rolling us so he's on his back. "You don't need to worry, my sweet Alpha," I coo. "Let me show you how amazing it can be. Just relax."

I roll my hips, and his eyes roll back as he grips my thighs tightly. I keep doing that for a little while, getting into a steady rhythm. It feels amazing as his cock massages my swollen inner walls, the tip bumping up against the right spot.

My orgasm is building, but I want to wait until the moment I lock down around his knot so we can cum together.

"Tia," he sighs. "I'm so close."

"Me too," I whimper as I start to move my hips faster.

"You're so perfect. You're riding me so good." His praise makes me whine as I race towards that feeling.

His breathing is growing ragged, his eyes wide and frantic. He's gonna cum any second now, and so am I. So as I bring my hips back again, I push a little harder. I moan as I feel his knot push inside, stretching me in the way I love. I scream out his name as he locks in place.

"Tia!" he roars, sounding more like an Alpha than my sweet Finn.

I whimper and whine, moaning and crying out as I cum hard, collapsing on top of him, unable to keep myself upright any longer.

He wraps his arms around me tightly, holding me close, like he never wants to let me go. His cum pumps into me like a never ending river, filling me up until I can feel it leaking out.

"So... was that okay?" I mumble into his chest a little while later after we start to come down from the high.

"Okay?" he chuckles, running his fingers lazily up and down my back. "Sunshine, it was perfection. Also, can we do that again? But this time, I wanna make love to you. I think I can do better."

"Alpha. You can take me all night long if you want," I tell him, moving so I can look at this handsome face.

"I need to bite you. Can I?" he asks, hope written all over his face.

"Of course," I tell him, kissing him. He gives a little thrust up into me, making me have a mini orgasm as I continue to tighten around his cock. He groans, breaking the kiss and moves his mouth to my neck, finding an open spot.

"I know I've said it so many times today, but I'll say it again and again. I love you, Tia," he mumbles against my skin before he bites me. I gasp, cumming hard around his cock. He growls, cumming again. A few seconds later, I can feel him, all his love for me. I can feel how nervous he is but thankful for my patience.

His knot deflates, and he slides out of me, my slick and his cum going with it.

"If my parents weren't coming home in an hour, I would take you up on that offer," he says, then blushes when he sees the mess we made. "Wow."

"Hope Spiderman doesn't mind cum on his face." I giggle, and he bursts out laughing.

We take a little drink and bathroom break before we go again. This time he knows a little bit more about what he's doing. He loses himself once he's inside me and has me cumming three more times before knotting me again. I bite him, marking him as mine too, and the noise he makes will forever be one of my favorites.

We must have fallen asleep because the next thing I know my eyes are snapping open as I hear someone calling out Finn's name.

"Finn, honey!" a woman calls out. "Are you here? I see some comic stuff on the table."

Shit! His parents are home. "Finn," I hiss, tapping his face.

"Five more minutes," he mumbles. "Then I can knot you again, Sunshine."

"As much as I'd love that, we can't. Finn, your parents are home."

His eyes snap open, turning to pure panic.

"Maybe he's in his room?" a male voice says.

"Oh no," he says, frozen in place. "No, no, no–"

"Finn." The door opens, and I seize up as Finn and I both look at each other in horror. "Oh... Oh. Billy!" his mom says, sounding way too excited. "Look! Finn is in bed, with a girl!"

"What?" his dad asks. "Well look at that. That's my boy."

I should want to die of embarrassment, but I burst into giggles, trying to smother them into Finn's chest.

"Get out, please!" he shouts.

"Oh, right. Sorry, honey! Can't wait to meet her!" she says, closing the door behind her.

Finn groans, and I gasp for air from laughing so hard. "So, that's gonna call for therapy," he says.

"Hey, at least the blanket is covering me and we're not knotted together."

"God. That would have made me want to die!" I burst into another fit of laughter.

We get up and shower. Thankfully, he has his own bathroom. When we get out, I start to strip the bed. "Sorry, Spiderman." I giggle.

"I'm sure he enjoyed it," Finn says, giving me a cheeky smile as he pulls on a pair of boxers.

He gives me a pair of sweatpants along with one of his t-shirts, and he puts on the same. Finn in gray sweatpants? Fuck, I need that more often.

"We need to get you some for home," I tell him.

"Really?" he asks. "You like them?"

"Yes, very much." I giggle, eyeing up the way his cock looks in them, and he's not even hard.

We take the dirty sheets and bring them to his laundry room. "I do not want mom touching these. I'm already embarrassed enough."

"Don't be," I tell him. "They seemed pretty cool about it."

"They're easy-going people," he tells me. "Come on, let me go officially introduce you to them... with clothes on."

Turns out, I love his parents. They are super nice. We eat pizza that they ordered and talk about how Finn and I met as well as the others. I tell them about what I want to go to school for and a little bit before starting my family.

When we bring the empty pizza boxes back into the kitchen his mother stops me. "I wanna say thank you."

"For what?" I ask her.

"For picking my son. For loving him like he deserves. He's been waiting for an Omega for a very long time. He was heartbroken every time he came home to visit, telling us it didn't happen for them yet. Eventually, he told me they pulled out of the program. They gave up, and it broke my heart. Made me want to find every snooty little Omega who hurt those boys and tell them off. They aren't like most Alphas, but I don't think that should matter because they have so much to offer. They are really good men, and I wish someone had given them a chance back then. I'm glad you did."

My eyes fill with tears. "I wouldn't have it any other way," I say, wiping at my eyes. "I love all of those men with everything that I am and for exactly who they are. I hate that they had to go through so much pain before they found their happiness, but if they had found someone sooner, then I wouldn't have them. The thought of being without them now physically hurts my heart. It's something I never wanna find out."

"You really are the perfect Omega for them." She smiles sweetly.

"Knox and I will take care of your son. We love him and will never let him want or need for anything."

"Everything happened at the right time. Without you there, I don't know if those boys would ever have admitted their feelings to each other. And you're so supportive of it."

"I just want them to be happy. I don't mind sharing if they are in love with each other. But no one outside my pack." I grin.

"Of course," she giggles.

We talk for a little while longer before they excuse themselves to head to bed, saying a brief hello to Knox when he came to pick us up.

"So. How was it?" Knox asks as soon as we get in the car.

Finn looks at me, an adorable blush taking over his face. "Perfect."

SAWYER

"Pretty girl, are you sure about this?" I ask as we stand in front of Tristan's car.

"Why not?" she asks with a shrug. "It's a car, it can't be that hard."

My brows raise as I let out a snort. "This isn't like riding a golf cart. There's a lot more to it."

"Have you read the driving manual that I gave you last night?" Tristan asks.

We're standing in the middle of an empty parking lot of a new mall that's not set to be open for a few months. Lots of room to teach our Little Omega how to drive.

"I did," she says, biting her lip with slight blush.

"How much of it did you read?" Tristan asks, narrowing his eyes at her.

She lets out a sigh. "Okay, so I fell asleep about forty pages in, and I don't remember much of it."

"Really, Love?" Tristan says. "You love to read, yet you couldn't read a hundred and fifty page book?"

"Listen here, Mr. Sexy Alpha Man. The books I read are full of sexy men with big dicks that make their partners cum like rivers. Oh, and tentacles. Lots of tentacles. Sorry, but knowing how fast I can go in a car and what the lines in the middle of the road mean doesn't interest me."

"But, Love, you need to know that if you wanna go out on the road in a car," he says, running a hand through his hair. "Alright, fine, I can tell you what you need to do today. We're only going to be driving around the parking lot, so we should be fine."

"Yay," Tia says, clapping her hands. "Alright, let's get this show on the road."

She moves over to the driver's side and gets in. Tristan looks to me, and I give him an amused grin. "How much you wanna bet she crashes your car somehow?"

"Screw you," he grumbles. "Have a little faith in our Omega."

I have a lot of faith in our girl for a lot of different things, but Tia doesn't seem very interested in learning how to really drive. I think she wants to try for the sake of saying she tried.

"Alright." Tristan hands her the keys. "It's in park. We keep it in park until we're ready to move, okay?"

"Got it," she says. "That's the gear shift thingie right?" she asks, pointing to the gear stick.

"Yes. There's park, reverse, neutral, and drive."

"Oh, I remember what those do!" she says excitedly. I

stifle a chuckle. *Poor Tris.* Oh well, I'm just along for the ride and to spend time with my Pretty Girl.

"Put the key in and turn it. The engine will start," Tristan instructs her.

She does what she's told, and the car revs to life. "I did it."

"You did." Tristan chuckles. "Now, do you know what the pedals on the floor do?"

"Duh," she says, rolling her eyes. "One is the brake, the other is the gas."

"Do you know which one is which?" I ask.

She looks behind her at me, giving me a devilish look that has my heart racing. I feel like I may need to fear for my life.

"Guess I'm about to find out," she says. She moves too fast for Tristan to stop her, putting the car into drive and flooring it. We lurch forward, Tristan having to catch himself from hitting his head on the dash.

"Whoa there, Love!" Tristan says as Tia slams on the brakes.

"You trying to kill us, Pretty Girl?" I laugh, eyes wide with excitement. We didn't move very far, and there's nothing near us, so we're fine. For now.

"Okay, so left is brake, right is gas," she says, grinning over at a very flustered Tristan. I gotta give the man some credit for his patience with her. If this was Knox or Dom, they would be losing their shit right about now.

"I could have told you that, Love, you just had to ask," Tristan says.

"Where's the fun in that?" Tia giggles.

We spend the next hour driving around the parking lot. I think I have whiplash, but I don't think I've laughed so much in my life. Poor Tristan is gonna need a stiff drink, and maybe Pretty Girl can give him some love to thank him for all his troubles.

Tia only has two speeds, slow as a snail or fast like a crazy person with a death wish.

"Oh look, that little, old lady on the sidewalk just lapped you three times," I tease as we do a simple task of going from point A to point B.

"What old lady?" she asks, looking behind her, not paying attention to where she's going. Her hands move, and the wheel spins making the car lurch. Her foot presses on the gas, and we end up spinning in a circle.

"Tia!" Tristan shouts. I'm laughing my ass off, and Tia is whooping.

"This is fun!" she shouts.

"You're gonna get us killed!"

Tia looks over at Tristan and slows down, seeing the real stress on his face.

She lets out a sigh and brings the car to a stop, putting it in park. "I have a confession. I know how to drive. Well, kinda. I just never could pass the test. I really didn't retain enough of the book to be able to answer enough questions for my learner's permit, but I know the basics. My friends and I used to do what we're doing now. I'm kinda self-taught."

"No way." I laugh. "You're joking right? Because it didn't seem like you knew shit all this past hour."

"It was fun fucking with you two," she says, giving us an adorable smile. "I'm sorry."

"So you know how to drive?" Tristan asks, not sounding convinced.

Tia nods her head, then puts the car back into drive and shows us that she does, in fact, know how to drive. She parks into a parking spot perfectly, and then shows us she can parallel park between two of the trash bins.

"Well," Tristan says. "I guess you don't need me."

Her face falls, and she turns the engine off, unbuckling her seat belt before crawling into Tristan's lap. "I'm sorry I kept the truth from you. I really do want to get my driver's license... someday. Maybe you can help me study? I know you're the best Alpha to help me."

"You really want to learn properly?" he asks.

She nods her head before leaning forward and kissing Tristan. He groans, and the car fills with her sweet perfume.

"What about me, Pretty Girl?!" I pout.

She looks over at me and grins. "You insulted my driving." She sticks her tongue out at me. "And there was no old lady!" That sends me into a burst of laughter as she crawls into the back seat with me. "I think you should drive now."

"Probably a good idea." Tristan chuckles, getting out of the car and moving to the driver's side.

"I'll make it up to you tonight, Alpha. I've been a

naughty Omega, and I think I deserve any punishment you wanna give me," she says in a voice that screams sex.

He growls, looking at her in the rearview mirror, and I groan, my cock growing hard.

"Can I watch?" I plead.

"If Daddy Tristan says it's okay." She flutters her eyelashes like she's some sweet little Omega. *Fuck, I love this girl and her dirty little mind.*

CHAPTER 27

OCTAVIA

"You're really not going to tell me where we're going?" I ask Dom as we drive away from Calling Wood.

"Nope." He grins, not looking away from the road as he takes my hand in his. Butterflies flutter in my belly when he kisses the back of my hand softly before setting it on the arm rest between us.

Life has been pretty relaxed since going home for the weekend. My time with Finn was perfect. Poor guy was so nervous, but he was quick to get over it after the second or third time.

When we left to come home, I got to briefly meet Knox's parents. They were just as sweet as Finn's and also just as supportive of Finn and Knox's relationship. The way Knox showed us off melted my heart, seeing him so proud to be with us.

A part of me still feels bad about tricking the guys and making them think I didn't know how to drive. I mean, it wasn't a lie, I don't have my license, and as much as I think studying with Tristan for my learner's permit might help, I won't hold my breath. I don't need to have my license because we use the carts around Calling Wood, and any time we leave outside the community, one of my guys is always with me. I'm all for being an independent Omega, but the fact is, I *am* an Omega, and mated or not, it's still always a risk to go out on my own. But I don't mind having one of my guys with me at all times because I love being around them. Also, I have Ivy if I ever need some girl time. She might be smaller than most Alphas, but she can hold her own.

And I made it up to Tristan... a few times. With a little help from Sawyer, which made me even more excited for my heat because I want all my men... at the same time. I might only have three holes, but hey, I got two hands too. No one needs to be left out.

My heart is almost complete. The only mate mark I'm missing now is my grumpy bear. Even though he's been a lot less grumpy lately, he's still growly, which I love.

That brings us to now. The truck is packed, and he's taking me somewhere, but he hasn't told me where yet.

He checks on me out of the corner of his eye and chuckles at my pouty lip. "Little One." He shakes his head. "It's not a surprise if I tell you."

"Fine," I huff and lean against his arm.

I end up falling asleep and am woken up sometime later

by a big but gentle hand caressing my face. "Time to wake up, Little Omega. You can sleep more on the plane."

"Plane?" I ask in a groggy voice as I blink open my sleepy eyes to see my Alpha looking down at me.

"Yes, Little One." He grins. "Come on." He scoops me up, my arms going around his neck to hold myself close to him. I snuggle my face into his neck, take a deep breath of his woodsy scent and sigh.

"I love it when you smell me, Little One," he growls.

"I love how you smell," I mumble against his skin before giving him a light kiss.

I hear the engine before I see the plane. My head lifts from Dom's shoulder to see a small private plane on an air strip.

"What is this?" I ask, looking at him with wide eyes.

"This is my plane," he grumbles. "And I'm using it to take you away for the weekend."

He carries me up the small steps into a very nice looking seating area.

Setting me down on one of the seats, he says nothing as he leaves the plane again. I take a moment to look around. *What the heck is going on? How did I not know he owned a plane?!*

I guess the same way I didn't know Sawyer owned a boat. I'm thinking it's safe to assume that all my guys have money of some sort and just don't like to flash it around.

It's their choice not to mention it, but I can understand why they don't. I know they know I'm not with them for anything else but them as a person. But some Omegas want the best in life, and they tend to gravitate towards wealthy Alphas.

That's not me. I don't want money, fame, or fortune. I want someone who loves me and can care for me when I need it. And I want to be able to offer the same thing back.

Dom comes back a minute later with all of our bags. "Sorry about that. I wanted to bring them on myself to make sure nothing was left behind."

He sits down in the seat in front of me, and I just stare at him, blinking.

"Dominic," I say.

"Yes?" he asks.

"Care to explain?"

"Right." He sighs, running his hand through his dark brown hair and scratching his beard with the other. "My family has money. I have money. I don't like using it, but this plane is the family plane, and I saw an opportunity to bring you somewhere special to me. I want our first time to be special. I know it sounds stupid, but I just... I didn't want to be around the others when I get you alone. I wanted you all to myself for the first time."

My body softens, and I give him a sweet smile as I get up and crawl into his lap. "I don't think it's stupid. I think it's sweet. I love that you wanted to do this for us, and I can't wait for you to take me... wherever the heck we're going." I giggle.

"So you're not mad at me?" he asks, his eyes flicking with worry as he grips my hips.

"No, Alpha," I purr, leaning forward and giving him a

heated kiss that has his cock growing underneath me. I grind down on him, my body ready for him right now.

"Little One," he groans deeply. "We need to be in the air first."

"I need you," I whine. I've waited for this man for as long as my body can take. I need him, his knot, his big hands wrapped around my thighs as he pins me down and devours my pussy. The thought has me perfuming like crazy.

Dom curses and the pilot pops his head out to tell us we're ready to take off.

"Sit," he says, picking me up and putting me in the seat next to me. He buckles me up, then himself.

I watch him, my body humming with need. *God, he's so sexy.*

"Stop looking at me like that," he grumbles.

"Like what?" I ask.

"You know," he says, not looking at me as he shifts in his seat and adjusts his pants.

"I'm sorry, but I'm also not. You're sexy, and knowing that I finally get to have your fat, Alpha cock deep inside me makes me a little horny," I say, acting nonchalant.

"Fuck's sake," Dom chokes out. "Dirty Little Omega, you are."

"Just you wait." I giggle.

I'm forced to sit in my seat until we're in the air, but the moment the pilot tells us it's okay to move about the cabin, Dom is ripping the seat belt off me as he drops to his knees.

"Dom." I suck in a breath as he rips off my shorts.

"You don't need these. Too cold where we're going

anyway." He grabs my legs, bending them at the knees and opening me wide. "Fuck me," he growls. "You're drenched, Little One. All of this is mine."

"Alpha," I cry out as I feel his tongue start to lap up my slick. My hands grip the leather armrests as I toss my head back.

"I've been waiting for this. For you. Do you have any idea how many times I wanted to just bend you over, shove my head between your legs, and eat you until you've soaked my face?"

"You should have," I whimper as he thrusts two, thick fingers inside me.

"I should have," he agrees. "And now, I plan to, every chance I get," he promises as he goes back down, sucking my clit between his lips as he fucks me with his fingers.

I'm gushing around him, my slick flowing onto his hand.

"That's right, Little One. Drip all over my hand, then I'm gonna make you lick it clean."

"Dom," I moan, my climax building to new heights. "It's too much," I say, tossing my head back and forth as he sucks and licks, his fingers reaching just the right place. I try to move away, but he holds me down with his free arm.

"Cum for me, Little One. Don't fight it," he growls against my clit, the vibration making me scream as my orgasm washes over me. My body tenses up as my pussy grips his fingers. "That's it, squeeze my fingers like you wish it was my knot. Fuck, look at all this slick, all for me." He removes his fingers and uses his sinful tongue to clean me up.

My heart is pounding, my head is spinning, and I'm gasping for air.

"Such a good girl, doing as your Alpha says," he praises, making me whimper. "Now, look at the mess you made," he says. My eyes flutter open to see him holding up his hand soaked with my slick. "Clean me, Little Omega. Taste how good you are."

I open my mouth, allowing him to put his fingers in. I suck them clean before taking care of the rest of his hand. I take my time, loving the pure hunger in his eyes.

"So fucking perfect," he growls, getting to his feet. My eyes find a very large lump in his pants. I whimper, my body heating up. "Not here," he says, my eyes flicking up to his. "I'd end up knotting you here, and I want to take my time with you."

"Then let me take care of you," I say, sliding to my knees. I grab at his pants, but he takes a hold of my hand. I look up at him to see an unsure look on his face. I wish he could see how I see him. "Please," I whisper. "Let me please my Alpha." It's a desire all Omegas have. We never want to see our Alphas needing for anything. Also, I love their cocks, their cum, their knots. It's not a hardship for me to be down on my knees with his dick down my throat. Fuck, the idea has me dripping again.

"You want my cock, Little Omega?" he asks, and I nod with a whimper. "Then take me out. Do with it as you please."

I'm quick to remove his pants, letting them drop to his feet. His cock bobs free, hitting him in the belly, the tip already leaking pre cum. My eyes trail down his long, thick cock. He's hard, and running up the whole length of him is a pulsing vein. Putting my hands on his thick, hairy thighs, I lean forward to run my tongue up the vein.

"Fuuuck," Dom groans, loud and deep.

I preen at the fact that I'm pleasing my Alpha. When I get to the tip, I suck it between my lips, moaning as his flavor hits my tongue. I need more, so I take him as far as I can, but he's big. Big enough that I'm able to wrap both hands around his cock while still hitting the back of my throat.

"Tia," Dom growls. "Your mouth feels so good. Just like that, Little One," he says as I grip him tight and start to bob my head.

The horny little Omega in me takes over. I suck him until he's cursing and his knees are shaking. He grabs a handful of my hair, gripping it hard as his hips start to thrust, shoving his cock further down my throat, making me gag. I run my hands up his belly, and he freezes. I whimper as I feel the tension rolling off him in waves.

"Your cock tastes so good," I moan as I pull back to gasp for air before taking him in again, trying to distract him from the unease he feels.

"I bet my cum tastes better," he grunts as I move my hands from his belly. With one hand I jerk him off, and the other I play with his knot. "Fuck. Tia, Fuck!"

He's about to cum, and I'm a greedy little bitch. So I give his knot a squeeze. He grips my hair almost painfully, but it just makes me moan as he holds me there, roaring out my name as he cums hard down my throat. I'm desperate to get every last drop, trying to swallow with every burst, but there's just too much. I choke, and he pulls me back. Gasping for air, I look up at him panting, trying to catch my breath. He looks down at me like I'm the most precious thing in the world, making me whimper.

"You really are perfect for us aren't you, Little One?" he coos, cupping my cheek. Using his thumb, he wipes at the cum dripping down the sides of my mouth and shoves it into my mouth. I suck his thumb clean, loving the growl that sends a shiver down my spine and slick leaking from my core.

He pulls me to my feet, bringing me to the little bathroom, and we both clean up. He goes to one of the bags, grabbing me a pair of leggings and a warm, fuzzy sweater.

"Where are we going that I'm going to need these?" I giggle as I change. I sigh, snuggling into the soft fabric.

"Someplace with snow," he says.

"SNOW!" I gasp, my face lighting up as I launch myself into his arms. He grunts before giving me a low chuckle. I kiss him hard as he brings us back to the seats. "I can't wait."

We take a seat on a little couch, and he pulls me onto his lap, wrapping his arms around me. "It's going to be a few hours, so let's watch something to pass the time."

"I could think of better things to do to pass the time," I purr, earning myself a growl.

"As much as I'd love to, I don't want the pilot to hear your cries again. Those are mine," he growls, and I shiver, my face heating up with the realization that people other than our pack heard us.

"So, I know we didn't have sex, but does this still count as joining the mile high club?" I ask, grinning at him.

"You naughty, little Omega," he chuckles, giving my butt a tap.

"Yes, but I'm your naughty Omega." I giggle, putting my head on his chest.

He holds me tight and kisses the top of my head. "Yes. Mine."

"Wow," I breathe out in awe, taking in the beautiful little cabin as we make our way up the driveway. Turns out, Dom took me to the Colorado Mountains. There's a fresh blanket of snow covering the ground, making the mountains behind the cabin and the trees look like a winter wonderland.

"So, the plane may have been my parents, but this cabin is mine. It used to be my grandparents, but they left it to me when they passed. The guys and I are the only ones who ever come here," Dom says as he brings the rental truck to a stop.

"Can we come here every holiday?" I ask, not taking my eyes off the sight before me.

"Anything you want, Little One," he says, reaching

behind us into the back seat. "Here," he says, handing me a big, puffy coat. "It's a lot colder here than it is in Cali."

With a big smile, I put the coat on. I'm about to ask about boots when Dom gets out and comes to my side. He opens the door, unbuckles me, then scoops me up into his arms. I giggle as he carries me up the steps. He takes a set of keys out of this pocket and unlocks the door.

"It's nothing big or fancy, but I like it," Dom says, placing me on my feet.

"I love it!" I say, taking a look around. The inside is mostly made of wood. The walls are logs; the couch, tables, and chairs are all made from wood. "It looks cozy. I hate big open spaces anyway. Omega, remember?"

"How could I ever forget, Little One?" He grins. "I'm going to grab our bags; feel free to check the place out."

And I do. I start off in the living room, admiring all the craftsmanship. Next is the dining room with a big wooden table, and the kitchen is a nice size with a fridge, sink, and stove.

I take off up a set of stairs in the middle of the cabin to the second floor. All the rooms seem to be up here, only four and a bathroom. But I'm sure the guys won't mind sharing when we all come up here.

All of them look almost the same, like typical guest rooms, but the faint smell of apple cider, cotton candy, and bubble gum tells me who each room belongs to.

Then the last one, the one with the big bed that could fit my whole pack, this one's Dom's. His scent is strong in here like it's had years to soak into every inch of the room.

"This is where we'll be sleeping," Dom says as he enters the room behind me and places the bags on the floor by the dresser.

"It looks comfy," I say.

"Don't worry, Little Omega, you can go steal something from the other rooms and make a cozy little nest in here if you want. But I did make sure to grab something from each of the guys for you, so you have something that smells like them."

My heart flutters, and I step up to him on my tip toes. Wrapping my arms around his neck, I kiss him. "Thank you for thinking of me."

"I always think of you, Little One. You're a permanent resident in my mind," he growls, kissing me deeply. "Come on, I'm gonna make you something to eat, then I'll chop some wood for the fireplace." Dom scoops me up into his arms, making me giggle.

"I can walk, you know." I smile up at him.

"I know," he grunts, not bothering to put me down. I just shake my head before placing it on his shoulder. He sets me down on the countertop before getting busy in the kitchen. "I had the caretaker come and stock the place with enough food for the weekend," he says, grabbing a frying pan and placing it on the stove before rummaging through the fridge.

"You have a caretaker?" I ask, raising a brow at his back.

"Yes," he says, turning around with a pile of ingredients stacked in his arms. He carries them over to the counter and dumps them. "The guys and I are only really here two times a year. A week for Christmas and a month in the summer. I have people come here and clean, get the place ready and stocked up. Saves us time."

I nod my head in understanding as I watch my sexy Alpha work. I love to eat, so watching him make me one of my favorite meals, chicken tacos with mango salsa, makes me clench my thighs together.

"Little One," he growls, lifting his gaze to mine slightly with a smirk on his lips.

"What?" I blush. "I'm sorry but watching you... well, do anything, turns me on." I shrug unapologetically.

He chuckles and gets back to work. I just sit there and watch. Once supper is ready, he raises one of the tacos up for me to try. I take a bite and moan. "Damn, that's so good."

"You really are going to make it hard to keep my hands off you this weekend, aren't you?" he growls.

"Isn't that the point?" I grin.

"Eat," he says, picking me up off the counter to set me on my feet. He taps me on the ass, pushing me in the direction of the table. I take a seat, and he brings over my food. We sit together and eat, not saying much but giving each other naughty looks every so often.

"Those were really good." I sigh as I lean back in my seat and pat my food baby.

"Seeing you appreciate food like you do makes my cock hard, Little Omega," he says with a rumble in his chest, and a look of approval in his eyes.

"Show me." I try to joke, but it comes out as a whimper.

"Later," he says. "You need your food to settle. And we need wood for the fire."

After putting on appropriate clothing for the weather and the boots Dom had someone get for me, we head outside and behind the cabin.

I sit on a little cord of already chopped wood and smile as I take in the beautiful sight before me. The sun is setting, but it's still closer on the lighter side out here, so the way the colors look on the mountains are breathtaking.

Grunting and groaning draws my attention to my Alpha. My lips part as I suck in a small gasp. Dom has his jacket off, his plaid shirt rolled up to his elbows as he stands in front of a chopping block. He brings the axe up over his head before letting out a sexy, manly grunt as he brings it down, splitting the wood in half.

I watch as he continues to chop more wood, and with every swing, every noise, every wipe of his brow, I get slicker and slicker.

After about the fifteenth piece, I decide I can't take it anymore.

"Dom!" I shout as he tosses the piece he just cut into the pile of wood. He looks over at me, wiping his brow again. He must see the look in my eyes, the need, the hunger for him because he lets out a growl that almost sends me over the edge before stalking over to me.

My eyes widen, and I let out a little squeal of excitement before taking off towards the front door to the cabin.

"Little Omega. Running just makes me wanna fuck you harder," he calls out.

Fuck, yes please! I almost make it inside when he grabs me around the waist, bringing my ass to his very hard cock.

"Looks like the big bad Alpha caught himself a little Omega. Whatever shall I do with you?" he rumbles in my ear.

"Eat me," I breathe out in a plea.

He growls and picks me up. Opening the door, he slams it closed as soon as we're inside. My heart is pounding in my ears, my pussy throbbing with the need to be touched by him.

He tosses me on the couch, rips off my pants, and gives me a repeat of what we did on the plane.

After he's made me cum three times and I've almost passed out from so much stimulation, he covers me with a blanket from the chair.

"Rest, Little One," he says, kissing my forehead. "I'll go get the wood and light us a fire."

I almost protest, demanding he stays here in my arms, but I'm too tired to argue. My eyes flutter close, and I drift off for a little bit, waking when I hear the crackle of the fire.

"Sleep, Little Omega," Dom rumbles as he brushes some hair from my face.

"But I want you," I whisper, half asleep.

"I'm going to go shower, then I'll be back." He kisses me softly before he's up and gone. I close my eyes again, sighing as I feel the warmth of the fire.

We still have tomorrow, we can have sex then.

CHAPTER 28

OCTAVIA

I wake up no longer on the couch, smiling when I feel the strong, warm arms of my Alpha. I wiggle back into him, pushing my ass into his hard length.

"Little Omega. If you don't stop with that sinfully, sexy ass, I'm gonna cum in my pants and embarrass myself," he says, his voice raspy with sleep.

"That's okay, I'd just help you clean up," I purr, wiggling my ass again. He puts his hands on my hips to stop me.

"Naughty girls get spankings," he warns.

"Have you talked to Tristan yet? That's not much of a punishment for me." I giggle as I roll over, bringing my face to his. Moving my hand to his cock, I give him a hard squeeze through his sleep pants before moving in for a kiss. He groans but turns his head away from me.

"Morning breath," he says. "I'm gonna go brush my

teeth." He gets up out of bed, but bends over to kiss my fore-head before heading to the bathroom, leaving me alone in this big bed.

Sitting up, I frown in the direction Dom takes off in. That was odd. He's never cared about morning breath before. None of my guys do.

Not wanting to make a big deal out of it, I get up and get dressed before going downstairs.

We eat and talk, and everything seems normal. That is until we get hot and heavy after we clean up. He eats me out on top of the table, but as soon as I move to climb him like a tree, to beg him to take me to bed and knot me, he's suggesting we go outside in the snow before setting me back on the table and taking off to get changed.

I sit there, horny and frustrated. But this is our time together, and there's still lots of time to have sex.

After getting into the proper clothing, we go outside for a little walk. He shows me the pond, saying it's perfect for the summer. Next, he takes me to a little tree house his grandfather built for him when he was a kid.

I almost burst out crying when he said he hopes our sons or daughters will love it just as much as he did.

We walk hand in hand as he shows me more of the property. I steal as many kisses as I can, loving the taste of him. But anytime things start to get hot and heavy, he puts a stop to it.

Now, I'm horny, annoyed, and confused because I thought this was our weekend to take that next step, to mark each other.

Bending over, I gather snow and pack it into a ball. Dom is in front of me, and without thinking, I chuck it at the back of his head. He stops, and my eyes go wide.

I'm sorry but I'm also kinda not. He's being weird today.

"Did you just throw a snowball at my head?" he asks, slowly turning to look at me with a raised brow.

"Yes," I whimper, hoping he doesn't hear my heart pounding in my chest right now.

"That's it," he says. But I don't get a chance to react before he's picking me up and tossing me into a big pile of snow.

He bursts out laughing, and I shriek as the snow starts to melt against my skin.

"You're an ass!" I shout back, but I'm laughing too.

"You started it, Little One." He grins as I stand up and brush myself off.

"And now, I'm gonna finish it." I grab another handful of snow and chuck it at him.

We end up having a snowball fight, running around the cabin as we duck and dive out of the way.

When we're done, we end up laying in the snow, panting to catch our breaths, bellies sore from laughing so hard.

"Look," I say, making a snow angel. He chuckles and makes one himself before rolling over in the snow to look at me.

"Thank you for coming here with me."

"I wouldn't want to be anywhere else," I say, meaning it.

We kiss for a little bit, and I feel my belly starting to

flutter with need. But like every other time we've kissed today, he stops it.

I try not to pout as we go inside. We change out of our wet clothes and into sleep wear. We eat supper, then cuddle in front of the fire.

This is our last night, and it's already late. We have to catch the plane back tomorrow because we have school on Monday.

"Come on, Little One," Dom says, picking me up. He carries me to the room, and by the time my back meets the bed my clothes are off, and I'm grinding against him, needing that release only he can give me.

I climb on top of him, kissing him until we're both moaning and panting. I move down to give him one of the best blowjobs I've ever given, not even bothering to try and take his clothes off, just filled with the desperate need for my Alpha's cum.

He cums hard, a roar of release that has me dripping slick as I greedily swallow everything he gives me.

He flips me over, taking care of that mess himself until I'm a sobbing mess on the bed. By the time we're done, we're both dripping in sweat, panting like we swam the length of lake and back with no breaks.

"I need to pee," I tell him, getting out of bed. He mumbles something as I take off into the bathroom.

This is it! I'm gonna finally get to be with the man I love. Mate him, and then we can all officially be a pack.

I'm quick to pee, hopping into the shower to clean up quick before going back to the room. My smile drops when I see Dom laying in bed, a fake as hell snore coming from him. I frown and take a moment, remembering everything today.

Then it hits me. He's not ready. Any time it comes to taking it to the next step, to the point that involves all of our clothes being removed, he shuts it down.

My heart hurts, but not because he's holding back. It's because he still thinks so low of himself even after I've told him a million times how sexy I think he is.

It doesn't matter how many times I tell him, I can't change how he feels about himself; that's something *he* needs to do.

The best I can do is give him my love, be supportive, and keep telling him how much I love how he looks.

So, I do something that hurts to do. I hold back the tears, and climb into bed. Kissing his cheek, I whisper goodnight before turning my back to him, and trying my hardest not to cry.

I wish my words were enough. I wish he could see how I see him, how I love him. I wish he knew how much I admire him. He loves hard and cares so much. He's everything I could ever want in an Alpha. My Alpha. And as an Omega, it pains me not to be able to take that pain from my Alpha. To help him see his worth. Because he's worthy of my love, my body, and my soul.

The next morning is awkward, and we aren't fooling anyone. He's been quiet and reserved. He won't talk to me, won't even look my way other than a kiss on the top of the head and a lingering touch like he's pissed at himself for how he's acting. It's like he wants me to know he still cares without having to face his feelings.

The plane ride was the same. We watched a movie, and I napped in his arms to pass the time.

Once Dom gets in the truck after loading our bags up and we're ready to go home, I decide that we can't go back home like this. I'm dying inside, and I miss my Dom.

"It's okay," I tell him as he stares out the front window, not meeting my eye. "I understand. I never want you to feel like you have to do something you're not ready for or uncomfortable with."

He lets out a harsh laugh that has me flinching back. "Okay? You think it's *okay* that I'm such a fucking pathetic Alpha that I can't even get naked in front of my Omega without feeling disgusted with myself? You think it's *okay* that I can't even do the one fucking thing I'm designed to do, knot and mate my Omega?" He shakes his head, and my heart breaks at his words. I bite the inside of my cheek to hold back the sob that is desperate to slip out.

"You are better off without me. Everyone is. I'm not the Alpha you deserve, Tia."

"Don't say that. Dom, I love everything about you," I say, my voice cracking. I just wanna crawl into his lap and shake him, kiss him, pour all my love into him. It feels like I can't breathe, like I'm having a heart attack.

"You don't need to say shit to make me feel better, Tia. I know you're amazing, and loving, and caring, and would never have the heart to tell me what you truly think. You're too good to do that. But don't tell me it because you think it's what I want to hear."

He starts the truck, and I turn to face out the window. With my hand over my mouth to hold back my sobs, tears stream down my face.

After an hour into the drive, I feel numb. *Is this really happening right now?* Did a weekend that was supposed to get me ready for the rest of my life turn out to be the thing that takes everything away from me?

When we pull up to Calling Wood gates, Dom finally speaks.

"Tia," he says, his voice sounding so broken. I look over at him and suck in a breath. His eyes are red, tear stains running down his cheeks. "I'm so fucking sorry for how I acted."

A sob bursts out as he pulls over onto the side of the road. I crawl into his lap, and he holds on to me like he's afraid I'll disappear. We cry together, and fuck if my heart doesn't shatter into pieces.

"I love you," he says when I pull back. He cups my face, wiping the tears from my cheeks. "I love you so fucking much it hurts. It scares the shit out of me because I felt for so damn long that no one would want me. There's only so many dirty looks and mocking laughs a person can take before they start to see themselves as the world sees them. Then you came along, this little spitfire, take no shit Omega.

You made us all fall hard and fast for you after we gave up hope. You helped each of my brothers heal and see their worth. I'm so fucking damaged that every time you looked at me with hunger, with love, with anything other than repulsion, I think it was too good to be true. That you were just being nice because of how fucking amazing you are. I want to see myself how you look at me. I really fucking do."

"But you're just not there, yet," I say, giving him a watery smile as more tears flow free. "It's okay, Dom. I'll be here for you, with you, as long as it takes. I'll NEVER give up on you. Never."

"But your heat is any day now. I don't wanna miss it." He lets out a mock laugh. "Actually, maybe our first time should be during your heat. You'll be too much in a haze to really see what I look like."

I'm about to protest when someone honks behind us. He lets out a sigh. "We should get going."

I crawl back into my seat, and he takes my hand as we continue down the road.

We pull up into our driveway and see another car. It's not any of my guys. "What the..." Dom says, looking around, then he curses. "You have got to be fucking kidding me."

"What?" I ask, "What's wrong?"

"Just wait here. My parents are here, I gotta get rid of them."

"Your parents?"

"They are assholes, not people I want you around. You're too good for them, Little One. Just... just wait here."

Dom gets out of the car and heads over to the man and

woman who are peeking into our house. *What the hell?* There's a woman standing there with them, looking like she would rather be anywhere else but here.

Rolling down the window a little, I try and listen to what they are saying. *Yes, I'm snooping, sue me.*

"Mom. Dad. What are you doing here?" Dom asks as he steps up to the older couple.

"Dominic, honey. Is that any way to greet your parents?" his mother asks.

"Sorry. But you gave me no notice that you were planning on coming here for a visit," he says, running a hand over his face. He's stressed. It makes my skin itchy, and a whine slips free. I hate seeing him like this.

"Do we need to have a reason to see our son?" his father asks.

"Look, now is not the best time. Can you please just tell me why you're here?"

"Can we go inside?" his mom asks.

"No. Like I said, now is not a good time. And who is this?" Dom asks, frowning at the girl who gives him a snooty look as she looks him up and down, not impressed. That gets a low growl out of me. How fucking dare she look at *my* Alpha like that. *Rude.*

She's got her black hair tied up into a ponytail with a black and white pantsuit on.

"That's what we came here to talk to you about. We think that you've had your fun here at this little school, but it's time for you to come home now. We know you don't have a major, so there's no real loss if you were to leave. We gave you four years to find an Omega, but it's clear that's never going to happen. So, how about you come home? This is Cindy, her parents work with your father. She would be the perfect wife for you."

I'm sorry, are my ears hearing this right? Is this lady for real? Rage starts to fill my body, and I see red.

But then this Cindy chick rolls her eyes and looks at Dom's mother and says, "He has a pack, right? It's not just him, I hope." She looks back at Dom and gives him a fake smile. "I'm sure you're a nice guy, you're just... not my type."

Oh hell fucking no! Nope, not happening. *Shouldn't have opened your mouth, bitch.*

I'm out of the car and storming up to them in seconds.

DOMINIC

I've never hated myself more in my life than I do right now. Not only did I fuck up my weekend with the girl I love more than life itself, but I made her fucking cry because I'm a selfish, insecure bastard.

I didn't mean to be so harsh back at the airport, but I was so on edge from how I was back at the cabin. I wanted her so fucking bad every second we were there. It took everything in my not to strip her down and rut into her, but every time we came close to having sex, I chickened out. I let my past rot my brain and my insecurities tell me that the moment I was bare to her, fully naked, she wouldn't see me the same way. She would be turned off and not want me anymore.

I know it's stupid. I know she loves me, I can see it in her eyes. And the way she's always perfuming just by one of my growls or the way I look at her when all I can think about is taking her sweet, sexy body makes it so damn obvious, but sometimes the mind just wants to see you suffer. I have a lot I still need to work on, but she didn't deserve how I snapped at her.

Knowing I made her cry, made her flinch, broke something in me. I don't cry, ever, but knowing I caused my Omega pain... fuck, it was just too much to keep in.

After I opened up to her a little bit a few minutes ago, I vowed to myself never to let her think for even a moment that I don't love her, that I don't want her.

What I didn't expect was for my parents to be here when we came back. I haven't seen them in a while. I don't like them because they've always made sure to remind me how worthless I was, even if it was in their own fucked up nice way. Like right now.

Are they for real? Do they really think I'm going to just drop my life and go home to marry some random woman. A woman who's looking at me just like all the Omegas who rejected my pack. Just like every girl who's looked at me.

Every girl but my Little One. My Omega.

Speaking of my Omega, the truck door slams, and she makes her way over here like a little, red haired tornado.

"Hi," she says to my mom with a fake smile, then looks to this Cindy girl. "First off, fuck you. Yes, he has a pack, my fucking pack. Because Dom is *mine*."

A rush of pride fills me at how she just claimed me as hers. I stand there, trying to hide the shocked look on my face. On the other hand, I also can't help but smirk as my little spitfire goes off on them.

She looks to my mother again. "Hi, I'm the Omega you think your son can't seem to get." Tia laughs and shakes her head. "You really are such a peach, aren't you?" I snort at that. "No, he's not coming home with you to marry this bitch. You don't seem to respect your son as a person who has his own mind or make his own choices, and that's fucking sad."

My mother gasps. "How dare you!"

"Like this." Tia snaps, then takes the glasses off my mother's face and tosses them at this Cindy chick. "Here, you must need these because I think you're having an issue with your eyesight if you can't see Dom for who he is, which is a hot as fuck Alpha by the way. I personally fucking gush like a damn river every time I look at him. And his personality? It's just the cherry on top of the beefcake that he is. You wish you could have someone like Dom. But honey, with *your* personality, the only thing you're gonna get is a dry vag."

A shocked gasp slips free, and I try to cover it up with a laugh.

Cindy sneers at Tia, raising her hand to slap her, but I reach out and grab her wrist before she can. "Don't you fucking dare," I growl. "I would never hurt a woman, but I'm not opposed to holding your arms behind your back while my Omega has a crack at you."

Cindy huffs, pulling her hand free.

"Dominic!" my father booms.

"No! Don't even. I'm not coming home. This is my home, with my pack. With Tia, my Omega. Yeah, that's right, I have an Omega, in spite of your lack of support and faith. So take this prude, and leave my property before I call the cops."

"Don't do this, Dominic," my mother says. "If you do, you're cut off. No more money from us."

"Do it," I shout back. "I don't even use your damn money, never have. I have my own that grandma and grandpa left me. Just go."

Turning my back to them, I ignore my mother's outburst as my father drags her away. My heart is pounding, and all the blood in my body has rushed to my cock from hearing my Little One defend me like that.

I'm done letting my self-doubt hold me back from being with my girl in every way I crave to be. She wants me, and I'm gonna give her exactly what she's been asking for.

"Fuck, Little One," I growl. "Seeing you get all worked up over me like that, it makes me fall in love with you all over again."

"I can't believe them! What they were saying, gah." She brushes her wild, red hair back from her face as she huffs in anger. "I love you, Dom. So damn much! And seeing them disrespect you like that, it made me all growly and whatever," she mutters, looking away with a blush.

I grab her chin, forcing her to look at me. "I'm done hiding from you, Little One," I growl, feeling myself grow more feral by the second.

Her eyes flash with heat, and she lets out a whimper as her perfume hits me hard. "You are?"

"I am. But Little Omega, I'm holding on by a string at the moment. I've been holding myself back from you for far too long. I need you. I need to be inside you, to fuck you, knot you, consume you," I say, chest heaving as I try to stay in control, the primal Alpha in me wanting to take over.

"Then do it," she breathes. "I'm yours, Alpha. Take me."

"Then run, Little One," I say, unlocking the door behind her, throwing it wide open. "Because when I catch you, I'm never letting you go."

She lets out a surprised whine, eyes going wide, her slick potent in the air. She turns around, taking off into the house.

Stepping inside, I slam the door and lock it behind me. My blood is pumping, my cock throbbing. The need to take my Omega, to mark her and make her mine is soul consuming.

"I'm gonna count to three, Little One," I call out, taking my shoes off and working my belt buckle. "Then you're mine." I start to walk into the house, her perfume thick around me, throwing me off. "One," I growl, finding her shirt on the ground, and stepping over it. I head further into the house and find her pants. "Two..." Licking my lips, I keep going, but when I see her panties on the ground, I pick them up. They're fucking drenched in her slick. Bringing it to my nose, I inhale deeply, my eyes rolling back, and a savage growl rips from my throat. "Three."

Now, I'm a man on a mission, my nose working over time trying to find her. I check every room, but the little vixen isn't in there, so I circle back to my room, where her scent is the strongest.

Standing in my doorway, I concentrate, listening for her. When I hear a little whimper coming from my closet, I grin like a wolf who's found his prey.

Taking a few steps back out of my room, I go next door to Sawyer's room and head into his closest. His connects with mine, so I move his clothes out of the way and find the door that's hidden back there.

I'm careful not to make any noise as I open it. Her perfume is crazy strong. Not only is she turned on, but I can smell her excitement and fear too. *My Little One loves to be prey, I see.*

"Gotcha," I say, grabbing a handful of her hair and pulling her to me. She lets out a scream that turns into a needy whimper. "Now, what do I do with you?" I purr, licking up the side of her neck, groaning as I taste her sweat and the slight hint of toasted coconuts.

"Anything you want," she moans as I grip her hair tighter. Smashing my lips to hers, I give her a bruising kiss that makes her knees give out.

I grab her by the waist with my arm, her back still to my front, and pick her up. Bursting through my closet door, I take the few steps over to my bed and toss her onto it.

She bounces a bit before she scrambles onto her back, propping herself up on her arms.

"So you want me, Little One?" I ask as I start to unbutton my pants.

"Yes." She nods frantically as she watches my pants hit

the ground, boxers with it, as I take my thick, hard cock into my hand. I slowly stroke myself, loving how her pupils are wide and lust filled.

"Are you sure?" I ask, letting go of my length. It slaps against my belly, getting my shirt wet with pre cum.

"Yes," she whimpers, watching me unbutton my shirt. I'm doing a damn good job at acting because even though I look confident as I stare down at my goddess of an Omega - her creamy skin on display, her red hair wild and untamed, her fucking curvy hips and luscious breasts that make my cock twitch- I'm scared as hell right now as I take my shirt off, revealing myself fully for the first time.

"Dom," she moans, falling back onto the bed. Her eyes roam my body, and I break out into a sweat. But when she brings her hand down to her pussy and starts to play with her clit, looking at me like I'm the hottest Alpha she's ever seen, it all melts away.

She doesn't see a fat, ugly man. In her eyes, I'm perfect, and I want, so badly, to see myself as she does. Maybe with time, but for right now, this is enough. As long as she wants me, it's enough, for now. But I will work on my self worth so I can be the best person I can be, for not only me but for her too.

"Alpha. I need you. Fuck, you're so sexy. I need you to touch me, fuck me, claim me. Knot, now."

"I'm all yours, Little One," I snarl, grabbing her ankles and yanking her to me. She yelps as she falls back. "I'd never hurt you, ever, so if I'm being too rough or you want me to stop, say red, okay?"

"Okay," she whispers.

With her approval, everything in me snaps. All the doubts about anything and everything are gone, replaced by her. Only her.

With a growl full of far too many emotions, I don't want to debunk, I throw her legs over my shoulders and lift up her back end. Grabbing a handful of her ass cheeks, I hold her in place as I line my cock up with her dripping pussy. Then I thrust into her with one hard, brutal thrust.

"Dom!" she shouts, her eyes rolling back as her pussy clamps around me. I lose all sense of who I am and start to fuck her hard and raw.

The snarls that leave me only make her soak my cock harder. "God, Little One," I growl. "So fucking perfect, so fucking *mine*!"

"Yours!" she cries out. "Always yours."

I fuck her into the bed until she's screaming my name, gushing around my cock as she grips me like a vice. The look of pure bliss on her face as she climaxes, like I'm her fucking hero, is the moment I know I'm hers a hundred percent. This girl owns me in every way imaginable.

"I want to fill you with my cum, Little One," I growl. "I want you so full it's leaking out of you for weeks. I want to put a baby in there. Not now, but someday."

"Yes," she moans. "I need your cum, Alpha. Please."

"Not yet," I say, pulling out of her. I flip her and pull her onto her hands and knees. Gripping her hips, I thrust back into her, her back arching as my cock fills her completely. I've never felt anything like this before, pure ecstasy.

Grabbing her hair, I pull her flush to me, my knot bumping against her opening as I thrust up into her. "You want my knot, Little Omega? You want me to stretch this perfect pussy as I lock inside you, making us one."

"Please," she begs.

"I will, Little one," I say, grazing my teeth against her neck. "But I want you to watch as I finally own you." We both look in the mirror that I have on the other side of the room.

She's never looked so gorgeous. Her body is flushed, so covered in sweat that it's soaking her hair line as her chest heaves for each breath.

"Alpha," she says with so much love it's my undoing. I growl, and at the same time that I thrust my knot deep inside her, I clamp my teeth down into her neck.

I roar, cumming so hard that I black out for a moment. Tia screams so loud her voice breaks. Her body starts to thrash in my hold as she cums again, but this one keeps going and going, milking my knot as I send streams of hot, thick cum deep inside her.

She's mine now, it's official.

Octavia Lockheart was an unexpected blessing in our lives. She saw a pack of broken men who were convinced they had no worth, and slowly, one by one, she put us back together, showing us we were worthy of love and acceptance. And I know for a fact that if it weren't for this woman, our Omega, we would still be those lost and broken men for the rest of our lives.

Removing my teeth, I lick my mark clean. She moans, another orgasm taking over as I move us to lie down.

"Fuck," I hiss, my cock almost hurting from how tight she's gripping me.

"Dom," she whimpers.

"Shhh," I soothe her, holding her tight to my body as we lay there in my bed. I'll be locked inside of her for a little bit, but I plan on doing this all over again. I think I'll have my Omega ride me so I can watch her perfect tits bounce with every roll of her hips. I groan, the thought making me cum again.

I kiss her cheek as I run my hand up and down her body, comforting her.

"I love you. I love you so much, Alpha," she cries, her emotions are out of control in this moment. "Thank you, thank you for finally letting me see you. You're so perfect, Dom. I wanna worship your body, every inch of it." I bite the inside of my cheek as I fight to hold back my tears.

"I love you too, Tia. You're my everything."

She grabs my hand and places it on her belly. "I used to think I was ugly. That I was fat and no one would like how I looked naked. It took a long time to get over that. So I see you, Dom, and I believe in you. I can't wait for the day that we look in the mirror together, and I get to see the moment when you see how stunning you really are. You guys remind me every day of how beautiful I am. That this..." she makes my hand squeeze the little pouch of extra weight. "Is sexy. That *I'm* sexy. We all look different, but we're all perfectly imperfect."

We lay like this for a little while longer, and when my knot slips free, she's on me in an instant, biting me, claiming me as hers.

Pack Ashood is now complete, and it's all thanks to our Little Omega.

CHAPTER 29

FINN

"Are you sure about this?" I ask Sawyer, rubbing the back of my head as I look up at the sign that says *tattoo*.

"Of course I am. I know exactly what I want, and it's going to be perfect," he says, grinning as he vibrates with excitement.

Tia is gone with Dom on their weekend getaway, so it's only Sawyer and me who are left at the house. Tristan had to deal with some last minute school work, and Knox is talking to the dean about other work he can do around Calling Wood now that Tia will officially have a pack and no longer needs a Beta guard.

He refused to take on another Omega, and I don't blame him. It wouldn't be fair to any of the parties involved.

About a half hour ago, Sawyer found me in my room,

reading, and asked if I wanted to go for a drive with him. I had no idea it was to come *here*.

"Alright, if you're sure," I say, following him inside.

Looking around, the place looks nice enough. I can see a few people getting tattoos lying down on the tables. Not much for privacy, but they all seem to be wearing gloves and have things wrapped up, so at least they're clean.

"Hey," a guy covered from head to toe in tattoos says, nodding at us.

"Hey. I have an appointment at six. Sawyer Ashwood."

The guy looks at his computer for a second. "Kevin!" he shouts, and another man looks up from the station he was cleaning. "Your six o'clock is here." He turns back to Sawyer. "You have any idea of what you want?"

"Yup," Sawyer says with a bright smile. I have no idea what he's getting done, and when I asked, he said it was a surprise.

Sawyer gets taken back to the guy who's going to be doing his tattoo, and they immediately start talking as Sawyer shows him something on his phone.

"You getting anything?" the guy at the counter asks me.

I look at him and blink. "Me?" I ask.

"Yes," he chuckles, looking me up and down. "I'm normally not one to assume, but I take it you don't have any ink?"

"Tattoos? No, but I like how they look. My boyfriend is covered in them." I bite my lip as I think about how Knox has almost no visible skin left. Along with the fact that his cock is tattooed. "It's just not my thing."

"That's cool," he says. "What about piercings?"

"Oh, no," I shake my head. "I don't think I could pull off any of them."

"Well, I think you would look hot with some plugs or a lip ring, your glasses might cover an eyebrow piercing. But not all have to be done where they can be seen," he says, wiggling his eyebrows.

My eyes widen as I think about Knox and how he has the tip of his cock pierced. "I don't think I could handle that kind of pain. My boyfriend has that too, and he told me it wasn't his best experience."

"There's always the nipples." He shrugs.

That has me stopping and thinking. *Could I handle that? Do I even want that?* It doesn't sound horrible.

Ten minutes later, I'm in the back, laying down with my shirt off as the guy holds a clamp to my nipple. My heart is pounding, my body breaking out in a sweat.

Why am I doing this? What is wrong with me? I should back out.

But when he says. "Ready?" I find myself nodding my head. "Deep breath in."

And once I do, he's quick. But fuck. I bite the inside of my cheek so hard to hold back my scream, I taste blood.

"You okay?"

"Yeah," I croak out before coughing and clearing my throat.

"Got some tears in your eyes," he says. "You ready for the other one?"

Oh, hell no! I can't do that again.

"Be honest, would it look weird with one? Because I'm gonna be man enough to say, there is no way I'm going to subject myself to that pain again."

The guy looks me over then shakes his head. "Nah, I think it looks fine."

"Thank god." I sigh, sitting up. "I'm good with this, then."

He chuckles and helps me up. "I'm honestly surprised you had the guts to get this far. Most people would have run once I took out the needle."

After carefully putting my shirt back on, he gives me care instructions. I groan when he says it could take months before it heals. I'm somewhat relieved when he mentions that since I'm an Alpha, the healing time should be cut in half. When we're done, I sit in the waiting area, trying not to panic about how the others will react. This isn't like me. I'm not the one who gets stuff like this out of nowhere.

"Ready to go?" Sawyer asks sometime later. I hop up out of my seat like I was caught with my hand in the cookie jar.

"You're all done?"

"Yup," he says with a big grin and lifts up his shirt to reveal a bandage on his hip.

"What did you get?" I ask, brows furrowed. It's not very big.

"Gotta wait until I show Tia."

When we get home, we see that Dom's truck is sitting in the driveway. I'm filled with nervous excitement. I missed my Omega, my Sunshine. It's just not the same without her around. Knox helped distract me in very... creative ways, but before going to bed, I still thought about her, wishing she was there in our arms.

"Dear god," Sawyer chokes out as he covers his face. I do the same as my senses are attacked by the very heavy, potent smell of our Omega's slick and perfume mixed with Dom's Alpha pheromones. "Looks like our girl brought the party home."

As we walk further into the house, I see Tia's clothes all over the place and look to Sawyer with a smile. "Something tells me we're officially a pack now."

"Almost, lover boy, you still have that Beta of yours to give a little love bite to."

I blush and look away. I want to mark Knox more than anything, but it's not something I've talked to Tia or him about. I think Tia would be okay with it, that's the kind of person she is, and it's one of the many things I love about her. My hand finds my mate mark on my neck, and I run my finger over it lightly.

"Hey there, Pretty Girl," Sawyer says, amusement lacing his tone. I look over to see my Sunshine fresh out of the shower with a towel wrapped around her perfect body.

She blushes as Dom steps out behind her. My eyes widen in surprise when I see him with only a towel around his waist. I haven't seen Dom without a shirt on since Tia came into our lives.

"Well, look at you two. Don't you looked well fucked and newly bonded." Sawyer chuckles, making Tia blush harder. Dom wraps his arms around her, pulling her to his chest. She sighs as she tilts her head to the side to let Dom place an open mouth kiss on his mate mark. "Alright, enough with that, or you're gonna send us all into a rut."

"Maybe not today, but soon," Dom growls into her neck. "I can't wait to watch them fuck you until you're a blubbering mess, Little One." She whimpers, looking up to kiss him. "Go say hi to your Alphas. I know they must have missed you. I'm going to get dressed."

Dom leaves, walking down the hall, and Tia comes over to us. "Where were you two?" she asks, wrapping her arms around my body. I almost worry she's gonna hit my piercing, but she's so short her head stops just below it. I squeeze her back, leaning my head down to breathe in her scent.

"We went out. And I'm glad we did because I have a feeling that what happened here wasn't meant for our eyes and ears," Sawyer says.

"Probably not," she giggles. Then looks up at me. "I missed you."

"I missed you too, Sunshine." I kiss her softly, loving how she melts into my touch.

"I missed you too, you know," Sawyer says with a pout. Tia laughs and heads over to him next.

"I missed you as well, Alpha." She smiles up at him, then moans into his mouth as he kisses her dirty. My dick is far too hard right now, and all these smells are driving me nuts. I need to open some windows.

"I have something to show you," he says, but then his face drops like he's rethinking everything.

"Oh really? What is it?" she asks excitedly.

Sawyer lifts up his shirt to show her the bandage.

"I got a tattoo," he says.

She gasps, her eyes lighting up. "Of what? Let me see."

"I don't wanna," he mutters. "Now that I think of it, I think it might have been a bad idea."

"What? Why?" she asks.

"I don't want you to think I'm stupid or crazy," he says, biting his lip. *Oh boy, what on earth did he get?*

"Sawyer," she says with an adorable growl. "I would never think you're stupid or crazy."

"What about now?" he says with a sigh, peeling back the bandage.

Tia and I both lean forward, then let out matching gasps.

"You didn't," I say, stunned.

"Sawyer," she breathes, looking up at him with tears in her eyes.

"You hate it," he groans.

"I love it," she whispers.

"You do?" he asks, his brows shooting up to his hairline. "Really?" Then he narrows his eyes. "You're not just saying that to be nice, are you?"

"You're kidding me, right?" she says, looking at the tattoo again. "Some people might not be into this, but me? Seeing my name tattooed on your skin, my Alpha's body..." she bites her lip, her eyes filling with heat. "So, can you still have sex, or is it too sensitive?"

Sawyer growls, lunging for Tia. She lets out a squeal of laughter as Sawyer starts to tickle her. I smile as I watch the two of them. A part of me wishes I could do the whole tattoo thing so I could do the same, seeing how much she loves the idea. But I couldn't even handle my other nipple getting done. I don't think I could sit still for an hour while getting repeatedly stabbed with a needle a million times a second.

"Did Dom not satisfy your needs, Pretty Girl?" Sawyer teases.

"Oh, I did," Dom says, giving Tia a dirty look that's all sex as he steps out of his room. "Trust me, I did."

Thankfully, Tia doesn't ask if I got anything before taking off into the bathroom with Sawyer to help him clean it. He can do it himself, but I think they both like the idea of her caring for him.

Will she be the same way with me when she finds out? Or will they think I'm the stupid one?

CHAPTER 30

KNOX

If you asked me a few months ago what I expected my future to look like, the life I have now wouldn't be the answer. I thought that I would continue to do my job and just take life day by day. Maybe find a nice Beta and settle down someday. But as I think about it now, watching my Kitten laughing as she and Finn play their video game, I realize that I would have been very unhappy, maybe even depressed.

I have no idea what I did in another life to deserve the two halves of my heart sitting in front of me, but I'm so fucking grateful.

Never did I think I would have such a loving, caring, amazing Omega to call mine. And not only that, she brought the man I've been in love with for as long as I can remember out of his shell and back into my life. I have so much love for these two, I'd lay my life down for them in a second. Even thinking of a life without them both fills me with rage.

My Little Omega has mated all her Alphas, and her heat is due any day now. I'm honestly excited to have a little more help with her heat this time. Tristan did an amazing job before, but my Kitten is a horny little thing. Right now, in our everyday lives, one at a time is enough. But during her heat? No, she's going to need all of her men to satisfy her needs, even though I think we're gonna be zombies by the end of it. But we're not complaining because sex during her heat is an out of this world experience.

"Hey!" Tia laughs. "You cheated."

"No, I didn't." Finn chuckles. "I just had that banana as backup."

"But you used it right as I was about to cross the finish line," she says, pouting as she looks up at Finn with puppy dog eyes.

"I'm sorry, Sunshine," Finn says, looking like he feels bad for upsetting her.

"Guess you're gonna have to make it up to me," she sighs dramatically, making me chuckle.

"We can play another round of Mario Kart? No bananas this time," he suggests.

"Nah. I'd much rather play with *your* banana," she teases, wiggling her eyebrows. Finn raises one of his own, giving her a grin before they both burst out laughing.

"I second the banana part," I say, smirking as Finn looks over at me, biting his lip. I love when he does that, it always makes my cock hard.

Tia moves to straddle his lap, making him drop the controller. She runs her hands up his chest, and he lets out a hiss of pain.

"Are you okay?" she asks, her eyes widening with panic. "Did I hurt you?"

"I'm fine," he says, but I'm not buying it, something is up.

"Finny?" I growl, getting to my knees. I guide him down, so he's laying flat on the bed with one hand while pulling his shirt up with the other. "What is this?" I ask, raising a brow as I look at the silver barbell pierced through his nipple.

He turns beet red, not meeting my eyes. "A piercing," he whispers.

"I know what it is, but why do you have it, and when did you get it?" I ask. Am I really seeing what I'm seeing? On my sweet Finny?

"You hate it," he says, resigned, and fuck, I feel horrible about how my reaction is coming off.

"No." I shake my head. "I think it's fucking sexy. But it's not really something you would do, even if I love it."

"Really?" he asks, his shy eyes meeting mine again, then he looks to Tia.

"I think it's hot," she states in a husky voice, and her perfume is quick to follow.

"You don't think it's stupid?" he asks, looking between the two of us.

"No." Tia shakes her head. "Did you get this done when Sawyer got his tattoo?"

"Yeah," he says. "I don't know what came over me. I was

talking to the guy, and the next thing I knew, I was laying there on the table while a needle was being pushed through my skin."

"Why only one?" I ask, eyeing up the barbell.

He looks away, his cheeks bright red again. "I was too chicken. The first one hurt so much, I backed out of the second one. I don't know how you've got all those tattoos and your piercing, but yeah, it wasn't something I wanna do again."

"I think it looks good with just one," Tia says. "Does it hurt?"

"Kinda? When I clean it or when it gets snagged on something."

"Have you been taking care of it? You should let me help you from now on," Tia insists, frowning.

Finn smiles like he was hoping she would say something like that. "I have been, but I could always use the help."

"Good," she nods. "But if you ever want to go get the other one done, I'd be happy to hold your hand the whole time," she winks with a grin. "Don't think you have to, though. You look perfect just like this."

"Thanks." Finn smiles back. "I just might take you up on that one day."

"Now, about your banana..." She grins. "I was serious. I want you, Finn," she says, rocking her hips against his crotch. Finn moans, his eyes rolling back into his head. Damn, watching the two of them has me hard as fucking stone.

"I want you too, Sunshine," he says, his breathing starting to pick up.

"But I want our Beta too," she says, looking up at me with hooded eyes. "Take me. Both of you. Please?" she whimpers.

"What do you say, Finny? Wanna take care of our Omega together?" I purr, looking at my man with hungry eyes.

"Y-yes," he swallows thickly. "But... can you..."

"Aww Finny, does my Alpha wanna be dominated?" I smirk, and he blushes but nods.

"Tell us what to do, Knox," Tia moans as she runs her hands up and under her shirt, giving her perfect tits a squeeze. "And we'll do it."

These two... un-fucking real.

"First, everyone needs to be naked," I say, pulling my shirt off.

Tia scrambles off Finn, almost tripping as she rushes to take her clothes off. She's naked and standing before us in seconds. I get up, take my pants off and drop them to the floor, kicking them to the side. "You too, Finny," I say, my voice a rumble as I step behind my girl. I run one hand up her body, grasping her breast while the other one slides down to her dripping pussy. "Kitten," I groan as she leans back into me with a whimper, bucking against my hand as I dip two fingers into her slick soaked cunt. "You're drenched for us."

"Yes," she moans.

Finn stands up, his cock visibly pushing against his

pants, watching as my fingers move in and out of our Omega. He takes his shirt off, then his pants. When he's completely naked, he reaches down and grips his delicious cock.

Thrusting my dick between Tia's ass cheeks, I groan as I watch Finn stroke himself. "You're so fucking sexy," I growl. "Both of you."

"Alpha," Tia whimpers, reaching for Finn. He moves toward us, his pupils blown wide with need, his chest heaving as he tries to keep himself under control.

"I want this," I tell her, moving my hand from her breast to her ass cheek, giving it a hard squeeze, making her moan. "This ass is mine. I'm gonna fuck you here while he takes your pussy."

"Please?" she sucks in a breath.

"Take her nipple into your mouth, Finn."

He leans forward, taking her into his mouth. Tia grips his hair, holding him to her. "Finn," she whines.

"Shhhh," I soothe her. "We have you, Little Omega. We know what you need," I growl, biting my mate mark, feeling prouder than ever. Finn looks up at me, seeing me lick and suck at it. I want one from him, but I need him to be the one to broach the subject. My eyes could be playing tricks on me, but the way he's looking at me right now tells me he wants it too.

"More," she demands, wiggling in my hold.

"Cum first, then we'll fuck you," I demand.

Thrusting my fingers in and out of her, I work her over as Finn switches nipples. He sucks and nips without being told. "Good boy," I purr, and he whimpers against Tia's breast.

I pluck at her free nipple while circling her clit. Her knees start to shake, and she whines and whimpers. "Oh, yes. Oh, I'm gonna cum," she cries, and a second later, when I thrust my fingers into her again, she's gushing onto my hand.

"Such a good girl," I praise her. "You always cum so perfectly. I can't wait until I'm cumming while we're buried deep inside you. How would you like that, Kitten?"

"Please," she whimpers.

I remove my fingers from her pussy and lick them clean. "Want some?" I ask Finn, and he nods frantically. With a surprised yelp from Tia, I lift her up so that my arms are under her thighs. Her back is against me, and I open her legs wide, exposing her dripping pussy to our Alpha. "Then taste."

Tia moans as Finn drops to his knees. He stares at her core, licking his lips before diving in and taking a lick.

"Fuck!" she moans. "Your tongue feels so good, Alpha."

I love how much she's enjoying Finn's tongue inside her pussy. "Alpha, make your Omega cum. Have her soak your face."

With a growl that's unlike Finn, he starts to devour her cunt. I hold her up as she writhes in my arms, her head thrashing against my chest as our Alpha's instincts take over him.

It doesn't take her long before she's screaming his name and cumming all over his face like the good girl she is.

Finn stands, and I see that his glasses have slick marks on them. "I should have taken these off." He chuckles, removing them from his face, setting them on the dresser. "But damn, Sunshine, your slick tastes like heaven."

"Need you..." she says as I place her on her feet. "Inside me, now," she says, and I grin because my Kitten is bringing out the claws.

"Yes, ma'am," I grin. "But first, I wanna do something." She moves to lay down on the bed and watches us as she plays with her breasts.

I stalk towards Finn. His eyes widen with a gulp. "So, is this sensitive to touch?" I ask.

"Y-yes," he breathes out, nodding.

"Then we need to take away that pain, don't we?" I grin.

"H-how?" he asks, blinking at me.

"Lay down," I tell him, and he stumbles onto the bed next to Tia.

She leans over, bringing her lips to his, kissing him while I go to the glass of water I have sitting on the bedside table and grab one of the ice cubes out of it.

"This is gonna be cold, but it's gonna feel so good," I tell him. He's still kissing Tia when I bring the ice down to his nipple, and he gasps into her mouth, his nipple tightening to a stiff peak. I watch as the water drips down his chest, leaning over to lick it up.

"Does that feel better?" I ask, blowing lightly on his nipple.

"So much better," he moans. I put the ice cube back on, holding it there for a moment, loving how he groans in pleasure. When it's all gone, I lean down and give him a slow sensual kiss before moving to lay back on the bed next to them. "Come sit on my cock, Kitten, but face away from me."

She scrambles up and reverse cowgirls me. We both moan as she takes my cock into her slick pussy, getting it lubed up. She lifts herself up, wrapping her fingers around my length. Giving it a few pumps, she shifts so that my head is kissing her back entrance before slowly lowering herself onto me, my cock filling her tight hole. Fuck, it feels so good, like she's strangling it.

"Come on, Finny," I groan. "Come feel how tight our girl's pussy is. I want to feel your cock rubbing against mine as we break our girl and put her back together."

"Fuck," Finn hisses, watching as Tia takes things into her own hands and starts to ride me. He better hurry up, or I'm going to be cumming in her ass way too soon. I'm so worked up right now.

He crawls around to face her, and I pull Tia down so that she's laying on top of me. Finn gets between her legs and waits for me to tell him what to do next.

"Cover her body with yours, slide that thick Alpha cock inside her wet cunt and fuck her until you knot her. I want her to be crying out when you pop that fat knot inside."

"Knox," Finn growls, making me grin. "Keep talking like that, and I won't last long."

"Good thing you're built to cum again and again. It's what I'm counting on during her heat because I want you to be locked to our Omega while I pound into you and make you both cum until you pass out."

"God, yes, please. I want that," Tia moans.

"Don't worry, Kitten, we will make it happen. But right now, fuck her, Finn. Let's drive our girl wild."

And we do. Finn thrusts into her, leaning his body over hers so that she's trapped between us. He starts to rut into her, grunting and snarling. I love this feral side of my man, and I can't wait to see what he's like when he's drunk off of Tia's pheromones during her heat.

Leaning up, I grab the back of Finn's hair, getting a good handful, and pull him to my mouth. Our kiss is dirty, all tongues and teeth. My cock throbs inside my girl as Finn rocks her back and forth on me as he thrusts wildly into her.

"God, yes!" Tia screams. "You both feel amazing. I'm so full."

"Our dirty girl loves our cum, Finny. She wants us to fill her up. Wants it dripping out of her holes. Let's give that to her. I wanna hear her come apart," I growl.

We kiss again, and my heart beats wildly in my chest.

"Knox," Finn pants as we break the kiss. He looks at me with pleading eyes. "I wanna bite you. Please?"

"Are you sure?" Fuck, I think I'm gonna have a heart attack from how fast my heart is going.

"Yes." He looks down at Tia. "Is that okay with you?"

"Yes," she whimpers. "He's not just mine, Alpha, he's yours too."

Finn kisses Tia until she's strangling our cocks with her orgasm. I growl as Finn rips his lips from hers and latches onto my neck. My eyes roll back as he bites into my flesh, and I cum hard, deep inside our Omega's ass. A feeling of pure euphoria filling my body.

He snarls against me, refusing to let go as he pops his knot into Tia. She screams a second time while cumming over and over again. I can feel Finn's cock jerk inside her, filling her with his seed. He's feral right now, so I rub my hand up and down his back to soothe him as he grunts, thrusting his hips in little jerky motions.

"Finn," I moan, his teeth pulling a little. I can feel his emotions. There's a lot of love there, but something more wild. It's like we unleashed a very sexy beast. "You need to let go, baby," I plead. He grunts but lets go, licking at my mark, causing me to send a few extra jets of cum into Tia.

"Sorry," he says, looking sheepish, his voice hoarse. "I don't know what came over me. It's just..."

"It's a lot to feel, I know," I say, kissing him and tasting my blood. "But we've got you. How are you doing, Kitten?" I ask Tia.

When she says nothing, we both look down at her. She's passed out, little snores passing through her parted, puffy lips.

Finn looks at me with a big, dopey smile. "I love you guys so much."

"I love you too, Finn," I tell him, brushing some of his red locks away from his face. "But why don't we let our girl sleep, and you and I go into the shower to... get clean." I give him a wicked grin, and his eyes flash with hunger. He nods, and we roll to our side. I slip out of Tia and go to the bathroom. Bringing back a washcloth, I clean her up the best I can with him still locked inside her. Once Finn's knot deflates, he slips out, leaving a big puddle of slick and cum.

"Why is that so fucking hot?" I growl, cleaning her up.

"Knox," Finn whimpers, and I look over, seeing him standing there hard again with a desperate look on his face.

We take a shower and once I'm done washing the cum off of us, we go back to bed to cuddle with our Omega.

I remind him what I plan on doing to them during her heat. Let's just say he very much approves of the idea.

Life is fucking perfect.

CHAPTER 31

OCTAVIA

I'm so hot. *Why am I so hot?* The shower is turned to the coldest setting, yet my skin feels hot and itchy.

"Ughh," I whine as I finish rinsing my hair and move to wash my body next. *Maybe I'm starting my heat?* Last time it wasn't like this. I was in pain, so much pain, and the only thing that took it away was a thick cock and orgasms.

Oh, those sound good right about now, I think as I run my hands over my breasts. They feel heavier and more tender than normal. I moan as I brush my fingers over my nipples, my legs squeezing together as slick runs down my legs.

I need my guys, but I also need to cum, right now. Sliding my hand down my belly, I brush my fingertips over my clit. My knees almost buckle, so I sit on the shower bench.

Tipping my head back against the shower wall, I open

my legs, allowing room for my hand. My fingers dip into my wet core while the other one plays with my nipple.

Chasing the orgasm my body so desperately needs, I work myself over until I'm biting my lip, holding back my scream as I cum around my own fingers.

It's not enough, but it will do for now until I can get out of the shower.

Turning off the water, I get out to see that my lips are blue. *Shit, was the water really that cold?* Yet I still feel like I'm standing at the gates to hell.

Grumbling to myself, I dry my hair the best I can, then wrap the towel around myself. With a huff, I start to scratch at my body, the fabric feeling itchy against my skin.

It shouldn't; I bought this because of how crazy soft it is.

"Fuck it," I growl, dropping the towel. The burning in my belly starts up again. I have to be starting my heat... *unless I'm dying?* No. *Who has the desperate need to have a good dicking when they're dying?* Although, what a way to go. I'd die one happy Omega. You know what? I think I'll go get me some of my sexy men, you know, just in case.

Giving my naked body one last look in the mirror, I shrug and leave the bathroom. I can hear the guys talking in the living room as I follow the sounds of their voices. Sawyer laughs, and the sound goes right to my pussy. Slick drips down my legs, and now all I can think about is my Alpha and his cock. I wanna ride it, taste it. His cum... fuck, I need it.

"Little One?" I hear Dom ask as I step into the room. They all go quiet, but the only one I'm looking at is Sawyer.

"Hey, Pretty Girl," Sawyer says, his voice like a soft caress. "Why are you looking at me like you wanna eat me?" he asks, a smirk spreading across his lips as he raises a brow.

Saying nothing, I prowl towards my prey. My mind is screaming *Mine. Alpha. Cock. Knot. Cum.* God, I'm a hot mess right now.

"Ahh... Pretty Girl," Sawyer says, sounding concerned.

Knox chuckles. "Holy shit, yup, can you smell her?" Knox groans from his place next to Sawyer. "She's dripping, her perfume is wild. Our Little Omega has gone full horny vixen as of now."

"What does that mean?" Sawyer asks as I drop to my knees between Sawyer's legs. He looks down at me with lust in his eyes, but it morphs into shock when I palm his hard cock. He groans. "Shit, Pretty Girl."

"It means all she wants right now is us, our cocks, cum, and your knots. Your sweet little Omega? Yeah, she's gone, so don't be surprised about the things that will come out of her mouth. It's fucking amazing," Knox purrs, making me shiver. But no, it's not him I want. He can fuck me later. Right now, I want this Alpha.

"What is she doing?" Sawyer asks as I make quick work of ridding him of his pants, clawing at them to get them out of the way.

"She wants your dick, dude," Knox scoffs. "Get your pants off before you lose the chance."

"Shit," Sawyer says, helping me with his pants. His cock springs free, and I whine as I see him hard and ready.

Shaking my head, I realize what I'm doing. Blinking up at him, I remind myself I'm not some heathen.

"I don't know what's wrong," I whine. "I'm so sorry." I move to stand, to run. I was about to take his dick without even asking.

"What? No. No, it's okay," Sawyer says, leaning forward and taking my lips. "You're in heat, and we know you can get lost in the haze. We don't mind you doing whatever you want with our bodies. Right?" Sawyer asks, and the guys all agree, reassuring me.

"If we weren't comfortable or it wasn't something we wanted, we would leave, okay?"

"Okay," I say, my voice soft. "I don't mean to come on so strong. It's just, damn it," I sob. "My body is on fire, and I just really wanna suck your cock."

Sawyer can't help laughing. "My cock is all yours, Pretty Girl. I was just taken by surprise." He leans back and grins, nodding down at his dick. "Take it, Little Omega. Take what you need."

SAWYER

Holy shit. Holy fucking shit. I've never seen my Pretty Girl like this before. My cock is painfully hard, my knot throbbing to be inside her. Tia is in full heat, there's no doubt about that. We knew this was coming, knew it would be any day now.

She's spent the past few days eating on and off all day, little mood swings here and there. One moment she would snap at us for something, the next, she'd cry about it and feel bad. Or she'd push us away to be alone, then whine that she was lonely.

And we all took it. We were there for her with whatever she needed. Just like right now. I felt bad for the look on her face when she realized how aggressive she was being. I was shocked, but my Pretty Girl can do whatever she wants with me.

Her hands slide up my thighs, and I shiver at her touch, sucking in a breath when she grasps my cock with her soft, slender hand. Leaning forward, she takes the head of my cock into her mouth. I moan as her hot, wet tongue laps at the pre cum before taking me fully in.

"Pretty Girl," I groan at how incredible her mouth feels as I watch my cock disappear down her throat. She gags a little before pulling back and taking me again. She starts to bob her head in a steady rhythm, sucking hard and caressing my length with her tongue as she goes. Gathering her hair in my hand and out of her face, I watch her big, green eyes stare into mine with heavy lust and need. She moans around me, making me bite my lip. If she keeps doing this, I'm gonna blow my load before I'm even inside her. Thankfully, she pulls back with a gasp, spit dripping down her chin.

"Need you," she whines, scrambling up my lap. She straddles me and leans forward, shoving her tits into my chest as she kisses me hard and dirty. She rubs her dripping pussy against my cock.

I growl into the kiss, my hand sliding into her hair,

getting a good grip and pulling a little. She moans, her hips working faster.

"You're gonna notice your Alpha come out more than ever. Go with it, you'll know when you've taken it too far. But she's up for almost anything and will be vocal about what she does and doesn't want. Be rough with her if she asks or if you feel the need to. She loves it," Knox says, chuckling when she claws her nails down my chest, making me grunt. Now, I know why they looked like they got attacked by wild animals.

"Let me take you to the nest, Pretty Girl," I say when she breaks apart, finding my mate mark from her. She stops and licks at it, whimpering.

"Now," she whines. "Please, Alpha. I need you." She reaches down, grabbing my length, and lifting herself up. She doesn't wait, taking what she needs by slamming herself down on my cock.

"Alpha!" she cries out.

"Fuckkkk," I groan as her tight walls squeeze me. Looks like my first heat with my Omega is starting.

"Fuck her, Sawyer," Knox growls.

I growl back, which only makes him chuckle. I don't need to be told to fuck my Omega. Gripping her hips, I snarl as I lift her up and slam her back down. "Yes!" she cries out. "More. Harder, deeper," she sobs, tossing her head back as she tries to move herself.

The need to consume her has me holding her close as I move us to the floor.

Grabbing her wrists, I raise them up and pin them above

her head. She looks so gorgeous with her flushed skin, wild eyes, and her breasts heaving as she sucks in air.

"You want my cock, Pretty Girl?"

"Yes," she moans. "Fuck me with your fat, Alpha cock. Split my pussy open with your knot."

"Fuck me, you *are* a dirty little thing, aren't you?" I growl, her words making my cock twitch.

"Told you," Knox chuckles.

"Look at you, Little One," Dom says, getting down on his knees. He leans over and kisses her. It's all teeth and tongue, and it makes me rut into her. "Taking his cock so perfectly."

She moans as I take her savagely, her back arching off the ground while she's trapped under me.

With my free hand, I lift her leg up, giving me a different angle. I pound into her, grunting and snarling, never have I felt more Alpha than I do right now.

She feels amazing, and I can't hold back the need to knot her.

"I'm gonna knot you, Pretty Girl. Lock you to my body and fill you with my cum," I growl, a deep rumble in my chest. The feeling of being inside her like this, in this moment, is indescribable, but so damn right, soul consuming.

"Please!" she screams.

"Take it," I growl, pushing my knot into her. "Take it like a good little Omega!" It pops in, and I drop my head to her chest, letting out a guttural roar as I cum harder than I ever have in my life.

Her body locks up. "Yes!" she screams, nails digging into my back as her pussy grips my cock, and I knot so hard that I black out for a moment.

I don't think I've ever cum this long. I didn't even know I had this much in me, but it's never ending. My cock is jerking violently inside her, filling her with my seed.

"Woah," I breathe as I start to come down. "That was…"

"Intense?" Tristan asks.

"And amazing," I huff out. Lifting my head, I let go of Tia's wrists.

"Hi," she says, her eyes growing sleepy.

"Hi, Pretty Girl," I grin down at her, my knot still locked in place. I love this girl so much.

"Thank you for filling me with your cum. And your knot. I love knots," she giggles softly.

"She's so damn adorable when she's dick drunk," Knox chuckles.

She slowly turns her head to the side and grins at him, eyes half lidded. "You're next. And I want both of you," she says, looking at Finn.

Finn blushes and nods. "You want me to make love to you while Knox makes love to me?"

"No, silly," she mumbles with a smile, making me grin. "I want you to fuck me into the bed while Knox fucks you in the ass so good you can't sit for a week."

Knox howls with laughter, and we all join him as Finn looks at our dirty girl with wide, shocked eyes. But the large lump in his pants tells us he loves it.

She lets out a sigh, her eyes finally closing, and a few seconds later, she's letting out sweet little snores.

"Damn it," I groan. "Can someone get me a pillow?" I ask, sliding my hands under her back and pulling her to me as I flip us, so she's laying on top of me.

Tristan gives me a pillow, and Dom grabs a blanket, draping it over us.

"I may as well take a nap with her until my knot deflates because I feel like I'm gonna need it."

FINN

When Sawyer is able to pull himself free from Tia, Knox scoops her up and brings her to her nest. But the moment he places her down, her eyes flutter open, and her perfume hits me. "Knox," she whimpers.

"Do you need more already, Kitten?" he asks her, stroking her face.

"Please," she begs.

Standing up, he strips his clothes off.

I step out of the room and into the bathroom to grab a warm washcloth. "Here," I say, coming back into the room.

"Alpha," she whines, reaching for me. "Need you."

"Come on, Finny." Knox takes the cloth from me and cleans Sawyer's cum from her pussy. "You ready for me to fuck you in the ass?"

My cheeks flush as I stare at him in shock at his dirty words.

"Yes!" Tia answers for me, making him chuckle.

"Yeah," I say, my voice shaky as I strip down.

"Give me," she says, making grabby hands towards my length.

I huff out a laugh, she's so cute. "I love you, Sunshine," I say, kneeling down on the bed between her legs.

"I love you too. But I also love your knot," she says, opening her legs wide. "So, put it to good use."

"Bossy little thing, you are," Knox chuckles as he moves next to us. Leaning over, he takes her lips with his, sucking on her bottom lip and giving it a good bite. She moans as he twists her nipple.

"Damn," I breathe. "You just made her soak the bed," I say, looking down at the slick that's dripping from her pussy.

"Now let's make her soak your cock," he groans as he grips his length, giving it a few strokes.

"Please, Alpha," Tia whines, giving me pleading eyes. I can't say no to her, ever. And why would I? I love being with her, inside her.

Lowering myself down, I shift until my cock meets her pussy. I look down at her with so much love, it makes my heart sing. I rub her thighs, making her moan, asking me again to fill her. Knox grabs my cock, making me suck in a gasp, and places the tip at her entrance.

"Thrust into her, Finny. Make my Kitten cream, make her scream, and everything in between," he chuckles, making me shiver, and I whimper, gripping her thighs. Knox grabs the back of my head and crushes his lips to mine. I moan, thrusting into Tia, unable to hold back any longer. She cries out in pleasure, my name on her dirty, little tongue. "Good boy," Knox praises me, moving behind me as I start to make love to her. With every snap of my hips and each pleading whimper from Tia, my Alpha side starts to show more and more. "How does she feel?"

"So good," I moan. "So fucking good."

"How about you, Kitten? How does it feel to have your Alpha's cock deep inside you?" he asks her. She doesn't answer, lost in the moment, as she whines and moans.

Knox gets up, going somewhere, but I don't pay attention, too lost in the green of my girl's eyes as she looks up at me with the desperate need to be thoroughly fucked.

My body is covering hers as I fuck her into the bed just like she wanted. Bringing my lips to hers, we kiss sloppily as I grunt and groan her name. She's clawing at my back, and I moan from the pain, loving that she's marking me as hers.

This isn't like the first time we were together. Even though that was amazing, and I'll never forget it, this time is different. I feel like I know what I'm doing now, know how to please my girl. Right now, I'm so glad my Alpha instincts are in control.

The closest I've ever felt to feeling like this was the other day with Knox and Tia. Something came over me when I marked Knox. Something primal that was so unlike me, but I didn't hate it. Nor did they.

I growl as Knox runs his hand up my back, taken by surprise by his return. "I'm sorry, baby," he soothes me. I look up at him with a little blush, but it only lasts a moment before I'm sitting up and grabbing his face. I need my Beta, my lover, so I tongue fuck his mouth, making our lips swollen. "Fuck my ass, Knox," I growl, overwhelmed with the need for both of them, making him groan. "I wanna feel you inside me for days after."

"Yes, Alpha," he growls back, giving me a quick, harsh kiss before I go back to fucking our girl.

"Knot," she demands with a moan. "I need a fucking knot in me now!"

I snarl, loving how she begs for me, before thrusting my knot deep inside her. She screams, the sweet cries of her orgasm overtaking her the moment she locks around me. My eyes roll back, pure ecstasy running through my veins as I moan, cumming hard with never ending spurts of cum.

"Knox," I moan against Tia's lips in a desperate plea, needing him too.

"I love when you beg for me," he growls, opening my ass cheeks and squirting something cold onto my tight hole. "I need to get you ready for me, this might sting."

I moan as he slides his fingers in my ass.

Removing his fingers, he places the tip of his cock to my hole. "I'm gonna press in now. Relax for me."

"It's hard for me to relax when our girl's pussy is choking my knot," I moan as Tia has another orgasm. So much pleasure it's almost painful, but I crave more.

Knox pushes his cock in, and I curse. "Shhhh," he soothes me, kissing down my spine as he massages my ass cheeks. "Look at you, Alpha," he groans. "Fuck, my dick looks so good in your ass."

"So full," I moan as I feel the slight sting of his cock.

"Fuck him!" Tia shouts. "I need more cum. I need to cum. Just, fuck!" she sobs.

"I got you, Sunshine," I say in a strangled voice as I try to calm her down. "You're doing so good."

"More!" she whines.

"You okay?" Knox asks me.

I nod. "It stings, but I kinda like it." I blush. What a time to be shy about what I enjoy in the bedroom.

"God, I love you both," Knox groans as he pulls back out before thrusting into me again.

"Knox," I whimper as Tia cries out. "God, yes!"

"Gonna own this ass," he growls as he starts to move faster, a little harder.

"Yes. All yours," I moan. God, I feel so full but so damn good.

Tia is unable to form any more words, just whimpering and whining, her hands grasping at me, at Knox. My knot is still locked inside her, so he's making me fuck her like this. It's intense.

I let go, letting the moment consume me, the feeling of her pussy around my cock, Knox deep inside me. So fucking tight and warm. I never wanna leave.

"I'm gonna cum," Knox growls.

"I don't think I have any more in me," I sob, but the moan that leaves me as he grips my hips hard, stilling as he empties his load into my ass, says I might just have a little left in me.

"One more, Kitten. Cum for us one more time," he tells Tia, who looks like she's barely hanging on. But after this, she should be good for another few hours before she needs one of the other guys.

Knox told us after Sawyer had his time with her that the best thing to do is give your Omega as many orgasms each round, tire them out, and give yourself time to rest because this is only the first few hours, we still have days. And I honestly can't wait.

Knox moves, laying down next to Tia, and slips his hand between the two of us. "I can't anymore," I say, feeling exhausted, fighting to keep my eyes open. I've been cumming this whole time, never really stopping for more than a few seconds as Tia drained my knot, milking me for everything I have.

"I know," he tells me. "I'll make her cum one more time, then you can both sleep." He kisses my forehead, and I nod. I can do that. I hope.

He plays with Tia's clit, giving it a few more rubs before she explodes again.

She doesn't even stay awake long enough to come down from her high.

"God, Knox," I whimper. "I think I'm all cummed out."

He chuckles, helping me roll onto my back with Tia in my arms.

"You're an Alpha, Finny. You will be ready to go in an hour. But next time, you're gonna be sucking me down while we watch our pack mates fuck our girl."

"Yes, please," I sigh sleepily, really liking that idea.

He kisses both of us on the cheek before leaving the

room. A few moments later, I hear the shower running, and I try to stay awake, waiting for him to come back to the nest.

I'm half asleep when I slip free from Tia, and my heart fills with love when I feel Knox carefully clean our cum and slick, careful not to wake us.

When he's done, he tosses the dirty cloth into the laundry basket before cuddling with us.

We fall asleep for a while, and when she wakes again, she's ready to go. But she's full of sweat and cum, so we take her to the shower. And in there, she begs to suck not only me but Knox and Sawyer off too. We take turns giving our Omega just what she needs before carrying her back to the nest. When we get there, the sheets are cleaned, and Tia busies herself fixing her nest again, grumbling about stupid Alpha's touching what they shouldn't. Knox tells Dom not to take it to heart, and it's only the heat talking.

After changing it a few different times, she's finally satisfied and snuggles into the blankets.

"Knox," she whines, looking at him, then to me and the others. "Alphas."

She's not asking for sex; no, she wants to be surrounded and secure, to feel protected while we sleep.

We all crawl in, so no spot was left open, and get some much needed sleep.

CHAPTER 32

DOMINIC

I'm awakened from my deep sleep by the sounds of moaning. It's not surprising, seeing how it's Tia's heat.

My girl has been knotted and fucked every way you can think of by now, but none of it is enough. She wants more. More cum, more knots. The more people fucking her, the better.

It's been a wild ride, and we're all getting to the point where we're glad that her heat is almost over. It's been three days at least. Knox has been a rockstar, making sure we're eating, drinking, taking showers, and sleeping.

We've been lost in the haze, only wanting to fuck our Omega, to please her, to hear her scream our names.

"God, Love," Tristan moans. I sit up on my elbow to see Tia sucking down Tristan's cock like he's gonna cum gold.

Her perfect ass is in the air, and I can see her pussy lips glistening with slick. The room is full of her toasted coconut scent, and I don't think any one of us will be able to get the smell out of our noses. *Thank god, she smells divine.*

I need another taste, crave her slick on my tongue.

Getting up on my knees, I crawl over to my Little One. "Doesn't it just blow your mind when her lips are wrapped around your cock?" I ask Tristan as he grabs a handful of her hair, holding her still as he thrusts up into her mouth.

"Mind fucking blowing," he groans as she gags.

I lean forward, swiping my tongue up her pussy, groaning as her flavor hits my tongue like an explosion. Tia cries out around Tristan's dick.

"Alpha," she moans as she comes up for air, wiggling her ass in my face as I lick at her some more. "Knot."

"I wanna taste you first, Little One," I growl into her pussy before dipping my tongue into her core.

"I don't care," she growls. "I want your knot. Knot me, fuck me. I need cum," she whines. I look up at Tristan, cocking a brow. He's got a smirk on his lips, but they part as Tia takes him back into her mouth, his eyes rolling back.

Moving to kneel behind her, I slap her ass, making her squeal. "Naughty Little Omega," I growl. "You didn't even say please."

She looks over her shoulder at me, an adorable little scowl forming on her face. "Fine. Can you pretty please shove that fat Alpha cock deep inside my weeping cunt, and fuck me until I cum, gushing slick around your knot? Please, oh please, wedge your knot inside me so that I can strangle it with my pussy until we're both cumming like our lives depend on it."

"Oh, my Kitten. My sweet, sweet Kitten. Your mouth is utterly filthy," Knox chuckles. I look over to see him, Sawyer, and Finn all watching, stroking their cocks.

"Not yet," Tia grins. "I still need to make my Alpha cum. Then I can choke on his seed, making my mouth truly filthy."

We all groan. Heat Tia is a little sex vixen, and we are all living for it. Some of the things she's said over the past few days would give a nun a heart attack.

"I guess since you did ask nicely," I chuckle darkly as I grip her ass. Lining my cock up with her sweet pussy. I thrust forward, making her take all of my cock in one go.

"Dom!" she screams.

"Now, that's not how you suck your Alpha off, Little One, no more talking." I grab her by the head and shove her back on Tristan's cock as I start to fuck into her.

She gags a little but is moaning and writhing between us. She loves it when I take control.

"Suck him dry, Little Omega. Then, if you're a good girl, I'll knot you," I growl.

She makes it her mission now, bobbing her head like crazy.

"Yes, fuck yes, just like that, Love," Tristan growls. "I'm gonna cum so fucking hard down your throat."

"And she's gonna swallow every last drop, aren't you,

our little cum slut," I purr, and she moans like the dirty girl she is.

"Shit," Sawyer groans.

"No cumming," I snap. "She's gonna need you next."

"Fuck yes," he says, letting go of his cock. "She looks so good sucking cock."

"Better being the one receiving it," Tristan moans. "Shit, shit, shit!" He thrusts up, and I hold her there as he lets out a roar, emptying himself down her throat. She does as she's told and struggles to swallow, but she gets every drop.

"Did I do good?" she gasps, pulling back.

"So good, Little One," I purr, pulling her up so that her back is against my chest. I nuzzle her neck, deeply inhaling her scent. "You're perfect, Tia. No one else was ever meant to be ours. Only you, Little Omega. You were born to take our knot, to suck our cocks, and drink our cum. It's all yours."

"Dom," she whimpers.

"Shhhh," I kiss her neck. "You can have my knot soon." I pull out of her, and her whine turns into an almost sob, but I flip her over so that she's on her back. "I wanna see the look in your eyes when I pop my knot inside you, Little One. It's one of the best sights there is."

OCTAVIA

Dom lifts my legs so that my knees are bent next to my face. "So fucking wet," he growls, looking down at my pussy.

"Knot," I beg, hating how they like to tease me sometimes. I'm not in a haze or the middle of a frenzy anymore, my heat is coming to an end soon. I don't remember much, just that my guys have taken really good care of me. This should be what finally satisfies the cravings because I'm still hot and horny but lucid.

"You're so impatient," Dom chuckles, rubbing the tip of his cock up and down my slit.

"Cock tease," I growl. It's mean to leave an Omega begging during her heat, but he knows I'm not in that state of mind anymore, so being the cocky asshole he sometimes is, he's gonna make me work for that knot.

"That's no way to talk to your Alpha," Dom says, slapping my breast. My eyes widen as I gape at him.

"Did you just slap my boob?!" I hiss.

"I did," he grins. "And I'll slap it again if you keep being a bratty Omega. Now, be a good girl."

"Fine, you wanna play it that way?" I look at Sawyer and put on the puppy dog eyes. He perks up, waiting for me to talk. "Sawyer, baby, can you come knot me, please?" I bat my eyelashes.

He goes to move, but Dom growls. "Sit," he hisses. "Her pussy is mine, and it will be filled with my knot."

"Well then, fuck me!" I snap, turning back to him and giving him my best glare. I'm horny, dripping, and I think I might die if he doesn't knot me. Okay, maybe that's a little over the top, but that's what it feels like!

Knox is chuckling next to me, making me glare at him next. "For laughing at me, I'm not touching your cock anymore tonight," I huff, lifting my chin.

"I'm sad, Kitten. But that's okay. I have Finny to take care of my needs," he says, grabbing Finn by the hair and pushing him down to his knees. Finn sucks in a breath, but when Knox brushes the tip of his cock against his lips, smearing them with pre cum, Finn moans, opening his mouth to suck the tip in. "That's it, such a good boy," Knox praises. I whimper, seeing the two of them like this has slick gushing out of me.

"Fuck," Dom growls, thrusting his cock back into me. I cry out, arching my back, but I struggle to keep my eyes on the two men next to me. Knox fucks Finn's face as Finn jerks himself off. "Watching them really does turn you on, Little One, doesn't it?" Dom groans. "You're squeezing my cock so damn tight right now."

"Why am I being left out?" Sawyer pouts.

I don't want my Alpha to feel left out, but I want to be able to watch Finn and Knox. "Come titty fuck me," I moan as Dom pounds into me a few more times before lowering my legs, settling them around his waist.

"Naughty Omega." Sawyer chuckles. "I love it."

Sawyer straddles my chest, and I push up my big breasts together.

"Here," Dom says, gathering my slick that's dripping out of me and wiping it onto my boobs.

"Fuck, that's hot," Sawyer says, sliding his cock between my breasts. "This feels so different," he comments, taking a hold of them himself. I run my hands up his thighs before dragging my nails down them. "But so damn good," he moans.

Dom and Sawyer work me over, making my body hum in ecstasy. The feeling of Dom's cock hitting me in just the right spot while seeing the look of pure bliss on Sawyer's face has my orgasm building again.

But it's not until Tristan tweaks both of my nipples that I cum, screaming out in pleasure as I gush around Dom's cock, making him curse. Fucker still hasn't given me his knot.

"Shit," Sawyer says, the tip of his cock weeping pre cum onto my chest. "I'm gonna cum," he grunts. Leaning forward, he thrusts towards my mouth. I suck the tip of his cock into my mouth, and when it pops out, he lets go of my breast to grab his cock, jerking himself off. A second later, he's roaring out my name, sending ropes of cum shooting out onto my breasts. I open my mouth and stick my tongue out to catch anything I can. I wanna cry at the wasted cum, but when he's done, breathing heavily as he tries to catch his breath, I bring my hands to my tits and rub his cum into my skin.

"Damn, Pretty Girl," he groans. "Now, I'm hard again." I giggle as he moves off me, falling back onto the bed.

"You still haven't knotted me," I pant out as Dom starts to fuck me again. He stopped to let Sawyer do his thing.

"You haven't earned it," he growls.

"I'm gonna cum," Knox groans. He starts to jerk off while Finn sits back on his knees, tongue out and waiting for Knox's cum. *I want some too!*

"Guess I'll just have to wait for that knot," I say.

"What?" he ask, brows furrowing as he stops fucking me.

I grin, wiggling out of his hold and off his cock before scrambling over to Knox.

"Fuck me, Kitten," Knox groans as I make it just in time, sitting back on my knees in the same position as Finn with my tongue out. Knox's cock erupts, sending jets of cum out onto mine and Finn's tongue. Knox curses as we moan. I better get that fucking knot after this because I'm so turned on right now that I'm gonna cry. It doesn't help when Finn grabs the back of my head and crushes his lips to mine. We share a filthy kiss as we swap Knox's cum.

"Dear god, the two of you are going to kill me," Knox hisses, getting down on his knees between Finn and me. I'm assuming he takes Finn's cock into his mouth because Finn is crying out into our kiss before breaking it and putting his forehead to mine. We look down to watch Knox sucking Finn off.

"Knox, I-I'm gonna...fuuuck," Finn moans, and Knox sucks faster. A few seconds later, Finn is cumming on a cry, and I'm ripped away.

I'm thrown over Dom's lap, his hand coming down on my ass, giving me a sharp slap. "That's for taking off on me just as I was about to knot you, Little One," he growls, flipping me onto my back and grabbing my legs, pulling me to him. He roughly thrusts his cock inside me with a savage look on his face. "Now, I don't think I will after you pulled that little stunt."

"If you're not gonna give it to me after I said please, then

I'll just take it myself," I sass back. I want that knot, and he's gonna give it to me.

"Yeah, and how are you gonna do that?" He lifts a cocky brow.

Wrapping my legs around him tightly, and with all the strength this horny little Omega can muster, I flip us, beaming down at him proudly when his back hits the bed with a grunt.

"Fuck," he moans as I take my chance and bare down on his knot, forcing it inside me. "That was hot. Okay, fine, Little One. My knot is yours," he moans as he locks inside me. I start to ride him.

I whimper, so fucking turned on. My mind is getting a little fuzzy because of the knot inside me. I'm knot and cum drunk at this point.

"Ride me, Little One," Dom growls. "I wanna see those tits bounce."

He grabs my hips, helping me fuck myself with his dick. I lean forward to brace myself on his chest, digging my nails into him as I whine and whimper. "I need to cum, Alpha," I plead, the sass in me completely gone. Normally, I cum as soon as I'm knotted, but I already did a few times before this, so it's taking me a little longer.

"I know, baby," Dom says, slipping a hand between us and playing with my clit. I cry out, falling onto him as I work my hips, trying to get that friction just the way I need it.

His thrusts are choppy because we are so tightly locked together, but it's just enough for his cock to hit me in just the right spot.

"That's it, Little One," he purrs. "Cum for your Alpha."

"Dom," I sob, an unexpected powerful orgasm rippling through my body. I writhe on top of him, overcome by the pleasure. He groans into the top of my head as he fills me with his seed. Thick, warm, sticky cum coats my insides. The thought of it has my pussy pulsing harder around him.

We stay like this for a little while, locked together and enjoying our little blissful bubble.

"Let's get you cleaned up," Dom says when his knot deflates. He slips free from me, a gush of both of our releases going with him.

"Nooo," I mumble into his chest. "Sleep. I wanna sleep for five years."

"Sleep after we clean you up," Knox says, coming to sit next to us. He smells like body wash and a hint of mangos. His hair is also wet; he must have just come from the shower.

"You wash me," I tell Dom.

"Of course, Little One," he chuckles, moving us off the bed and into the bathroom. He washes me with tender touches and so much love, but we don't do anything more. I didn't ask. I didn't feel the need, so when Dom lays me down in my bed and not our nest, I know this heat is done.

"Sleep, Little One," Dom kisses my head.

"Good night, Pretty Girl," Sawyer says, giving me a sweet, lingering kiss.

"I love you, Sunshine." Finn is next.

"Sweet dreams, Love," Tristan says with a kiss of his own.

"Dream of me, Kitten, and all the things we can do next time," Knox chuckles, making me give him a sleepy grin. I tell them I love them as they all gather around me to sleep.

As my men lie around me, I'm happy and content with a massive smile on my lips, and I know everything is going to be okay.

My guys aren't who they were before. No longer are they broken because I did everything I could to put them back together. Are they perfectly healed? I don't think so, only time will tell, but I do know that they are good.

And I will spend the rest of my life reminding them that everything that others have deemed flawed or wrong about them are the things I love the most about them.

My silly Alpha, who never fails to make me smile on my darkest days.

My sweet Alpha who cares for not only me but all of us, keeping us a pack.

My shy Alpha who's opened up so much not only to love others but to love himself.

My grumpy Alpha, who learns to love a piece of himself every day, and over time, I think he'll see what I see.

Then my Beta, my best friend. He may have acted like nothing ever bothered him, but I saw how much it meant that I bit him. To see how happy he is, not only to be mated to me, but Finn as well makes me so happy that we could give that to him.

And me, the Omega, who didn't settle for just any pack. I knew my worth, and I knew what I wanted. I held out until the universe tossed me into the right pack, the pack who I was meant to be with. The person who once thought she would never be what Alphas wanted is now being looked at every day like she's a Queen.

I don't know what life has planned for us yet, but I know as long as we're together, everything will be alright.

EPILOGUE

Two years later

TRISTAN

Life has been amazing these past few years. The guys and I graduated from Calling Wood while Tia stayed to start her classes to become a teacher.

We have all been doing our own things to keep ourselves busy while Tia is in school.

Knox started up his own small security firm, and Dom ended up working for him, taking a job here in Calling Wood so that he doesn't have to be far from our Omega.

Finn is living his dream and bought a little space here in Calling Wood, opening his own comic book store. It's doing really well and has become a big hit with the students.

Sawyer started working for his parents, going away every few weekends to do photo shoots for the magazine.

Sometimes he takes Tia, or we all go. It's been amazing seeing new places.

As for me, I've just been helping out here and there around Calling Wood because what I want in life hasn't happened yet.

Well, until now, I hope.

"Guys," Sawyer says, watching Tia scurry around the house, grabbing anything soft she can find. "Is she nesting?"

We all look up to our girl, watching her as she mutters to herself. She's glowing, her breasts are getting bigger, her hair shinier, and she has been a little snappy the past few days.

"Her heat shouldn't be here for another few weeks," Dom grumbles, looking at her with a confused look.

With each heat, Tia's body has leveled out from a heat every month to every two months. As time goes on and a pack becomes more settled, it tends to happen, so her doctor says.

I know something they don't. I've been waiting for this day, done all the research that needed to be done on my part because my dream is to be a stay at home dad and watch our kids.

That's why when she started adding anchovies to pretty much anything, including ice cream, I started to get curious. The guys think it's just some random new thing she enjoys, and I can't help but laugh at the looks they make when she eats it as they try to act supportive while trying not to gag.

I'm trying not to get too excited because she should still be on birth control. However, it's not something we've brought up in a long time. She said the implant was good for two years. It's been two years, and I don't think she's gotten it replaced. It didn't cross my mind until the other day. This nesting she's doing is proving my suspicions to be true.

I don't want to say anything to the guys and get them excited or worked up until I talk to Tia.

Ignoring the conversations that started up between them, I get up and follow my girl into her nest.

Leaning against the door frame, I grin as I watch her move pillows and blankets around.

"God," she grumbles, looking back at me. "Is it hot in here? Can you turn up the air conditioner?"

"It's already as high as it can go, Love," I tell her as she takes off her shirt. She's not wearing a bra, and her already large breasts are even bigger. There's no way no one has noticed.

"What?" she says, her eyes filling with tears. "No," she whines, starting to cry. Damn it. I didn't mean to upset her.

"Shhh," I coo, pulling her into my arms, not wanting to touch her nest and make it worse.

"But I'm so hot," she sobs.

"I know," I rub her back, kissing the top of her head. "Tia, baby, are you okay?"

"What do you mean?" she asks, sniffling as she looks up at me.

"You're nesting, and your heat isn't due for another few weeks."

"Oh," she says, brows furrowing. She looks around like she's just realizing what she was doing. "Maybe I'm going into heat early?"

When Tia goes into heat, she's always turned on, even when she's nesting, moody, and binge-eating.

"Well, are you in the mood?" I smirk, and she gives me this adorable little nose scrunch.

"No," she shakes her head. "I kinda wanna sleep. But it's so hot." Her eyes go wide. "Am I broken?" she starts to cry again. I shouldn't laugh, but she's so... all over the place.

"No, Love, you're not broken. But do you think you could be pregnant?"

"Pregnant?" she asks, wiping her fresh tears. She stares at me for a long moment before the expression in her eyes turns to panic. "Shit, shit, shit." She runs over to the pile of blankets on the floor and starts throwing them around, looking for something. When she finds her phone, she frantically starts to look through it. "I missed it."

"Missed what, Love?"

"The email from my doctor telling me I need to get a new implant and that the other one expired," she whimpers, and I feel an excited thrill race through my body as I try to hold back my smile.

"When was it sent?" I ask.

"A month before my last heat," she groans. "We were on a trip with Sawyer that weekend. Then my email got swamped with class assignments. It got lost."

"Tia, Love. Do you want to take a test?" I ask her. When her off behavior started up, I went to the store and got her a few tests just in case.

"No," she whimpers. "Because what if I am? I want kids, but I still have two years left of school, Tristan."

"If you are, everything will be fine, Love. You have five mates to help you. You don't have to give up anything. And Tia, this is what I signed up for, hoped for. This is exactly what I want to be doing with my life. Helping raise our kids so you can have everything you want out of life, including a family."

"Really?" she asks. "I'm so scared."

"Everything is going to be fine. It's okay to be scared, but you're not alone Little Omega. We're here for you, always."

She takes a deep breath and nods. "Do you have a test? Or do we need to go get one?" she asks, putting her shirt back on.

"I have one." I grin, rushing off to my room. I grab the bag I have in my side table and rush back to her. Grabbing her hand, I drag her into the bathroom and dump the tests onto the counter.

"One?" she laughs. "Babe, I think you need to learn how to count."

"Okay, so I may have gone overboard." I chuckle.

"I think it's cute," she giggles, then picks one up. "Well, here goes nothing."

Five tests later, we both lean over them. Staring back at us are five positive results. My eyes fill with tears, and I feel a different kind of joy as the fact that I'm gonna be a dad hits me.

"I'm pregnant," she whispers, looking up at me with watery eyes. "We're going to have a baby."

"Yeah, Love," I croak. "We are."

She jumps into my arms, crying, what I hope are happy

tears, into my neck. I hold her tight, never wanting to let her go.

"I'm so afraid because, God Tris, babies are a lot of work. But I'm also so happy," she cries.

"Me too." I chuckle. Pulling back a little, I look into her eyes, wiping the tears as she smiles widely up at me. "Everything will be okay," I promise her. "This baby will never want for anything. He or she will be so loved."

"I know." She nods. "And not only do I have you guys here with me, I have Ivy, Everlee, and her pack. Plus, Spencer is starting in a few weeks. All the people I love will be in one place. Well, except my parents. Oh my, my parents." She laughs. "They are gonna be so excited. I can't wait to tell them."

I chuckle, happy to see her so excited when moments before she looked terrified. "How about we tell this little one's daddies first, eh?" I say, placing my hand on her belly. She puts her hands over mine and gives me a shy look.

"Do you think they would be mad?" she asks, her voice small.

"No, Love," I say without a doubt. "They might feel a little like you do, because this is a big change, but they love you so much, Tia. Starting a family is something we've all wanted more than anything."

She nods, and leans against the counter. Looking into the mirror, she says, "Let's go tell them."

We walk into the living room, and the guys are all bickering, in each other's faces. I have no idea what is going on or what they are so worked up over, but they all stop the moment Tia walks into the room, eyes finding her.

"What's wrong?" Dom growls, getting up off the couch and taking a step towards her.

"Kitten?" Knox asks.

"Sunshine, are you okay?" Finn asks, looking from Tia to me.

"Pretty Girl, your silence is making me freak out," Sawyer says.

Tia looks up at me, and I smile down at her, nodding.

"What's in your hand?" Dom asks. They all look at what Tia is holding.

"So... Anyone up for being a daddy?" she asks with a shy laugh, holding the pregnancy test up.

"What..." Sawyer says, his eyes going wide in shock.

"Baby?" Finn whispers. "We're having a baby?"

"Fuck yeah, Kitten," Knox whoops, running across the living room and scooping Tia up. He spins her around before setting her back down on her feet and peppering kisses all over her face, making her giggle.

"So there's a baby in there?" Finn asks, pointing to her belly, making Tia laugh.

"Yes," she nods with a nervous smile on her face.

Finn looks up at Knox with a big grin. "There's a baby in there," he laughs, pointing to Tia's belly.

"Yes, there is, Finny. Our baby," Knox chuckles, pulling him in for a kiss.

"Do you think they'll like the water?" Sawyer asks. We

all look at him like he's crazy. "What? I wanna take them sailing!"

"Of course, that's how you react," Finn chuckles, and they both start to talk excitedly.

"Really?" Dom asks her, looking at her like she's the most precious thing in the world. "You're really pregnant?"

"Really." She nods, grinning like crazy. Dom drops to his knees and puts his forehead to her belly.

"Hi, Little One," he whispers. A little sob escapes Tia, but Knox kisses it away. "I'm your daddy. Well, one of five," he chuckles. "I just want you to know, you will never have to worry about being loved or wanted, because no matter who you are, who you love, or what you like, we will always support you for exactly who you are. Remember, Little One, you are worthy."

We Are Worthy.

ALSO BY ALISHA WILLIAMS

Wondering about Tia's brother? Well, good news, he's getting his own story. Pre-Order We Are Destiny!

Complete Series

Emerald Lake Prep

Book One: Second Chances

Book Two: Into The Unknown

Book Three: Shattered Pieces

Book Four: Redemption Found

Blood Empire

Book One: Rising Queen

Book Two: Crowned Queen

Book Three: Savage Queen

Ongoing series

Silver Valley University:

Book One: Hidden Secrets

Book Two: Secrets Revealed

Book Two: Secrets Embraced (November 2022)

Angelic Academy – Series:

Book One: Tainted Wings

Book Two: Tainted Bonds (December 28 2022)

Black Venom Crew:

Book One: Little Bird (January 28th 2023)

Stand-alones

We Are Worthy- A sweet and steamy omegaverse.

We Are Destiny A steamy omegaverse (2023)

ACKNOWLEDGMENTS

I wanna thank all my readers who are used to my contemporary writing for giving my first omegaverse a chance.

As always, beyond grateful for Jessica, Jennifer, and Amy. You ladies are family more then anything! Thank you for all the time and energy you put into all my books. And a big shout out to Tamara. Thanks for being there for me, and helping me with everything you do, you're the best wifey! Also, I wanna welcome Cassie to the alpha family! Thanks for being an amazing friend who started off as an ARC reader but turned into someone so important to me!

Many thanks to my Beta and ARC teams for your time and efforts in help each of my books be the best they can be!

And to any new readers I gain from this book, please know omegaverse isn't something I plan on doing a lot of, how ever I do have a few stand-alones planed for the future. But if you're willing to give my contemporary stuff a try, I'd be grateful.

ABOUT THE AUTHOR

Writer, Alisha Williams, lives in Alberta, Canada, with her husband and her two headstrong kids, and kitties. When she isn't writing or creating her own gorgeous graphic content, she loves to read books by her favorite authors.

Writing has been a lifelong dream of hers, and this book was made despite the people who prayed for it to fail, but because Alisha is not afraid to go for what she wants, she has proven that dreams do come true.

Wanna see what all her characters look like, hear all the latest gossip about her new books or even get a chance to become a part of one of her teams? Join her readers group on Facebook here - Naughty Queens. Or find her author's page here - Alisha Williams Author

Of course, she also has an Instagram account to show all her cool graphics, videos and more book related goodies - alishawilliamsauthor

Sign up for Alisha's Newsletter

Got TikTok? Follow alishawilliamsauthor

Made in United States
Troutdale, OR
04/11/2024

19125505R00289